Series by Julie Johnstone

Scottish Medieval Romance Books:

Highlander Vows: Entangled Hearts Series
When a Laird Loves a Lady, Book 1
Wicked Highland Wishes, Book 2
Christmas in the Scot's Arms, Book 3
When a Highlander Loses His Heart, Book 4
How a Scot Surrenders to a Lady, Book 5
When a Warrior Woos a Lass, Book 6
When a Scot Gives His Heart, Book 7
Highlander Vows: Entangled Hearts Boxset, Books 1-4

Renegade Scots Series
Outlaw King, Book 1
Highland Defender, Book 2

Regency Romance Books:

A Whisper of Scandal Series
Bargaining with a Rake, Book 1
Conspiring with a Rogue, Book 2
Dancing with a Devil, Book 3
After Forever, Book 4
The Dangerous Duke of Dinnisfree, Book 5

A Once Upon A Rogue Series
My Fair Duchess, Book 1
My Seductive Innocent, Book 2
My Enchanting Hoyden, Book 3
My Daring Duchess, Book 4

Lords of Deception Series
What a Rogue Wants, Book 1

Danby Regency Christmas Novellas
The Redemption of a Dissolute Earl, Book 1
Season For Surrender, Book 2
It's in the Duke's Kiss, Book 3

Regency Anthologies
A Summons from the Duke of Danby (Regency Christmas Summons, Book 2)
Thwarting the Duke (When the Duke Comes to Town, Book 2)

Regency Romance Box Sets
A Whisper of Scandal Trilogy (Books 1-3)
Dukes, Duchesses & Dashing Noblemen (A Once Upon a Rogue Regency Novels, Books 1-3)

Paranormal Books:

The Siren Saga
Echoes in the Silence, Book 1

Highland Defender

Renegade Scots, Book 2

by
Julie Johnstone

Highland Defender
Copyright © 2018 by Julie Johnstone, DBA Darbyshire Publishing
Cover Design by The Midnight Muse
Editing by Double Vision Editorial

All rights reserved. No part of this book may be reproduced in any form by any electronic or mechanical means—except in the case of brief quotations embodied in critical articles or reviews—without written permission.

The characters and events portrayed in this book are fictitious. Any similarity to real persons, living or dead, is purely coincidental and not intended by the author.

The best way to stay in touch is to subscribe to my newsletter. Go to www.juliejohnstoneauthor.com and subscribe in the box at the top of the page that says Newsletter. If you don't hear from me once a month, please check your spam filter and set up your email to allow my messages through to you so you don't miss the opportunity to win great prizes or hear about appearances.

Dedication

This one is for my brother. I feel certain that he'll know why.

As always, I have to thank a few people. First my assistant Dee, without whom I would be a hot mess. And of course, I need to thank my editor, Danielle Poiesz for always helping me dig deeper. Without her, I'd be lost! And lastly, I need to thank my husband and my kids. They put up with my distraction and my obsessive writing. I love you guys!

Author's Note

This book presented an interesting challenge. After coming to know Angus and Lillianna as secondary characters in *Outlaw King*, I absolutely knew that I wanted to write their story. However, I also was certain that I wanted their book to start from the first day they met, which meant I literally had to start the second book in the series back in time from where I ended the first book. This actually turned out to be easier than I first imagined it would be.

The other challenge of the book was building the rules of the brooch you will encounter in this story. I don't want to say too much to avoid plot spoilers, but it took some doing to create the legend of the Brooch of Lagothmier! But, oh, what fun it was doing it!

I do so hope you enjoy the book!

If you're interested in when my books go on sale, or want to be one of the first to know about my new releases, please follow me on BookBub! You'll get quick book notifications every time there's a new pre-order, book on sale, or new release. You can follow me on BookBub here: www.bookbub.com/authors/julie-johnstone

All the best,
Julie

Chapter One

1302
Central England

Laird Angus MacLorh lived by three rules: put king above self, protect his family at all costs, and never become entangled with a lass again. He appreciated lasses as much as any man did, but he had no desire, nor place in his life, for the soft emotions an attachment to a woman would bring. He'd allowed a weakness for a woman to rule his head and heart once, and his poor judgment had resulted in his father's death. It didn't matter that Angus had been a mere nineteen summers and he'd thought less with the head on his shoulders than the one between his legs; he should have realized what was happening. His gut had warned him, and he'd chosen to ignore his instincts. That one foolish decision had changed not only his life but those of his mother, siblings, and his entire clan.

He didn't let himself forget it. Ever. Even if he wanted to, which he didn't, guilt had become his shadow. He awoke to it every day, and it followed him with silent footsteps. At night, shame haunted his dreams. He'd become accustomed to the heavy feeling that pressed upon his heart, mind, and soul. In fact, he'd decided long ago that it was best to nurture the guilt, lest he ever meet a lass that made him want to forget again. As laird, he could not allow himself to be distracted by a woman and fail in his duties to his clan ever again. Especially with that devil Edward, the King of England, systematically and brutally subjugating the Scottish people in an attempt to steal Scotland's empty throne. Now, more than ever before, Angus could not falter.

"Angus, did ye hear me, man?" Robbie growled from Angus's right. Black eyebrows arched questioningly over Robert the Bruce's probing dark eyes as the Scot stared at him.

Angus paused on the pebbled path that led from the great hall of the Palace of Westminster through the gardens and into the woods. Rocks crunched underfoot when he turned to face his longtime friend and if his instincts were correct, which they always were, the future King of Scotland. The question in Angus's mind was not *if* Robbie would one day sit upon the throne; it was *when* the Scot would fill the void left when the damnable English king had driven John Balliol, Scotland's most recent ruler from power. Angus's surety of that eventuality, as well as the fact that he literally owed Robbie his life after he had saved Angus years before, was why he'd agreed to come to England, into the very heart of their enemy's domain, and pretend to submit to King Edward as his liege lord. The vile thought of actually bending the knee to the wishful usurper made Angus's chest tighten.

A cool breeze stirred, and a shaft of sunlight momentarily fought its way through the thick clouds gathered overhead. Robbie cleared his throat, and Angus forced himself to concentrate on his friend. "Nay, I did nae hear ye."

Robbie arched his eyebrows a fraction higher, and irritation scratched at Angus's insides. He prided himself in always being focused, always paying attention, and remembering every detail, and he decided then and there that it was Robbie's fault that Angus's attention was so strained.

Angus motioned toward his friend's eyebrows. "Dunnae give me that look," he grumbled.

"What look?" Robbie asked, his eyebrows arching still higher.

"This one," Angus snapped and arched his own eyebrows. He had known Robbie since they were very young and had trained to be warriors together. Long ago, they had even formed a small group of tight friends they called the Renegades. These men fought for Scotland's freedom, and they knew one another better than they knew their own brothers, so Angus understood well what Robbie's gestures meant. "Ye see what I'm doing!" He tapped hard by his right eye. "I ken ye do." Robbie's thick brows immediately lowered, and Angus continued, his annoyance ticking in time with his heartbeat. "I may nae have heard ye just now, but I heard ye last night when ye announced yer plan for me." Angus still could not believe that Robbie expected him to take some helpless lass Angus did not know or trust with him to Ettrick Forest to warn Robbie's men they were in danger.

"I did nae ever say Elizabeth's cousin Lillianna is helpless, nor did I *announce* what ye were to do." Robbie's eyebrows dipped together in a scowl. "I conveyed what I *wish* ye to do."

Angus snorted. "Ye did nae have to say the lass is helpless. It's in yer tone. And ye conveying what ye wish is the same as an order. Ye will be my king one day, and ye ken well I live to serve king above self." He waved a hand at a pesky bee buzzing around his head.

Robbie flashed a smile, revealing just how aware he was that Angus would submit to what was asked of him. There was too much at stake. When Robbie's ailing father finally passed, Robbie would rise up, throwing off the cloak of feigned submission to Edward that Robbie's father had long demanded. And when that happened, Robbie would lead Scotland to freedom and take his place as the rightful King of Scotland. Angus had to do what he could to help.

Robbie set a hand on Angus's shoulder. "Ye know I'd nae ever ask ye to do something without fully considering it first. Ye trust me, aye?"

Angus clenched his teeth on the urge to immediately respond. He did trust Robbie—implicitly. Yet he also believed that, in this instance, the Scot was being led more by his desire for Elizabeth de Burgh than logical reasoning. Angus blew out a frustrated breath. He'd made his concern clear to Robbie last night, so there was nothing more to say. Except…

God's teeth! The need to state his opinion again was too much to keep inside. He may later regret the anger he would likely incur from Robbie, but Angus would never forgive himself if he kept his silence now and Robbie died because of it—or he did. He preferred to be aboveground as long as possible.

Though only green trees surrounded them on the path to the garden, Angus leaned closer, ever aware that just because they had been careful when coming out here this day, enemies could well be lurking.

"I came here to guard yer back from our enemies, and now ye demand I leave ye unprotected with a too-bonny lass working her spell on ye."

Robbie frowned. "I asked. I did nae demand. And Elizabeth is nae *ban-druidh.*"

"Who said she was a witch?" Angus asked. "She is beautiful and has captured ye in her web—"

"Elizabeth is nae a spider, either," Robbie protested.

Angus smirked. "That remains to be seen." He swatted at the bee again, and this time he got it, smacking it between his palms. He flicked the dead bee off his hand. "She is a distraction, much like that bee I just killed."

"Are ye suggesting I kill her?" Robbie asked, laughing.

Angus frowned at his friend, who was clearly—and dangerously—enamored of the goddaughter of the King of England, their mortal enemy. "Ye ken I believe it is a mistake to trust the word of the de Burgh lass in regard to most anything, and certainly when it comes to what *her godfather* will do. But it is my duty to protect ye, and I ken well ye will ride to Ettrick Forest yerself to warn yer men that Edward is coming for them if I dunnae go, and I kinnae allow that. If one of us has to ride into an ambush, better me than ye."

"Ye are nae riding into an ambush, ye stubborn Scot!" Robbie hissed. "If ye had been listening a moment ago, I made this point to ye as ye scowled and stalked ahead. Do ye think Elizabeth would send her beloved cousin with ye if ye were being sent to yer death? She would nae chance Lillianna's life."

Angus turned on his heel and continued his trek down the path, shoving branches out of his way as he went. Behind him, Robbie's footfalls resounded and Angus's need to make Robbie listen grew. "How the devil do I ken what Elizabeth de Burgh would chance? And for that matter, how the hell do ye?" Angus demanded, feeling his anger rise. He huffed as he strode ahead, straight through a spider web that he'd failed to see. God's teeth! Robbie being distracted by the de Burgh lass was even affecting Angus! It was as if it were seeping into him.

He gritted his teeth. "We have been at this court less than a month, and from yer own lips to mine, the lass admitted she was ordered by her godfather and father to seduce ye for information." Angus paused long enough to glance over his shoulder and catch a glare from Robbie. Assured that his friend was listening, Angus turned and continued walking. "For all I ken, sending her cousin— whom she claims needs to be taken from here to protect her from Lady Elizabeth's father—is yet another lie, another layer of the king's plan against ye, against us." He thumped his chest for emphasis.

"'Tis nae a lie," Robbie said, his voice hard.

"Ye desire the de Burgh wench," Angus accused.

"Aye, I do desire her," Robbie agreed. "But I'm nae controlled by my desires any more than ye are."

Angus stiffened. His friend had shot an arrow intended to make Angus question himself, and doubt flooded him for a breath. Was he allowing his own guilt from the past to color what he saw of the current situation? Or maybe he simply could see the danger more clearly than Robbie because he did not lust after the de Burgh lass as Robbie did. If Angus were a wagering man, he'd bet it was the latter.

"Ye must pledge to me that ye will see Lillianna to safety after ye have warned the men in Ettrick Forest," Robbie said.

Angus scowled. It was bad enough Robbie was demanding that Angus leave him unprotected here in this den of manipulative liars, but to ask him to take even more time to see some half-Irish, half-Scottish, English-loyal lass to safety he was not positive she needed? It was crucial to return to Robbie's side where he could protect him. Anything else was foolish. Yet Robbie *was* asking him not to.

Angus swallowed the desire to refute Robbie. *King above self.* "I'll take the lass," he said, stopping and facing Robbie. "As I said, I ken if I dunnae, ye will attempt to, which would likely either get ye killed or destroy the illusion we've worked to create that ye are here to submit to Edward."

Robbie winked. "Verra astute of ye, Angus."

"Tell me of the lass," Angus said with a sigh. "If I'm to travel with her for the sennight it will take to reach Ettrick Forest, I need to ken more about her."

Robbie shrugged as he motioned for them to start walking again. Angus nodded, and they continued on. "Ye already know she's Elizabeth's cousin," Robbie said. "She's like a sister and verra important to her."

Therefore the lass had become important to Robbie…

Angus did not like it one bit. Robbie was convinced Elizabeth de Burgh was not conspiring against him with her godfather simply because she had admitted to Robbie that she was supposed to be learning his secrets. But that could actually be a plot to make herself seem innocent. Angus would not condemn her or her cousin of duplicity in his mind *yet*. He was not a heartless brute, after all. He'd wait for the solid evidence he was fairly certain would be forthcoming, and when it arrived…

"What else can ye tell me of her?" Angus asked, winding down the narrowing path to where they would rendezvous with the de Burgh lass and her cousin.

"Her mother was a MacLeod," Robbie said.

"A MacLeod?" Angus frowned. "I thought I'd heard years ago that de Burgh had a bastard daughter, one not with his wife, who was the daughter of the MacLeod laird."

"Nay," Robbie responded. "That was a lie Elizabeth's father and uncle concocted because they believe in the legend of the daughters of the MacLeod lairds. They conspired to keep Lillianna's identity secret until they could use her. Ye know of the legend, aye?"

Angus snorted as he continued to walk and swiped at another spiderweb that had just hit his face. "I ken a bit about the foolish legend. All in the Highlands do."

"Ye do nae believe it?" Robbie asked.

"Of course nae." Angus scoffed. "Saying that MacLeod lasses born to the lairds of the clan—and any daughters they bear—become seers when they find true love is fae nonsense. It was likely made up by a bunch of drunken warriors watching a lovely lass dance a hundred years ago. I believe in things I can see, touch, and taste."

"Like a woman in yer arms," Robbie said with a chuckle.

"Oh aye. I believe I have a warm, willing lass in my arms when I can see her, taste her, and touch her, but that dunnae mean I can *trust* her."

"Ye're a cynic," Robbie said.

Angus shrugged. "If being a cynic allows me to do my duty as laird, then aye, I'm a cynic."

"What of the part of the legend about the lost magical Brooch of Lagothmier? Do ye believe in that? Ye can see and touch a brooch, after all."

Angus guffawed at the mere thought of a magical brooch. Honestly, he'd never paid much heed when people spoke of the legend so he did not know all the details, but even if he did, it would not make him a believer.

"I'll take that as a nay," Robbie said.

"That is how ye should take it," Angus said. "I kinnae believe that ye would give credence to such nonsense as a story of a fairy falling in love with a mortal MacLeod laird and then being forced by her fae father to leave the MacLeod and their newborn lass to return to the fae world."

Angus rolled his eyes. "And then she supposedly gave a magical brooch to her infant daughter?" He stopped and glanced over his shoulder to smirk at Robbie. "I thought ye more rational than that."

"Ye can mock," Robbie said, frowning, "but the legend makes sense."

"It's *nonsense*," Angus shot back, feeling ridiculous even arguing about it.

Robbie moved to thump Angus on the head, but Angus caught his friend's hand easily and laughed. Robbie yanked his hand away and scowled. "The original fairy Lagothmier *did* give a magical brooch to her infant daughter," Robbie said. "She did so to protect her and so the lass could defend her clan after Lagothmier's father ordered her to leave her MacLeod lover."

This was preposterous. "Robbie," Angus started.

Robbie waved a hand at him. "Let me finish. When Lagothmier broke the rules of the fae world and fell in love with a mortal, her father—the king—ordered her to leave her daughter."

Robbie gave Angus an expectant look, so Angus said an obligatory, "Aye," though he felt like a clot-heid doing so.

Robbie gave a satisfied nod. "When Lagothmier realized she had no choice but to do as he commanded, she gave her brooch—the heart of her power—to her daughter. The brooch could be used by anyone the fae loved to tell the future if they possessed it." Lagothmier's father was furious because he believed the MacLeod had only wanted to wed his daughter to use her."

Again, Robbie gave Angus an expectant look, and Angus dutifully replied, "Naturally."

Robbie took a deep breath, and impatience filled Angus. "Lagothmier's father thought he saw what his daughter had failed to: men were evil and power hungry, and would go to great lengths to possess the brooch and the women who wielded the power."

"Do ye personally ken the fae king?" Angus joked.

"Nay, but my three times great-grandfather knew the MacLeod laird. He was a good man. Lagothmier's father was wrong."

Angus had to bite his tongue to keep from laughing. He understood that Robbie must have heard this story a hundred times growing up, and likely from his grandfather, whom Robbie had adored.

"So," Robbie continued, "the fae king did two things: he limited the powers of the brooch while also punishing his daughter for her foolishness by cursing her descendants. The brooch would no longer give the gift of sight to any but the fae who wore it. And the female descendants would only come into their powers when they fell in love. But if that love was destroyed by a betrayal from their beloved, the lass would lose her gift and only see the future when she wore the brooch."

"Ye talk as if ye were there a hundred years ago, Robbie. Ye sound ridiculous."

"What is *ridiculous*," Robbie said with a scowl, "is to dismiss something because it seems impossible. If that's yer attitude, ye should dismiss the possibility that I might one day be king."

Angus threw his hands up. Robbie chose to believe in impossible things because of his own difficult situation, but the difference was that, with Robbie, there was no magic involved, just determination.

"Convince me, then," Angus said, deciding it was best to let his friend finish the story.

Robbie nodded. "My father said he once saw the Brooch

of Lagothmier on Lillianna de Burgh's mother, Kara, when the woman was nae more than fourteen summers. This was before it was lost, ye see."

"Well, obviously," Angus said, half snickering at Robbie's entrancement with his fanciful story.

Robbie's eyes narrowed. "My father said the brooch swirled in the middle like a storm and that Kara MacLeod—she was nae a de Burgh at the time—touched my father and told him he would win a great battle the next day. And he did."

Robbie's story intrigued Angus but not enough for him to abandon reason and embrace the nonsensical idea that Lillianna de Burgh would have the power to see the future if she fell in love or miraculously obtained the magical Brooch of Lagothmier. Not to mention Robbie's father was a known liar.

Angus blew out a breath, thinking how to debunk his friend's fantastical belief without angering him. "If that legend were true, the conniving King Edward and Lady Elizabeth's father, would be searching high and low for the Brooch of Lagothmier. They'd want to find it and force the lass Lillianna to wear it, so she could inform them of what's to come—battles, ambushes, everything."

"They probably did search for it and could nae find it," Robbie said, his face growing serious. "Which is another verra good reason to aid Lillianna in fleeing to Scotland. Then if they do find it, they kinnae use her to win the war."

"Let us pretend ye're correct," Angus said, always one to think things through completely before dismissing them. "Her father would nae have ever allowed her out of his control if she had the potential to be a seer."

"He would if she had nae fallen in love or if he thought she would nae ever get her powers for some reason.

Especially with the brooch lost."

That did make sense, but...

"Why reveal her identity now? Or when did they reveal it?" Angus asked, realizing he actually did not know.

"Who the lass really is was made known a year ago. I do nae know the answer to yer other question: I can nae read King Edward's or de Burgh's minds. If I could, we would be in control of Scotland already, not playing the part of traitors to our country."

"Ye have a good point," Angus admitted.

"Mayhap they revealed her identity hoping to draw out whoever has the brooch. Or mayhap they revealed her identity hoping a man would capture her heart, and they'd nae need the brooch." Robbie paused, brow furrowed in thought. "Though the last part of the legend does say that if the lass is betrayed by love, she will lose her seer powers. That is why the brooch is imperative if the lass is nae in love or feels betrayed."

"I dunnae believe," Angus declared, having listened patiently to it all and now deciding he could most definitely dismiss the legend.

"It dunnae matter," Robbie retorted. "The brooch is lost, and Elizabeth says that Lillianna is verra wary of men and their intentions."

"What does the lass look like?" Angus asked. It was probable that there were many foolish men who'd likely tried to capture her heart simply because they believed in the legend. She could look like a toad and the English fools would still want her.

He could only imagine how they'd react if she was bonny...

Robbie shrugged. "I can nae say for certain."

"What do ye mean ye kinnae say for certain?" Angus

asked incredulously. "Are ye so besotted with Lady Elizabeth that ye kinnae even recall what her cousin looks like?"

Robbie scowled at Angus for a moment before answering. "Nay. I told ye, Lillianna has been kept in the dungeon since she and Elizabeth arrived at the Palace of Westminster. This is how Elizabeth's father has controlled her and forced her to do his bidding. He threatened to kill Lillianna if Elizabeth did nae submit to his wishes."

"He'd nae kill her if he truly believed in the legend," Angus pointed out.

"He would if he thought there was nae any hope of her getting her powers," Robbie said. "As for what she looks like, I have nae met her in person, and the only time I've ever seen her was from a distance in Ireland. So nay, I can nae say what she looks like. I think she has brown hair."

"Well, if she did nae make any impression on ye that means she is nae especially bonny, and that is just fine with me."

Robbie chuckled as they rounded a turn in the path. "When will ye let go of yer foolish rule about lasses?"

"Nae ever," Angus replied, ducking a particularly low-hanging branch.

"Ye realize how foolish it is to cling to the belief that an attachment to a lass will make ye repeat yer past, do ye nae?"

"It's nae foolish," Angus grumbled. "It's wise." If he'd never allowed himself to become distracted by Isla Belfaine, he would have battled beside his father rather than having gone to meet Isla in the woods when he'd thought she was in danger.

"Do ye nae get lonely?" Robbie asked, his voice pitching oddly.

"Nay," Angus said. "Do ye?"

"Aye, since I met Elizabeth. She makes me feel the loneliness because I wish to be with her," Robbie said to Angus's dismay. He feared Elizabeth de Burgh was going to lead Robbie straight to his downfall, but Angus held his tongue and allowed Robbie to talk. "Ye will feel the loneliness, too, when ye meet a lass who ye can nae resist. And I do nae mean one who simply stirs yer desire. When ye meet a lass who tightens yer chest, that's the lass ye should fear."

"And do ye fear Elizabeth?" Angus asked carefully, thinking briefly of Isla. She had not tightened his chest, but she'd tightened his manly parts. He'd thought that love, and perhaps it had been, just not so very deep. And that meant anything greater would be even more trouble.

"I did," Robbie admitted, voice low. "Now I fear that I kinnae be without her. Can it be stopped, ye think?" His voice was so earnest that Angus knew for certain they were no longer speaking of him, which he was heartily glad for.

"It can," Angus said, though in honesty, he had never personally tried to stop feelings for a lass he was enamored of, quite simply because he'd not allowed himself to become attached to anyone since Isla. He did not yearn for the women he joined with in any way but raw desire, which was why he allowed himself the pleasure of the moment. "Keep yer guard up always. Vow it to me."

"I do nae believe I need to," Robbie replied.

"Christ, man!" Angus exploded. Robbie was their best hope to unite the nobles under one man who would one day lead Scotland as their king. Robbie was honorable and would be a good king, and Angus could not believe his friend would be so foolish as to risk a woman—even one as lovely as Elizabeth de Burgh—jeopardizing all they had worked for.

Angus glanced up to the sky as he kept walking. "I swear, if ye're nae careful, she will be yer ruin. God, make him use his eyes," he muttered.

"I *am* using them," Robbie grumbled, "which is why I can see ye're about to run into a branch."

Angus jerked his gaze down, ducked the branch, and then came to a shuddering stop. Five paces away, where the gardens met the woods, stood a lass. She was surrounded by lush green foliage from the garden on either side and at her back was the towering woods. She stood under the golden sunbeams, and she was the bonniest lass he'd ever seen. She had hair the color of a leaf turned by the changing season. It was not simply brown, as Robbie had said. Long, thick strands of copper, gold, and mahogany veiled her face on one side and tumbled over her slight shoulders on the other to nestle against her chest.

His fingers twitched with the sudden urge to know how the slide of those locks upon his skin would feel. He curled both hands into fists, desire beating within him. High cheekbones and skin like snow framed eyes the color of fresh moss. He hissed in a breath, arrested by her eyes, not for the brilliance of the color but the wariness shining from them. Her gaze was narrowed like a skittish barn cat who'd been attacked by a vicious dog and was ever watchful—and fully expectant—of another assault. Dark shadows cushioned her eyes as if she'd not slept in days.

His protective instinct stirred to life, along with a flare of caution. He turned to Robbie and lowered his voice to ensure the women would not hear him. "Nae only are ye sending me on a fool's errand with the lass, but she's surely descended from Aphrodite herself."

Robbie clapped him on the shoulder. "I give ye a fortnight. Nay, make that two—ye're stubborn."

Angus grinned. "Two fortnights for what?"

"'Til yer chest is tight."

"Bah," Angus growled in return. He shrugged Robbie's hand off and stopped in front of the lass with whom Angus was soon to be saddled.

"Robert," Lady Elizabeth said in greeting, before looking to Angus. "This is my cousin Lillianna. I put her in your care."

Lady Elizabeth's words rang in his ears: *in your care.* Those three simple words bound him to the lass for better or worse until he saw her to safety. As he stared into the lovely lass's guarded gaze, he found himself thinking of the distrust of men Robbie had mentioned. It was likely best for both of them that men made her wary. They could travel together without her wishing to get to know him.

"It's normal to make your greeting when you are introduced, Angus," Lady Elizabeth chided with amusement.

"Pleased to meet ye," he said, hearing the gruffness of his own tone.

The lass flinched, and guilt stirred within him. God's teeth, he didn't want to scare her; he simply didn't care to become involved overly much. Yet he supposed he could manage to be polite. But what the devil did one say in making polite conversation?

He scanned his mind, trying to remember. These days, whenever he spoke with a lass it was because it was clear they both had joining on their mind, and that was all. Polite conversation was not needed. He tried to think of something to say, but her lush body only brought to mind words he could never utter. Then he recalled where he was to eventually take her, and he nearly exhaled with relief that he had a topic to speak on.

"I'm told yer mother was a MacLeod," he blurted.

Her eyes narrowed with obvious wariness, and he realized she must be thinking of the legend surrounding her and the men who likely had tried to woo her because of it. Though, even without the legend, she was the sort of woman who would lure men with her beauty.

Best to ease her fears directly, he decided. "I dunnae hold stock in the ridiculous legend surrounding ye, so ye need nae fear I'll want ye."

"Angus!" Robbie and Lady Elizabeth said as one. The lass, however, cracked a smile, though her gaze kept its distrustful glimmer.

He winced. That had not come out correctly at all. One look at her was all it took for desire to spark within him. But he had no time on this mission to sate his desires, and he did not think her one who would be willing to have a romp in the hay and nothing more.

"How refreshing," she said, reaching up and tucking a lock of hair behind her right ear. A dark-purple bruise marred her creamy skin.

He recognized the mark of a lass hit by a man. "Who struck ye, lass?" he demanded, his mind turning with ways to repay the offender with a lesson he'd never forget.

She stared at him for a long moment with her large, suspicious gaze, and then she tilted her chin up in a defiant gesture. "Stephen. He *does* believe in the legend and thought seducing me and bedding me would capture my heart. I did not wish to oblige, so I fought him."

The lass's sarcastic bravado showed a strength of spirit. She may have been beaten, but she had not been broken. Admiration tightened his chest, and he rubbed absently at it, catching Robbie's gaze on him. The smirk on his friend's face made Angus immediately recall their earlier conversation. All he could do was scowl.

Chapter Two

The giant Highlander in front of Lillianna made her instantly wary. What was his plan? Did he think telling her he did not believe in the legend surrounding her would make her trust him? Or perhaps he thought offering to kill the king's horrid guard Stephen would make her so grateful and him so heroic to her that she would fall in love with him.

She wanted to tell him that she had no use for a hero, or a man at all for that matter, but instead, she forced a smile and said, "It's refreshing to meet a man intelligent enough not to put stock in a legend likely created by men who had imbibed too much mead."

He gaped at her for a moment, making her think her bluntness had shocked him, but then he announced, "That's exactly what I said, but I think it was by men who had imbibed too much while watching a lovely lass dance."

"Mayhap," Lillianna said and smiled tightly.

This was either the cleverest attempt to gain her trust she'd encountered in the past year—and there had been hundreds of attempts—or this man truly did not believe in the legend. But since she'd known him for the space of a breath, she refused to let down her guard and discover which it was. The legend was true, though, and she would proceed with him as she would any other man: as if he was a threat to her well-being. Men had attempted to gain her heart ever since she'd been sent to live with her uncle, and not because they wanted her for *her*. They had wanted her dormant seer abilities.

Men cared nothing for women but what control they could have over them. Her mother and her grandmother— God rest their souls—were stark examples of what happened to women who allowed themselves to fall in love. Both of them had been betrayed by the men who had claimed to love them, and both women had come to discover the men only wanted to use their powers. And Lillianna's father and uncle, men who should have wanted to protect her, had only ever wanted to use her, too.

Ever since she was a child, her father had told her that her only worth lay in the way he could use her to punish her mother for losing both her powers and the Brooch of Lagothmier, and one day, when she would finally fall in love, that worth would lie in how he could tap into her powers. When she had proven too wise to fall in love, and he'd tried and failed to find the brooch, he'd sent her away in disgust.

In her mind she could still hear the last thing her father had said to her: *I care not what happens to you. Your uncle can use you as he pleases. You have no value to me.*

And her uncle had used her, indeed. He'd been willing to kill her when he, too, had failed to find the brooch and awaken her powers.

She caught her cousin's gaze and raised her eyebrows questioningly, but when Elizabeth frowned in obvious confusion, Lillianna looked to the powerful, dark-haired, gray-eyed Scot before her. Then she touched her index finger to her heart briefly. It was her and Elizabeth's secret code so she could inconspicuously ask Elizabeth if she thought a man was trying to use Lillianna. When Elizabeth's eyes widened and she shook her head, Lillianna let out the breath she'd been holding. She had to travel with this man, and she wanted to trust him, as much as she dared to allow herself.

"I'll see that devil swine Stephen punished for hitting ye," the warrior said, his voice like the rumble of an impending storm.

His words interrupted her musings, and Lillianna eyed the imposing man before her. Why would he offer to risk himself for her if he did not believe in the legend? Elizabeth believed Bruce to be so very honorable, and she had vowed that this man, Bruce's friend, was as well, yet Lillianna did not trust it. She'd be a fool if she did.

She crossed her arms over her chest and narrowed her eyes. "I do not need your protection, nor do I want it. You will not gain my heart with feigned acts of gallantry."

"Thank God for that," he said, the amusement in his voice surprising her.

"I beg your pardon?"

"I dunnae want yer heart, lass."

He said it in such a matter-of-fact tone that she almost believed him. She noticed Elizabeth and Lord Bruce gaping at her. "There is no such thing as the Brooch of Lagothmier," she lied adamantly.

"Aye," he said, arching his eyebrows at her. "I quite agree, despite what others claim the *legend* says."

His mocking tone on the word *legend* truly made him seem believable, and it was suddenly rather irritating that he appeared to be making fun of her. She bit her lip at her ridiculousness. If his disbelief was real, she should rejoice. But if this man was attempting to seduce her, to try to make her fall in love with him so the seer powers within her would spark to life, it truly was the most cunning way to go about it. Despite herself, in her gut she wanted to believe him.

She didn't know much about this man, except that he had very reluctantly agreed to take her to the safety of her mother's family. And there was no time to discover more about Angus MacLorh, or Laird MacLorh, as Elizabeth had informed her before the men had arrived. They had to make haste, and whatever she learned of this Highlander, good or bad, would have to be discovered on their journey from England to Scotland.

A smirk settled on Angus's face, and when he cocked his head and a thick lock of black hair fell over his right eye, her belly fluttered in a way that she didn't care for at all. She'd seen women lose every bit of sense they possessed over a too-handsome face, and Angus MacLorh had such a face. She could never allow herself to be such a simpleton. She was not like other women. Love could never be part of her life, in spite of the lies she had told Elizabeth. It was easier to play the part of a young woman hopeful about love than to admit to her cousin that she feared it with every bit of her soul.

To fall in love meant risking doing so with the wrong man, one who wanted to use her and strip her of all control and freedom. It had happened to her mother. First, she had fallen in love with Laird Drumlan, who had turned out to only want her for her powers. She had escaped him but had lost the brooch to him in the process, only to be forced to wed Lillianna's father, who'd been furious to discover after they'd wed that her powers were gone because her heart had been broken. Her mother's life with her father had been horrific. No, Lillianna would trust no man more than she needed to in order to survive.

Yet she found herself unable to look away from Angus when he raised his arm to shove his hair back. His upper arm muscles, and those of his abdomen, rippled in a raw display of power with his easy movements. Her father, his knights, and her uncle used their weapons and titles to wield power, but this man would only need the strength of his body. The thought left her somewhat dry mouthed and in awe.

When he cleared his throat, her gaze flew from his stomach to his face. Heat infused her cheeks and neck as she realized he had been watching her scrutinize him. The tan skin around his piercing eyes crinkled momentarily with what appeared to be amusement, as if he was used to women staring at him, and his mouth curled up into the start of a smile. He pressed his lips together, banishing his mirth with what seemed purposeful will.

Feeling acutely self-conscious, she cleared her own throat. "If you are telling the truth about not believing in the legend, then I'm extremely glad," she said. "That will make things much more pleasant between us."

He surprised her with a hard look. Most men she had encountered since her identity had been revealed practically slobbered all over themselves to feign niceness at first. It usually took about a sennight before they showed their true selves—around the same time they realized she would not be losing her heart to them. Angus didn't seem to be bothering to pretend at all, which truly *was* reassuring.

His eyes narrowed as her thoughts turned, and then he said, "I'm glad ye think so. In order to keep things pleasant, ye need to ken a few things."

"Such as?" she asked, looking to Elizabeth and Lord Bruce and seeing them glance at each other.

Angus offered a tight smile. "Since I'm the man tasked

with taking ye from England to Scotland, ye do, indeed, need my protection, so ye will do as I say or I will leave ye here for yer uncle to return ye to the dungeon." His tone, as unbendable as steel, was that of a man used to being obeyed.

She tensed at the Scot's words, at his reminder of the dungeon. It had been filled with beady-eyed, scuffling rats and the stench... She nearly gagged recalling the cell in which her uncle had imprisoned her below the castle. Though she had bathed repeatedly after being released last night, her skin still crawled from the filth, and when all was silent, she swore she heard the scuttle of rats on the floor. She could not go back there, and not simply because it was horrid, dark, and dank. She refused to be a pawn to manipulate her cousin—or for anyone to use, for that matter.

"Well?" Angus demanded, breaking into her thoughts. "Are ye going to obey my commands, or will I be leaving here without ye?"

The hopeful look he gave her, the one that wished she would be stubborn and therefore, left here, would have been off-putting to most, she suspected, but it filled her with relief. She recalled her mother speaking about the men in her clan with such awe and telling Lillianna how honorable and protective of women they had been. Honestly, Lillianna could not imagine such a man; yet there was a part of her deep within that wished to believe such a man existed. The mere thought was reckless given who she was and what falling in love would mean for her.

Lillianna drew herself up to her full height, shoving thoughts about honorable men away and focusing on the need to escape so she could live her life on her own terms. "I have no intention of staying here in my uncle's grasp."

"Then ye must agree to abide by my every directive," he replied. "One false move and—"

"Angus," Lord Bruce growled, but the Scot spared only a brief look for the man who would one day likely be his king. Angus speared her with his probing eyes once again.

She sucked in a sharp breath with a sudden realization. "You don't trust me," she said, hearing her surprised tone. Honestly, she was used to being the one to feel that way.

His gaze upon her was unflinching. "Trust must be earned," he confirmed, cutting his eyes to Elizabeth for a moment. Lillianna felt herself gape. He did not trust her cousin, either!

"Whatever could you think?" she murmured. "That we are leading you astray?" She had been half joking, but when his lips pressed together and his nostrils flared, she knew that was exactly what he believed.

"I am not your enemy," she said through clenched teeth.

"Ye are," he shot back, "until ye prove otherwise. And if ye ever fail to abide by one of my wishes, I will leave ye and nae look back."

Here was a situation unlike any she had ever encountered. This man distrusted her just as much as she distrusted him. It should have made her ecstatic. They could travel together and ignore each other. Yet she did not feel overly happy. She felt ridiculously hurt. She had lost more than sleep in the dungeon; it seemed she had lost her logic. She needed to recover it immediately. Having injured feelings over being judged duplicitous by a man who did not know her was irrational, and she was not an imprudent woman. Not to mention guilt was niggling in her. She had judged him, as well, and it was hard to deny in the face of his similar treatment.

She'd rather eat dirt than let the man know he'd managed to wound her heart in the few short minutes they'd known each other. It was supposed to be encased in iron! Plopping her hands on her hips, she said, "Perhaps it is I who will leave you in the woods if you prove too much of a hindrance to me."

Elizabeth laughed beside Lord Bruce, and he chuckled. Angus frowned at her, but before he could offer a reply, Elizabeth tossed a priest's frock at him. It was meant as a disguise so that he could safely ride into the woods to flee the castle with her and Elizabeth. No one would question her riding out with Elizabeth and a priest, but they would stop Angus.

"Put these on," her cousin demanded.

Lillianna was vaguely aware that Elizabeth had turned her back to the men, and Lillianna meant to do the same but she could not seem to wrench her attention away from Angus. Everything about the man commanded notice. It wasn't just his size, though his stature was impressive. He had his massive arms crossed over his wide chest as he stared at her. His powerful legs were spread in a wide, battle-ready stance, and the fingers of his right hand grazed the handle of his sword, as if he thought he might need to use it, while his left hand gripped the priest's frock. But perhaps more than that, it was the tilt of his head, the slight cocksure curl of his lip, as if he were ready to refute any opposition to his command.

Suddenly, a very alarming, rather challenging, purely wolfish smile pulled the corners of his lips into a grin that could only be described as sinful. "If ye wish to watch me disrobe…" he said, slinging the priest's frock over his shoulder and then hooking his index finger underneath the material of the braies that clung to his powerful hips. He arched his thick, dark eyebrows while tugging the material of his braies out just a bit. "I can oblige ye."

She turned swiftly away, heat burning her cheeks, and quickly walked to where her cousin stood gawking at her. Lord Bruce moved past her toward Angus and growled, "Must ye be so antagonizing?"

"Aye," the swine Angus replied, laughter clear in his voice. She did not hear any more of his response, as Elizabeth grabbed her by the hand and led her some feet away.

When they stood face-to-face, Lillianna said, "Can you believe he distrusts me? Us!" She could hear the incredulity in her own voice.

Elizabeth quirked up an eyebrow, and her blue eyes danced with merriment. "No more than you do him," she chided. "As for his skepticism of me, honestly, I'm glad he's so cautious. It heartens me to know Robert has such a careful man as a loyal warrior."

"There is that benefit," Lillianna agreed.

"And if my father or yours should come for you, Angus will protect you with his life."

"Neither of them will come for me, and you know it. They deem me worthless without any active seer powers. Uncle Richard only took me in last year because he had hoped exposing my true identity would bring forth whoever has the brooch." Lillianna bit her lip, her guilt threatening to expose itself. She had never told her cousin that she knew who possessed the brooch, or at least who *had* been in possession of it—Laird Drumlan. The necklace had been ripped straight from her mother's neck when she had escaped the man.

She forced a shrug when Elizabeth gave her a pitying look. "You know as well as I do that your father would have seen his threat through to kill me if did he not think you were complying with his order to seduce Lord Bruce and gain information. As for my father…"

His voice and image were suddenly in her head.

He loomed over her as she stood before him shaking, a mere child of eight summers. He kneeled so that his face was a hairsbreadth from hers. The flush of anger stained his cheeks, and his eyes narrowed ominously upon her. "Don't ever forget your place," *he hissed, grabbing her chin.*

She tried to nod. Though his grip on her chin was painful, the fear of the pain to come made her overcome the terror of the moment.

"Your only worth lies in the gift of sight that will one day be awakened in you. Until then, I do not want to be bothered with you. That includes you trying to flee me to see your wretched mother."

Her mother whimpered from the corner of the bedchamber in the isolated castle in which her father had imprisoned her. Lillianna darted her gaze to the corner, wanting one last glimpse of the mother she so rarely was permitted to see, but the glimpse she got made tears fill her eyes. Her mother's face was battered. Her lip split. Her eyes swollen. Hatred filled Lillianna, and she brought her gaze back to her father, wishing it could wield the blow of a sword.

He smiled maliciously at her. "Every time you dare to defy me, dare to make me even realize you are alive, until the day I need your power, your mother will suffer. Do you understand?"

"Lillianna?" Elizabeth's voice cut through the memory, and Lillianna started. Fear tingled across her spine, though she looked around and could see she was not at the castle where her mother had eventually died. "Lillianna, are you all right?"

"I will be," she assured Elizabeth, determined to make it so.

"Oh, Lil," Elizabeth said, hugging her.

Her cousin's use of the moniker that Lillianna's mother had given her stirred her restless memories once more.

"*Ye're safe now, Lil,*" *her mother said, pressing a shaky hand against Lillianna's cheek.* Lillianna swallowed as she looked down at her frail mother on her deathbed. "*I convinced yer father I had a vision that ye would nae ever fall in love. He will nae try to use ye any longer since the brooch is lost. Ye're safe.*"

"Lillianna!" Elizabeth's fraught cry was like ice-cold water being thrown in Lillianna's face.

"Shh," Lillianna hastened, seeing Lord Bruce and Angus glance their way. "It's just memories. Memories cannot hurt me."

Elizabeth gave her a disbelieving look. "We both know that's not true," she said quietly.

Lillianna sighed and linked her arm with her cousin's. "No, it's not. But let us pretend it is."

"If ye two are done whispering, we need to make haste," Angus boomed across the space that divided them.

Lillianna glanced at him to find him staring at her. His penetrating gray gaze felt as if it delved into the recesses of her mind, and she didn't care for it one bit. He seemed to be the sort of man who could discover secrets one would rather not reveal. Even still as he was, he exuded power. It rolled off him almost like a hot wave of air to caress her from the distance.

As he strode toward them with Bruce by his side, a half smile curled Angus's mouth. "How do I look?" he asked her, stopping in front of her.

"You are entirely too lean and too handsome to be a priest," Lillianna blurted, disconcerted by the intensity of his gaze upon her.

When he gave her a suspicious look, as if her words hid

some nefarious purpose, she had to swallow her laughter, and a little of her ever-present wariness slipped away. If he truly was just as suspicious of her as she was him, she could relax her guard a little, which would be a welcome respite. It was tedious always worrying about men's intentions.

"Did ye just compliment me?" he asked.

"Not purposely," she said, her amusement hitting her full force and causing her to smile.

His brows dipped together in a scowl as Elizabeth went to Robert, and the two of them walked toward the edge of the line of trees that marked the forest. Likely, they wished to speak in private. Angus's size seemed to swallow up all the open space in the small area of the half circle of the garden in which she stood with him. "I dunnae ken what ye find amusing," he said. "We're about to embark on a deadly mission during which our lives will be in constant danger. Ye are a liability to me, and ye must take our situation seriously at all times."

His words stung and infuriated her. She was heartily sick of being considered worthless. "I do," she bit out, banishing all traces of her amusement. "Give me a weapon."

"What for?" he demanded.

"So I will not be a *liability*," she snapped.

He surprised her by whipping out a dagger from a holder on his hip and handing it to her. She gripped the hilt as he said, "I assume ye ken how to use a dagger."

"I do," she assured him as she took it.

"Who taught ye? Yer father?"

His question stilled her for a moment as the clamoring memories rattled in her head.

"*I can hear you, Lillianna,*" *her father said loudly enough that the talking in the great hall ceased. She tensed in her seat at* the back as her father stood. He slammed his goblet against the table. "You know I do not like to hear your voice!" he roared. "You sound like her! You sound like your ban-druidh mother!"

The people around Lillianna gasped. Heat consumed her face, neck, and chest. They thought her father was referring to the woman he supposedly bedded and got with child—and she was that child. Her father had spread the lie, so no one would know that Lillianna was a MacLeod descendant, like her mother. He wanted everyone to believe that Lillianna was the result of a liaison outside of marriage. Lillianna knew the truth. There had never been another woman. Lillianna was no bastard child, and her mother had most definitely not fled her father as he had led people to believe. Her father had sent her mother away to torture her and Lillianna. Her mother had wanted to flee him, of course, but she never would have left Lillianna.

"Lass?"

Lillianna blinked back to the moment at hand and the powerful Scot before her. She swallowed as their eyes locked. "I taught myself," she replied. She had done so with the intention of one day escaping her father's home, but then she had been sent away. Feeling as if Angus could see the truth in her head, she turned from him and searched for Elizabeth and Lord Bruce. They still stood near the woods in an embrace.

Suddenly, Angus's heat enveloped her from behind. His body brushed her backside at the same moment his arm slid around her waist, and he handily relieved her of the dagger she held before she even knew what had occurred. His arm tightened around her like a band of steel, and he pulled her gently against him. He pressed his mouth close to her ear as he raised the dagger in front of her face. She was helpless to reach for it with her arms penned at her side. "Yer first lesson of the dagger is to nae ever lose it."

With those words, he released her and spun her to face him. She gasped as his fingers caught her wrist. He raised her hand and set the hilt of the dagger in her palm. He positioned her fingers so that her index finger pressed against the hilt while her other fingers curled around it. "This is the most secure way to hold a dagger. Do ye ken?"

His fiery gaze locked on her, almost searing in its intensity. "Yes," she whispered, her heart pounding.

An almost gentle look swept his face, and he nodded as if satisfied. "I will teach ye more, as we travel."

"Thank you," she whispered, touched. No one had ever offered to teach her anything.

He frowned and then shrugged. "Dunnae make too much of it, aye? I'd simply rather have ye able to protect yerself so I dunnae have to fash myself over ye every moment of the day."

"Of course," she automatically replied, sensing that he would anyway. She suspected that Angus MacLorh was instinctually protective, but for some reason, he did not want her to think so. There certainly was more to this man than the gruff Highlander he appeared to be.

Chapter Three

Richard Og de Burgh hiked up the willing Lady Grace's skirts and found, to his delight, that she had worn nothing under them. "You," he said, pressing his mouth to her ear, "are a most naughty lady-in-waiting to the Queen of England."

"And you," she said, "are a noble dutiful to the king *and* queen and a naughty husband. I doubt your wife would be pleased to learn you are joining with me."

All of Richard's good humor left him in a flash. He grabbed Grace's lovely neck and squeezed. "Are you threatening me, Grace?"

"Richard, no," she said, her voice pleasantly beseeching. "I was teasing you. Only teasing, my love."

Love. He hated that word. His wife bemoaned the fact that he did not love her. His willful daughter Elizabeth bemoaned the fact that he asked her to wed as he needed her to for the good of their family, even if it included the wretched Bruce. Elizabeth wished for love. Bah! And his niece, Lillianna, ironically, could not seem to find love.

By God, the one time he'd hoped for it for someone! He had even fallen on his knees and prayed to God to bestow it upon her so her powers of sight would come to her. Damn Lillianna's dead mother! Richard was certain that his weaker brother Brice's now deceased wife Kara had somehow put a curse on Lillianna so that the girl would not find love. Damn the word *love*. Damn the concept of it. Damn all the weak people in the world who were ruled by it. And damn the Brooch of Lagothmier, which he had spent a year searching for since Brice had admitted to him that Lillianna was really a MacLeod.

"Richard?" Grace whined, annoying him.

He set her down hard and motioned to her. "Leave me."

His appetite for her was gone, his mood dark once more. His time was at an end. He could no longer delay telling King Edward that he had failed to find the brooch that would bring the seer power to his loveless niece.

"Richard, let me please you," Grace begged, which only irritated him further. He hated beggars.

"Get out before I have you flogged," he threatened, enjoying the fear that suddenly lit her eyes.

She gathered her slippers and raced to the bedchamber door with them in her hands, but at a knock, she suddenly turned to him, looking like a scared doe. He despised fear almost as much as he despised love.

"Open the damned door," he ordered. She did so, skirting Donovan, the guard who stood in the doorway, and then she disappeared down the hall. Richard frowned. "Why are you bothering me at this hour?"

"I received a message I thought you would like to read," Donovan said, smiling.

Richard waved the man in with a frown and watched Donovan stride toward him. The man was bold. Perhaps too much so. Maybe he should kill him? No. He'd already thought about this. He had not killed Donovan when he had delivered the news that the spy Richard had sent to Laird Drumlan's castle in Scotland had failed to find the brooch. He'd allowed Donovan to live because he could be quite useful. Perhaps one day Richard would send Donovan to kill that nasty Scot Drumlan. Richard would wager his life that the man had the brooch. It made the most sense since Kara had been seen wearing it years before when Drumlan had captured her, according to Brice. But when she had escaped and then Brice had gotten his clutches on her, the brooch had been gone. Brice had been such a damned fool to believe he could make Kara MacLeod love him and gain her powers. His brother had been an even bigger fool not to confide all this to Richard before last year. Maybe if he'd known sooner, he could have retrieved the brooch.

Donovan held the note out, and as Richard grasped it and turned it over, he saw the seal of the spy he'd sent to Drumlan's castle right after Richard had found out about Lillianna and the brooch. Richard frowned. Thornsby was supposed to be imprisoned for failing to find the brooch. "What's the meaning of this?"

"It seems that Thornsby escaped the prison some months ago, according to his note," Donovan said, taking a step backward, as if he expected Richard to lash out at him.

Richard chuckled, but his humor was short-lived as he considered the news. He unfolded the note and began to read of the escape. Then his breath caught.

> I have seen the brooch, my lord. It is in Drumlan's possession, but his castle is well guarded. If you are reading this note instead of my telling you in person, I have been killed. I beg you, as I proved your loyal servant, to take care of my wife and my son. Send them the money you promised me.
>
> Your humble knight,

Thornsby

Richard smiled slowly, his heartbeat speeding up. He folded the note and glanced up at Donovan. "Bring me Lillianna. I cannot wait to see her face when she understands she has been outwitted by me. I have the lady, and soon I will get that brooch, even if I have to storm Drumlan's castle myself."

As Angus rode away from the Palace of Westminster and into the woods with the lass Lillianna by his side, he looked back over his shoulder. He did not like leaving Robbie alone with their enemies, but the time to argue had passed. Robbie had decided, against Angus's advice, to trust Lady Elizabeth. Now Angus would do the best he could to ensure he did not lead the king's men directly to Robbie's vassals hiding in Ettrick Forest. Those men were outlaws because they had followed Robbie and Angus and the other Renegades in revolt against King Edward, and Angus felt a deep responsibility to do all in his power to ensure they were not killed or taken prisoner.

He scanned the lush, green forest around them, searching always for enemies and a way out in case they were attacked. He was not yet willing to dismiss the notion that Lady Elizabeth might be scheming with her father and her godfather, and that the scheming included her lying to Robbie to make him believe the king knew where Robbie's men were hiding. If Angus were the King of England—

"What are you scowling about?" Lillianna asked.

He looked to his right where she rode on her horse. He was not in the habit of revealing his inner thoughts to a lass, and he was not about to change that now, especially not with a lass as alluring as she was. Yet, he had learned over the years that one could often discern truths one's enemy wished to hide by revealing a bit of oneself.

"I was just thinking that if I were the King of England, I would have instructed my goddaughter to convince Robbie that I kenned where his men were so that my knights could follow him or one of his comrades when they went to warn those in hiding, and then ambush them." He arched his eyebrows in expectation of her response, but when she arched hers back at him, he had to bite his cheek against the unexpected desire to laugh. He'd give the lass this—she didn't seem to scare easily. She had to know he was accusing her and her cousin of scheming with the king. "Is that what is happening here?" he pressed.

She quirked her mouth into a half-amused, half-contemptuous look. "Do you honestly think my cousin would send me with you if she was conspiring with her father and the king to lead you to your certain death?" He opened his mouth to answer, but Lillianna spoke before he could. "Elizabeth loves me, and she would never put me in danger, which is why she sent me away even though she is putting herself in peril by doing so."

He could not deny that Lady Elizabeth did seem to care for her cousin. Still, he knew from experience that lasses could be deadly deceptive. "I dunnae ken what to believe. It would seem yer cousin cares for ye, but can ye say for certain that I'm nae being used to lead the king to my comrades in hiding?"

Her gaze grew almost frigid, her knuckles white where they gripped her horse's reins. She appeared frightened, but the expression swiftly disappeared and a steely look, one he could hardly believe such a gentle-looking creature could conjure, replaced it. Cool air hit his teeth, making him startle. He was not sure a lass had ever caused his mouth to gape with such surprise.

"I can say nothing with full certainty," she said. "I do not have the power to see the future, nor am I currently or was I ever privy to the plots of the king and my uncle." She paused and stared at him for a long silent moment, as if she were trying to discern something about him.

"I did nae guess ye to be lippy," he grumbled to cover up his continuing desire to laugh. He was surely going daft. The lass had not given him an answer; rather, she had very cleverly made her point.

He should be irritated, not amused. And he should be wary, as there was something about a beautiful and highly intelligent woman that stirred his blood. The thought had him sitting rigid in his saddle. The only other time a lass had affected him like lightning striking through his veins had been Isla, and that she-devil had robbed him of his good sense, the consequences of which he had to live with every single day.

He stole a sidelong glance at Lillianna and found her staring back at him, distrust in the depths of her gaze. Her vulnerability struck him hard in the chest, making it tighten. It called to mind Robbie's earlier words.

Devil take it! He was a warrior, not a man to be brought down by lust. Because that's what was attempting to invade his body, mind, and soul—desire. Nothing more. It was entirely too bad that Lillianna was not the sort of lass with whom to have a romp in the hay. If she were, he could do so and then be rid of the desire she had ignited.

"How long do you think the journey to Ettrick Forest will take?" she asked.

"A sennight," he replied, his voice gruff in an attempt to

cover any hint of what he was feeling.

She frowned at him. "And how long will we ride until we stop for a respite?"

"One stop at midday and then tonight," he said, motioning to a branch hanging low in their path so she would duck.

She did, her hair cascading over the side of her face to hide it for a moment, but when she sat upright once more, she shoved her hair back and scowled at him. "One stop," she echoed. "Will not the horses get tired?"

"Aye, but they are bred for war and used to riding for long periods without rest."

Her forehead creased, and she nibbled on her lower lip, as if concerned about something.

"Can ye nae ride that long?" he asked. He'd not considered it at first, but it made sense. She was not a warrior. He assumed that she'd never ridden from somewhere possibly pursued and hunted, and most definitely not without the luxury to halt for a respite. But no matter her answer, they could not stop, so if she said she did not think she could manage it, he would have to put her on his horse with him, in front of him, between his thighs.

God above...

He mumbled a prayer for sense and strength as images of her lush bottom pressed invitingly against his groin filled his head and heated him. He had been without a woman for too long. That had to be why she was affecting him this way. He was not normally like a whelp who had not yet had his first tumble in the hay.

She lifted her chin. "Of course I can," she assured him. "I was merely worried for the horses."

Her suddenly splotchy neck revealed her lie, but he did not dispute her words. In fact, a bit of admiration filled him for her willingness to try to ride for that length of time. Most women he had known in his life would have put up a fit upon hearing the news that they would stop only once before nightfall. There was a full day ahead, after all. His youngest sister, Mari, would have been wailing at the discovery of how long she was expected to ride, but then, she was a particularly spoiled lass. It was his fault for indulging her. He'd always felt so guilty for her having to grow up without their father and mother. He had a sudden memory of seeing his father lying in his own blood from the wounds he'd received in the battle that Angus had missed. Guilt battered him and grew stronger when an image of his mother, wasting away of heartbreak after his father's death, filled Angus's head. He forced the memories down and thought upon his sisters. Mari was the baby of the family—if one could still call a lass of eighteen summers a baby—and he'd treated her as such. Greer, his other sister, was different. She was as tough as any warrior he knew—except himself, of course.

"Glad to hear ye will nae have trouble staying upright upon yer horse, for ye likely have all the morning and into the afternoon to do so." He watched her face, eager to see her reaction. The lass was not particularly good at disguising how she felt, which suited him perfectly.

Her eyes narrowed, and her lips pressed into a hard line. Clearly, she did not like seeming weak. That was good because she was soft and feminine, and therefore, naturally weak, but if she was prideful and she wanted to be strong, she had a much better chance of survival.

"Oh, that's perfectly fine. I'll have no trouble," she replied.

The quiver in her voice contradicted her bold words, and for a brief moment, he considered offering to put her on his horse right then. But three things stopped him: the longer they could travel on two horses, the better to keep from overtiring one horse; the more distance he could maintain between himself and Lillianna, the easier it would be to control his desire; and lastly, he needed her to have a burning desire to survive because he had a gut feeling they were going to come up against not only severe conditions but battle.

He glanced up toward the sky and thought about the best way to get to Ettrick Forest. From here to Ettrick, it was nothing but land controlled by King Edward. "We'll have to keep to the woods and remain guarded at all times," he said. "If ye feel weak and need to stop, simply say so."

"I will not feel weak," she grumbled.

The lass had fire, which he was purposely stoking because she would need it. They had hard riding ahead of them for the sennight it took to get to Ettrick Forest, not to mention a lass such as she would not be used to cold winter nights in the outdoors. She'd likely never slept on the hard ground in her entire life.

"Let's see what ye're made of then," he said, goading her.

She thrust back her shoulders, and he could practically see the determination coursing through her. "Do you fear we will be pursued? Is that why you don't wish to halt for respites?"

"Partly," he said. "But I also need to warn my comrades as quickly as possible."

She nodded, then cocked her head in apparent thought. "My uncle will not bother himself to come after me, so you can at least set that worry out of your mind."

Pity stirred in him that her uncle, her blood, obviously did not care for her. "What of yer father?" he asked, guiding his horse toward a path that looked more traveled and would be less dangerous to set the horses to a gallop. When she didn't answer, he looked to her. The scarlet tint coloring her cheeks revealed her embarrassment.

"My father will not be coming for me. He...he simply won't, so you have no need to fear him."

Angus had a sudden desire to learn the details of her relationship with her father, but he clamped his teeth together on the question. The first rule of not becoming entangled with the lasses he joined with was to only ever join with lasses who clearly seemed to only want him for his body. The second rule was to never ask—or answer—personal questions.

"That's good," he said, instead of telling her he was sorry or asking any questions. As the trail opened up before him, he felt relief to be able to ride so fast that all he could concentrate on was that. "We gallop!" he announced, then nudged his horse and took off without glancing back at her. He did not need to look back. Her horse's hooves pounded behind him, but even if he could not have heard them, her presence warmed his back like a beam of sun, silent, unseen, yet encompassing. It was disconcerting and alluring at the same time.

Lillianna gritted her teeth at the constant jarring motion that sent pain through her tailbone and seemed to reverberate up her spine. She glared at Angus's back as he rode ahead, his dark hair fanning behind him with the fast pace he had set them to hours ago. The high-handed Scot had simply announced what they were going to do and had not even bothered to wait for her reply. He'd taken off like a blur and had them galloping across the hardest terrain she'd ever ridden in her life.

Her hands were cramped from her death grip on her reins, and the skin stung as if it had been chafed raw, but she dare not look to confirm her suspicions. She was certain Angus was testing her to see just how long she could ride. She would stay on the blasted saddle until he called for them to halt or she fell off from exhaustion. She was heartily sick of feeling that she had no value beyond the powers she might possess, and now that she was leaving England, she would prove otherwise. She stared at Angus's back. She was going to show him—and herself—that she was no millstone.

So when Angus picked up the pace even more, she squeezed her thighs together on her destrier and pressed her lips shut on any desire to utter a complaint. Yet, as morning slid toward day, the tender skin of her inner thighs throbbed and burned, and she feared what sort of chafing she would find there when he did finally call for them to halt.

As he rode them through valleys thick with trees, the little bit of sun that was out became hidden and the temperature dropped. Her teeth chattered as they galloped across the rocky bank of a stream, and the water splashed up on her skirts, soaking them and causing gooseflesh to sweep across her entire body. Not daring to release her reins to warm herself, she hunched forward, nearly touching the horse's mane with her nose.

"We'll stop here," Angus suddenly barked from ahead of her. Before she could even so much as right herself, Angus had halted his horse and whipped around to look at her. "That's nae a proper way to ride," he announced.

Multiple sarcastic responses flowed through her mind, but first she had to stop the chattering of her teeth. She clenched down hard on them, sat up, and rubbed her hands vigorously over her arms to warm herself while Angus stared at her. A frown appeared on his face, which deepened to almost comical proportions, except she was entirely too cold to laugh.

"Ye're cold?" he asked, sounding astonished.

She forced her freezing lips into what she hoped was a smirk. "Of course not," she replied, purposely exaggerating her words. "My teeth always chatter, and I always rub myself like I'm trying to put out a fire on my skin."

"I suppose I should nae be surprised," he said, managing to sound utterly insulting. "Ye people who are nae full blooded Scot are nae made of hearty stock."

Fury blazed through her, and before she knew what she was doing, she had taken off her slipper and threw it at his head. He caught it easily, but he gaped at her, his astonishment clear. Frankly, she was shocked at herself, too. She'd never allowed herself to lose her temper with a man in her life. She'd never dared for fear of the punishment she would receive, but for whatever reason, she realized with a start, she did not fear Angus would harm her. Was it because he claimed not to believe in the legend? It was foolish to let down her guard because of that.

"Lippy and bad-tempered," he grumbled, waving her slipper at her.

"I'm neither of those things," she bit out. "I simply do not like being seen as a burden. I'm plenty hearty, and I'll prove it."

"Oh, aye? This should be entertaining," he said with a chuckle as he dismounted his horse and walked over to her. He looked at her for a long moment, and as his gaze held hers, a flame sparked in his eyes, warming her. Slowly, he held her slipper out to her, but when she grabbed it and went to tug it away from him, he held firm. "If ye intend to harm someone when ye throw something at them, ye need to be quicker about it."

She felt her eyes widen in shock that this gruff man was giving her advice. "I was not intending to harm you," she replied. "I lost my temper."

His lips pulled into a smile that contradicted his mostly cold attitude—thus far—and made her heart stutter. His smile was teasing and slightly dangerous at the same time. "I ken," he replied, "which is why I'm willing to offer ye advice now. If ye are intending to harm someone when ye throw something at them, never hesitate. Acting quickly is the best way to overcome their defenses. And aim for the middle of the forehead."

"I'll remember that," she said, her curiosity awoken by him. He showed the world a gruff exterior, but he seemed to be hiding a naturally protective side that hinted at some softness. "Do you have sisters?" she asked, thinking perhaps that's what made him so protective.

His eyebrows dipped together. "Aye. Why?"

"Well," she said, leaning to her right to try to put her slipper back on, but when she started to tilt a bit, she instinctually held her hand out to stop her fall and met with what felt like rock. Her eyes flew from her foot to Angus's chest where she half clutched her slipper and him. "I'm sorry," she mumbled, trying to push away, but he caught her wrist, snagged the slipper from her clutch, and bent down. Before she knew what was occurring, his fingers, strong and warm, encircled her ankle.

She stilled, but her heartbeat exploded at the contact of his hands on her ankle. Never had she been touched there by a man. Her belly clenched, and heat pooled deep. She was not naive. She had heard the servant women gossip and giggle about men and desire, and she knew unequivocally that's what she felt in this moment. Did he know? God, she hoped not! She did not dare look at him, but suddenly, his jagged inhalation caressed her ears, and his fingers, which were curled around her ankle, momentarily tightened, as if he too had some strong emotion coursing through him.

"There ye go," he said, the slipper sliding onto her foot. His voice was rough and strained to her ears. Instantly, he released his hold and stood. "Why did ye ask me if I have sisters?"

She immediately looked down and fidgeted with her reins, trying to think how to pose what she'd thought, without revealing too much. She could feel his stare upon her head like a fire at her back, unseen but no less hot. Swallowing hard, she forced herself to look up and meet his gaze. The intensity of it stole her breath.

"I... Well, you seem to have a gentle side," she blurted, thinking of his offer to teach her the proper way to hold and use a dagger, and then his advice on the best way to throw something at someone with the aim of injuring them. His appalled look at being called *gentle* made her want to chuckle, but she suspected he would not appreciate that.

"I dunnae have a *gentle* side," he replied, as if the word were an insult. "Dunnae mistake my nae wishing ye to die under my care for a soft side. Can ye dismount without aid?"

"Of course," she said breezily, biting her tongue on pointing out that an inconsiderate man, a hard man, would likely not even have asked that question. He gave a curt nod, turned, and started toward his horse. Lillianna set her palms, which were almost numb from the cold, to the horse's flesh to shove off and dismount, but a niggling pain through both her palms stopped her.

She turned her hands over and gaped. The flesh was

raw, cut and bleeding from gripping her reins so hard. She hated being so cold, but in this instance, it was a good thing because it numbed the pain. Yet, now that she was aware of her wounds, they started throbbing. She clenched her teeth and once more positioned her hands to dismount, but as she swung one leg over the horse, excruciating pain raced from her inner thighs to her mind and made her want to scream. She barely contained it and was rather proud of herself for her show of fortitude. But the moment her feet hit the ground, she knew she was in trouble. Her legs buckled, and she grasped the horse in order not to fall flat on her bottom.

The beast neighed a startled protest, and suddenly, heat consumed her from behind and the smell of pine surrounded her. "What's wrong, lass?" Angus asked, not touching her, yet he may as well have been. Her body tingled in memory of his hand on her ankle.

"Nothing," she said, her voice sounding thick to her own ears. "My legs are a little numb from all the riding, but I'm good."

"Ye're certain?" Angus asked, his warm breath tickling the back of her neck. She willed herself not to react to him. "Did ye hear me, lass?"

His breath whispering across her neck made her shiver. She nodded. "I'm perfectly capable of standing on my own two feet," she snapped, irritated at herself that he made her react to him at all. She shoved away from the horse, and her legs promptly buckled again. She flailed her hands in the air to try to grasp the horse once more, but Angus's arms slid deftly around her waist, and before she could protest, he had hauled her off her feet. She found her legs caught by one of his arms, her right shoulder pressed against his chest, and his other arm securely across her back with his fingers curled around her shoulder.

She struggled to put space between herself and the hardness of Angus's body, but it was no use. He pulled her a little closer and tighter. "Quit squirming," he ordered.

She'd been ordered about all her life by her father, his men, and then her uncle. She refused to be dictated to any longer. This was a new start to her life, and she was going to take it. She was no longer a burden, no longer meek, no longer afraid—well, except to let herself love, but that was not fear, that was being prudent.

"Put me down," she responded.

"I will when I'm certain ye can stand," he replied.

"What do you care if I can stand or not?" she asked, poking his sculpted chest. Angus had to spend hours every day training with his sword to be so cut. He was like a rock that had been chiseled with the utmost attention.

"I *care*," he replied, surprising her when he hooked a finger under her chin and forced her gaze to his, "because if ye fall and hurt yerself, ye will become even more of a burden to me."

"I am not a burden," she bit out, smacking his hand away from her chin. Pain lanced through the cut on her hand, causing her to wince. When his gaze darted to her hand, she drew it protectively to her chest and laced her fingers.

He stared at her for a long moment, his brow furrowing. She was sure he was going to demand to see her hand, but then he said, "So ye keep saying. Yet here ye are, unable to stand on yer own two feet."

She would have been offended by his words, except his cool, gray gaze grew smoky with what appeared to be merriment. "I had a moment of needing to adjust," she said, lifting her chin. "There is no shame in that. I've not ridden as long as we just did in quite a while."

"How long?" he asked, hitching up his dark eyebrows.

Not since she'd been ten, but he did not need to know that. When her father had decided she was leaving her girlhood behind, he had ordered her contained to the grounds of his estate until the day she had been sent to live with her uncle. She recalled well the day her father had given the dictate. He had told her it was because his castle was on the border of England and Scotland, and he feared the savage Scots would abduct her.

Initially, she'd been touched by his admission and hope that he might truly love her sprouted within her, but then he had gone on to say that he could not have someone taking her and her potential powers from his control. Her heart squeezed at the memory, but she steeled herself against allowing any pain to seep from the old wound.

"How long?" Angus repeated.

"At least several fortnights," she lied.

He gave her a disbelieving look, and she held her breath, waiting for him to accuse her of lying, but then that same gentle look from before settled on his features. "When ye ride for a long time, ye must be certain to loosen yer grip on the reins or else they will cut into yer skin as sharply as a well-honed blade."

Now he told her. Inhaling a long breath, she said, "Yes, I'm aware." She had to get him to put her down so she could get away from him and see how bad her injuries were. "I can stand now. Please—" she swallowed against a wave of pain "—put me down."

There was something wrong with the lass. All the color had left her face, and she was digging her nails into his shoulder as if she was struggling to suppress something. She was injured. He was almost certain of it, but she'd never readily admit it. And she had been lying about her experience riding long distances; her chest and neck had become splotchy with her attempt to deceive him. He'd learn why after he found out what was wrong with her.

Without a word, he set her down, grasped her wrists, and turned her hands palms up. Deep gashes ran the length of both her palms. "God's teeth!" he roared, more worried for her than angry. "Why did ye nae ask me to halt? Why did ye nae tell me ye were injured?" It was one thing to want the lass to try to be strong, but it was quite another to allow her to injure herself badly in the process.

Her chin came to a stubborn tilt. "Because I did not have need."

Guilt slammed him in the chest. He'd done this. He'd goaded her, thinking to make her stronger, but this was foolish. "Ye had need, lass," he said, gentling his tone. "If these cuts become infected ye'll grow verra ill, and then we'll have to halt for certain. And for a much longer time than we can spare."

"Oh!" Her cheeks pinked. "I'd not thought of that... I'll find a stream to wash the cuts and then bind them."

"I'll aid ye. We will set out again after." She'd have to ride with him to protect her hands now, but he suspected she'd fight him still, so he'd simply not tell her. He'd sling her on the horse, and that would be that.

"You'll aid me?" Her eyes had grown wide, and a distinctly uneasy look crossed her face. "I do not need your aid."

"Nay?" He cocked his head. "Do ye ken the healing arts? Are ye so impressive that ye can bind yer own hands?"

Her shoulders sagged, but then her brow furrowed. "Do

you know the healing arts?"

He chuckled. He couldn't help it. She sounded so completely surprised. He was aware it was unusual for a man to know the healing arts. He'd received this reaction many times in the past. "Aye," he said. "In truth, I ken just a bit. Enough to keep me alive if my wounds are nae too grave. If the wounds are dire, then I'd need a true healer like my sister Greer."

"Is your mother a healer, then? Did she teach you both?"

He hesitated. This was a personal conversation, but as it was not about his feelings—or lack of them—he decided it was all right to answer her. "She was a healer. She's dead."

"Oh. I'm so sorry." She reached for him then, her fingertips grazing his arm before she let her hand quickly drop away. His skin tingled where she had touched it, and the genuine sorrow in her voice wormed its way into his chest and made him feel oddly as if he wanted to soothe her.

He shrugged. "Dunnae be sorry," he said, intending to leave it at that.

"You don't care about your own mother dying?" she asked on a gasp.

"I do," he assured her. But he refused to be baited into any more personal conversation.

She stepped back, a look of fear sweeping across her face, and he let out a disgruntled sigh. He'd have to give the lass a few details, so she didn't think she was traveling with a cold-blooded man who she needed to fear. Not wanting to be entangled with lasses was one thing, but scaring them witless was another.

"Her death was a blessing of sorts," he explained slowly, watching Lillianna's face for any sign that she was more at ease. As soon as he saw it, he'd give no more details. "She fell verra ill with grief after my father was killed, and she could nae even get out of bed."

The memory of it struck him like a swift punch to his chest. He'd never talked of his mother's death, nor the guilt he felt over it, to anyone, not even his siblings. His shame for his actions, his decision to go to Isla to ensure her safety instead of riding to his father to aid him in battle against the Belfaine, ate at him daily. He had been distracted by Isla, as she had intended, and he had failed to see that he was being deceived. He had failed in his duties as the laird's son. He had failed his family.

He blinked, focusing on Lillianna once more. "My mother stayed in her bed for months, just wasting away. She would nae eat. I forced broth in her mouth, but eventually…" He swallowed, his throat suddenly very tight. He looked down at his hands, guilt pressing ever more heavily on him. It was his fault his father had died, and therefore, it was also his fault his mother had died. "Eventually she died," he finished.

"I am so very sorry, Angus."

Her trembling voice caused him to look up, and he was shocked to see her eyes glistening with unshed tears. She was a tenderhearted creature. He purposely never bedded such lasses; they were not the sort to want to join simply for pleasure. He felt a strong desire to shield her from harm, both physical and mental. This is what personal conversations would get him.

"Thank ye," he said stiffly, needing to reconstruct the barrier between them.

She exhaled a long, slow breath, her gaze moving past him as if looking somewhere else. "I cannot imagine feeling a love that powerful."

"A curse to be certain," he said. He shoved his own

memories away, as her eyes met his. He expected her to refute what he'd said, as his sister Mari always did. She was a tenderhearted lass, too.

"I could not agree more," Lillianna replied, shocking him for the second time in a very short expanse of time. "Shall we find a stream to cleanse my wounds?"

The woman was perplexing, and he could not help but think that figuring out a complex creature such as Lillianna would be rewarding, almost like winning a battle. He scowled at the weak thought and turned from her. "Follow me," he said, determined not to allow them to get to know each other any further. She was a mission, plain and simple.

Chapter Four

Lillianna was immensely relieved that Angus was stalking ahead of her. The mere act of walking nearly brought her to tears. Her inner thighs burned fiercely, making her certain the skin there looked much like the raw, bleeding skin of her hands. She had to get a moment of privacy to look without him knowing she might be injured there, as well. It would be mortifying.

He made quick work of securing their mounts, and then he motioned toward the thick brush. "There's water that way."

"How do you know?" she asked, looking in the direction he'd indicated. She saw only huge, ancient, moss-covered trees with large trunks and naked limbs. Winter had taken the bright-green leaves of summer, but this forest was so crowded with trees, vines, and shrubs that it was still impossible to see very far, even with so many bare tree limbs.

"I heard it," he replied without stopping. He shoved a branch to the side, the underbrush crunching beneath his feet, and then he paused. "Are ye coming?"

She stilled to try to hear it. "I don't hear anything," she answered.

He turned to her, a resigned expression on his face, as if he was used to needing to further explain himself. Mayhap his sisters often asked for clarification from him? She had never been part of real family, so she could only muse that this was what family loyalty and love looked like; doing things you didn't necessarily want to. Her mother had loved her and had been loyal, as best she could, but they had not lived together and never had a chance to truly become acquainted.

"Are you close to your sister?" she asked.

"I protect them." His answer was evasive as he motioned for her to keep following him.

"You have two sisters?"

"Aye."

"What I meant," she said, trying again, "is, do you care for them?"

"Aye," he said, stalking ahead. "What do ye think I mean by protecting them?"

"How am I to know," she grumbled. "Protection can be given out of duty and no love at all."

"*Love* is nae a word warriors use, lass. That's a woman's word." He held a branch back for her as he walked.

His responses were gruff, but his actions were honorable. She bit her lip, wanting to ask him more, and then decided she simply would. "Do you have other siblings?"

"Do ye always talk this much?" he demanded, his exasperation clear in his terse tone.

"With my cousin," she said. She did not want to reveal that she'd had no one else to ever talk to. Her father had made certain she was isolated.

"Besides my two sisters I have two brothers. Now, move faster. We kinnae linger here."

He picked up the pace, clearly not considering that she might not obey his dictate, so she stopped and allowed him to walk away, wondering how long it would take him to realize she was not lapping at his heels like a puppy. It took three steps.

When he faced her again, a warning cloud had settled on his features. "Are ye always this uncompliant?"

"No," she answered honestly. He need not know she'd previously feared not obeying orders.

"Ah, so yer behavior is just for me?" He rucked up his eyebrows and glared at her.

"Well," she said, "yes and no." When his eyes narrowed dangerously, she knew she had to explain herself. Otherwise, she feared he'd lose his patience and simply throw her over his shoulder and take her to the stream. Her mother had said Scottish men were a hotheaded lot, who got what they desired one way or another. "I was always obedient before."

Please, please let him leave it at that.

He opened and closed his mouth several times, almost as if he were fighting against himself to continue the conversation. "And?" he finally spit out.

"And as you are neither my father nor my uncle, I don't feel compelled to obey you," she said, purposely not mentioning that she did not fear him as she had them.

"Nay, I'm nae yer relation. But I am yer protector. We've been through this. It's my duty to deliver ye safely to yer mother's clan, and I mean for ye to be alive when I do it. Now come along."

"I will. I simply want to know—"

"Now," he ordered.

She bit her tongue on calling him a few choice foul names. "I'm not a dog to be ordered about. Do you hear me?" she demanded, surprised at the anger she felt. She pointed her finger at him. "Men think to order women always, and we must obey for fear of punishment. I tell you,

I refuse to be fearful anymore." She ended with a huff.

The anger on his face slipped away, and a somber expression replaced it. "Were ye fearful, then? Before? That's why ye were obedient?"

She'd not meant to reveal so much, but now that she had, she could not take it back. "Yes."

Cold fury lit his eyes and twisted his mouth. "Did yer father hit ye? Yer uncle, too?"

"No… Well, not often." The look on his face changed from furious to deadly. She suspected if her father or her uncle had been standing in front of Angus right now, they would have had to deal with his wrath.

"There is nae ever a reason for a man to hit a woman," he growled.

There it was again—the fierce, honorable protector hiding behind his gruff exterior. That was the sort of man a woman could develop a tendre for, if she was so inclined. Of course, Lillianna was not. How different she might be if her father had been a good man. He was not, though, so there was no point in dwelling on it. He had not hit her often, but whenever she had displeased him, he had hurt her mother, so Lillianna did all in her power not to anger him.

"There are other ways to hurt people," she said, surprising herself. She'd not intended to utter her thoughts out loud.

"And what ways might yer da have used?"

She could not see the harm in revealing a few things to a man she would soon part from, one who did not appear to believe in the legend. "He hurt my mother when I displeased him. I learned very early on to never challenge him, never disobey, and always do as he asked."

"I'm of a mind to visit yer da after I see you settled at

the MacLeod castle," he said, his voice like ice.

His words startled her. No man had ever offered to be her champion, not even the ones who had tried to win her affection over the last year. Angus's selflessness and courage filled her with awe, but also fear for him. "I appreciate it. I really do, but don't ever do such a thing. You must vow it."

"I'll nae vow such a thing. Yer da deserves a lesson."

"He does, I agree. But his castle is well fortified and his men well trained." Angus scowled at her. She'd offended him! She rushed to clarify. "I'm not at all saying you could not fight him and win, Angus. It's just, avenging his wrongs against me is not worth your life."

"I'm nae in danger of losing my life, lass," he said, winking at her. "I'm fairly handy with a sword."

"Oh, I'm certain you are," she replied, her gaze drawn to his powerful shoulders and then his battle-honed arms. She imagined he was fearsome in a fight. When he cleared his throat, she realized that she'd once again been caught staring at him. This man was a danger to her, and he wasn't even trying to be. She needed to break the moment and the hold he seemed to have over her. "Should we not make haste?"

"Aye." He agreed so readily that she sensed he was uncomfortable, and no wonder! He must have been fawned over quite a bit and rather tired of it. And she'd likely been staring at him with her mouth agape!

He turned once more and started walking so fast she had to run to keep up with him, which made her grit her teeth against the pain in her thighs she was trying to ignore. In no time, they broke through a patch of thick brush, and the bank of a river was before them. He faced her, a smile hovering at his lips. "Do ye ken why ye did nae hear the water earlier?"

"No," she replied, forcing herself to ignore the pain.

"Because there is listening and then there is *hearing*."

"What the difference?" she asked, intrigued by the way he thought.

"I'll show ye," he said, and then he stood very still and quiet, so she did to. She thought it would be but a second, but when it became apparent that he meant for them to stand there for a few minutes, she tried to really hear everything around her. After a bit of time, he said, "what did ye hear?"

"Water rushing, the leaves blowing, an owl hooting in the distance," she said, rather proud of the last one.

He shook his head. "Ye listened, but ye did not hear. Hearing involves making yerself one with yer environment."

"All right," she said. "What did you hear?"

"Crickets chirping, a small animal hunting for food near us. Wood crunching under their feet."

That startled her. "How do you know it's not someone coming to pursue us?"

"People have heavy footfalls. 'Tis a much different sound than that of an animal. Come, ye can practice hearing while I clean yer wound."

The thought of him holding her hand to clean her wound started a flutter in her belly. "I can clean my own wound," she assured him.

"Nae as good as me, ye kinnae," he replied. "Now either come willingly to the river's edge or I'll toss ye over my shoulder and—"

"I'll go willingly," she interrupted. If he tossed her over his shoulder, her chest would be pressed against his skin and her bottom in his face. That seemed a decidedly intimate position, and she had no intention of becoming intimate with Angus.

"Wise choice." He turned and made his way to the steep river bank, then started to reach for her waist, likely to aid her down the incline.

"I can make my own way down, thank you." she said, not wishing to seem helpless.

"As ye wish," he replied, turned on his heel, and with graceful agility, snaked his way down the embankment in the time it took for her to inhale and exhale. She was determined to descend the bank with as much dexterity as he had shown, but when she stepped into the brush, her slipper landed on something squishy. She glanced down and saw a slithering snake underfoot. Screaming, she jerked away from the reptile, lost her balance, and went flying face forward down the embankment, only to be caught at the bottom by Angus. Her legs, where they rubbed together, and her hands, where she tried to catch herself, screamed in pain.

Her body collided with his, knocking the breath from her in a *whoosh*, and then his arms, warm and well-formed with muscle, encircled her in his protective embrace. He clutched her to his chest for but a brief second, but in that moment, she felt the thundering of his heart.

"Are ye all right?" he asked as he set her on her feet upon the flat, sandy bank.

"Were you worried?" she asked, her words coming out snappish due to her embarrassment.

He frowned. "It's polite to ask, aye? At least yer scowl showed me ye'd nae injured anything. Ye did nae hear the snake, I take it."

She gasped. "You knew that snake was there!"

"Aye," he replied, surprising her when he lightly took her elbow to lead her to the water. "Because I *heard* it," he said, his lips curling into the briefest of smiles.

She was intrigued by his ability to hear things she could not, but first... "Why did you not warn me?" she asked, starting to kneel as he had done by the water's edge, but he stopped her, and without a word, he stripped off his plaid, folded it up, and placed it on the ground beside him. He turned his face to the water so that she could not see it.

"For yer knees," he said, his tone hinting at his discomfort. "There are pebbles." He motioned to the sand. "My sisters always whine that the little things dig into their skin, and I'd rather nae hear ye whine."

She knew she was gaping again when the cool air hit her teeth, and she quickly clamped her jaw shut. No one had ever done such a thing for her before. It was a simple gesture, a thoughtful one, and it moved her to her core. She studied the back of his head for a moment, aware he was likely waiting for her to respond. His thick black hair hung just over his shoulder in waves. The muscles of his back strained against the tan skin. She allowed her gaze to wander downward, stopping on a long scar of about eight inches that ran from below his shoulder blade to the lower part of his ribs. She kneeled, not realizing how close she was, until her shoulder brushed his as she came to her knees. He turned his face to hers and his smoldering gaze snatched her breath. But when he blinked, it was as if ice-cold water had put out the flame that burned within him.

"Thank you for your plaid."

He nodded, his gaze assessing her. "Ye may wear it. It will get bitter cold when the sun goes down, and my sisters always whine when they're cold. And as I'd rather not hear ye whine—"

She pressed her lips together on the wish to laugh at his obvious attempt not to seem overly thoughtful to her. Why he wanted her to think he was simply being kind out of a desire not to hear her whine like his sisters, she did not know, nor was it her place to prod. She understood what it was to want to keep one's secrets.

She glanced to the sun. He was right about the impending chill. Winter was upon them. In fact, the new year was close. How near, she could not recall. "How many days until Hogmanay?"

"Ye ken Hogmanay?" His surprise was evident in his voice and upon his face.

"Of course," she replied.

"It's tomorrow," he said, his tone full of wistfulness. "Give me yer hand."

"Tomorrow? I had no idea," she murmured, not realizing she'd even offered her hand until his warm fingers closed gently around her bones.

"I'm nae shocked since ye were locked in a dungeon." His earlier anger surfaced in the vibration of his words. "This will sting a bit, but it's necessary."

She nodded and steeled herself against the pain as he tilted the wine skin she hadn't seen him take out. As he poured the liquid over the cut of her left hand, she clenched her teeth against the need to scream, but she could not stop the tears from filling her eyes. She held her eyes open wide, refusing to allow a single tear to escape.

"Ye're a braw lass," he said, releasing her hand and startling her by taking the edge of her skirt in his fist.

"What are you..." Before she finished the sentence, she understood his purpose and allowed her words to trail off. He ripped the material of her skirt quickly, took the long strip, and wound it around her left hand.

"To protect the wound from dirt and allow it to heal," he explained.

She nodded, her hand throbbing so severely now that waves of dizziness washed over her. When he reached for her right hand, she instinctually jerked away from him and brought her hand protectively to her chest.

Sympathy filled his eyes, which stunned her; she'd assumed he'd be irritated at her show of cowardliness. His gentle, understanding gaze rested on her and took the sharp edge off her fear, but not to the extent that she planned to willingly offer up her other hand for torture. She feared if she had to endure any more pain, she'd simply pass out. "I'm detaining us," she said as an excuse. "The wound on my other hand is not as terrible, and we should depart." She expected him to argue, but his eyes held hers, a look upon his face as if he was waiting for something. She had no notion what.

She licked her lips, her mind conjuring a thousand possible reasons. "If we linger too long and someone is following us, they'll catch up to us."

"Aye," he said, his voice as steady as his gaze.

"Let us ride, then. I'll hold the reins with one hand." The moment the words were out of her mouth she heard how ridiculous they were, and a dismaying thought struck her. "I'm being the burden I swore I'd not be."

"Aye." That hint of a smile pulled up his lips once more before he pressed them together, as if he had no time for smiling or the emotions that came with it. "Are ye ready to continue proving that ye can be braw?"

"Yes," she croaked, not at all sure she was, but she was not about to crumble on their first day together. "Distract me, please," she said as she held her other hand out to him.

He nodded, took her hand, and immediately moved his thumb gently back and forth over her wrist so that she concentrated on those small motions and the way they made her feel. Her stomach tightened and gooseflesh swept her arm, and then his voice rolled over her like a hot wave. "Pain is a state of mind. Tell yerself ye feel nothing, and ye will nae."

"Is that what you do?" she asked. Their eyes met, and a tingling sensation commenced in the pit of her stomach.

"Aye. Every time ye start to feel anything, simply tell yerself ye dunnae."

She nodded, unsure it would work.

Slowly, he released her hand and reached once more for his wine skin. "How do ye ken about Hogmanay?" he asked, bringing the wine skin to hover over her hand but not tilting it yet. She tensed all over.

I will feel nothing. I will feel nothing. I will feel nothing.

"Hogmanay?" he prodded, interrupting the litany in her head.

"My mother was a MacLeod, as you know. She told me of it. I've not ever participated in it, though. How do you celebrate it?"

"Oh, 'tis grand," he said, his happy memories and enthusiasm obvious. "We've the Saining of the Castle."

"The Saining?"

"The blessing," he said. "Now dunnae talk. Just listen and continue to chant in yer head that ye feel nothing."

She nodded and commenced the chant.

"We get water from the stream, and the priest, Father Dunlap, blesses it. Then he sprinkles the water around the castle and on our livestock. The whole clan is gathered, ye ken. Then my sisters, Greer and Mari, and some other womenfolk whose fathers or brothers sit on the MacLorh council with me and my brothers carry burning juniper branches around the castle to purify the rooms with smoke."

It sounded to her like his clan believed in a bit of magic, just as her mother's clan had. If he believed in magic, then why did he not believe in the legend surrounding her? She frowned. It didn't matter why he did not believe the legend; it was simply fortunate that he did not.

"Once the castle is good and smoky, we throw open the windows, and that's when the real celebration begins," he went on.

She studied the genuine, and rather large, smile on his face. If she mentioned her thoughts to him, she was certain that smile would disappear, as it did not match the hardhearted Scot he seemed determined to claim as his true self. A sudden longing pierced her heart, wishing to experience the celebration with him and his family, and feel just a bit of that happiness, that closeness, that love. She wanted to ask him what he meant by the "real celebration," but he'd told her to listen, so she waited, hopeful he'd tell her.

"We have reviving drinks, ye see, so wine flows freely. My sisters, brothers, and I—well, everyone—dance and sing and act foolish, but none judge. Then I tell a tale around the fire in the great hall to end the celebration. It's the best night of the year. The wine especially," he said with a chuckle. "It is the most special of wines, and we only drink it on that one day. It slides down yer throat gentle-like to warm yer belly."

She could feel it going down her throat as he spoke, and then she realized with a gasp that he'd poured the wine over her free wrist. Suddenly, he took her fingers in his, his eyes impaling her. "Ye feel nothing."

"That's not true," she whispered, caught in the moment of his tale, the image he'd created of him, his family, and his clan dancing, singing, gathered together for his story. "I feel envy. You seem so close to your family. I've never had that."

And I never will." She bit her lip as he frowned. She'd revealed too much. Slowly, she pulled her hand out of his, and he once again took up a corner of her skirt, tore it, and wound the material around her hand.

He took hold of her waist then, and guided her to standing with him, and then he looked down at her, something intense flaring in his eyes. "Ye will have that. I will make certain ye reach yer mother's clan, and ye will meet a man." He stopped suddenly, swallowed audibly, and continued. "Ye will meet a man, marry, have bairns, and create the family ye did nae have with the one God gave ye."

He was so wrong, yet she could not say so without him questioning her, so she simply nodded and then looked away. "We should make haste," she said to fill the silence.

"Aye. We've lingered too long," he agreed. He released her, reached down, grabbed his plaid, and then handed it to her. "Wrap this around ye."

"Will you not be cold?"

"Nay," he said, winking, his moment of playfulness surprising her and making her wonder if he was carefree like this with his family, when his guard was lowered. "I'm a Scot." He paused for a moment, as if considering if it was safe to say more, and then she could practically see him decide that it was. He gave an almost imperceptible nod. She suspected it was meant only for him and that he was unaware he'd actually physically nodded. "My mother used to shoo my siblings and me out of the castle as wee lads and lassies in nothing more than our bare skin. She said we had to learn to embrace the cold. She'd wait for a good heavy snow and send us out. The first one to venture back in would be sent to bed without supper, but the rest of us got a feast, a warm fire, and stories from my ma into the wee hours of the night. So the chill of a winter's night air in the winter 'tis nae a thing to me after a good five years of romping bare-arsed in the snow."

She smiled at the picture of him and his siblings out in the snow, bare as the day they were born. "Your mother sounds like she was a most unusual woman," she said as she fashioned the plaid around her body. She had no notion how to do it correctly, and she knew she'd mucked it up when Angus shook his head at her, undid the knot she had just done, and rewrapped her snugly in his plaid with deft, speedy hands. In a few breaths, he nodded with obvious satisfaction and motioned for her to follow him. He turned on his heel and started back toward the embankment, and her eyes were drawn to the scar on his back once again.

"How did you get that scar?" she asked.

Silently, he turned, encircled her waist, and before she could protest, he fairly lifted her onto the side of the ridge. "Grab hold of the vines and pull," he told her instead of answering her question. Apparently, he had decided he no longer wanted to speak of personal matters. It was probably for the best.

She did as he instructed and quickly made her way to the top of the mound. Once, there she set her hands on the cool, damp forest floor and pushed herself up and over the ledge, glancing behind her to see that he was starting the climb. She rose to her feet, looked up, and screamed.

There stood Donovan, one of her uncle's guards, with his sword at the ready. "Hello, Lady Lillianna," he said, his voice as chilling as his cold gaze.

Chapter Five

Angus stiffened at Lillianna's scream. He opened his mouth to call to her when a man with a heavy English accent bid her a greeting, and then said, "You have caused me a great deal of trouble. Your uncle is most displeased with me that you fled the castle. Tell me, are you alone?"

"Yes," she immediately responded, and Angus sighed with relief. Now he still had the element of surprise to take down the English guard sent to track her.

Angus scanned his surroundings, looking for the best place to scale the embankment and take the man unaware. Angus could easily climb the bank to his left and then circle through the brush to overcome the man from behind.

"Give me your hand, Lillianna," the man demanded.

Loud rustling came from above. "You bloody bitch!" the man roared.

Angus clenched his teeth that the man would call Lillianna such a thing. Not wasting another moment, he belly-crawled as quietly as he could toward the area where he intended to climb. His hands sank into the damp soil and the thick brush made his progress slower than he cared for, but he could hear Lillianna screaming so he knew she was still able to talk and had not gone far.

"Release me!" she bellowed.

"You tried to stab me," the man bit out.

Angus grinned at that news, then grasped on to the vine before him. Thorns sliced open his palms, but he clenched his teeth, curled his grip around the vine, and scaled the embankment as all sorts of horrible images of what the man was attempting to do to Lillianna filled his mind. The lass was his responsibility, and he was not about to let her come to harm.

He came up into a patch of deep vegetation, and he glanced to his right, following the man's voice, but he could not see Lillianna or the stranger because of the overgrowth. He withdrew his sword as he jumped over a fallen tree and then ducked under a low-hanging branch. As he came up, Lillianna shrieked again, and the fury within him pounded like the beat of his heart. He barged through the trees, shoving limbs out of the way, and ran back through the woods far enough to come out behind her captor. Then he angled to his left and began backtracking toward them, his grip on his sword so tight that he could feel every pulse of his heart in his fingertips.

When the male voice drifted to him again, he knew he was close, and he slowed his steps, careful to ensure the man did not hear his approach.

"Your uncle said to bring you back to him, but he also said I could use you. If you attempt to fight me, I'll not make this pleasurable for you."

Angus ground his teeth so hard he thought they would break. He would kill the man.

"You imagine that you could?" Lillianna's voice was full of contempt. Then she gasped, and a thump sounded, as if a body had hit the ground.

"Did that hurt?" the man sneered.

Angus peered through the trees and found them. The man was on the ground with his sword lying near his feet.

He hovered over Lillianna and had her hands pinned over her head, his fingers locked around her wrists. One knee was between her thighs and the other was by her right hip. She bucked, and the man raised his hand to hit her. Without thought, Angus retrieved his dagger from the holder at his left calf and sent it through the air, pleased when it lodged in the man's back.

Immediately, he stiffened, released Lillianna's wrists, and went for his sword, but Lillianna was faster. She scrambled around him and grasped the sword as Angus ran toward them. The man shoved her back and snatched his sword from her just as Angus reached them. Their swords met with a clank, and the knight—the man's chainmail told Angus that's what he was—surprised him with his ability to still fight nimbly with a dagger stuck in his back.

He shook off the shock and channeled his rage into a full-blown attack. He swung his sword from the left, the man's blade meeting his again, and then from the right, slicing the knight across the stomach. He turned and lunged at Angus, and when Lillianna screamed, Angus was momentarily distracted long enough that the tip of the knight's sword grazed him. Still, he managed to swivel back, deflect the sword, and send his blade back around to catch the knight across his right arm.

The man dropped his sword, his face frozen in shock.

Angus pointed his sword at the man. "I can make it hurt, too," he growled. And then he plunged his sword into the knight's chest just far enough that he would die a slow, painful death rather than a speedy, merciful one. Lillianna gasped and turned away.

The knight dropped to his knees, clutching at his chest, and Angus moved toward the man, pulled his dagger from the man's back, and then gave him a push. The knight fell to his back, turning pale and wheezing. Angus stared down at him dispassionately but offered a quick prayer for his departing soul before stepping around him. Instinctively, he took her by the elbow to lead her around the now-gasping knight, but she paused and turned to look down at the man. "Will he... Will he die?"

"Aye," Angus said, "painfully. Much like the pain he promised ye. Come, let us make haste from here in case he's not alone."

She nodded, giving the knight one last lingering look.

They walked in silence to the horses, and when he looked at her, tears were brimming in her eyes. His gut clenched. "Lass," he said, encircling her in his arms without thinking. He brought her toward his chest, hoping to ease her fear.

She clutched his shoulders and buried her head against him, her trembling subsiding after a moment, though his own heart raced. God's bones! Holding her, soothing her, felt as natural as having his sword in his hands. It scared him, but he did not push her away. Instead, he found his hand upon her head and he stroked his palm down over her silky hair while whispering to her. *"Chailin chalma,"* he whispered.

She pulled back from him, her small bandaged hands pressed to his chest. He was certain she did not even realize her hands were there, and he willed his heart to still so she'd not know she was affecting him. "What does that mean?" she asked. *"Chailin chalma?"*

"Brave one," he replied, moving her palms that were crazily stirring his desire. If she were not injured he would keep them on separate destriers, but she could not ride on her own in her condition. "Come. Ye dunnae need to fear that he'll follow us, but as I said, there may be others nearby."

She nodded but stood there, unmoving. Was she in shock? "Did he hurt ye?"

She shook her head. "No, not really. I—" She swallowed audibly. "I did not think my uncle would send someone after me. He must—" She stopped suddenly and bit her lip.

Angus frowned. "He must, what?"

She looked away from him, her shoulders pulling up with obvious tension. "He must still wish to use me, and if that's the case, he'll not stop. He'll send more men, and more, and—"

"Dunnae fear," he said, turning her face back to his. Terror shimmered in her gaze. "I will protect ye with my life."

She stared at him for a long moment. "You truly are honorable," she whispered.

Before he knew what he was doing, he ran a gentle hand down her cheek, but when she stiffened, he withdrew it, cursing his momentary weakness. Silence stood between them and grew uncomfortable. "Should I take yer shock at my honor as a compliment?"

"Of course," she said easily.

He nodded, feeling his own shock at how pleased he was that she was growing to trust him. He should not care at all. "Do ye need help mounting?"

She shook her head and started toward her horse. He was about to tell her that she was riding with him, when he noted she was moving very slowly. "Are ye certain that he did nae hurt ye?"

"I'm a little sore from riding, that's all."

"Oh," he said, glancing down at her. "How sore? Can ye straddle the horse for the rest of the journey today?"

"Yes," she replied, starting to grip the saddle, but Angus

stopped her with a hand to her shoulder. It was a clear lie.

"Nay. Ye'll ride with me."

"With you?" She gasped, her gaze raking over his chest and warming him considerably. Far too considerably for man on a mission with a lass he could not join with.

"Aye," he said. He cleared his throat when he heard how husky he sounded. "Yer hands are injured, and I'll nae risk ye hurting yerself more. We have to ride hard the rest of the way."

"I'll ride alone," she protested, crossing her arms over her chest in such a way that it accentuated the lush roundness of her breasts. He barely held in his groan. Desire shot through him like liquid fire searing his veins as it flowed. God's blood, the lass spoke to him as no lass ever had. Irritated with himself, he took hold of her waist, ignored her protest, and lifted her up onto his saddle.

"Ye will ride with me, and that's that. I've nae the time nor the patience to argue."

"You will never get a wife being so bossy with women," she growled, glaring down at him.

"That's nae yer concern," he retorted.

Turning his back to her, he quickly tied her horse to the rear of his saddle and then swung up behind her. The minute his thighs pressed against the curve of her bottom, yearning spiked again so that he had to clench his jaw against it. She glanced over her shoulder and scowled at him before she scooted as far forward on the destrier as the beast allowed. They no longer touched, but it did not seem to matter. Her body called to him like a siren song. It was not until they were well away from the river that he felt in control of himself enough to speak.

"What do ye think yer uncle wishes to use ye for? If he believes yer cousin is complying with him, what else could he want from ye?"

"Marriage perhaps," she said, her voice sounding strained.

He frowned. The odd pitch of her tone told him she did not believe what she was saying. Why would she lie?

"Ye think yer uncle sent that knight—"

"Donovan," she supplied.

"Donovan. Ye think yer uncle sent Donovan to find ye because he decided to marry ye off?" When she nodded, Angus felt his frown deepen as he remembered what Robbie had told him. "But why would yer uncle threaten to kill ye if yer cousin did nae do as he wished and then suddenly decide to marry ye off when he thinks yer cousin *is* doing as he wishes?"

"It's simple," she said. Her voice still held that same strained sound, but it had a new edge to it now, something almost fearful. "Now that he thinks Elizabeth is complying, my uncle has decided I am not quite as worthless as he so often told me. He can use me in marriage for his gain, or perhaps as a favor owed. Other than that, I *am* worthless to him. Women have been used in marriage since the dawn of time, Angus. Certainly, this cannot come as a shock to you."

She had a point. He didn't know why he didn't think she was telling him the whole truth. Mayhap he was just too accustomed to being distrustful, or mayhap she truly was hiding something...

He stared at the back of Lillianna's shining head as he thought. Robbie's foolish story about the legend entered his mind. Was it possible that the legend was true? He felt foolish for even asking himself the question, and he quickly dismissed the thought. "Nay, it dunnae come as a shock." He wanted to ease the hurt she must be feeling, but he had never been one for soft words, and the desire to soothe her meant he was becoming too embroiled, despite himself. So instead of saying anything more, he clicked his heels and sent them galloping over the terrain in hopes they'd reach a village before nightfall.

The ride was excruciating, and Lillianna had concluded that she might die before Angus decided it was safe to halt. The cold wind had turned her face numb hours earlier, no longer stinging her skin. She felt nothing there, and she wished to God above that she could feel such numbness in her thighs. They throbbed and burned in a way she had not known possible. She was certain, without even having to look, that the skin had chaffed away.

Angus had set them to a fast pace not long after they had ridden away from the forest, and he had not let up since. She'd not protested. In fact, she'd been relieved not to talk. Fear had lodged in her throat, and when she spoke she could hear it in her voice, and she was certain Angus heard it, as well. Her uncle had sent Donovan after her. Why? Why would he do that? She had told Angus it was likely to marry her off, but that was a lie. The only reason she could think that her uncle would bother to send someone for her was if he had found the brooch. Her breath caught at the thought. If he had found the brooch, he'd go to great lengths to get his hands on her. She prayed the MacLeods would protect her, for she had nowhere else to turn.

The pain in her thighs pierced her thoughts for a moment, but when Angus shifted and his thighs pressed more firmly against hers, she considered the day—what he had done for her and all he had told her. She pictured his family celebrating Hogmanay, and she imagined herself there.

Wistfulness filled her. What would it be like to have a family that you knew loved you, that you could count on? She'd never know. Though she was going to her mother's clan, she did not expect to ever truly be considered a MacLeod. She'd not been raised there, and she had no intention of every marrying, which would serve to alienate her from many people. They'd see her as odd and question why, but she'd never be able to give a good answer.

She couldn't help but wonder what it would be like to be married to a man such as Angus. He would die to protect whomever he loved—of that much she was certain. His wife would be part of a big, happy family. Jealousy and longing settled in her gut like a hard rock as the road grew rough and the jostling became worse. Her pain became nearly intolerable, but she clenched her teeth, determined to stay on the horse as long as Angus required it of her.

Her mind drifted to her past, and suddenly, her father was looming over her, and she was wheezing and shaking with a fever on her bed.

Her father stood by the medicine woman who had treated her mother at her death. "She'll die soon if we do nothing," the healer said.

"What do I care?" her father snarled. "She's worthless to me now. Her only worth was in the seer powers she would come into when she fell in love, but now that I know that will never happen, she matters not to me."

"Your wife could have been wrong," the healer suggested.

Her father looked down at her dispassionately. "No," he said, "I'm certain she was right. Lillianna has been nothing but a burden. Let her die. I care not. The brooch is lost, and she will never have worth. Never."

The healer nodded, and as she and Lillianna's father left the room, Lillianna cried out over and over, but no one came back. She was too weak to move, too weak to help herself. Daylight turned to night, and back to daylight, and then night once more. She drifted in and out of sleep, waking only to a dry, burning throat. Suddenly, a hand was on her forehead, and the healer's face was in front of her. "Your uncle has written. He's searching for the brooch now, so I'm to keep you alive. You must be quiet as I treat you, though. Your father is not happy. He thinks you should be left to die."

The horse jostled, and the memory was gone in a blink, but sadness invaded every part of Lillianna. She did have worth. She had worth beyond her powers. Why could her father not see that? Why did he not love her?

After some time, the sun started to fade, and in the distance, she thought she saw the dim glow of lights. Hope that they had reached their destination flared in her, and when Angus began to slow the horse, she nearly wept with relief.

"This is Bedord," Angus said, leaning closer to her ear, his chest brushing her back and warm breath caressing her neck.

Gooseflesh swept her body, but the pain of her legs washed over her anew, banishing any yearning that he had sparked. She supposed she ought to be grateful for the pain. The thought almost made her laugh. Almost.

"Will we stop here?" she asked, praying she didn't sound as desperate to get off the destrier as she was. Her head was swimming, and she was suddenly so very hot. It had to be the plaid.

She started tugging on it, but Angus's hand came over her fingers and stopped her now-frantic efforts. "What are ye doing?"

"I'm burning up!" She gasped, trying to shove his hand away, but her fingers felt clumsy and the world around her tilted precariously.

Angus's palm settled on her forehead, and he stiffened behind her as he swore. "Ye've a fever."

She let her head sag into his palm, glad to no longer be holding up her heavy skull. "I don't feel well," she mumbled. Bright silver dots appeared in her vision, and then it felt as if she'd taken a great leap off a cliff with nothing between her and the earth but blissful sky. Her body swished through the air as all went black.

Chapter Six

Drunken laughter, music, and light flooded out of the King's Head Inn as Angus approached. He held an unconscious Lillianna close to him, his heart thudding hard with every step. How could he have not realized a fever had overcome her? Anger at himself nearly choked him. He'd been so busy trying to ignore his attraction for her, he had completely disregarded her in the process.

He prayed Simon Fraser still kept a room at the inn. His comrade, another Scot who feigned allegiance to King Edward in order to gain information of Edward's plans, used this tavern to privately meet with his contacts who took his messages to their allies in Scotland.

Angus kicked open the door and stepped into the rowdy tavern. Smoke from the fireplaces filled the air, along with the pungent smell of ale. Everywhere he looked Englishmen and women stood, some dancing, some laughing and talking, and some engaged in flirting. These were not wellborn people. These were the commoners, the servants, the people who worked 'til they nearly broke to barely scrape by. King Edward ruled them with an iron fist, and he wanted to do the same to the Scots. These people probably despised Edward as much as Angus and most other Scots he knew, but they were too afraid to rise in rebellion, and rightly so. Edward had a reputation for killing any who dared to stand against him.

Angus curled his fingers more tightly around Lillianna, and the desire to protect her took a firm hold. If anyone realized who she was, they'd try to take her and carry her back to the castle in hope of gaining the favor of the king or some reward. Or if her uncle had sent other men after her, they could be here looking for her. All Englishmen knew that de Burgh was a close personal friend of the king and one of his favored advisors.

Curious gazes came their way from the men nearest to the door, but Angus narrowed his eyes and shifted Lillianna just enough that his grip on his sword was firm. He'd taken his plaid off her and stuffed it in the pouch tied to his horse. He did not want unnecessary trouble, and this was just the sort of place being a Scot would bring such drama.

A group of three men to his left—ruffians by the scruffy look of them—stopped talking and the biggest man took a step toward Angus. "Who's the lovely lady?"

"My wife," Angus said.

The man leered at Lillianna. "Wore her out, did you?" The man's friends snickered, and fierce anger pounded through Angus. If he didn't put these men in their places now, he knew he could expect trouble. Gripping Lillianna tightly, he hauled her up higher so he could kick out. His shoe connected with the man's chest and sent him flying backward into his friends. One fell hard to the ground, and three, including the man who'd first approached Angus, remained standing. One of the strangers scuttled away and threw up his hands.

"I want no trouble," the man said, backing away.

"Good decision," Angus growled. "What of ye two?" he demanded, noting that the man who'd fallen was moving toward the other man. He focused on the man who'd approached him and the one still standing by his side. "Do ye wish for trouble?" He pinned the dark-headed man and the fair-haired one with his gaze.

The dark-headed man smirked at Angus. "I'm always in the mood for trouble. Especially when I've been kicked in the chest. You should take a care about whom you kick."

As much as Angus wanted to beat respect into the men before him, if he could avoid a fight he would. But he was wise enough to be prepared in case he could not. Angus scanned the crowd. Most people had not even taken notice of the brewing fight, likely because brawls occurred here regularly. He needed somewhere to set Lillianna down, but he did not want her far from him. Everywhere he looked were men similar to the ones standing before him or wenches here to make some coin.

"I'll watch her," a man said from the shadows to his left.

Angus narrowed his eyes toward the darkness as a tall, lithe man came into the dim light of the tavern. Angus examined the man. Something about him was familiar, but there was no time to question him now. The man wore no plaid, but his Scot's accent told Angus enough.

Angus tilted his head in thanks, unsure he would need the man's aid. Lillianna groaned in his arms, and her eyelids fluttered open for a brief moment before closing once more. Lillianna needed immediate attention. "I'd rather nae fight this night, so if ye'll go on yer way and dunnae give me problems—"

"You gained a problem the moment you kicked me," the tall, dark-headed man said, withdrawing a dagger and drawing nearer to Angus. His two friends followed suit.

Damnation. Angus had no doubt he could defeat these three men, but he feared the delay in tending to Lillianna. He'd have to be quick about it. He turned to ask the stranger to hold her, and the man was there, reaching out his hands. Angus frowned. He didn't like how eager the man was to take Lillianna from him.

"If ye touch a hair on her head—"

"I ken, Angus."

Angus's frown deepened. The man knew him.

"I'll keep her safe. I vow it."

Angus would have to accept what the man told him. He leaned close to Lillianna, the heat coming off her body in waves. "Hold on, lass."

Her eyes fluttered open, but they were cloudy and a crease appeared on her forehead. "Angus," she croaked.

"Aye, I'm here, and I'll nae be far." He handed her to the stranger, who took her with a gentleness that both eased Angus's fear for her and unreasonably stirred his jealousy. He reluctantly turned from her, took out his dagger, and bared his teeth. "Come on, then," he snarled, motioning the men forward with his fingers. "I've nae all night to best ye."

They launched at him at the same time. One man came from the right, another from the left, and the taller man straight on. Angus jerked his arm up and rammed his elbow into the nose of the man on the right. Bone crunched with the hit, and to be certain he put the man out of commission, Angus reared back his right arm again and sent his elbow into the man's now-bloody nose once more. At the same time, he whipped up the dagger he clutched in his left hand, sprang forward, and made a clean sweep of the blade across the chest of the dark-headed Englishman who'd launched at him head-on.

With a cry from his right and a bellow from in front of him, both men fell, one on his back clutching his nose and the other to his knees. Angus turned to deal with the man who'd come at him from the left, but no one was there, and when he was grabbed from behind, he knew it was the third assailant.

"You Scots need to learn your place," the man snarled in his ear as a dagger came to Angus's throat.

Angus was just about to flip the man over when a voice came from behind him, but not directly. "Do ye think so?" a man asked slowly.

Angus could not see the speaker, but he knew it to be his countryman by his accent and by the tone of his voice. The man was supposed to be watching Lillianna! Alarmed, he cut his gaze to the left and found her sitting in a chair, her eyes barely open. A redheaded woman sat beside her, seeming to half hold Lillianna in her seat. Before he could even question what the devil was happening, the Scot behind him said, "Throw down yer dagger or I'll slit yer throat."

The music and most talking in the inn ceased. All attention appeared to be upon them. "Slit my throat?" the Englishman demanded. "I'll kill your friend before you can even flinch."

Angus grabbed the man's wrist that held the dagger to his throat. He squeezed the nerve with his thumb and forefinger and felt the dagger tilt forward away from his skin as the man's fingers likely went numb. With his right hand, Angus grabbed the man's dagger as it started to drop, slid it open-palmed so that he was holding the edge close to the blade, and reared the hilt back into the man's nose. Then he swiveled around and sent his forehead into his attacker forehead. The man's eyes went wide and then dropped shut. As the Englishman's body started to collapse, Angus caught him just enough to shove him out of the way.

He brought his dagger up to the heart of the Scot who was supposed to be watching Lillianna, just as that man brought his own dagger up to Angus's chest. "Ye were to watch the lass," Angus said, voice low and his anger barely contained.

The music in the inn started again, as well as the talking and singing. The men who had confronted him but moments before had all slunk off, except for the one Angus had just knocked unconscious, so he felt no compulsion to divide his concentration between the man in front of him and anyone else.

"Ye appeared to need my aid."

"I did nae," Angus assured him. "And just for future knowledge—" he lowered his dagger and strode toward the table where Lillianna was propped with the wench "—if I tell ye to guard this lass, ye will do just that. Her life comes before mine." Without a word, he took Lillianna from the serving wench, then snagged a few coins from a pouch at his hip to give to her before waving her away. Her eyes alighted on the coin, and she scurried from him without question. Angus lifted Lillianna into his arms once more and turned toward the Scot.

The man had a cocky grin on his face that seemed vaguely familiar. "I would have nae ever expected to hear the renowned, ferocious Laird Angus MacLorh say something that sounds like he cares for a lass," the stranger said in a voice barely above a whisper. "From my memories of ye and my brother's tales of ye, it used to be that ye did nae have use for the lasses unless they were lying on their backs with open arms and thighs."

Angus got as close to the man as he could without allowing the stranger to so much as graze Lillianna. Yes, he cared for her, damn it, but only because he'd given his vow to see her to safety. "Who the devil are ye, and who is yer brother?"

The man smirked. "My brother is Simon Fraser," the Scot said so quietly that Angus knew no one had heard but him.

Angus studied the man. He had an open, honest face but looks could be deceptive. He had brown hair, whereas Simon's was red. Nor did they share the same eye color, though the shape was the same. And that smile, only half his lip curled up, was identical to Simon's. Angus had a vague memory of a very young lad with blue eyes and brown hair coming to see Simon at the castle when Simon, Angus, Robert, and their other comrades had completed their warrior training.

"Turn yer wrist up," he ordered. He knew before the man did so that he was who he claimed to be because a knowing smile lit the man's eyes and his eyebrows shot up in surprise. Still, the stranger turned his wrist, and Angus got the confirmation he'd been looking for. Grant Fraser, Simon's younger brother, had long ago branded himself with the Renegade mark their small circle of Renegade comrades wore. Grant was no Renegade, though, and he believed his brother Simon a traitor, just as Simon had needed him to. And as Grant and Simon's clan had turned their backs on Simon—and Grant hated the English—it made little sense why Grant was here in the heart of England.

"Satisfied?" Grant asked.

Angus scowled. "What brings ye into English territory?"

Grant gave him a look that indicated it should be obvious. "I've come looking for my brother."

Angus was surprised to hear the news. It had to be of grave importance for Grant to come searching for the brother he had disowned. "What news do ye bring?"

His mouth twisted unpleasantly. "His wife has died,

though I doubt he'll care."

That wasn't true, but it was not Angus's place to reveal secrets Fraser would rather keep to himself, so Angus just shrugged. "I kinnae say. Only yer brother could tell ye how he feels about that."

Grant snorted. "I see ye lie as easily as ye always have, Angus MacLorh. I ken verra well that ye Renegades are closer than a band of brothers. Ye tell one another everything—things I'm certain the lot of ye dunnae share with yer blood relations."

Grant's tightly controlled tone revealed his long-held resentment that Angus knew was born of Fraser making Grant feel like an outsider of the Renegades and unwanted. But Fraser had done it to protect his brother, even if Angus had not agreed with the decision. It was not his to make.

Angus sighed and gripped Lillianna tighter. "I dunnae ken exactly where yer brother is." At Grant's dejected look Angus leaned in and whispered, "But he's likely headed to Ettrick Forest, as am I."

Grant's eyes narrowed. "I heard rumor that ye and Bruce also turned traitor." He shook his head. "I'm disappointed. I should have let those men kill ye."

Angus glared at Grant. He did not have time to set him straight about him and Robbie. "If I see yer brother, I'll tell him of his wife." He started to brush past Grant, who grabbed his arm. Angus glanced at the hand on his forearm and then down at Lillianna, who had grown paler than he'd thought possible. He had to get her to a room and care for her. "Release me. I need to aid the lass."

"I've a room," Grant offered.

Angus's eyebrows shot up in surprise. He was going to refute the offer, but the realization that he could help Lillianna a great deal quicker if he accepted Grant's aid had him nodding. "Thank ye."

Grant motioned to Angus, and Angus held Lillianna tightly as he followed the man.

"Who's the lass?" Grant asked, pausing to look over his shoulder at Angus and Lillianna with interest.

An odd feeling of possessiveness overcame Angus. "My responsibility," he replied.

Grant smiled suggestively. "Seems she's more than an obligation by yer face and tone." Grant turned on his heel and continued through the crowd that parted for him.

Angus feared Grant was right. Lillianna was becoming more than just a mission, and he had no notion how to stop it from happening.

The small room reeked of ale and sweat, and the single bed in the room was old, the wood chipped in many places, but the covering appeared clean. It would do as a place to see to Lillianna's wounds. After Angus situated her on the bed, he scrubbed a hand over his face, contemplating what needed to be done. He had to figure out what was causing the fever.

He could feel Grant watching him silently from the corner, but Angus ignored him for the moment and sat on the bed by Lillianna. Her small, delicate body rolled toward him when his weight settled on the mattress. Her eyes did not flutter open, nor did she make a sound, and that worried him greatly.

He carefully unbandaged one of her hands and then the other to inspect the wounds. They were bad but not so much so to cause the sort of fever that was gripping her. The cuts were still swollen and would become infected if he did not properly cleanse them, though. He set down her hands beside her thighs and thought. She'd gotten the cuts on her hands by squeezing the reins so tightly for so long; if she was so tense there as to injure herself, where else on her body might she had tensed and caused injury? Hadn't she mentioned her legs hurting? He carefully inched his gaze down her body until his attention landed at her thighs.

Christ's teeth. He thought he knew where she might be injured.

And if that was the case... His chest tightened thinking on the tender flesh of a woman's inner thighs and how sensitive she would be. He was a damn, unthinking fool for not considering her needs more. He remembered the herb pouches he carried with him, glad he'd replenished them before he'd come to England with Robbie. He'd have to make some Liquid Death to cleanse the wounds and battle the infection.

First he needed to ascertain if her inner thighs were indeed where she was injured, but he'd be damned if he was going to ruck up Lillianna's skirts with Grant standing behind him gawking at her. Just the idea of Grant seeing Lillianna's legs bared to her hips, let alone her legs spread, made Angus's temples throb.

Slowly, he twisted toward Grant, not surprised to find the younger man studying him. Grant had always been curious, and smart as a whip, but Simon had denied Grant admission into the circle of Renegades because Simon said his younger brother was too rash and needed to learn to think things through carefully and critically.

"Could ye fetch me some water, a water basin, a rag, and some ale?" Angus asked.

Grant crossed his arms over his chest as a sardonic expression twisting his lips. "Why should I aid a traitor? I should kill ye," he growled. "Each one of ye I leave alive is another treacherous Scot to help King Edward crush Scotland with an iron first. Ye all may have turned yer backs on Scotland, but I have nae."

The man's passion for Scotland was obvious in his burning, accusing glare. Angus understood why Fraser wanted to protect his brother from walking the same treacherous line of duplicity that Fraser himself was now walking as a spy, but Angus doubted the wisdom in continuing to allow Grant to think Fraser's loyalty now lay with the King of England. Fraser had sacrificed a great deal to further the Scottish cause, and no one knew the steep price he had paid except the Renegades. Fraser had made his betrayal very believable, so much so in fact, that his clan had become divided into two factions: those who had been glad when Fraser had bent the knee to the Edward because it had saved the clan from being attacked by the English as many of the other Scottish clans had been, and those who had called for Fraser to no longer be laird of the clan because they felt betrayed by him. Grant was now acting laird of that faction.

Angus made a decision, and he prayed it was the right one. "I'm nae any more loyal to the King of England than ye are. These things ye've heard about Bruce and me are exactly what Bruce wished people to believe so that King Edward would believe it."

Swift surprise flashed across Grant's face, but it was gone so quickly that Angus would have missed any reaction at all if he hadn't been staring at the man.

Grant unfolded his arms but kept his gaze steady on Angus. "What proof do ye have that ye and Bruce are nae traitors to the Scottish cause?"

"I'm on my way to warn Bruce's men in Ettrick Forest that Edward is on the way to capture and kill them. That's my proof. I rode away from the English castle in a priest's frocks to disguise myself so I'd nae be followed."

"Ye expect me to believe ye after my brother's betrayal? He's like yer own brother."

"Aye," Angus said slowly, losing patience. "He is. So if I still hold him in high regard..." He let the words fade, reminding himself it was not his secret to share, but the time for Fraser to reveal it was close at hand. Soon all the Renegades would throw off the cloak of deception and rise against King Edward.

Angus could see Grant's jaw go rigid and then relax, and then repeat the movements, clearly struggling to control his reaction. "Are ye telling me my brother's duplicity was a ruse so he could become close to Edward and gather information?"

Angus felt a shaft of pity for Grant. He could hear the hope in the man's voice. "I'm nae telling ye anything. If ye wish to ken the truth, ye'll have to get it from yer brother."

"Where *is* my brother?" Grant demanded.

"On his way to Ettrick Forest with a host of King Edward's men."

"And ye say my brother is nae traitor," Grant said, disgust in his voice.

Angus glanced toward Lillianna. Her face was flushed, and when he set a hand to her cheek, heat seared him. He had no more time to waste with words or diplomacy. He'd never been a man to tread lightly with words, and he certainly did not feel like starting now. "I did nae say that. What I said was that if ye wish to ken the truth, ye must ask yer brother."

"I will," Grant said evenly. "I'll travel with ye to Ettrick. I assume ye intend to thwart King Edward from finding Bruce's men."

"Aye. I pray I reach them in time. I dunnae ken how long nursing Lillianna may take."

"Leave her in the care of an inn wench, and ye and I can ride out this night."

"Nay," Angus said, feeling the finality of his decision down to his bones. Lillianna was his responsibility, and he'd not leave her behind. The lass deserved better than that. "If ye'll fetch me the things I asked for—"

"Aye, I'll go now," Grant interrupted.

Angus nodded his thanks, then added, "When ye return, knock on the door before ye enter."

"Why?" Grant asked. "Surely, ye dunnae intend to bed the—"

"Dunnae be a clot-heid," Angus snapped. "Lillianna is a lady, and her injuries may be somewhere indiscreet. I'm going to have to examine her."

Grant nodded. "I'll knock."

The minute the door closed behind Grant, Angus looked to Lillianna, letting his attention fall to her thighs again. As he reached for the edge of her gown, he paused and searched out her face. "I'm sorry, lass," he whispered, knowing she would likely be outraged when she learned he'd done this, but better outraged than dead. He pulled her gown up over slender ankles and long legs, holding his breath with worry as he slid the material to her thighs. He froze and then let out a ragged breath and swore.

"God's teeth!" he muttered, staring down at the caked blood that had run down her legs to mar her creamy skin. With care, he parted her legs just a bit and hissed. Rage at himself poured over him, and he shook. "Christ, lass."

A sweat broke out on his forehead. She was raw on the delicate skin of her inner thighs. The wound there already looked to be festering. He could not imagine how she had withstood the pain and remained on the horse without complaint. He'd known hardened warriors to complain about less. Admiration beat in time with his heart as he reached a hand to her forehead and gently swept her damp hair off her hot skin.

"I vow to ye to take better care of ye, Lillianna," he whispered fiercely. She groaned suddenly, her eyes moving rapidly under her eyelids, and he suspected she was having a nightmare. "Shh, lass," he cooed, surprised at himself. He'd never tried to soothe a woman in his life, other than his sisters. He had no notion where the feeling that he wanted and needed to comfort Lillianna was coming from, but it was there, lodged in his chest, and devil take it, his chest tightened.

Pushing away all thoughts that currently did not matter, he loosened her gown and slipped it over her head, leaving her in only her underclothes, which clung to her and momentarily drew his gaze to her curves. Lillianna was a stunning woman, but she was also a sick woman and one he had no right to stare at in her present state. He jerked his gaze to her face, silently begged her forgiveness for his momentary indiscretion, and then situated the coverlet over her in case Grant did not knock before he came into the room.

"Angus," Grant called, knocking.

"Enter." Angus got up off the bed and met Grant at the door. Grant was carrying a full washbasin and tucked under his arms was a rag and a jug of ale. "I'll take those." Angus grabbed them before Grant could agree or disagree. "Now ye can go." He moved to the table by the bed and set the items down.

"Ye expect me to leave my own room?"

"Aye," Angus replied, motioning toward Lillianna. "The

lass's injury is on the inner skin of her thighs. 'Tis bad enough that I'll be where nae a man should be without a woman's consent, but I'll be damned if I allow ye to watch while I tend to her."

"Ye sound jealous, Angus," Grant said, eyeing him. "Does the lass mean something to ye?"

"Nay." But the minute the denial left his lips, he knew it to be false. "I mean, aye," he said, feeling the fool. "It's my duty to get her safely to the MacLeod clan, so she matters to me. Now get out," he barked, irritated with himself because he sensed in his gut that the explanation he'd just given was not quite right, either.

"Angus, if ye are trying to reach Ettrick before the English—"

"I ken," Angus growled. They needed to depart. But he could not do that tonight and risk Lillianna's life. "I'll stay here until tomorrow. Then we'll ride." He had already accepted that Grant would be going with them.

"I'll return in the morning," Grant said.

Angus gave an absent nod before turning his attention to the herbs he needed to make the medicine for Lillianna. He quickly took a pinch of yarrow, myrrh, and saffron, and added it to the ale, then stirred the mixture. When he held up the golden Liquid Death, he felt a moment of hesitation at pouring it on Lillianna's wounds. It would cure her, but it would pain her terribly, even in sleep. Yet, it could not be helped.

He crawled onto the bed, gently pushed her legs apart, and set his open palm against her left inner thigh. Her gasp had him jerking his gaze to her face. Her eyes were open but glassy, and she appeared to be staring at him but not seeing him.

"This will help ye," he assured her, "but it will hurt."

Understanding seemed to dawn on her face, and her fingers trailed across his shoulder, light as the touch of a butterfly.

"I want to be a MacLorh," she mumbled.

He frowned, realizing she had no notion what she was saying, but if he distracted her, then maybe the pain would be more bearable.

"And why would ye wish to be a MacLorh?" he asked, angling the jug where he needed it exactly.

"You love your family, and I'm certain they love you," she said, her words slurred. "I have no one." Her voice grew fainter. "No one who cares for me. Only what I could—"

He tilted the jug so that the liquid poured onto her leg. Her words broke off, and fire lit the depths of her gaze. Her back arched up, and she started to scream. "Son of a devil! Satan's spawn! You're killing me!"

"Shh," he said, quickly pouring the concoction over the other leg and praying she'd quit shrieking. The last thing they needed was attention drawn to them, but her yelling got louder than he'd imagined possible for such a delicate creature.

"My thighs! You have burned my thighs!" she screamed.

A pounding came on the door, and before Angus could answer, it banged open.

"For the love of Christ," Grant said. "Get the lass to hush. Ye can hear her all the way down in the tavern. If she keeps it up, the English will return to give us trouble."

Angus gripped her legs as she started to thrash and recalled that cooling the wound helped. So he did the only thing he could think to do: he blew steadily on her left thigh and then her right.

Her screaming stopped, and she settled, going from panting to murmuring. "Candles," she muttered, her head moving restlessly on her pillow. "A man who wanted my heart would know I loved candles. Tons of them to make a room glow and chase away the nightmares. And, and—" her eyelids fluttered closed "—flower petals. They make a room smell so lovely. God," she bellowed, making him twitch in surprise, "I need a bath. I love to soak in a bath, which is sinful, I know." Her breathing grew deep, and she fell silent.

Angus heaved a sigh of relief, and beside him, Grant said, "I do believe the grip of fever is making her confess her innermost thoughts."

Angus nodded, thinking about what she had said. A man who wanted her heart would know she wanted candles, flower petals, and baths. Too many baths would make the lass sick, but he'd not be the one to tell her.

"I think," Grant said, "she must trust ye on some instinctual level."

Angus drank in Lillianna's appearance. Her skirts were still rucked up her legs but not so far as to show her injury, only the enticing curves of her calves. Her mead-colored hair was in wild disarray, hanging loosely about her shoulders and over her chest, and the outline of her full breasts was visible through the thin, damp cotton of her underclothing. She was the picture of alluring, irresistible innocence. And she wanted to be a MacLorh? Her confession tugged at him in a way nothing ever had, though he knew she never would have said such a thing if she had been thinking clearly.

He tried to recall why he should keep a wall between them, but he could not. Instead, he found he wanted to help her heal some of the wounds on her heart. The best way he knew to do that was to show her she had worth. Thankfully, he could do that without becoming entangled with the lass.

Lillianna could not cool off. She kicked at the blankets that suffocated her, but each time she did, the heavy covers settled on top of her again. It filled her with such irritation and anger that she struggled with all her will to open her eyes. They felt nailed shut, but finally she got them to open. She blinked to clear her vision. Two men stood before her, one she didn't recognize, so she immediately shifted her blurry gaze from him to the taller, bigger man standing beside him.

Dark eyebrows rose, and the man's gray eyes seemed to bore into her. A look of relief swept across his face and a satisfied smile turned up his lips. This man she knew. Her brow furrowed, and she swallowed against the scraping dryness of her throat. "You," she said, trying and failing to raise her heavy hand and point an accusing finger at him. "You did this to me!" Her words were like a horn in her ears, they seemed so loud. He winced, and there was a part of her mind that whispered that she was wrong, but her body was on fire, and she was certain it was because of him. "You are killing me, you big clot-heid," she shouted, thinking of a time she'd heard her mother call her father such a thing. "Do not cover me again or I'll bloody kill you."

She was panting with the effort it took to speak. A sweat had broken out at the base of her skull, and on her lip and her forehead. He seemed to be leaning toward her in slow motion, the room around him spinning. Concern lay heavy in his gaze.

"Ye're nae decent, lass," he said, his lips so close to her earlobe that the skin tingled there. Then again, it tingled everywhere. She'd gone from devilishly hot to bitingly cold.

Her teeth began to chatter, so when the heavy coverlet dropped over her body once more and Angus's hands molded it around her, tucking all of her in but her arms, she did not protest.

"I'm decent," she grumbled, feeling as if she wanted to say something else, make some other point, but her thoughts would not cooperate with her mouth. Her father's voice was suddenly in her head. She saw herself lying on a bed, hair matted, face ashen, and leeches on her skin.

She shuddered. She was dying. She was dying, and the only reason that she was not dead yet was because her uncle had written that he was now searching for the brooch and would be coming for Lillianna.

The fever was burning her from the inside out, and hot tears trickled down her face. Her mother had died not long before, and now Lillianna would be joining her.

"Let her die," her father had said to the healer about her mother, and he had said the same of her.

Her father stared down at her, his face twisted. "You're worthless. My brother is a fool to think he can find the brooch. Does he not think I have tried for years?"

She was too sick to answer her father, yet she feared the repercussions if she did not try. Her mother was gone now, so her father would likely hit her. She tried to shake her head in response, but the room spun.

Her father leaned close to her and took hold of her chin, her skin so tender from the fever that she moaned. "Your mother was worthless to me, and you are no better. Without the brooch, you might as well be dead." With that, he'd pulled the coverlet over her face as if she were already gone from this world and strode out of the room. She heard the clack of his shoes on the floor and the door slam.

"I've worth," she mumbled as heat once again swept across her skin, scorching her from head to toe. She kicked with all her might, feeling tangled and panicked, worried the healer would let her die. Or was it Angus who would let her die? Suddenly, she was confused about who was caring for her or where she was. Was anyone caring for her? She began to cry, and more memories invaded her.

"I got you a gift for your birthday," her father said.

She blinked in surprise. Her father had never gotten her a present before. "What is it?" she asked hesitantly, taking the pouch he handed to her.

His eyes were alight with eagerness as he motioned to the pouch. "Open it."

She did. Then she took out the thin chain with a brooch on the end of it.

Fear tightened her belly as she raised the brooch, but she exhaled with relief when she realized it was not the Brooch of Lagothmier. She knew what it looked like from her mother's description.

"My man brought this to me. He's sure it's Lagothmier's brooch. Put it on."

"But Father—"

"Put it on!" he roared.

She flinched but quickly slipped the brooch on. Her father immediately grasped her hands. "Tell me my future. I'm riding this eve to take Drumlan's castle. Will I win?"

She knew it would cost her greatly, but she shrugged, for if she lied, her father's anger would be worse. "This is not the brooch, Father."

His answer was a swift hit that sent her reeling off her chair. The great hall fell to immediate silence, and a bench scraped against the floor as one of the servant wenches stood and moved to aid Lillianna.

"Leave her!" her father bellowed. "She is not worth picking up off the floor. Leave her to fend for herself."

Humiliation heated her from her scalp to her feet, but she got *first to her knees, and then pushed up to a stand. She walked with her head as high as she could hold it as she exited the great hall, but no one looked at her and no one spoke. She knew it was out of fear of her father, but even knowing this, she felt insignificant and invisible, and she vowed to show her worth to her father.*

A hand brushed her forehead and jerked her to the present for one brief moment. Angus swam in and out of her vision, and the memories she hated to recall swirled around her and encircled her with dark fingers to pull her into the depths of guilt and misery.

Her father shoved her through the bedchamber door of her mother's room. When her mother turned, her eyes lit for a moment, but then fear skittered across her face. "I wasn't expecting you," she said to Lillianna's father, "but I'm so glad you brought Lillianna to see me."

"Your daughter defied me," her father roared, shoving Lillianna forward so that she fell to her knees. "She snuck into the stables and attempted to ride my new stallion, and in the process, she got the stallion killed."

Her mother gasped as her gaze moved to Lillianna.

Lillianna's heart thundered in her chest. No one had been able to tame her father's new horse, and she had thought if she could, that maybe, just maybe, he would think she had worth, maybe even be proud of her.

"Tell her!" Father roared.

"The horse would not listen and raced across a ravine. He fell and broke a leg, and they had to put him down." Tears coursed down Lillianna's cheeks, and her father stalked toward her mother. Lillianna started screaming, knowing what he would do, how her mother would be punished for Lillianna's actions. He slapped Mother once, so hard that she lurched sideways and tripped. Lillianna began to race to her mother, but a guard grabbed her from behind and dragged her out of the room at her father's orders. The man held her there, just outside the door, and

she could hear every hit, every cry from her mother, until she heard no more.

"Let her in," her father bellowed.

Lillianna was released and ran back into the bedchamber. Her mother was on the floor, unmoving. Lillianna ran to her and took her in her arms, sobbing at the blood on her face. "What have you done?" she screamed at her father. "What have you done?"

"Me?" he said from above her, his voice indifferent. "I did not do it, Lillianna. You did."

Chapter Seven

As the first rays of dawn streamed through the tiny window in the bedchamber at the King's Head Inn, Angus held Lillianna in his arms, painfully aware of how her body shook with her tears. The remaining heat of her weakening fever seemed to be burning into his very soul.

"Shh," he whispered. She twisted in his arms, her eyes shut and lips cracked, and kicked at the coverlet once again. He leaned sideways, grabbed the rag out of the washbasin, and with one hand, he wrung the water from the dripping cloth and then laid it on her head. At the moment she was mumbling about being hot, but he knew in another few minutes she'd be raging at him about how her fevered state was his fault before she started shivering and her teeth started chattering. Then she would bellow that he was trying to kill her by freezing her to death. It was a pattern that had occurred all night.

A knock came at the door, and though Angus was nearly certain it was Grant, he picked up his dagger from the table by the washbasin before saying, "Aye?"

The door creaked open, and Grant entered the bedchamber looking well rested. His gaze fell first on Angus, then on Lillianna. "She's nae any better?"

"A bit," Angus said. And she was, but she was going to be weak, and he feared the rest of the journey would be difficult for her.

"We must leave," Grant pressed, the urgency that Angus felt in his own chest coming through in Grant's tone.

"We will. We'll wait until nightfall to give her more time to rest."

"I could go," Grant offered. "Ye could stay here with her, and I could head to Ettrick. Ye would simply need to tell me where to find Bruce's men."

Suddenly aware that he still held Lillianna in his arms, he settled her on the bed, careful to cover her immediately. As inclined as he was to stay here to allow her time to heal, he could not be further detoured from his mission for Robbie. Too many lives were at stake. "I have to be the one to warn the men." Angus stood. "We all leave at nightfall," he said, deciding that he would take her with them. Leaving her was more dangerous than taking her.

Grant nodded, as if he'd been expecting that answer.

"She'll slow ye down, Angus. She'll be a burden, weakened as she is."

Anger burst within Angus at Grant's words because he knew how much they would hurt Lillianna. He opened his mouth to reply, but Lillianna spoke first. "I don't know who you are, but if you ever call me a burden again, I'll stab you with my dagger."

Grant's mouth gaped open, and Angus chuckled as he turned toward her. Then his own mouth slipped open. Lillianna had sat up, likely not realizing that she was in only her undergarments. The outline of her full, lush breasts was all too visible, even the hard buds.

"Turn yer back," he ordered Grant in a harsh tone, and when he looked at the man and saw desire on his face, it was all Angus could do not to pummel him. He would have if Grant had not turned red and swiftly faced the wall.

Lillianna frowned, then looked down at herself and gasped. Slowly, she raised her head and fixed her gaze upon him once more as she drew his plaid up from her lap and around her shoulders to cover herself. She looked so lovely and natural in his plaid, as if she were meant to be wrapped in it. He shoved the ridiculous thought away. "Ye've been sick," he said by way of explanation.

Her eyes narrowed. "My illness required you to undress me?" she snapped.

"Aye," he snapped back, suddenly angry that her stubbornness had risked her life. "It did, ye wee muleheaded lass. And I had to spread yer thighs and touch yer delicate skin to treat ye," he said, spitting out the truth. "So unless ye wish me between yer thighs again—"

She gasped again. "No!"

God's teeth, a vision of her creamy thighs spread, her back arched, and her head thrown back in the throes of passion filled his mind. He shook his head almost violently to rid himself of the image, but it stuck like honey. The alluring picture seemed to almost drip across his vision and whisper in his ears of the pleasure to be found in her arms. He couldn't. She wouldn't.

Would she?

The thought rattled him. He clenched his teeth, irritated at the weakness she was bringing out in him.

"Yer gown's just there," he growled, motioning to the chair while purposely not looking at her. He wanted to order her to dress immediately so he'd quit lusting after her, but he was keenly aware that she may be too weak to dress herself. "Do ye need my aid dressing?"

Lillianna felt as weak as a chick just hatched, but she'd rather swallow nails than admit it to Angus or the man who had said she was a burden. Not only that but she was not quite over her embarrassment of Angus undressing her and tending to the wounds on her thighs. Her stomach tightened just thinking upon it. "I can dress myself, if you will but give me privacy."

He nodded, avoiding her gaze, and since she certainly did not believe him to be embarrassed over what he'd done after the frank way he'd told her what had happened, she had to wonder why he was purposely not looking at her. Since she was positive she would not get an answer, she shoved the question to the back of her mind and watched as the two men departed the room. Without turning back to her, Angus said, "I'll be right outside yer door in case ye need me."

"I won't need you," she bit out, feeling irritable and helpless.

His response was to shut the door. Once she was alone, she threw back the covers and glanced at her wounds, biting her lip at how horrible they looked. She'd be scarred for life probably. Useless, ridiculous tears welled in her eyes. There was no time for tears over something that did not matter. She would never be intimate with a man, so what did she care if she had scars where no one would ever see? She'd be alone, an outcast likely. She sucked in a breath. Never had she allowed herself to consider what she was giving up by purposely avoiding love, so she did not know why she was thinking upon it now.

She rose on shaky legs and clumsily walked to the chair to get her dress, the pain throbbing as she did. She bit her lip when she considered the notion of riding a horse again. She didn't know how she'd do it, but she would have to. She would not be the reason that Angus did not reach Ettrick Forest in time to save Bruce's men.

By the time she managed to don her gown, her forehead was damp with the effort and her skin was cool and slick. She sucked in a deep breath and willed herself not to be sick. "You may come back in," she called.

The door banged open, and Angus stalked in, stopping mid-stride. He shook his head. "Ye look like death."

"Does that silver tongue woo many women?"

He chuckled. "Come," he said, walking to her and taking her by the elbow. "Sit." He said it so gently that she did not mind complying and sat on the bed, her body nearly sagging with relief. "Grant is fetching ye something to eat, which should make ye feel a wee bit better."

Her skin tingled where he'd touched her, which she attributed to it being sensitive from the fever. "I can eat a hunk of bread and cheese as we ride."

"Nay," he said, his unyielding tone leaving no room for argument. "I'll dress yer wounds, then—"

"No! I will not allow you between my thighs again!" When he burst out laughing, she scowled at him a moment, but then she gave in to the tickling feeling in her throat and chuckled with him.

Once they both grew quiet, he sat beside her, the bed dipping under his weight and omitting a small squeak, which elicited a flash of memory of his fingers upon her forehead. She could not recall what he'd said, but it had soothed her. His thigh brushed her leg, and he quickly put space between them. Yet she had the feeling that no matter how much distance separated her from this man, she would feel consumed by him. He was big in size, yes, but it was more in the way his very presence overwhelmed everything around them. Everything about him from the glint in his eyes to the curl of his lips suggested he demanded—and expected—people to take notice of him, respect him, and obey him.

"I must dress yer wounds so they dunnae become infected once more. If that were to happen ye would need to stop traveling."

"And you'd leave me," she guessed.

His gaze captured hers, contemplative and resigned at once. "Nay, Lillianna. I will nae leave ye behind until the day I have brought ye to the MacLeods as I promised. Dunnae forget that. Ye can rely upon me."

A lump formed in her throat. She had never really had anyone to count on other than Elizabeth—certainly never a man. Her mind warned her not to rely on Angus, but there was another part of her head that whispered to simply let go. He did not believe the legend, and he had proven himself a good and honorable man. Simply relying on him certainly did not mean she planned to allow him into her heart. Soon, he would leave her at the MacLeod holding and they would part ways forever.

"I will depend on you, if you will depend on me," she said shyly.

He looked at her as if she was daft. "How could I possibly rely on ye?"

She wasn't offended by his question because she honestly had no idea how he could rely on her, either. She didn't really have any skills that would be particularly useful for their journey, except—"I can cook," she said, though admittedly it had always been in a fully stocked kitchen.

He grinned. "I'll take ye up on that offer. I'm a terrible cook. I do what I must when on a journey, but when I'm home…" He shrugged. "My sisters have our kitchen running like the women are part of a well-trained army, and they ensure that my men and I dunnae ever go hungry."

It was settled. She didn't have much to offer, but at least she could offer that. "Will you teach me how to defend myself and use the dagger as you mentioned before? I want to be able to rely on myself for survival."

"I'm still pleased to teach ye," he said, his genuine tone reinforcing his words. "My sisters all ken how to take care of themselves." She liked that he was not opposed to a woman learning to defend herself. Some men seemed to be, but he was different. He motioned to the bed. "I'm going to need ye flat on yer back so I can tend to ye."

Her stomach clenched, and a flush swept over her as she thought about him tending to her wounds in such a private place while she was awake and knew what was occurring. "Angus, I cannot—"

"Ye can," he insisted. "I vow to ye that when I'm practicing the healing arts, that is all I'm thinking about." Her flush grew even hotter, but she nodded, crawled onto the bed, and lay on her back. "Unless ye wish me to ruck up yer skirts for ye and—"

"No, no, I'll do it. If you could avert your eyes for a moment?" She knew it was foolish given he was about to be situated between her legs, gazing at her inner thighs, but she would rather get prepared for him without his staring at her.

He immediately did as she'd asked, and when she had pulled her skirts past her wounds and opened her legs just a bit, she swallowed, gripped the bedcovers, and said, "You may look." Though her eyes were squeezed shut, she knew the minute he moved by his soft footsteps and then the dipping of the bed as he kneeled upon it. His heat came between her thighs, and then he touched her, ever so gently, not on her wound but near it. She sucked in a sharp breath as her pulse skittered alarmingly.

"Am I hurting ye?" he asked. The concern in his voice made her smile. This big, gruff, deadly Scot was also the gentlest man she had ever met.

"No," she said, wincing at how breathless she sounded. She hoped he did not notice.

"I'm going to apply a salve and then wrap yer thighs. I vow to be gentle."

"I trust you," she said, shock going through her as the words left her lips. She did trust him, at least until he proved he could not be trusted.

"My first lesson for ye on survival is nae to ever easily give yer trust to a handsome Scot," he said, and then his fingers were smoothing something cool over her wounds. She tensed, but once she realized how gentle his touch was and that it did not hurt overly much, she relaxed.

"Are you saying I've given you my trust too easily?" she teased.

Then she realized she'd inadvertently admitted that she thought he was handsome. She opened her eyes to see his reaction and released a relieved breath. He was utterly absorbed in what he was doing and did not appear to have even heard her. A line of concentration had settled between his brows, his thick hair hanging on both sides of his face, and he was biting his bottom lip as he worked.

When he finished, he sat up, and his gaze caught hers. His eyes darkened to almost black, making him appear lethal. He said nothing, but even if he had, she was unsure she'd hear his words. Her heart beat like a drum in her ears, pushing her blood through her veins at a heady rate. He assessed her slowly, thoroughly, and she had the fleeting thought that this had to be what it felt like to be consumed by someone. There was nothing else in the room for her in this moment but him.

His bold stare assessed her frankly. "Dunnae ever tell a man who is between yer thighs that ye find him pleasing unless ye wish for him to show ye just how much pleasure he can really bring ye."

His strong, velvet-edged voice sent a chill racing across her skin. She swallowed, her mouth suddenly dry. "I'll remember that," she said, surprised she was able to form a coherent sentence. This man, this Scot, was seducing her without even attempting to. Thank God he did not believe in her powers, and thank God neither her father nor her uncle was in a position to use her if she should succumb to the feelings stirring in her for Angus.

Chapter Eight

Angus had thought being between Lillianna's tempting thighs and having her admit she thought him pleasing was the greatest temptation he would ever face, but he had been very wrong. As darkness descended to welcome night, Lillianna was situated between his legs with her bottom pressed against his stiff cock, his arm secured under her heavy, lush breasts to hold her in place. It was all he could do to clench his teeth against the painful desire she had lit in him.

Each time the horse's hooves jostled her and her body rubbed against his, he got a clear picture of her on her back, thick hair trailing over her bare shoulders and breasts, and her thighs open to him. She was inviting him to partake of the sweetness he knew would be found in her arms. Never had lust so besieged him as it did now. He wanted her with every fiber of his being, but to take Lillianna would be far more than a simple tumble in the hay. He could not allow himself to venture down that lane.

"When will we halt?" Grant asked from the horse to Angus's right.

They had made very good progress since they had left the inn shortly after Lillianna had eaten. Angus had fashioned a blanket and his plaid over his horse to make the riding softer for her; between that and his insisting she lean against his chest and completely relax, he felt confident that her skin was not being chafed much, but the personal price had been high. His desire to give in to the temptation she presented was great, and in this moment, he needed a reprieve.

"We halt now," he replied, looking toward the thick woods. He'd wanted to reach the village of Northampton so that Lillianna would have a soft bed and would not be subjected to the cold, but tonight, this would have to do.

"Having trouble fighting yer desire for the lass, are ye?" Grant asked in a teasing tone.

"Aye," Angus said, not bothering to deny it. Lillianna was sound asleep, and Grant obviously could see the struggle on his face.

"Surely ye ken the best way to slate yer desire is to bed the lass? Ye'll nae want her near as much once ye've had her. Simply woo her into yer arms."

Likely Grant was correct that joining with Lillianna would slacken his desire for her, but Lillianna was not the sort of lass to be used. "It's more complicated than that," Angus said.

"Aye, I ken. My brother told me long ago that ye dunnae allow lasses close to ye. He said one betrayed ye once, which caused ye to do something that harmed yer clan and ye have nae ever allowed a lass close since. Is that the reason ye are nae wed?"

Angus would ring Fraser's neck when next he saw him for speaking of Angus's personal matters to others, not to mention that Fraser was wrong. The only thing keeping Angus from becoming truly angry with Fraser was that his friend had most certainly spoken of it years before, as most of his friends had long quit mentioning his refusal to become entangled with any of the lovely lasses he joined with.

"Yer brother did nae have his information correct."

"Oh nay? So ye did nae do something to harm yer clan?" Grant asked, slowing his horse as Angus did.

"Aye, I did," Angus growled, unwilling to hide his guilt like a coward.

"Then what information did my brother have wrong?" Grant asked.

"I am nae wed because I dunnae need the distraction." He clamped his jaw shut, unwilling to say more.

Grant frowned. "Why would a wife be a distraction? Unless ye fear that ye are weak and will repeat the mistake of yer past?"

"I'm done talking of this," Angus said, his guilt about the past loud within his head.

Grant threw up his hands. "We'll nae speak of it any more. I'll just say that my father did nae trust himself, and he was a weaker ruler for it. Simply trust that ye are stronger and wiser than in yer youth, and ye will be."

"Ye ken when ye say 'I'll just say' that ye are still speaking of something we just agreed nae to."

"Aye," Grant replied with a laugh. "I ken it. I learned that trick from my brother."

Angus liked Grant. Hell, he even admired the man. He clearly cared for his brother—Grant had almost idolized Fraser—but when Grant truly had thought that Fraser was betraying the Scottish cause, he had turned from him. That had taken bravery. Angus was glad the rift between the brothers could soon be mended, but the good feelings did not outweigh one important thing. "If ye ever suggest I'm weak again, we will fight."

"Then dunnae be weak," Grant replied, and before Angus could reply, Lillianna started screaming.

"Are ye all right?" Angus asked as he kneeled beside Lillianna at the campfire where she was tending the fire to cook the rabbit Angus had caught. She startled, having been lost in the memory of her mother's death and burial. No one had attended the burial but her and the priest. Her mother had lived separate from her father and Lillianna by his will and force, and though she had been kept in an isolated castle almost like a prisoner, just without a dungeon, there had been people there she could have become friends with, but her mother had confessed to being afraid—afraid to make friends, afraid to allow any sort of love in because she'd said if she did, mayhap she'd succumb to loving a man again, and then history would repeat itself.

In her memory, her mother's face in the casket had disappeared and it had become Lillianna's. She was being buried, and there was no one to put her in the ground, or cry for her, or remember her. There was not even a child because she'd never had love or a husband. Unexpected doubt about her decisions for the future besieged her. Was she doing the right thing? Yes, of course she was! It was just fear stirring these questions, nothing more.

"Lillianna?" A gentle touch to her arm made her jerk.

"I'm fine," she said, turning the stick to evenly cook the rabbit.

Angus sat on the log beside her, his presence overwhelming her as it always did, but it was comforting. That in and of itself worried her. She was developing an attachment to Angus, and startlingly fast. She stole a sideways glance at him and found him staring straight ahead into the fire. The flames cast shadows across his face, and she could just make out his concerned expression and the lines of weariness around his eyes. He'd held her the entire day as they rode to ensure that she did not have to clench her legs to stay on the horse. Gratitude swelled in her throat, as did a longing to learn this man who she was traveling with. She thought about it for a moment, silenced the warning in her head, and opened her mouth to speak, but Angus spoke first.

"Where did ye learn all those bawdy words ye yelled at me?" he asked.

She felt her jaw fall open. "I do not use bawdy words! And when did I yell at you?"

"When ye were in the grips of the fever, and ye do use bawdy words. So"—he speared her with his unwavering gaze—"where did ye learn them?"

"My father," she said, unsure why she would reveal such an embarrassing thing, except that she oddly felt that she could confide in Angus and he would not think less of her.

"He taught them to ye?" Angus asked, frowning.

"What? No!" She laughed at the mental picture of her father teaching her bawdy words. "My father never taught me anything except to fear him," she blurted. "He would yell such things at me when I irritated him, so…" She shrugged. "I learned the words."

"Ah, lass," Angus said, his sorrow for her reaching out across the small distance between them and caressing her like a reassuring touch. "Ye dunnae have to fear yer father ever again."

"I hope not." Her mind turned that statement over. "I don't think he'd ever come for me. But my uncle…" She shuddered. "If he discovers where I have fled to, he will likely come. What if the MacLeods won't protect me? They don't even know me."

"Ye're kin. Besides that, ye will likely meet a man and take him as husband, and he will protect ye."

She shook her head. "I'll not take a husband."

"Dunnae be daft."

She feared wedding and giving a man control over her. Especially if the man duped her, and she thought she was wedding a good, honorable man. And then she found herself in love only to discover the man's true nature. And say the man was good and honorable, she feared she would naturally grow close to the man and fall in love, and then her powers would come out and the potential for the man to change and wish to use her would be there. Such a thing would destroy her.

No, wedding was not for her.

"A woman needs a husband to watch over her," Angus said.

"I'll do that myself. You're going to teach me, remember?"

"Aye, but ye must take a husband. Ye are a gentle creature. I can teach ye things, but it will nae ever make ye truly a match against a fierce warrior. What I can show ye would allow ye time to possibly escape, but ye must have someone to flee to."

"Well, then I shall hope the MacLeods grow very fond of me and will do all in their power to protect me."

Angus grunted. "I'm certain the MacLeod laird will extend his protection to ye, but there is protection born of fondness and obligation and then there is protection born of love."

His way of thinking fascinated her, and as it would happen, she agreed. She'd seen her mother sacrifice herself to shield Lillianna, and she'd watched her father give her protection only because he wished to use her. When she no longer seemed useful, he no longer felt that obligation. What sort of obligation would the MacLeods feel to her? Would it be strong enough that they would protect her, endangering their own wives, daughters, and sons if her father or uncle ever came for her?

"What do you suppose the difference is?" she asked, wishing to hear more.

He scrubbed a hand across his face as he stared into the fire. "Well..." He turned to her, and flames danced in the depths of his eyes. "Protection born of fondness and obligation is nae as strong. When ye love someone, ye will sacrifice yerself to protect them. Ye will put their welfare above all others'."

His words tightened her chest almost painfully. She had to swallow past her desire to be enfolded in such protection and speak. "And someday you will protect a wife that way?"

"Nay."

His quick, vehement answer surprised her. "You don't wish for a wife?"

"Nay, I dunnae."

She frowned. "Why?"

He looked distinctly uncomfortable. "I dunnae wish for entanglements."

"From anyone?" she asked, probing.

"From any woman," he clarified.

Her chest squeezed at his words. "Why is that?" she asked gently, sensing a hurt in him.

"When a woman takes yer heart, she takes yer good sense, as well. I'll keep my good sense, thank ye verra much."

"You sound as if you speak from experience," she ventured, shocked that she was being so bold.

"I do," he said, his voice almost raw with emotion.

She wanted to reach out and squeeze his hand, so instead, she fisted her own. "Mayhap you gave your heart to the wrong woman," she blurted, thinking that it would be a shame if this man never loved again.

"Of course I did," he said with a chuckle. "But that's the problem as I see it: when ye have been robbed of yer good sense, ye dunnae see that ye are making a bad choice."

"Well," she said quickly as Grant approached, "I'm certain there are signs. You must simply watch for them. A bad person cannot hide their true nature all the time."

"I have nae ever thought of it that way," he said reluctantly.

Feeling especially bold, she said, "I told you I had worth. I have just given you a new way to contemplate your past to help decide your future."

His hand caught hers and snatched the breath from her lungs. His warm fingers circled all the way around her hand easily, and he squeezed her gently. "Ye dunnae need to prove ye have worth, lass. I see it."

"Am I interrupting something here?" the man Grant asked boisterously as he kneeled across from them.

Lillianna went to pull her hand away from Angus at the same time he did. They exchanged a look, which to Lillianna, ridiculously felt rather like two children caught being naughty.

"Nay," Angus responded. "I was just telling Lillianna about the MacLeod clan."

She could not say why precisely, but Angus's words made her feel suddenly melancholy.

Grant nodded. "The MacLeod laird is a good man. He'll be kind to ye, and I'm certain he will find ye a husband right away."

Angus watched Lillianna's face. Grant's statement made her look downright terrified. He didn't stop Grant from talking because Angus was curious why she did not wish for a husband. Had she been hurt by a man before? The idea of a man harming her physically or mentally made anger heat his blood. Her father and uncle were already on the list of men that would pay for hurting her, and he'd be more than glad to add the name of the man who had wronged her.

God's teeth. Perhaps a man had seduced her and stolen her innocence, so she felt she could not marry? That would go a long way in explaining why she felt unworthy. The notion filled him with rage. "Lillianna," he interrupted Grant with no notion of what the man had been saying. "Were ye seduced, lass?"

"What?" Her jaw dropped open. "No!"

Angus sagged with relief. "Then why in God's name do ye nae wish to marry?"

She looked suddenly like a deer caught in a trap. "I have my reasons," she said quietly, "and they are private." Her tone went steely, and it made him want to grin. Lillianna had more grit than five Highlanders.

"Ye'll need to marry, lass," Grant said gently.

"Dunnae bother," Angus grumbled, irritated though he knew he had no right to be, that she would not share her reason with him. "I already tried to convince her to marry, and the lass is foolishly stubborn."

She narrowed her eyes on him. "I find it rather hypocritical that you insist I should wed when you have no intention of doing so yourself."

"I'm a man; 'tis different. I dunnae need someone to protect me." Not to mention he did not need the distraction of a wife, though Grant's words from earlier surfaced in his mind. Mayhap a wife would not necessarily be a distraction.

Just because he wed did not mean he'd need to allow soft emotions. It was something to consider.

"I do not need someone to protect me, either!" Lillianna insisted.

Grant quit skinning the rabbit and frowned at Angus. "The lass is wrong. She must have a husband to protect her."

"Aye, I ken it, but she thinks she will protect herself."

"You do both recall I'm sitting here, don't you?"

Angus purposely ignored her, hoping if he could not directly sway her thinking, then perhaps this conversation could show her the importance of a husband. As Grant did not even blink an eye at Lillianna's words, Angus suspected the man had come to the same conclusion, which made Angus like him even more.

"What do ye suppose made the lass think she could protect herself?" Grant asked.

From the corner of Angus's eye, he saw Lillianna's lovely eyes narrow with irritation. "I suppose 'twas my unthinking words," he replied to Grant, having to fight the urge to chuckle. Lillianna was a stunning woman, and as her irritation mounted, she was quickly becoming a sight to behold. Her flashing eyes and head tilted in challenge made him want to grab her and kiss her and see if he could melt her anger. He was not even involved with the lass and already she was making him a clot-heid.

"What did ye say?" Grant demanded, his words clipped, but Angus saw the briefest hint of a smile before it disappeared.

"I told her I'd teach her to protect herself, but that she would nae be a match for a fierce warrior."

"Aye, none. And a pretty lass like her will nae last long in the Highlands before a Scot decides he wants to marry her and simply takes her and makes her his."

Angus stilled, all his humor vanishing in a flash. Grant was right. Women were forced to marry against their wills far too often. There would likely be a man, even among the MacLeods, who would do such a thing when faced with a beautiful lass like Lillianna. The time for kidding was over. "Ye must take a husband immediately so it will at least be yer choice."

"I thank you for your concern," Lillianna said rising, her tone stiff, "but I will not take a husband." He opened his mouth to argue, but she spoke again. "Even if I did wish to take a husband, as you say—which I most adamantly do not—there are no men to be taken on this journey."

"I'm available," Grant said, standing swiftly and capturing Lillianna's hand in his. Angus sat rigid. What in God's teeth was Grant doing? He glared at the man and decided he disliked him immensely. When Grant brought Lillianna's hand to his lips and kissed her delicate skin, skin that Angus happened to know felt like silk and was so creamy one could see the faint traces of her veins underneath, he had an intense desire to pummel Grant into the dirt.

"That's very kind of you, Grant, especially since we really do not know each other."

Angus surprised himself by exhaling at Lillianna's words, and he must have done so loudly because both Lillianna and Grant looked toward him. Lillianna's brow was furrowed, but Grant smirked at him. Angus clenched his fists and pictured punching that smile from Grant's face. His growing desire for the lass was making him think illogically.

"Let me speak, Lillianna," Grant said.

"The lady did nae give ye leave to call her by her given name," Angus bit out.

Grant grinned at Angus, then at Lillianna, and the devil of a Scot did not release her hand. "Angus has a point. Will ye give me leave to call ye Lillianna? If we are to be wed—"

"She's nae going to wed ye!" Angus roared, jumped up, and shoved his way between them. A knowing, almost smug, expression settled on Grant's face. Lillianna gaped at Angus, and he could feel the slow burn of embarrassment from his neck to his ears.

"And why nae?" Grant demanded, trying to step around Angus to get to Lillianna, Angus was certain, so he blocked the man with a forearm to his chest.

"Because," Angus growled, "the lass told ye she dunnae wish to marry!"

"But ye agreed that she ought to," Grant said, which annoyed the devil out of Angus and caused his temper to snap.

"I've changed my mind, and if ye dunnae cease pestering Lillianna, I'll hit ye where that smirk is."

Grant had the bollocks to grin at Angus, and Angus knew in that instant the man had pushed him into showing that he had some sort of affection for Lillianna. Damn the Scot.

"Gentlemen," Lillianna said, her tone exasperated. "Please do not fight over this. Grant, Angus is quite right. You are sweet to offer, but I have no wish for a husband. But you may—" she gave Angus a stern look that reminded him of one his mother use to give him when she would lecture him "—call me Lillianna. If we are to travel together and face danger together, you may certainly call me by my Christian name."

"I'll protect ye from danger," both men said at the same time. Angus glared at Grant, and Grant winked at Lillianna, who giggled unexpectedly. The musical, joyous sound made Angus's chest squeeze mercilessly.

"I appreciate the protection from both of you. Tomorrow, Angus"—she looked at him once more—"if there is time, would you show me one move with the dagger before we ride?"

"Aye," he said gruffly. "I'll make the time."

"Excellent." She grinned, and he had the wish to press his mouth to hers. God above, the woman truly was making him daft. "I'm going to retire," she said. "I'm weary and not at all hungry."

Angus frowned, stepped toward her, and set his palm to her forehead. "Ye're nae hot with fever. Are ye certain ye dunnae wish to eat?"

She nodded and tapped his hand, and he blinked, realizing he'd not moved it. Slowly, he withdrew his hand from her skin, the warmth of her forehead tingling his fingers.

"But ye spent all that time cooking," Grant protested.

"I did it for the two of you. I knew you'd be hungry."

She started to turn, and as she did, Angus asked, "Shall I make ye a pallet?"

"No," she said firmly. "I'm quite capable. I'll just be right beyond the trees where I may obtain privacy."

Angus started to protest, but then he recalled his sisters and their insistence that women liked privacy for things such as relieving themselves, so he clamped his jaw shut and nodded. He'd check on her in a bit, but he suspected if he admitted that, she'd argue with him. He'd learned with his sisters that sometimes it was easier just to do what he knew was best and not tell them. If they wanted to argue after the fact, he could simply walk away.

After Lillianna departed, Grant and Angus sat down to eat. With a mouthful of rabbit, Grant said, "Any woman who would cook for a man when she is nae hungry is a good woman. A woman that a man could join himself to. A woman who—"

"Shut up," Angus snapped, not because he thought Grant was wrong, but because he thought Grant was right.

Chapter Nine

Lillianna's thighs were on fire, but she'd eat dirt before she admitted it. She wanted to strip off the bandages and cleanse her wounds with cool water, but she knew if she told Angus, he would insist on accompanying her. She glanced back over her shoulder, glad to see both men had their backs to her, and they appeared to be in deep discussion. She shoved a low-hanging branch out of her way, and then she hesitated, to see if she could hear water. The faint rush of a stream met her ears. Angus had taught her that. She smiled but quickly tried to force it away. It would be far too easy to fall for the man, and she could not be so foolish.

Yet, as she walked toward the sound of the water, she could not help but think of the anger on Angus's face moments before when Grant had offered to marry her. Angus had almost seemed… She stilled for a moment, searching her mind for a word to describe what she was thinking. Well, he had almost seemed *jealous*, but that could not be, could it?

When her belly fluttered with the thought of Angus being jealous over her, she shook her head. She needed to concentrate on the most important matters at hand and shove the image of the too-handsome Scot out of her mind.

As she continued to walk, her thoughts turned to what

the men had said in regard to her needing a husband. What if they were correct? What if taking a husband was the only way to protect herself from unscrupulous men who would kidnap her? She sighed softly. There had to be another choice. She could not risk repeating her mother's fate.

She took a deep breath to settle the storm brewing inside her. She refused to tie herself in knots with speculation. The men could be wrong, and she *did* have another choice. She would protect herself!

She was not helpless. She just needed to think more like a man. Determined to do so, she bent down, took her dagger from the holder at her ankle, put it between her teeth, and hoisted up her skirts to unwrap the bandages from both her legs. Then she removed her slippers, tied her skirts into knots at her waist, put her dagger in her left hand, and waded into the moonlit glistening water.

The cool temperatures provided immediate, much needed relief. She stood for a moment, the water gently lapping against her legs, and stared up at the moon. To her dismay, her mind wandered to Angus once more. Try as she might, she could not block her thoughts of him. She'd never known a man like him—a man of complete honor and total bravery, a fierce warrior more than willing to die for what he believed was right, who could be ruthless one moment and gentle the next. He was also a man capable of great love for his family and, she thought with a twinge of jealousy, for a woman. He'd given his heart to someone, by his own admission, and she'd somehow betrayed him. She'd wounded him so greatly that he did not want to give his heart to another again.

It occurred to her suddenly that they had such fear in common, only for different reasons. She had told him that he simply needed to look for the signs that he had chosen a good woman before giving his heart. Could her advice to him be applied to herself?

No, no! There she was being weak again. She could not risk being used merely for the legend.

The sharp point of something cool at her neck snatched her thoughts, and fear exploded within her.

"Hello, Lady Lillianna," a familiar deep voice with a heavy English accent whispered in her ear.

The hairs on the back of her neck stood on end at the sound of Donovan's labored voice. Shock held her silent for one breath, and when she opened her mouth to scream, he clamped a hand over her mouth. "Now, now. I cannot have you bringing your companions to us," he wheezed. "I regret that I'm in bad shape since my last encounter with you and that nasty Scot. I'm going to remove my hand from your mouth, but if you scream, I vow to you, I'll manage to kill at least one of your companions when they come for you, preferably the one who left me for dead," he finished, panting.

She swallowed. She could not risk screaming and getting Angus or Grant killed. She would have to see if she could take him down herself. At least it was clear he was fighting his injuries. She nodded that he could remove his hand, and he did so, transferring his hold to her upper arm once more. As he slowly started to turn her, she lowered her dagger to her side and prayed he'd not seen it. Her heart pounded and thoughts raced. She had to wait for a good opening to use her dagger. Trying to do so with his weapon at her throat was not the time.

When she faced him fully, she saw the pain that twisted his features, and she regretted that it gave her hope. He glared down at her, his dagger piercing her skin. The sting of her flesh being cut made her eyes water and tightened her throat with fear. "You," he said, his voice filled with obvious hatred, "have proven harder to return to your uncle than I imagined, but return you, I will."

Her skin prickled at his words. She tried to pull back a bit, to give herself space to bring her dagger between them when the time was right, but Donovan gripped her tighter. She grunted at the pain, and he smirked. "That is but a small sample of what I will do to you if you cause me one more bit of trouble. You're going back to the castle with me *now*."

His words seeped into her mind and set true terror in her heart. She jerked back, but he surprised her with the strength he still wielded and yanked her hard against his chest, his dagger digging even deeper into her skin. She clenched her teeth against the need to cry out in pain. Warm blood trickled down her neck, and her heart pumped blood through her veins with such force, she could feel the rapid movement of her pulse.

Something brushed her foot under the water, causing her to startle, and she yelped involuntarily. The sound echoed in the silence of the night, and birds flew from the thick trees that surrounded the stream, squawking as they took to the sky.

Donovan's lip curled back, and even in the darkness, she could see the anger erasing the pain from his expression. When he lifted his free hand to hit her, she brought her dagger up, but instead of planting it in his gut as she intended, it grazed his arm. He howled with the contact and then knocked her dagger out of her hand. The weapon splashed into the water, and she lunged for it. But before she could even fully bend down, she was yanked back up by her hair. The dagger hit her foot underwater and then she no longer felt it.

"Lillianna!" Angus cried out in the night.

"Do not call back," Donovan commanded. "I promise you I still have the strength to kill one of them."

"I won't," she assured him, her scalp screaming with pain. Her blood roared in her ears as she tried desperately to think what to do. She had to get that dagger, and she had to get Donovan to release his hold on her in order to do so. "Let me go, and I vow to run with you. You cannot defeat them both, and I'll not chance one being killed. I can even tend your wounds," she lied.

"If you do anything..." he threatened, desperation heavy in his voice.

"I won't," she insisted.

The moment he released her, she brought her knee up between them, connected it with Donovan's groin, and shoved him while he was off-balance from his pain. She fell to her knees, water splattering in her face as she frantically swept the moist sand of the streambed for the dagger. As her fingers curled around the hilt, water splashed beside her. She glanced up and gasped as Donovan shoved her head underwater. Liquid filled her lungs, and she kicked and clawed at the air.

Pressure seemed to come at her from everywhere. Sound was muted, and everything was a silvery-black color. The blood pounded in every part of her skull. He was going to kill her.

―⁂―

Angus barreled through the trees, cursing himself inwardly for not realizing that Lillianna had wandered off from their campsite. Moonlight glinted across the stream and made the silhouette of a man clear. He was bent over holding something under the water. Angus's blood froze.

Behind him, Grant said, "There."

"Aye." Angus grunted, closing the distance to the water as fast as he could, yet it seemed to be the slowest he had ever moved in his life.

Lillianna's thrashing echoed through the night. She was fighting for her life, and he had to save her. Suddenly, the man howled in pain, and a loud splash brought Lillianna up and out of the water. Coughs wracked her body, but as Angus splashed his way toward her, she raised her arm, and the moonlight shone off the blade of her dagger. Hope and pride expanded his chest.

His leg, his leg, Angus thought. *Go for his leg.*

The man would not expect it. It also would not kill him, but it would give Angus time to reach them and then finish the man.

When she brought her dagger down and plunged it into the man's leg, Angus roared his approval. The man cried out and lifted his hand to hit her, but Angus barreled into him with a thud, sending himself and the man crashing backward into the water. They went under as one, freezing water and blackness enveloping them. Rage was Angus's heartbeat, fear for Lillianna, his breath. He brought his dagger up through the water, and struck the man in the gut, plunging his blade deep and yanking it up to pierce the lung, which would kill the man quickly.

The body in Angus's arms went limp almost instantly, and as he shoved the enemy away, he felt a hand close around his arm. His battle instincts took over, and he drove his elbow up as he gained his feet and surged out of the water. His elbow connected with what felt like bone. Understanding he'd gained an opportunity over his opponent, he took hold of his sword, arced it up, and started the swing of death, but at the last moment, Lillianna's shriek cut through his red haze and he realized he was not fighting an enemy, but Grant.

All noise around him crashed in at once. Grant cursing. Lillianna screaming. The rush of his blood in his ears. His heavy breathing. "Dunnae ever grab a man in the heat of battle," Angus ground out by way of an apology.

Grant swiped a hand across his bloody nose and nodded. "Aye, I ken that. It was a fool's mistake."

Angus nodded. He did not need to say more. Grant would not forget he'd almost died; he'd not make such an error again. Grant was already reaching for Lillianna, who was visibly trembling, and without apology or explanation—and not totally knowing what he was going to do—Angus stepped between them, scooped her up and out of the water, and enfolded her in the protection of his arms.

She trembled violently, but between chattering teeth, she said, "My dagger. Please. I must have my dagger back. It's, it's in his leg."

Angus thought she might be in a bit of shock. His gaze met Grant's, and Grant silently responded to the unasked question by nodding. "Grant will retrieve yer dagger, lass," Angus said. "Let's get ye to the fire and warm yer bones."

She did not speak or truly acknowledge him. Instead, she buried her head into his chest, put her arms around his waist, and clung to him as if he were her lifeline in a violent storm. Something in him ignited, but before he could even analyze it, she said, "It was Donovan."

"What?" he asked, shocked, and looked to the body, now bathed in moonlight. He motioned to Grant, who took Lillianna by the arm, and Angus released her, splashed his way to the body, and turned it over. Donovan's face was slack in death. Devil take the man. Angus could hardly believe the knight had survived the previous fight and managed to follow them here. How long had he been tracking them?

Angus looked to Lillianna. She had almost been killed, and it would have been his fault. He was supposed to protect her, but clearly, his desire for her was a distraction that was making him less vigilant and less effective than he should be. He had to do better.

Leaning over, he felt for a pulse to ensure the man was dead, though clearly he was. Nothing. If Donovan came for them again, the man would have risen from dead to do so. Angus yanked Lillianna's dagger out of the man's leg and sheathed it. Then he walked back to her and, without a word, took her from Grant and led her out of the water, down the path he had taken to get to her, and to his horse.

Her wide eyes met his. "Can ye stand?" he asked.

"Yes, of course," she said, her voice cracking to reveal the depth of how what had occurred had rattled her. He set her down but slid one hand around her waist, as much to ensure she could stand as to keep her near. He withdrew the small blanket he'd brought and the priest's frocks. Grant emerged from the path and raised a hand, giving Angus the sign that all was well, and then turned and headed back down the path he'd just come from. Angus assumed to offer privacy to Lillianna.

"If ye will undress, ye can put these priest's frocks on," Angus said. "They're dry."

She bit her lip in clear uncertainty but then nodded and took the clothing that he held out to her. Her wet gown clung to her body, displaying the lushness of her breasts, and his mouth went dry.

"Would you mind turning around?" she asked after a moment.

"Aye," he said, realizing he'd been staring, and when a

frown came to her face, he shook his head. "I mean, nay, I dunnae mind turning around." He did so immediately, but he'd never been more keenly aware of a woman in his life.

"I stabbed him," she said, guilt heavy in her voice.

"Aye, ye did. But ye did nae kill him. I did." He paused. "And I'm sorry I failed ye before."

"You did not fail me," she said, clothes rustling, so that he thought perhaps she was now undressing. The mere notion of her removing her clothing had him contemplating her state of dress, and his desire grew like a fire raging out of control. His mind conjured an image of a lovely perfect shoulder, skin as smooth as silk. She would slip the gown first over one shoulder, then the other, and slide it ever so slowly down—

"Angus?"

He twitched out of the daydream. "Aye?" His voice was deep and thick with wanting to see her, touch her. He prayed she did not notice.

"I...I cannot get the last of my laces undone."

Please dunnae ask for my aid. But then again, please do.

"Could you aid me?"

He could not decide whether to cry out in joy or real fear that he would do something foolish and unwise such as kiss her...

"Aye," he grated out. He turned to find her back to him, her gown off and puddled at her feet. She stood there in nearly sheer underclothing that had laces undone almost to her arse. He held back his groan as he moved toward her.

The smell of the stream, wildflowers, and woman hit him at once. He brought his hands to her laces, but his gaze stayed fixed on the creamy expanse of back visible to him. Surely there was not a woman alive who had a back this lovely and alluring. He wanted to trace a finger down the perfect curve of her spine, to feel what made a woman who looked so fragile actually be so incredibly strong. Her underclothes billowed, caught by a sudden gust of wind, so that he got a full view of her tiny waist and round bottom. He swallowed repeatedly, and untied the knot at the end of her laces that was prohibiting her from taking off the drenched undergarment. When he had clumsily undone the last of the laces, he hesitated to tell her.

"Angus, are you finished?"

He squeezed his eyes shut and tried to extinguish his desire. But when he inhaled, her intoxicating scent consumed him, and a vivid picture of her naked in his arms filled his mind. Suddenly, her hand was on his back and the closeness of her body was like a drug, lulling him to euphoria and overpowering his control.

"Angus? Are you all right? Do you feel guilty, too?" Her soft hand slid over his shoulder, and the last vestige of restraint he had snapped.

He spun around, plunged his hands into her hair, and then hesitated long enough for her to demand she release him. But when she closed her eyes and her lips parted, triumph, the likes of which he'd never felt, took hold of him. He spread his fingers in her thick, silky hair at the curve of her neck and drew her to him, silencing the doubt and vanquishing the distance that separated them. He traced his tongue over the soft fullness of her upper lip, and her arms came to his shoulders. She twined her hands around his neck, and then she entangled her fingers in his hair. When he repeated the movement on her lower lip, she whimpered, the sound the most erotic thing he'd ever heard in his life.

His heart thudded, but he forced himself to move slowly for fear of scaring her as much as fear of losing his control. He brushed his lips to hers once, twice, and when she moaned again and crushed her lush body against his, he moved his mouth over hers, devouring her softness, drinking her sweetness, and consuming her heat. Their tongues tangled and retreated for him to explore the velvet warmth she offered to him as the greatest gift.

When she quivered and her hips pushed into his hardness, he forced himself to pull back, to put distance between them, before he crossed a line from which there was no retreat. Her dark, thick eyelashes slowly rose, revealing a gaze burning with desire. He wanted to possess her body, but she was not the sort of woman to simply bed. He swallowed hard, his lust burning him from the inside out.

"I'm sorry. I should nae have kissed ye."

She pressed her fingers to her lips. "No, I should not have allowed you to."

His mind searched for something to say, some way to explain what had just occurred, other than the obvious fact that he desired her with an intensity he had never experienced in his life. "Sometimes after a battle, when yer life was at risk, there's a need to feel alive."

"Oh, yes. That makes sense!" She said it with such enthusiasm that it was obvious she too wanted a reason for what had just occurred, other than that they had not controlled themselves, that was. "It's a need to feel connected to another person."

"Aye," he eagerly agreed, deciding it was not simply his desire that had overcome him. It was that need to feel alive. "We can simply forget the kiss."

"Yes." She nodded so quickly that he frowned. They did need to forget the kiss, but did she need to be so eager to? He shook his head at his own ridiculousness.

"I'll make ye a pallet while ye change."

She nodded, and he walked around her to the fire, spread the blanket on the ground, and scowled down at the meager place for her to sleep. "I'm sorry I kinnae offer ye a better place to rest."

"I'm certain I'll be fine," she replied. "I'm all changed."

He turned to her and chuckled. "Ye are the loveliest priest I've ever seen."

Her wide, genuine smile made his heart thump hard against his ribs.

"Thank you," she murmured, and then offered a mock curtsy. The lass was playful, which unfortunately made his lust-filled brain wonder if she would be playful in the bedchamber.

Grinding his teeth back and forth in frustration at himself, he motioned to the blanket. "Yer bed, my lady," Angus said.

"Where will you sleep?"

"On the ground," he answered.

She looked from the blanket to him, then bit her lower lip. "The blanket is large enough for both of us. If you wish to—"

"Nay," he cut in. It came out sharper than he had intended, but once again, a picture of her twined in his arms had filled his mind. "I'm used to sleeping on the ground from years of battle, and besides that, I dunnae get cold."

She smirked at him. "Everyone gets cold."

"Nae me," he assured her. "My sisters say I give off an unnatural heat." Some of the women he'd bedded mentioned it, as well, but he certainly could not say that.

"I see." She sounded altogether unconvinced, but then she shrugged, moved to the blanket, and settled herself there. "Goodnight, Angus," she offered, lying down and facing the fire, which put her back to him.

"Goodnight, lass," he said. He forced to himself look away from her, though he wished to stand there and stare.

Grant emerged from the path once more and as Angus made his way to him, the man situated his plaid on the ground. Angus kneeled beside Grant as the man lay down. "The man, Donovan, was a guard who her uncle assigned to watch her at the Palace of Westminster," Angus said, knowing Grant would be wondering. "He attacked us once before, and I was certain his injury would kill him, but clearly it did nae."

Grant sat up. "Why was she assigned a guard at all?"

Angus quickly told Grant of her uncle and about him using Lillianna to try to get Elizabeth to do as he wished. He also told him what he knew of Lillianna's father. He left out the part about the legend, though. It was too ridiculous to repeat.

When he finished, Grant said, "Well that explains why she is fleeing to the MacLeod clan. Did she tell ye why she dunnae wish a husband?"

"Nay," Angus replied. He'd been wondering about that himself.

Grant snorted. "Likely that was because ye were busy kissing her."

"Were ye watching us?" Angus demanded.

"Nay," Grant said. "'Twas a guess, but now I ken I guessed correctly."

That was a well-known trick to acquire information, and something he would not have previously fallen for, but Lillianna was muddling his thoughts. "It was momentary loss of control," Angus offered, though he had no notion why.

"If ye say so," Grant said with a laugh. "One of us should sleep here at the edge of the woods and one of us should sleep close to the lass. If ye fear ye kinnae control yerself, I'll be happy to be the one to sleep close to her."

"Nay," Angus growled. "I can control myself." Not only that but he'd be damned if he was going to allow Grant to sleep near Lillianna and ogle her.

"If ye need me, call out," Grant teased.

"I'll nae need ye," Angus snapped, turned, and walked back toward Lillianna. When he approached, he could hear her deep, even breathing and knew she had fallen asleep. Good. He'd feared she would not be able to sleep with how cold it was outside, but the fire—now almost dead—had likely given her enough warmth. Hopefully, she would not awaken in the night when the warmth from the fire was gone.

Chapter Ten

Lillianna lay facing the fire, willing herself to sleep and not think of Angus and the kiss they had shared, but it was useless. His kiss was the only thing she could think of. Despite her desperate tiredness, her mind would not allow her to rest. She could still feel his lips on hers. She'd never been kissed before. Oh, she'd imagined what it would be like, but nothing, absolutely nothing, could have prepared her for the way Angus's lips on hers, their tongues twining, would make her feel as if warmth enveloped her from head to toe and a fire burned in the pit of her belly.

Her lips still tingled from his searing kiss. Her belly felt tied in knots, though her pulse had finally calmed to a slower, steadier beat. He'd tasted slightly of mead and smelled of wood and fire and horse and water. He'd felt… She sighed as she recalled the ripple of his muscles under her fingertips, and then she frowned as she recalled his words.

He'd said he was sorry for the kiss, and she didn't doubt he was since he didn't wish to be entangled with her any more than she wished to be with him, but he desired her. He desired her for her and only her. Maybe his kiss had been driven by a need to affirm their lives after the fight, but the kiss had been full of passion. A kiss that searing had to be fueled by pure attraction to her. A heady sense of power she'd never felt filled her, but then she gave herself a little shake. She could not allow him to kiss her again, no matter how good it felt, no matter how good he seemed. Because if he wasn't as good as he seemed and she allowed her heart to become engaged, she knew instinctually that he would break it.

She forced herself to draw deep breaths, yet it did not seem to help quiet her thoughts. She flipped onto her back and lay there for what seemed like forever, and then she rolled onto her right side, making sure to keep her eyes shut in case Angus's were open. At first the fire kept her back warm, but after she'd been lying there for a bit, she no longer felt heat from the fire. Cold seeped from the ground into her skin and seemed to burrow to the center of her core, and she started to shiver, but finally, after a long while, she fell asleep.

She awoke the next morning no longer cold. In fact, she was cocooned in heat and the ground was not near as hard as she recalled. Something tickled her forehead, something warm. And then something moved, and the long, distinct sound of a slow inhale filled her ears. Her heart started to thud, and she opened her eyes, seeing only a wide expanse of very well-muscled chest.

She lay facing Angus, and he had his arms wrapped around her. Her heartbeat went from thudding to thundering as she glanced up and saw his face peaceful in sleep. His broad shoulders rose with another deep breath. She needed to move, to disentangle herself from him, for she could now feel that even their legs were tangled together. One of his heavy, hot legs was slung over hers and his other leg was under hers as was one of his arms.

He was cushioning her, she realized with a start. Even in sleep the man seemed to be honorable. She glanced down at the sliver of space between them. The blanket he'd given her was underneath them. So he had come over to her and lain down with her. But why?

She ought to move, yet his closeness was so bracing, so comforting. She allowed herself to examine him, knowing it would likely be the only chance she got. He had a small, half-moon scar on his lower abdomen near his hip bone, and up a little farther he had another scar, this one in the shape of an almost perfect circle. The muscles of his stomach cut slabs across his abdomen, and unable to help herself, she reached out and touched him. He was hard as steel. She could hear his breathing, now harsh and uneven, but instead of moving her hand, she traced it light as a feather over a long scar that ran almost the length of the left side of his stomach.

His chuckle froze her breath in her throat. "I'm verra ticklish."

Her cheeks burned instantly, but she forced herself to look up into his face. His gray eyes flashed like silver lightning as he swept them over her, then caught her gaze once more. Her toes curled at his hungry expression. At the base of her throat, her pulse beat and swelled as though her heart had risen inside her.

Without a word, he caressed his thumb over her sensitive skin of her neck. "It's verra dangerous for us both for ye to touch me like that," he said, his voice rough and deep.

"I...I'm sorry," she said as she disentangled herself and sat up. His eyes did not waver from hers. He watched her steadily with an almost wary look. She cleared her throat, pretending not to be as affected by him as she was. "How did you come to be over here?"

He sat up with ease, his strong body moving fluidly, the muscles rippling. "The chattering of yer teeth was keeping me awake, and I had to do something. I came to wake ye, and when I touched ye, ye were ice cold."

"So you enfolded me in your heat," she said, almost mesmerized by the notion of him wrapping his body around hers to keep her warm.

"Aye. I could nae think of another way to warm ye."

She nodded and motioned to his stomach. "Your scars. How did you get them?"

His eyes widened with surprise. "Ye're the first lass to ever ask me that."

She smirked at him. "I take it many lasses have seen your scars."

He suddenly looked disconcerted. "Well, I kinnae truthfully claim to be a saint."

She chuckled. "I don't suppose you could."

A slow, wolfish smile came to his lips. She doubted he had any idea how devilish he looked when he smiled like that. He was so handsome, so magnetic. She imagined he had no trouble finding an eager woman to warm his bed.

Distinct jealousy stirred in her gut and made her uneasy. She had no business feeling jealous, but she did. "So how did you get the scars?"

"Well," he said, looking down at his abdomen while kicking his long, powerful legs out in front of him and crossing them at the ankles. He leaned back on his right hand and pointed with his left. "This scar here—" he touched the half-moon near his hip bone "—I got saving Simon Fraser, Grant's older brother, from being trampled by a horse when we were lads of seventeen summers. And this one here—" he moved his hand farther up to graze his thumb over the almost perfect circle "—I got from a woman."

He looked away from her, and her heart squeezed. "The woman who betrayed you?" she blurted, sure that only the woman he had once given his heart to would have ever caught him with his guard down. Angus was the sort of man who was always careful.

"Aye," he replied, bringing his gaze back to her. His gray eyes were hard and full of dislike. "Isla Belfaine."

His voice betrayed nothing but disgust, yet she had to wonder... "Do you... Do you still care for her?"

"What?" His eyebrows shot up. "Nay. Whatever I felt for her died the moment I discovered her betrayal."

She wanted to ask so much more, but she decided it was probably too personal and she knew they had to ride out soon. She focused on the scars again. "What of the long, jagged one?"

He did not look at the scar but kept his gaze locked on her. "I got that scar the day I killed Isla's father."

The lethal calmness in his eyes made her swallow hard. "Why did you kill him?"

"Because," Angus said, standing up, "he killed my father."

Angus looked down at her and held his hand out to her. She took it, her skin tingling where his touched hers. He hauled her to her feet, and they stood face-to-face, only a hairsbreadth between them. "My father died because I was nae at a battle to guard his back, as I was supposed to be." Grief twisted Angus's features. "I was with Isla, instead. She had called me to her, and I went, like a fool. Her father had used the opportunity to kill my father and try to take our castle. If I had been where I was supposed to be my father would still be alive, as would my mother."

The guilt she heard in his voice, the torment, astounded her and made her heart twist for him. "I imagine," she said slowly, quietly, "that you've made penance for the choice you once made."

She could see that he was clenching his teeth by the muscle of his jaw flexing. "Nae enough."

Dear God. His hurt was heavy upon him. She wished she could ease it and give him peace. "How much is enough?"

"There is nae an amount, ye see, because the dead kinnae be brought back to life."

"No, they cannot. But punishing yourself the rest of your life is not the answer."

He scowled at her. "I'm nae punishing myself. Now, enough talk. We need to ride."

She opened her mouth to argue, but his face became closed. She knew he would not speak more on it, so she simply nodded and said, "If you'll give me a moment to change?"

"Aye." He glanced over his shoulder, and she looked to where he did, toward the stream. Grant was striding in their direction.

"Did you hear him approaching?" she asked, curious.

"Aye." He smiled. "Did ye?"

"No," she admitted. "I was too distracted by you."

Heaven help her! Had she just said that?

That wolfish smile appeared again for the briefest of seconds, before he gave her a stern look. "Dunnae ever let yerself be distracted." He winked suddenly. "Nae matter how braw the Scot."

She laughed at that. He was a complex man, so serious one moment but joking the next. She wished... Well, she wished her circumstances were different and that she could open up her heart to him and his to her. But they were not. "I'll only be a minute," she said, then collected her gown, which had been thoughtfully hung on a tree branch to dry. "Did you do this?"

"Aye. I've sisters, remember? I ken well that women dunnae like to don a damp gown and undergarments."

"Just your sisters have taught you that?" she teased. "Not other lasses?"

"I dunnae ken the preferences of any lasses but my sisters," he said, his tone serious.

She didn't doubt his words. Likely, he'd never let a woman close enough to learn her likes and dislikes. The notion made her happy that no one else knew him intimately, which disturbed her. She hurriedly grabbed her gown and brushed past him and Grant, murmuring, "Good morning," as she went.

Just as she reached the thick trees, Angus said, "Dunnae go farther than ten paces. We'll nae be able to see ye, but I'll be able to hear ye."

She bit her lip on a grin that he was concerned for her welfare, but then she shook her head at herself. She really had to get control of how good he made her feel.

─❦❦─

Angus could not tear his gaze away from Lillianna as she walked away, shoulders back and head held high. He frowned as his body heated for her. He could not act upon his yearning again, and it was putting him in a foul mood. He thought he'd gotten control of it lying on the hard ground last night, but when he'd had to lie beside her to warm her, his desire for her had flared brighter than ever.

Even more disconcerting was how easy it had been to

fall asleep with her in his arms. It had felt so right to have her there, unlike anything he'd ever experienced with a woman in his life.

It was likely because they had shared personal stories about themselves, and he'd spent more time with her since he'd met her than he'd ever spent with a woman. She was certainly getting to him.

Grant stopped in front of him and smirked. "Sleep well?"

"The lass was freezing," Angus said in defense.

"Well, if she's freezing again tonight and it's too much temptation for ye, I'll be happy to wrap myself around her as ye did last night."

"Dunnae even think of it. And I'll nae be doing so again. We can take turns keeping the fire stoked through the night tonight."

"That sounds like less fun than tangling myself up with a bonny lass like Lillianna."

Angus narrowed his eyes upon Grant. "Lillianna is nae a wench for ye to bed, do ye ken me?"

"I ken ye," Grant said, his tone light. "It's nae all right for me to bed her because ye want to."

Angus wanted to throttle the younger man. "No one will be bedding the lass, and if they do—" he eyed Grant "—they'll be marrying her."

"I could nae agree more," Grant said with a wink. "I simply needed to be certain ye were as honorable as I recalled."

Angus found himself gaping at Grant. "Did ye honestly think I'd allow myself to bed the lass and nae marry her?"

"I'd hoped nae because from what I see, the fire burning between the two of ye is about to consume ye both."

Angus grinned. He couldn't help it, but he quickly got

control of himself and wiped away his smile. "We may desire each other, but nae anything will be happening."

Not again.

"If that's the case—" Grant began, but Angus cut him off.

"Nay. I'm nae going to stand around and watch ye try to woo the lass."

"Why nae?" Grant demanded. "'Tis better I woo her than some man ye dunnae ken, is it nae? Ye ken well that I'm honorable. I'd treat her well, and—"

"Nay," Angus said again, more forcefully this time. He damn well refused to watch Grant woo Lillianna and then possibly wed her. His blood was now rushing hard through his veins. If he felt so possessive of Lillianna now, how would he feel in the next sennight it would take to get to the MacLeod hold? He could not allow himself to think on it because however he felt would change nothing. She was his mission, and that was all. He said it in his mind over and over, even as his gut twisted.

"Fine. I'll nae argue it," Grant said. "There are plenty of lasses to woo."

Nae like Lillianna, Angus thought to himself.

"We need to ride," Grant said.

"Aye. We will shortly. I promised the lass a quick lesson with the dagger."

Grant cocked an eyebrow at Angus. "Do ye always make promises to lasses that dunnae mean anything to ye?"

"Shut up," Angus growled, at which Grant chuckled.

"I'll go ready the horses," Grant said as Lillianna came strolling back to them, half-dressed in her now-dry gown. It hung loosely from her, telling him she needed help lacing it.

Angus gave Grant a distracted nod, his gaze glued on Lillianna. Her hair was a tangled, tumbled mess around her shoulders. Her gown was sullied and torn. She had a smudge of dirt on her right cheek, and she held her slippers in her right hand, swinging them as she walked. And never had a lass looked lovelier to him... He wanted to kiss her until she was breathless. He wanted to learn every inch of her body and then show her the ways a man could bring pleasure to a woman. He wanted to—

Christ's blood. This mission was going to kill him. He was going to be felled by lust instead of a sword.

He yanked his hand through his hair and breathed deeply until his pulse slowed and his body did not feel flushed. Lillianna stopped in front of him and presented her back. "I'm ready after you lace me," she said, and his mind immediately leaped to what he was ready for. He swallowed hard, deftly laced her, and then turned her toward him.

"Bring up yer dagger," he commanded. She did as he asked. "Good. Now point it at my heart."

The sharp edge of her weapon came close to his heart. "Like so?" she asked, her tongue darting out to lick her lips.

"Aye," he croaked, trying to will himself to concentrate on the task at hand. "Now, try to keep hold of yer dagger while I try to take it."

"All right," she said, grinning, which made him grin. She was a funny lass—so delicate yet so eager to learn to defend herself. He whipped his hand up and snatched the dagger from her before she could even blink.

She frowned. "I did not even see you coming for it until it was too late! You're very fast."

"Nae any faster than many men. Ye need to clutch yer dagger so tightly that it will nae be taken. But yer grip is wrong and too loose to do so." He took hold of her hand, set the hilt of her dagger in it, and situated her fingers around it. "Hold it like that, but verra firmly, like it's the one thing between ye and death, which it verra well could be."

She nodded, and he watched as she did what he said. She cocked her head at him, admirable determination shining in her eyes. "I want to try again."

He nodded, but instead of giving her any notice, he simply repeated the motion from moments before and came away with her dagger again. She gasped. "You did not tell me you were about to try to take my dagger!"

"Of course nae," he replied with a snort. "Will yer enemy warn ye before he tries to kill ye?" He handed her dagger back to her.

She took her dagger as she sucked in her temptingly plump lower lip and then released it. Yearning engulfed him. He needed to think of anything else but how he wanted her, so he concentrated on what could happen to her if he did not teach her to properly defend herself. He grew angry, imagining a man trying to defile her and succeeding because Angus had failed her in this lesson today. It worked. His desire waned beneath the fierce anger.

"Answer me," he demanded, wanting to make certain she understood the importance of this.

"Of course not," she said, raising her dagger. "I—"

Once her dagger was fully up, he snatched it from her again.

She gasped. "Angus!"

"Again," he ordered, his fear for her suddenly throbbing through his entire body. He held the dagger out to her, and she took it, anger and resolve settling on her face. He stole it from her four more times, but on the fifth time, she managed to hold on to it.

"I did it!" A smile stretched across her face, and she

launched herself at him, hugging him and laughing. He could feel her hammering heart through the fine material of her gown—along with every feminine curve she possessed—as her soft body molded to the length of his. Her scent of wildflowers swirled around him, and he had such an intense wish to fist his hand in her hair and cover her mouth with his that he shook as he pushed her away.

Her eyes widened, and he wondered if she knew the effect she had on him. "Angus, I'm sorry," she whispered, splotches of red appearing on her porcelain cheeks.

"Dunnae be sorry. It's just that I kinnae—I mean, ye should nae—" Devil take his damned tied tongue. His frustration exploded. "Ye are nae the sort of lass to bed and forget, and I'm nae the sort of man for more than that. And every time ye touch me, ye tempt me. A man can only take so much when faced with a woman like ye."

She frowned. "What sort of woman is that?"

"Ah, Lillianna." Despite the fact that he knew he ought not to, he cupped her cheek, telling himself it would be the last time he touched her intimately again. "Beguiling. Bold. Brave. I wish... I wish—"

"Wishing is for weaker people than we are," she interrupted, her tone steely. "I'll ride with Grant."

With that, she turned on her heel and walked away from him. And he did not stop her because he feared he'd forget all the reasons he could not pursue her, and simply do so anyway with the zeal of man starved for one particularly fetching, fiery lass.

Chapter Eleven

The next several nights were not as cold as it had been the night Angus had wrapped himself around Lillianna to keep her warm. Thank God for the increased temperature, because despite how hard Angus fought his yearning for Lillianna, it did not wane. If anything, it grew with each leg of their journey. They were another day away from Sheffield, the next village, and from there, they'd only have three more villages to pass through until they reached Ettrick Forest.

Lillianna had elected to ride with Grant each day, and Angus had let her, but he'd also speared Grant with a look that said if the man touched her in any way other than to hold her on the horse, Angus would cut off his hands. Grant had proven more than honorable, with only one joking comment that if her thighs became too chafed again, he would personally rub Angus's salve on her. Angus had not had to do a thing or say a word to put Grant in his place, though. Lillianna had brought her dagger to Grant's groin herself, and in the sweetest voice, she promised to relieve him of his bollocks the next time he made a lurid comment like that. Angus had never been prouder, and Grant had apologized profusely and said he'd clearly been among his warriors too long and had forgotten his manners.

At night, Lillianna slept on Angus's blanket, wrapped in

his plaid. He pretended to fall asleep immediately, but the moment her breathing turned deep and even, he'd open his eyes and watch her sleep. It was the most beautiful sight he'd ever seen. The most tempting, too. His body ached. It was almost as if he was torturing himself by watching her, but he could not seem to stop. He'd never seen a woman sleep before. Hell, he'd never stayed the night with a woman, and neither he nor they had ever had any interest in doing so. That was the beauty of those relationships. As for Isla, they'd never slept the night together, either. Their clans had been enemies, and his relationship with her had been forbidden. They'd only had brief snatches of time together. Sometimes, when he thought back on those days so many years ago, he wondered if he'd got entangled with Isla less because of love and more because his father had forbidden it, and Angus had been young, stubborn, and foolish. He could not recall Isla making his chest feel the way Lillianna did, and he'd never even joined with Lillianna. They did not even have any sort of relationship, really, other than protector and protected.

On the fifth day of their journey, they rose early, as they did every day, and Angus and Lillianna made their way to the riverbank. They trod through thick mud, as it had rained continuously for the past two days and the ground was drenched. Angus eyed the deep, fast-moving river and the thick brush that hung over the water.

He looked at the ground to his right and picked up a long, thick, sturdy stick. "Dunnae wade far, and poke down with this stick before ye step forward, to make certain ye're nae taken by surprise and fall off a steep incline. In that heavy gown, ye'd find it hard to regain the surface."

She nodded. "I'll be careful."

Angus turned his back so she could wade into the river

and wash herself. The lass was very particular about being clean, which was likely why she smelled so very good.

Though he did not like the fast movement of the river this day, he forced himself to keep his back to her, as much for her privacy as his sanity. She was a smart lass and would be careful, and seeing her completely clothed was temptation enough. If he got a glimpse of bare legs or her dress loosened for her to wash her chest, well, that would be torture. So when Lillianna yelped, Angus flinched but he did not turn around. Instead, he called out, "Are ye all right?"

"Yes," she replied. "The water is freezing. I'll not be long."

He got a mental picture of her lovely, perfect skin covered with gooseflesh, and then he imagined all the ways he could warm her. He groaned, but the sound of his torment was muffled by another yelp.

"What is it, lass? Too cold for ye?"

When silence greeted him, his protective instincts roared to life. He swiveled around to find her, but she was nowhere to be seen. And then her head popped up down the river for one brief moment before she went under again. A black fright swept through him as he yanked off his boots and splashed into the water. The frigid temperature snatched his breath. If it was cold to him, it had to be near unbearable to Lillianna. How long could she survive in this freezing water?

Ten steps in, the slimy ground beneath his feet gave way, and he started to swim. His heart pounded viciously, causing his blood to roar in his ears. He cut through the water, feeling as if he was swimming for his life, but it was her life he was swimming for. He scanned the distance and saw her head pop up again, but it disappeared more quickly than the time before. She was closer to him now, though, and that gave him great hope.

He concentrated all his determination, all his will, on reaching her, so when she next came up, coughing, his fingertips grazed her, but she was just out of his grasp. His lungs burned with the effort, but he'd die before he quit trying to save her. He surged forward just as she surfaced again, but it was her back that appeared, not her head, and dread, which felt far too much like what he'd felt before discovering his father was dead, filled him. He caught her by her shoulder and held on tight as the water carried them forward at a clipped pace.

He allowed the water to move them for a moment as he pulled her to him, flipped onto his back, and positioned her on hers to slide his arm around her waist. Her head lolled backward, and anguish nearly choked him. He glanced to his right toward the riverbank. His greatest hope to save her was to get her to dry ground and get the water from her lungs. He'd done such a thing once before, so he knew saving her had something to do with getting the water out of her lungs. Once he got the water out, the next worry would be the cold.

Roaring his anger at fate, he swam sideways toward the trees that hung over the river, and when he got near enough to one that was nearly in the water, he grabbed for it. He was pushed past but managed to hold on to the branch and Lillianna at the same time. His arms burned with the strain. Gritting his teeth, he pulled them forward until he was in the thick of overhanging limbs. He gripped her tightly to him, found purchase with his feet against the tangle of tree roots under the water, and slowly climbed them out of the water and onto the bank. He collapsed, bringing her down upon him, then taking a deep breath to calm his thoughts so he could methodically decide what to do next, he rolled her to the ground and onto her back.

He scrambled to his knees beside her and slid one hand under her neck while cupping her chin with the other, and then he sealed his mouth over hers and blew his breath into her, willing her to live. He did this several times, and when she did not respond, his control snapped, and he pressed hard against her chest, desperate to get the water out. Still, she lay unmoving, white, clammy, and cold.

"Ye kinnae die, damn ye," he cursed down at her. "Ye are too amazing to die. Dunnae let go, do ye hear me?" he roared and bent down to blow into her mouth again. He came up panting after a moment and began to press on her chest again as he yelled at her. "Dunnae be weak. Hold on! Come back to me. I'll protect ye. I vow I will. I'll protect ye with my life, and I'll nae ever let harm come to ye again!" When she continued to lie there lifelessly, he bellowed his grief. He blew into her mouth once more, pulling away only when bright silver spots appeared in his vision. "Lillianna de Burgh, I thought ye stronger than this," he growled, pushing once more on her chest.

Suddenly, she began to cough. Water spurted out of her mouth, and her eyes fluttered open, locking on him. He gathered her into his arms, forgetting the vow he'd made about not touching her intimately again, and he pressed his hand to her head and into the cradle of his chest. He wrapped his arm around her back, needing to feel her breathing, to assure himself she was alive.

His heart beat so hard his chest ached, and after a moment, her hands came around his back, and she clung to him as much as he held her to him. That she had the strength to do so filled him with such relief he wanted to weep like a bairn.

"Did you curse at me?" she asked, amusement in her

voice. The warmth of her breath washed over his neck. He felt joy like he'd never known. It scared him, but not enough to make him release her.

"Aye," he replied. "Ye were trying to die, and I could nae let that happen." When she shivered, he wrapped his arms tighter around her. "I vow, ye make keeping ye safe difficult, but I'll be damned if I let harm come to ye again."

Angus's words sparked something in Lillianna's head. She heard his voice speaking in her mind, yet she could see his lips, which were not moving. *I'll protect ye with my life, and I'll nae ever let harm come to ye!* He'd said those words. She was certain of it. He'd risked his own life to save her, and then he'd brought her back to life. She froze as her senses and her awareness of him leaped to life. Her heart fluttered wildly in her chest as gratitude, awe, and his nearness kindled a flame within her that she'd only ever felt with him.

She was drawn to him certainly, yet she sensed it could be more, so much more. And within her, the desire to allow it to blossom made her ache. Could she truly trust him? If she gave into what he was making her feel, would it be the biggest mistake of her life as it had been for her mother and her grandmother? She didn't have the answers, not yet anyway, but she knew one thing for certain, she wanted him to kiss her as he had before. She needed to feel alive after having been so close to death yet again.

She looked up at him, and their eyes locked. Their breathing came in unison. Everything vanished but him, and the emotions swelling within her destroyed whatever fear she had of kissing him. He made no attempt to hide the fact that he was watching her, yet if she asked him to kiss her would he deny her?

"Angus," she began, licking lips that felt suddenly dry. Before she could form the rest of her sentence, he gave a growl, and then his mouth claimed hers. One hand came to the small of her back and the other fisted in her hair to bring her closer to him. His tongue breached her mouth, and she welcomed the invasion, meeting the intensity of his kiss with her own desperation.

Their tongues twined and retreated, and his kiss became demanding, sending the pit of her stomach into a wild swirl. He broke the kiss, leaving her mouth burning with fire and a protest on her lips. Yet, before she could voice it, his lips came to her neck and his hands slid across her belly. He worked magic across her skin with his mouth, and his light touch up her stomach to her breast made something in her surge at the intimacy of his touch. His fingers brushed over her hard buds, and her breasts grew instantly heavy and her core tightened almost painfully. Her heartbeat throbbed in her ears as his fingers found her buds again and circled them once, twice, sending dizzying currents of need through her.

"Angus," she moaned, delving her hands into his hair and tugging him closer. She didn't know what she wanted, yet she knew she wanted something that only he could give.

His answer was to slip his fingers under the shoulders of her gown and pull the wet material down until her breasts, hidden only by her undergarments now, spilled out from her gown. She should be shocked, she knew. She should stop him, certainly. But she was too far gone, too desperate with the need to feel his hands on her bare skin to care what danger she was courting.

Cool air whispered across her breasts as he pulled her underclothing down with another yank, and then his mouth, hot and seeking, came to her right breast and took her into his warmth. His tongue swirled around her bud, and then he suckled her in a way that forced a scream of pleasure from her lips. She arched toward him, needing more, wanting more, feeling she would die without more. And he gave it with long, luxurious pulls of his mouth and teasing, tempting slides of his tongue over her sensitive flesh.

His hands settled on her outer thighs then moved lower, her soaking skirt being pulled up over her hot skin, and then her hands were on his aiding him. She didn't care about anything, not even the dull ache from her wounds, but the sensations he was creating for her. He was suddenly hovering over her, and she was on her back, imprisoned by her growing arousal. He caught her left breast with his mouth this time and flicked his tongue against her hardened nipple as he gently parted her thighs fully, and then his body pressed against hers, flesh to flesh, man to woman. She felt the full length of his desire against her stomach, and she froze, the reality of what they were doing crashing in around her.

She put a hand to his chest, her breaths ragged, her chest heaving, and a tormented groan escaped him as he rolled off her and onto his back beside her. "Christ," he muttered, the word raw. "Christ," he said again, the word now drenched in self-loathing that stole the last bit of the warmth their passion had lent her. A chill swept her body as she drew her undergarments and then her gown up over her breasts. The dull ache of her wounds became more pressing, but she shoved the pain away, more concerned with Angus. She wanted to look at him, but she feared doing so. What must he think of her? What had she been thinking?

"I'm sorry," he whispered. "I did nae have a right to touch ye so, but I wanted it. I want ye so damn much that I lost my good sense."

She'd lost hers as well, and she feared he was on the verge of stealing her heart, whether he wanted it or not, whether she wished it or not.

Chapter Twelve

Angus drove them almost relentlessly the entire day and stopped that night to rest in a tavern, for Lillianna looked bone weary and he feared she would fall ill again. As he dismounted, he looked to her and Grant, who aided her in dismounting the horse she had ridden with him. Jealousy stirred, but Angus knew her riding with Grant had been best. After what had almost happened in the forest, he could not be so close to her until he was certain he would not lose control once more.

"Will ye see to a room for Lillianna?" Angus asked Grant, who had wisely not commented to Angus when he and Lillianna had emerged from the woods that morning. Grant nodded, though Angus could see the questions in the man's eyes.

Lillianna had been unusually quiet all day, likely as numb with shock as he was that he had almost taken her innocence. She followed Grant, and as she passed Angus's horse, her scent of wildflowers tickled his nose and filled his mind with memories of her lush breasts in his hands, her silky skin, her perfect buds, the way she made little moans when he sucked her breasts. Heat seared him. God's truth, he needed a drink.

He quickly secured the horses at the inn stables and found a seat in the dark, nearly abandoned tavern. He was glad no one was at the inn this day. He could feel himself itching for a fight, and it would be foolish to draw attention to himself. A buxom blond serving wench sauntered over to him, batting her eyelashes. She leaned forward far more than necessary to speak to him, and he got a full view of her breast, but oddly, he felt nothing, which was surprising given the constant state of unfulfilled desire in which Lillianna left him.

"Can I get you something?" the lass asked, winking. "Mayhap some mead and me?" She offered him a suggestive smile. This was exactly the sort of lass he had bedded in the past, one who clearly wanted a tumble in the hay and no more, but tonight her invitation held no appeal.

"Thank ye," he said, not wishing to injure her feelings, "but I've been traveling for some time, and I'm bone weary. All I require is mead."

Her lips formed a pretty pout. "You're certain?" she asked, brushing her breasts against his upper arm. "No need to fear I'll desire more than this night," she added with another wink. "I'm wed, but the rotten man cannot pleasure me proper."

"I'm sorry for that, lass, but I'm certain," he said.

Her pout turned to a scowl, and she frowned at him. "As you wish," she grumbled.

As he watched her walk away, her hips swaying, Lillianna filled his mind once more. It was her hips he saw, her mouth in a pretty pout, her perfect body writhing under his. When the lass came back with his mead, he drank it down in four gulps. Two more meads later, he felt slightly less like a taut bow about to snap, but when Grant came strolling toward him and pulled out a chair, the tension returned to Angus in full force.

He gaped at Grant. "If ye are here, who is guarding

Lillianna?" he demanded.

"Grant's eyes widened. "Does she need guarding? I left her in her room about to go to sleep."

"Ye were in her room?" Angus growled, his hands reflexively clenching into fists.

Grant's gaze flicked between Angus's fists and his face. "I did nae enter the lass's room," he said carefully.

Angus blew out a long breath, realizing how unreasonable he was being. "I'm sorry, Grant."

The man nodded. "If she's gotten to ye so badly, I kinnae see why ye dunnae simply bed her. Clearly, the lass wants ye as much as ye want her."

"I told ye," Angus said through clenched teeth, "Lillianna is nae the sort of lass to bed and nae wed."

"Then ye best consider wedding her. I'm fairly certain with the distracted state ye are in now, that yer enemies could easily fell ye, and I heard talk by two tavern wenches I passed coming in here that Belfaine stayed at this tavern last night with a group of his men. Is Belfaine nae yer enemy?"

"Aye," Angus growled, thinking of Isla's brother who was now laird Belfaine since Angus had killed the man's father. Angus shoved back from the table, not wishing to talk about his shortcomings or Lillianna, and most especially not the fact that Belfaine had been here. If the man had happened on Angus earlier when he'd been caught up in thoughts about Lillianna, Belfaine could have easily taken Angus by surprise.

"Did the wenches happen to mention where Belfaine was headed?"

"Nay, but does he nae have to ride through Ettrick to get to his home?"

"Aye." And with that, Angus dismissed thoughts of Belfaine. It was very likely the man had simply been on his way back to his stronghold. Angus had enough to concentrate on with Lillianna's safety and warning Robbie's men to add Belfaine to the list when it was, in all probability, a coincidence. "I'll guard Lillianna's room for the first half of the night, if ye will watch it for the second?"

Grant nodded as Angus rose to leave. He only got three steps away when Grant said, "I've nae ever met a man so determined to protect a lass that he did nae care about."

"She's my duty," Angus replied, plain and simple, without breaking his stride.

Outside her bedchamber, he slid to the hard ground and crossed his legs and arms. He would conquer this constant desire, this distraction. Methodically, he began to recount the first battle he had ever been in, and then the next, and the next, and hours later, when he was finished recounting details of his battles, he thought upon the day he had failed his father.

By the time he had finished with that, Grant was there, relieving Angus of guard duty. Angus departed quickly and found a patch of nice, soft grass under the stars to take a respite. He closed his eyes, and it was not long before sleep overcame him.

But when he awoke in the morning, his first thought was of the green-eyed, brown-haired siren. He took a quick dip in the freezing cold loch, and when he returned to the stables, Lillianna and Grant were already there, mounted and ready to ride. Early-morning light shone on her, making her hair almost appear as if spun with strands of gold. Her gown was rumpled and there were dark smudges under her eyes, but his breath still caught.

"How is it that even in travel, even after sickness, ye are so blessedly beautiful?" he blurted, unaware he'd spoken aloud until her mouth parted, surprise crossing her face.

Grant chuckled.

"You must have hit your head last night, and today it's affecting your vision," she said, a blush staining her cheeks.

He'd been hit, all right, but not in the head. In the groin by a gnawing, unwavering, all-consuming yearning for this woman.

He set them again to a grueling pace, which they kept the entire day and well into twilight. When they camped that night, Grant took over all duties having to do with Lillianna without Angus even asking.

The next morning, they started out at a gallop, but no matter how hard and fast he drove them, he could not outride thoughts of her. Images of them entwined in the forest filled his mind, and the same shock he'd felt after first almost taking her innocence blanketed him. If he had done that, if he had joined with her, there would have been no choice but to wed her, and the deep, troubling thing was that he found himself contemplating it, considering it. She had become a constant distraction. If he could simply keep control until he left her with the MacLeods... His entire body rebelled at the very thought.

He tugged a hand through his hair as they galloped toward Ettrick Forest through most the early day, and when the sun was directly overhead, the edge of the forest became clear. Soon they would be with Robbie's men, and Angus's obligation to them would be complete, leaving only his promise to take Lillianna to the MacLeods.

He stole a glance at Lillianna, who was situated in front of Grant on his horse. She sat stiffly, as she had every day. He wanted to halt them suddenly, knowing their time together was drawing close to finished. He wanted to bring her onto his destrier with him, wrap his arms around her, smell her, feel her.

It felt as if a tight band had been wrapped around his chest and was squeezing all the air out of his lungs. He could not let her go. The realization struck him hard, and he sucked in a breath. If he could not let her go, only one choice remained: wed her. As he saw it, he now had two main problems: he needed to figure out how to convince Lillianna to stay with him and trust him enough to tell him why she did not wish to wed, and he needed to remedy the problem of her being a distraction. Wedding her and bedding her would surely make it so his every thought would not be consumed with her. Satisfied that it would be so, he focused his attention on the looming forest.

Discovering Lillianna's secret and convincing her to wed him would have to wait until after he warned Robbie's men. He needed to be completely focused. The forest was thick, and therefore, an excellent place for enemies to hide. So if the king's men had already arrived here, he needed to be aware at all times so he did not lead them to Robbie's men or to get himself captured. His one reassurance was that Simon would be one of the men leading Edward's knights, and Angus knew Simon would do all in his power to lead Edward's men away from Robbie's.

Looking at the edge of the forest, a blanket of silver and red leaves met his eye well into the air, and lower, near to the ground, thick shrubs were clustered everywhere. He raised a hand to slow them, and as Grant halted his horse, Angus removed one of his daggers and directed his destrier near Lillianna and Grant.

Angus held the dagger out to her. "Dunnae lose this again," he said.

She scowled at him, and even irritated, she was the most beguiling creature. She took the dagger from him and put it in the holder at her waist. "I did not lose it. I left it in

Donovan's leg, and you know it."

"If it's nae in yer possession, it's lost," he said gently, wanting to make her understand his point without injuring her feelings. "Yer weapon could well be the thing that keeps ye from death. Guard it as ye would a limb. If ye stab someone with it, immediately extract it after turning the blade good and deep."

She snorted. "My limbs are attached to my body, therefore much harder to lose."

"Ye're a cheeky lass," he said, pleased that she felt so comfortable with him that she could be so.

She grinned, the first playful gesture she'd offered him since he'd nearly joined with her. He was glad to see the wall of ice she'd built around her was melting, especially given his recent decision.

She tossed her hair over her shoulder. "You see me as cheeky, and I see myself as unafraid."

"Good," he said, chuckling when her eyes widened in surprise. "Now—" he looked to Grant "—I'll be making my way to Robbie's men alone."

"Why?" Grant demanded.

"Because," Angus said evenly, "if the king's men are in this forest, and they have nae found Robbie's men, I dunnae want to lead them to our comrades. I can move with stealth much more easily on foot alone than with the two of ye. And," he added, holding up his hand when Grant opened his mouth as if to protest, "I'll nae risk putting Lillianna in danger. I wish her away from a possible battle. If it becomes clear there is a battle, or that I'm captured and we are losing it, ye must vow to me on yer honor that ye will take Lillianna and ride—"

"Angus, no!" Lillianna protested, but he ignored her and continued, keeping his gaze locked with Grant's.

"Ye will take her and ride straight to my home," he said. "My brothers will keep her safe. But if I'm killed, take her to the MacLeods." They'd have more of a stake in protecting her than his brothers.

"I vow it," Grant said with obvious reluctance. Angus knew the reluctance was born of not wanting to miss a battle, not reluctance to keep Lillianna safe.

"Let me and Grant come with you, Angus. We can aid you!" she protested.

Angus looked to her, knowing he had to be careful with what he said. He did not want his words to make her think she was a burden, yet if it came to a battle, she would be a weakness, a thing that distracted him, which ultimately made her a burden.

"Ye kinnae come with me," he said, trying and failing to find words to smoothly explain why. Instead, he decided to opt for the commanding approach he often used with his siblings. "Ye will stay here," he said and dismounted.

"You cannot order me about like some…some hound!" she snapped and dismounted herself. The moment her feet hit the ground, she strode past him and toward the thick trees with a glare.

Grant dismounted last and stood beside Angus. "She dunnae appear to ken she should listen to ye," he commented, amused.

"Ye're verra humorous," Angus snapped, starting after her as she disappeared into the thickness of the woods. He was halfway to the spot through which she had entered when she screamed. As his own sword sang from its holder, Grant's did, as well. Angus barreled toward the woods, shoved branches out of the way, and came to a shuddering halt. Lillianna stood with her dagger to his youngest brother's throat.

"Allisdair," Angus growled, moving between them and pushing Lillianna's dagger down.

"You know this boy?" she asked, releasing a shudder.

"Aye, this is my brother. Allisdair, this is Lillianna," Angus said, mussing his brother's head of russet curls. The boy was fourteen summers, but he still looked more like a lad of ten summers, much to Allisdair's frustration, and much to the delight of many of the MacLorh boys Allisdair's age. They teased him for his small size, and he took the bait every time.

"I'm very sorry I held a dagger to you," Lillianna said in a voice as sweet as honey. "You frightened me, and I had no notion you were related to Angus."

Allisdair scowled at Lillianna. "Ye took me by surprise, too," he said. "I was waiting here for my brother Ross."

"Ross is here, too?" Angus asked, scanning the thick forest beyond him. "Then who the devil is acting as laird in my absence?" He'd left Ross in charge of protecting the castle and leading the clan while Angus was away.

"Aye. Ross is bossy as ever," Allisdair muttered. "I wanted to go with him to locate Bruce's men, and he threatened to whip me if I so much as moved from this spot. Can ye imagine that?" His cheeks reddened with his ire, and Angus sighed. Allisdair was his usual quick-tempered self.

"I can imagine," Angus barked, cuffing the boy on the head.

"Angus!" Lillianna chided and moved protectively in front of Allisdair. "If you dare to touch this child again—"

"I'm nae a child!" Allisdair protested and thumped his chest. "I'm almost a man."

Lillianna's mouth formed a perfect O. "I beg your pardon. I thought—"

"Dunnae beg this miscreant's pardon," Angus said.

"Angus MacLorh, do not call your brother a miscreant!" Lillianna snapped.

Allisdair's gaze widened upon Angus as he peeked around Lillianna. "Ye let this lady talk to ye that way?"

It made him damn happy that she felt brave enough and comfortable enough to do so, but he could not let that be known or his brother was sure to misbehave. "I'll deal with the lady at a later time," he assured his brother and scowled at Lillianna for good measure. She, of course, scowled back. "Why are ye and Ross in Ettrick Forest?" Angus asked.

Allisdair looked at him as if he were a clot-heid. "Because ye sent for us, of course. Ross received a message from ye last week, instructing us to come here immediately and meet ye where the Bruce left his men."

"Christ's blood," Angus swore, meeting Grant's gaze. "Ross has walked into an ambush!"

"Aye," Grant agreed. "We best make haste and see how many men we can save."

Angus glanced to Lillianna and Allisdair. They would be safer here than headed into an ambush with him and Grant, though the thought of leaving them alone twisted both his gut and his heart. He took a dagger out of a sheath at his right thigh, and then he stepped around Lillianna and held the dagger hilt first toward Allisdair. A proud look settled on Allisdair's face as he took the dagger, as if he knew what was about to happen. His brother, with his keen blue eyes and cheeks still plump with the pudginess of youth, seemed to grow taller as he gripped the dagger.

Angus cleared his throat, which felt clogged with a swell of emotion, and gripped Allisdair's left shoulder. "If I dunnae return, I'm either captured or dead."

"Angus!"

He ignored Lillianna's gasp. Time was of the essence. "Dunnae search for me. Dunnae let her, either," Angus added, motioning to Lillianna and catching her gaze for one brief moment. It was wide with fright, and her face was pale as the moon. He feared she was just impetuous enough to do such a thing as charge into battle. Angus focused on Allisdair once more. "Do ye ken?"

"Aye," his brother croaked.

Angus released a sigh, his mind turning with what else to say in the next few breaths. "Stay hidden until one of us or Ross returns for ye. Ye'll ken it's us by the call of the red bird." Angus made the call to remind Allisdair, but the boy already knew. All his siblings had been taught this signal at a young age. "If none of us come for ye by nightfall, head for Fraser's stronghold, as he is our nearest ally. It's an hour's ride from here, and the Fraser men will give ye shelter and help ye make yer way home. If ye discover that I'm dead and Ross is dead, however, take Lillianna straight to the MacLeods." If he and Ross should fall, they would be better able to protect her than Allisdair, who would be a young ruler and at the mercy of the MacLorh council for a while.

"Simon Fraser is a turncoat!" Allisdair protested, then paled and looked to Grant. "I'm sorry to speak ill of yer brother."

Angus impatiently waved his brother to silence. He'd wanted to let Simon tell his brother his secret, but there was no option for that now. "Simon is nae a turncoat. He has played the part, and done so well, in order to gain information from the King of England that will aid us in taking back our land."

Out of the corner of his eye, he saw Grant grin and then frown. "Why would ye simply nae confirm the truth before?"

"I did nae feel it was my place, but I feel ye need to ken it now, so ye ken for certain ye can trust him. He did nae want to endanger ye, and his betrayal had to be believable to everyone. It still does," Angus emphasized, "until we dunnae have a need for him inside the king's castle anymore. Allisdair, we must make haste. Guard Lillianna with yer life, Brother."

As Allisdair nodded, Angus turned to Lillianna. No longer did she look fearful; to his shock, she looked determined. She set her palm to Angus's chest. "I will guard your brother with my life," she vowed vehemently.

He had a great deal he wanted to say to her, like would she wed him, but it would have to wait. Instead, he said, "I ken ye will, lass, but guard yerself, as well, and hold on to that dagger for all ye're worth." And because he could not resist the temptation, he reached out and tugged her to him, reveling in the brief feel of her soft body against his. Her lips parted with surprise, and he swooped down to kiss her. And it was no normal kiss. He possessed her mouth in those few breaths as he intended to soon possess her.

When he pulled away from her, she appeared to sway, and he turned without a word, motioning to an unusually quiet Grant to follow him into the woods. He glanced back once as the canopy of the forest swallowed them. Lillianna stood facing him, her fingertips to her lips and a look of happy confusion on her face. If he died this day, he could not think of a better image to be his last.

Chapter Thirteen

Richard Og de Burgh glanced at the Scot before him, a traitor to his own kind. Though Richard hated the Scots with a venom that left a bitter taste in his mouth, he was happy to use them when they came calling. And Hector Fraser, cousin to Simon Fraser—who was also a traitor but one who had gained Richard's trust—had recently arrived at Westminster and requested to see Richard. It seemed the Scot wanted to be laird of the Fraser clan, and he had traveled here to make a bargain. He'd secure information for Richard if Richard would ensure neither Simon nor his brother Grant, who were both ahead of Hector in the line to be laird, ever returned to the clan. Richard raised his wine goblet to his lips and studied the man, deciding what to reveal and what to truly do.

It wasn't that he liked Simon necessarily, but the man had proven useful. But in order for Richard to get his clutches on Lillianna, he'd sell each and every offspring he had to the devil himself. The king needed his niece to tell him whether to go forth with the attack on Edinburgh or not, and if he didn't find her, he feared he'd become engaged in a battle with Edward.

What to do, what to do…

Richard took a long drink of his wine, enjoying watching Hector start to fidget. A fidgeting man was a desperate man, and desperate men would do whatever was asked of them. Donovan had not returned with Lillianna, and he should have by now, so what Richard needed most was someone who could find her and bring her to him.

His mind made up, he set his wine goblet on the dais, where he sat alone, and leaned his elbows on the table. "This is what I require from you," he said, his voice echoing in the empty great hall. "My niece has disappeared with a Scot named Angus MacLorh. I wish you to find her and bring her to me. I am sure you know him," Richard said. He had been informed just recently by another one of his spies that a wench at the King's Head Inn had made mention of a sick English lass with a Scot, and the lass and Scot fit Lillianna and MacLorh's description.

"Aye, my lord," Hector said. He tugged at his red beard, which annoyed Richard. Unkempt people disturbed him. "Do ye ken where MacLorh was headed with her?"

"Ettrick Forest," Richard replied easily. "It seems MacLorh took her with him to warn Bruce's men that King Edward was coming for them."

Hector's eyes widened at the news, but the man wisely held his tongue. Richard would not say more. He did not need to relate that MacLorh had been used by them and was riding, hopefully, to his death.

"I imagine the man would send her to safety," Richard went on. "Perhaps to the MacLeod hold or to his own home. Find her and bring her to me, and I will ensure that Simon Fraser meets his death, and I'll aid you in ending the other Fraser's life, if he does not die before then."

Richard stood then, circled the dais, and went to stand in front of the man. At six foot two, Richard normally looked down on men, but he was eye to eye with Hector, which made him think the man might need a good glimpse into what Richard could do to him if he failed. "Fail me," Richard said slowly, "and I'll ensure the Fraser clan knows you are plotting to become the next laird by murder."

He expected Hector to look surprised, perhaps even slightly nervous, but a razor-sharp smile came to his face. "I'll nae fail ye."

Lillianna sat on the forest floor with her knees pulled to her chest and her arms encircling her knees. One hand rested there while her other hand gripped her dagger. Allisdair sat quietly beside her, holding his own weapon. Every so often, he would clear his throat and nibble on his lip. It was obvious he was scared but trying not to show it. She knew how frightened she was and could only imagine how fearful a young lad of fourteen summers must be.

Tentatively, she extended her hand. "I'm awfully frightened. Will you hold my hand?"

He nodded, sitting up a bit taller, which made her smile inwardly, and then he more clutched her hand than held it. He leaned close to her. "They will return," he whispered. "And soon, I expect. Angus is the brawest fighter in all of Scotland. He has nae ever been defeated in combat or a tournament," Allisdair boasted.

She didn't doubt the truth of what he said. She could recall the feel of Angus's muscles under her fingertips, and she'd watched him move with the speed and grace of a warrior, born and bred. Honestly, she'd never seen a man as quick with his hands—or his lips—as Angus. Heat consumed her as she recalled the kiss he'd given her before he'd left, and her lips started to tingle all over again. What had that kiss been about? Had he lost his senses again because of his desire for her? She seemed to lose hers nearly every time he was near, and when she thought about the possibility of never being near him again, never being kissed by him again, she felt hollow, like a shell of a person who had never been loved.

What if one or both of them died today? Suddenly, a lifetime of being too afraid to love seemed the worst fate she could imagine. If—*no, when*—they were together again, she would speak to him and see if he was willing to discover if anything more lay hidden under their passion. For her part, she was certain there was something there, and she thought she might want to take a chance with Angus. Her greatest fear had always been of being duped as her mother and grandmother had been, but Angus did not even believe, or seem to care, about the legend of her powers. If one day he awoke them in her, after she was sure of his love, she would tell him. Before she could consider anything else, Allisdair's hand suddenly grasped her tighter, and her breath caught as she listened.

In the distance, to their right, the distinct sound of metal clanging against metal echoed in the looming night. She swallowed the large lump in her throat. The fighting had begun. She and Allisdair huddled closer together, both of them breathing heavily with worry. Anxiety flowed through her, and every clank, every clash, every cry in the night made the cold knot in her stomach grow bigger and harder, and made her more aware with each passing moment that she simply could not imagine never seeing Angus again.

The urge to jump up, to defy what he had said and run to fight beside him was so unbearable that she had to choke back a cry. Instead, she let out a moan. Allisdair patted her hand. "Dunnae fash yerself. My brother will return."

God, she hoped so.

By the time Angus got to the fork in the river where Robbie's men were hiding, it was too late. Everywhere he looked Scots fought the king's men. Swords swished and arced through the air, and men fell as blood splattered to cover the ground. It appeared that the English outnumbered the Scots three to one. Angus did not know if his brother had led the king's men to the hiding place, if Edward's men had found it by luck, or if they had discovered the men some other way. It mattered little, though. All that mattered now was saving as many Scots' lives as possible.

The deafening roar of battle filled the normal silence of the forest and hummed in his ears. He turned to shout to Grant that they should stay together, but as he did so, Grant gave his own shout. "Behind us!" he bellowed.

Angus spun around and swore. A line of at least twenty English knights was closing in on them. It seemed he himself had led some of the enemy to Robbie's men! He could not think how, but then he saw Simon, a giant of a Scot with a chest like a barrel, at the front of the line, and Angus felt a blow of betrayal to the center of his chest. With a savage cry, he raised his sword to deflect any blow Simon might deliver, and when his sword met that of his longtime friend, his fellow Renegade, rage and sorrow exploded within him.

Horses raced past Simon and Angus as they fought, but Grant remained by Angus's side and raised his own sword to fight his brother. Yet, when the last English knight had galloped into battle, Simon's swings became less accurate, less forceful. But one would only know it if they were on the receiving end; a mere spectator from a distance would never be able to tell.

A moment of uncertainty to whether Simon was friend or foe made Angus pause, and as if Simon could read Angus's doubt, he snarled, "Flee the damn forest! This cause is lost!"

Angus jerked his sword back just before it connected with Simon's skull. "Are ye a turncoat or nae?" he demanded, his voice vibrating with anger.

"Ye ken damn well I'm nae a traitor," Simon said, his blue gaze moving to Grant. "Brother," he said. He swung his sword again, but this time Angus was certain it was for show. Simon's gaze was pleading. "I'd hoped to meet ye soon and mend the rift between us, but nae here, nae now. Ride away, both of ye. King Edward's men are everywhere. We rode here ten thousand strong."

"Christ's blood," Angus muttered, apprehension coursing through him. "Robbie's men will be massacred if we kinnae aid them in escape."

"Ye kinnae save them all," Simon said, swinging his sword again. Angus did the same in case anyone looked to them.

"We'll save as many as we can," Angus replied, knocking his sword against Simon's. "How did ye come to ken Robbie's men were in Ettrick Forest?" He needed to discover the traitor among them.

Simon glanced toward the melee, as did Angus. If anyone had been watching them, it was doubtful now. Men battled each other on every space of the ground, and where there was not a battle, men lay dead.

"I dunnae ken who told the king," Simon said, "but it was Elizabeth de Burgh's idea to tell Bruce so he would send ye to warn his men, and some of the king's men would follow ye."

Angus faltered at the news, and his thoughts swung immediately to Lillianna. Had she known this about her cousin? Did Lillianna have a hand in leading him to this treachery? He could not believe it of her.

Unaware of the doubts and questions in Angus's mind, Simon continued. "And it was her father's idea to send a message to yer brother Ross in case ye did nae come. Half of us rode straight here to wait for him. That is how we found Robert's men, or most of them, not long ago. We lay in wait for Ross, who led us to them."

"I knew Elizabeth de Burgh would be Robbie's downfall," Angus growled. "Where is my brother? Where is Ross?" When Simon's face fell, Angus's chest squeezed.

Dear God above, dunnae let Ross be dead.

He shook as he asked, "Captured or dead?"

"Captured," Simon said, and Angus let out a relieved breath that his brother still lived. "But the English mean to kill all who have been captured," he hurriedly added.

"Let them try," Angus snarled. He would not fail his brother. Ross would not die this day. "Where are the captured men?"

"Just over the hill," Simon said, nodding to the left. "They are only guarded by four knights. If ye can kill the knights…"

"You two head into battle," Angus said, already preparing to go to his brother. "Grant, the Scots will need your sword arm, and Simon, ye must maintain the pretense as long as ye can that ye are on the side of the English. Robbie needs King Edward to think ye loyal until the very moment ye rise against him."

Simon nodded. "It sickens me daily, but I will do it."

Angus nodded his understanding, then focused on Grant. He had to ensure Lillianna and Allisdair had someone to watch over then. "Grant, if I'm felled this day—"

"I'll guard Lillianna and yer brother with my life," Grant swore, "until the day I dunnae have breath left in me."

Angus nodded, noting Simon's frown. He would have no notion about Lillianna and her presence here with Angus, but there was no time to explain it now. Two English knights had turned their way and were galloping toward them.

"Ye've company," Angus warned just before he swiveled on his heel and raced in the direction Simon had indicated. The woods were thick, but when he glanced behind him, Grant was fighting the knights. Simon pretended to swing at Grant but, at the last minute, felled the knight who was lunging at Grant.

Angus turned away, flooded with relief that Grant had survived. It gave him peace to know that if he died, the man would do all he could to protect Lillianna and Allisdair, and God willing, Ross would survive to aid him. Angus raced up the steep slope of the forest, grabbing at rocks and vines to speed his ascent. He barreled through shrubs and jumped logs, never reducing his pace. He had to get to Ross and Robbie's men before the battle was lost and they were executed. At the top of the ridge, the ground leveled, and between rows of tall trees, near a cave, he spotted an English knight, then another, followed by two more. They stood facing the Scots they had captured. A quick scan showed twenty Scots tied to a post that had been driven into the ground. "God's teeth." The English had planned this carefully.

Angus slowly took out two of the four daggers from the holders at his thigh and sheathed his sword. If he was quick, he could fell all the knights in two breaths, which would give them no time to sound a warning or kill any of the

Scots. Angus judged the distance between him and the knights, then carefully aimed the daggers in his left and right hands. Thank God the English were so arrogant as not to fear a man might approach them from behind.

Clenching his teeth, he said a prayer for accurate aim and then released the daggers, grabbed the other two as the thrown ones struck his intended targets in the back of their heads, aimed the other two daggers just as the remaining started to move, and threw those daggers, as well. One hit true in the third knight's skull, but the other knight proved quick, ducked to the ground, and came up. But by the time he'd gained his feet, Angus was there, plunging his sword deep into his enemy's gut. The man grunted, his eyes went wide, and then he fell to the ground to join his three comrades in death.

"Angus!" his brother Ross cried out.

Angus swept his gaze over the men to cries of thanks and found Ross at the very end. Blood and dirt smeared his face, but as Angus went to his brother, he could see that Ross did not have grave injuries.

"Brother," Angus said, his voice cracking under the weight of what he felt as he untied the knot that bound Ross to the stake. Everywhere Angus looked there were stakes in the ground with men tied to them. When Ross's hands were freed, the men clasped arms, their eyes locking, and silently acknowledged the bond that had almost been severed. Angus swallowed back a wave of emotion.

Ross swiped a hand across his face, leaving a trail of blood. "The king ordered his men to kill us here, cut off our heads, and then put them on the end of the stakes," Ross said derisively. "King Edward said to line the forest with our heads."

Angus clenched his fists, his rage so hot he felt he would

burn to ash. Taking a deep breath, he spat at the ground, as did his brother, to show that they thought Edward had no honor.

"Come," Angus said to his brother, "let us make haste to free the others."

Soft words of gratitude came from the men as Angus and Ross untied them and answered their questions about Robbie.

"Ye all need to flee this forest," Angus told the men. "Bruce will be rising soon, and he will unite us all against King Edward, but ye need to continue his fight where ye can win. Make yer way to Loch Doon Castle. The castle keeper Gille abandoned it to the English because he did nae see any hope." Angus's heart pounded. "Go there! Take back that castle from the English. Ye outnumber the men King Edward left to hold it. Take back that castle for Robbie! Take back that castle for yer future king and for Scotland!" Angus brandished his sword in the air, and the men roared a cheer. They started toward him one by one, some clasping Angus's arm, some clapping him on the shoulder, some just meeting his gaze with gratitude. Angus saw the tide of change rising before him like a great wave in a violent, unstoppable storm.

He turned to his brother. "Ross, make haste to where ye left Allisdair."

"Ye saw Allisdair?" Ross asked.

"Aye, ye should nae have brought him here, but there will be time to discuss yer mistakes later."

Ross nodded. "I'm sorry, Brother."

"Dunnae be. Learn from this. Ye will find a lass with Allisdair," he said, motioning the men standing around them toward the six horses he'd seen tied in the distance. "Take five of those horses there." The king's colors were draped on the beasts, and Angus was more than happy to relieve Edward's knights of their destriers. Some of the Scots would have to double up on a horse, but they would survive. He focused on his brother once more. "Take Allisdair and the lass, Lillianna, to our home. Dunnae stop until ye reach it, and then rouse our men to be battle ready."

"I kinnae leave ye," Ross protested. "Ye need me—"

"I do need ye," Angus interrupted. "To keep our brother, the lass, and yerself alive. If I fall, someone must lead our clan, and as the next eldest brother, that someone is ye. We are far outnumbered here. Ye must flee." Angus pointed to the last horse in the distance. "Ride that beast and when ye get to Allisdair and the lass, take my horse as well. It's tied close to them."

"And what will ye ride when ye escape?" Ross asked.

"An Englishman's horse," Angus said with a wink. "Now away with ye!" He gave his brother a gentle push. "I'm to the battle, and my mind will be easier and more focused if I ken the three of ye are away."

Ross nodded, turned, and headed to the horse. He mounted it in a flash, and Angus watched his brother just long enough to ensure he got safely away. When Ross was out of sight, Angus quickly removed his daggers from the dead men, sheathed them, and gripping his sword, ran back toward the battle. As he cleared the trees by the fork in the river, he spotted a destrier without a rider. The horse would not only give him an advantage in the battle but he'd need it to escape. He approached the horse, mounted it, and then charged into the fray, swinging at English knights as they came at him. One by one, he cut men down, but it seemed for every Englishman he felled, three more appeared.

The fight was lost, and the only hope now was for him

to help as many of his fellow Scotsmen get away as he could. "Ye!" he shouted to a nearby group of Scots battling some of Edward's knights. "Mount the destriers and follow me! Spread the word."

"What destriers?" someone cried out.

"These, man!" He shifted on his horse and shoved an unexpecting knight off his mount. "Take it," he roared to the nearest Scot. He turned his horse around to the left, and with two swings of his sword, he stabbed an Englishman in the gut and slashed another across the back. The men fell, and Scots scrambled out of the shadows to mount the horses. By the time Angus started to fight again, the three Scotsmen beside him were involved in their own battles. Four more Englishmen fell, putting seven Scots on destriers, and then the tide changed.

It was as if someone had realized what they were doing. A line of riders was headed for them. "Take to the woods!" Angus ordered the Scots mounted alongside him. "If we can lose them, we can survive."

※

The thundering of horses' hooves sent a prickle of fear down Lillianna's spine. She did not think a contingency of men would be coming for them. "Stay here," she ordered Allisdair. "I'm going to peek out and see if I can tell if enemy or foe approaches."

"I'll go," Allisdair said. "I'm the man."

"No," she said, using her sternest voice. "I'm your elder, so—"

"We go together," the boy insisted.

"Fine," she relented, knowing he'd not yield, just as she wouldn't.

The minute they crept from their hiding place, she knew it was a mistake. Five English knights rode hard toward them, and the one in the front spotted them. He pointed and yelled, "Capture the woman and boy."

"Allisdair, run!" Lillianna screamed. She turned and nearly barreled over Allisdair. She caught him by the hand, and they raced toward Angus's and Grant's horses tethered in the distance. Hooves pounding against hard dirt vibrated the ground beneath Lillianna's feet, and the intensity increased rapidly. The English were closing in on them. "Get to the horses!" She released Allisdair's hand and turned, yanking her dagger out of its holder.

She sucked in a sharp breath of shock at the sight of a large Scot with thick, shoulder-length brown hair, who seemed to appear out of nowhere. He had come from the woods on a destrier, straight onto the path between her and the English, and brandishing his sword, he glanced to her for one moment and shouted, "Go with Allisdair. Flee here!"

She hesitated for one moment, not wishing to leave this man, who she assumed was Angus and Allisdair's brother Ross, to fight the English alone, but as the knights approached him and he easily cut two down in the time it took her to blink, she felt more confident that he would survive. Still, she could not abandon him without aiding him at all. Gathering all her courage, she ran toward Ross and the three knights he battled. One of the knights broke away from the foray and headed toward her.

"Please," she called, waving her arms at the Englishman, "help me!" When he drew close and slowed his horse, she wasted no time. "These filthy Scots took me! Please, please, you must save me."

"*You're English,*" the man said, his surprise evident, but

his sword was still poised to strike her down.

"Yes," she said. "De Burgh is my uncle. I was stolen from the forest near the castle."

And that did the trick. The man lowered his sword and leaned toward her with his hand extended to her to swing her onto his horse. She reached her own hand out, and when his fingers grazed hers, she whipped up her dagger and plunged it into his chest.

He dropped his sword, and his hand went to his chest, but then with a roar, he lunged toward her. Yelping, she jumped back, turned, and ran, glancing behind her only once to see the man struggling to right himself. She barreled through shrubs and trees, the limbs scraping and cutting her as she went. Finally, she burst through the thick bushes to almost run smack into Allisdair. He sat atop a horse while holding the reins of another.

"What are you still doing here?" she demanded, equally angry and glad that he'd not listened to her.

"Coming to save ye," he gloated.

She mounted the horse, automatically went to sheathe her dagger, and then remembered she'd left it in the knight's chest. "Your brother Ross is behind us."

They looked at each other for a moment, and as if by silent consent, they turned their horses back toward where they had just fled. But as they did, they heard a shout from the distance. "Ride! Ride! I'm surrounded!"

"That's Ross," Allisdair said in a frightened voice. "If he's surrounded…"

He was defeated, and she with no dagger and Allisdair with only one would be no match. "Let us ride to the Fraser castle and get aid for these men."

Allisdair nodded, and they turned, taking off into the descending darkness. Behind them, the sound of horses giving chase thundered in her ears. When she glanced back, she could see the English were close. She urged her horse faster, ducking trees and racing across a stream. Cold water splashed up between her and Allisdair, and they drove their horses across a wide expanse of rolling hills at a gallop and then back into the thickness of woods with the English still close behind.

They wound down another hill and toward a shadowed valley between two steep inclines, when horses suddenly neighed from in front of and behind them. Lillianna pulled her destrier up sharply, thinking they were trapped, but Allisdair waved at her. "Those are plaids ahead. Scots. Those are Scots. Keep riding."

Lillianna's heart beat viciously against her ribs. She gripped her reins and urged her horse back into a gallop. Ahead, the Scots pulled their mounts to a stop and seemed to create a line across the narrow valley. At first she was confused, but then she saw them withdraw bows and arrows, and as she ducked, arrows flew through the air, hitting the pursuing Englishmen. Men fell to the ground, and she nearly wept with relief as she continued to thunder toward the Scots. By the time she reached them, there was no one behind her but a lone rider, more hanging from his horse than sitting upright.

She squinted to get a better look. "That's Ross!" Allisdair shouted. Lillianna started to urge her horse toward Ross MacLorh, but the man beside her shot out his hand and grabbed her reins.

"Ross?" he said, his Scottish accent thick. "Ross who?"

"MacLorh," she answered, certain the Scot wanted to ensure he was not letting an enemy approach.

"I'm Allisdair MacLorh," Allisdair added proudly.

"Are ye now?" the man asked. Something in the way he

drew out the sentence set fear in her heart. The man moved his horse to Allisdair and took the lad by the chin. "Where is yer brother, the laird? Is he near?"

"I dunnae ken," Allisdair said, fear sweeping his features. He obviously sensed something was wrong, as well.

"Ross MacLorh!" the man suddenly roared. Lillianna flinched at the sound, and she looked toward Ross. He was struggling to right himself, obviously wounded. "Tell yer brother that the laird of Belfaine has wee Allisdair, and if he wants him back, he'll have to relinquish his castle to me."

She gasped. They had ridden straight into the arms of Angus's enemies.

"Who are ye, lass?" Laird Belfaine demanded.

Lillianna felt as if she were being strangled. What could she say in order to survive and protect Allisdair?

"She dunnae matter to my brother," Allisdair sputtered, giving her a warning look.

"Dunnae fear, lass," Belfaine said, but his words had a threatening ring to them. "I'll take ye anyway." He released Allisdair, motioned for one of his men to grab the boy, and then grasped her by the jaw. "I'm in need of a plaything for my bed."

Lillianna tried to jerk free at that ominous threat, but Belfaine held tight and snickered.

"Nay!" Allisdair shouted. "My brother will kill ye."

"Will he now?" Belfaine grinned wickedly. "Why would he care if the lass dunnae hold worth to him?"

There was no answer Allisdair could give to save her. If this man thought she had worth, he'd use her to strike at Angus, and if he thought she had no worth, he'd simply use her for his pleasure. Her only hope was for them to escape, but even as she thought it, Belfaine leaned over, gripped her around the waist, and yanked her off her horse as if she weighed no more than a feather. His men chuckled as he pulled her onto his horse instead of setting her on the ground. She immediately twisted toward him and brought up her fists to hit him. He captured her wrists with his hands and moved his face a hairsbreadth from hers. Eyes like a cold blue wave fastened on her, as if she were being pulled under by evil.

"I look forward to learning all about ye," Belfaine said, making her stomach turn. When he released her wrists, she slapped him.

A menacing smile spread his lips, and his hit came so fast across her face, she had no time to react. The force of it sent her flying to the left, but Belfaine caught her and tugged her back into the saddle and hard against his chest. A wave of nausea rolled over her as he brought his lips close to her ear. "I like a feisty lass," he said.

Escape was her only hope.

Chapter Fourteen

Angus and the men he'd rescued managed to escape being caught through the night, and as daylight fell, they made their way to the other side of Ettrick Forest, to the cave where half of Robbie's men had gone to hide. But at the midpoint to the location, a neighing alerted him that they were being tracked.

"Ride hard!" Angus bellowed. He urged his mount into a gallop and took off across the treacherous terrain.

He turned his horse, riding in the opposite direction of the other Scots' hiding place, but not all the men with him were expert riders. When he glanced back, he cursed. The Scot at the end of their line was being overcome by the English. One by one, his comrades were outridden, until only Angus and a man named Caleb remained. Angus urged his horse faster, but an arrow struck him in the back, and the sharp pain shot from the point of entry to the fingers of his right hand like liquid fire. They instantly went numb. He grabbed his falling sword with his left hand and guided his destrier as best he could, but more arrows flew at them, now hitting the beast. His horse reared, and with no free hand to grab the reins, Angus flew backward off the animal. His back slamming against the ground took his breath, but it was the blow to his head from whoever stood over him that sent him into oblivion.

Angus awoke to darkness, jostling, pain, and the world upside down. Thick fog filled his head, and it took him a moment to sift through his thoughts and remember what had happened. Hooves clopped against the ground, and the smell of the animal, as well as the warmth of the beast against his belly, told him he was on a horse. He tried to move his wrists and legs, but both had been bound, prohibiting him from doing so. He turned his head left and right, seeing the flicker of torches against the darkness in both directions. The English were traveling through the night, that much was certain, even if nothing else was. His head pounded, and the upper right section of his back burned where the arrow had pierced his skin. But when he attempted to curl his fingers into a fist, he could still do so.

Relief poured through him. He'd need his fighting arm if he had any hope of escaping, and he had to escape. Questions raced through his mind, and each one twisted his insides a bit tighter. Had Ross found Allisdair and Lillianna, and gotten them to safety? What if he had not? Images of Lillianna being abused and Allisdair tortured filled Angus head. He ground his teeth and shook his head in an attempt to rid himself of the images. Yet more questions hit him. Was Grant alive? Where was Simon? How many Scots had been killed?

Christ's teeth. He could not allow himself to contemplate the possibility that his brothers or Lillianna were dead.

"We halt!" someone ordered from the front of the line. "We'll make camp here."

Hands came to his arms, and he was pulled off his horse and thrown to the ground with a thud. Then he was dragged over roots, thorns, dirt, and rock, and left by a tree.

The smell of wet soil and blood tickled his nose. He glanced up, sensing a man standing near him, but it was so black out he could see nothing. Boots clomped toward him, and a flickering torch cut the darkness, and then Simon appeared, his face illuminated by the torch he held. Beside him stood a young guard of perhaps twenty summers.

"My lord Fraser," the young guard began, "is this where you wish us to keep the prisoners tonight?"

Hope filled Angus. Simon being in charge boded well for him. "Aye," Simon answered, kneeling down to stare at Angus face-to-face. "But nae this one, nor his brother."

Damn it all to hell! Either Ross or Allisdair had been captured.

"Bernard!" Simon shouted. "Bring over the other Scot I told ye would be trouble."

After a moment, the sliding of a man being dragged over the ground, grunting as he went, filled the silence, and then Ross was unceremoniously dropped like a log beside Angus. Their eyes locked, but neither man said anything. Simon waved a hand negligently between them. "Take these two to Alex's shelter and tell Alex I said to personally guard them."

"Alex is already guarding a man who caused trouble," the guard Bernard responded.

"Alex can handle three men," Simon bit out. "Make haste. I'm weary and need some rest."

Another guard joined the younger one, and Angus and Ross were dragged past rows of tied-up Scots. Angus swept his gaze over the men, guessing there were possibly two hundred there. "Where are the rest of the men?" he asked, dreading the answer, as he was dragged past the last man in the row.

"Killed," the Scot said flatly. A mixture of rage and

regret twisted Angus's insides as the Scot continued. "Their heads are on spikes," the Scot spat. "Satan's spawn wants to show his victory to his court."

Angus's rage pounded in his head, and when the Scot who had called the king "Satan's spawn" received a brutal kick from one of the guards, Angus jerked helplessly with the need to kill the Englishman. There was no hope. He yanked furiously on his binds, but they were well tied. Impotent rage nearly choked him, and left with no ability to help, he memorized the guard's face. He would kill the man eventually.

A few harsh bumps and scrapes later, Angus and Ross were deposited in front of what Angus assumed was the man Alex's shelter. It looked to be animal skins fastened to four sticks that rose from the ground.

A man kneeled in front of another man in the shelter, and just as the younger guard spoke, the man they called Alex stood, his massive body unfolding to rise, and he came out of the tent, to stand in front of Angus. Angus stared at the mud-crusted boots. Who was this man? Was he friend of foe?

"Who do ye have for me now?" Alex asked the English guard. The man was a Scot, that much was certain, so friend perhaps. Could it be Simon and Grant's cousin Alex? It almost seemed too much to hope.

"More men my Lord Fraser says might cause trouble," the guard answered.

Alex snorted. "Doubtful. That one in there has nae even awoken from the beating he received. But I simply do as I'm told, so leave them and I'll keep them quiet, even if I have to cut out their tongues."

"You realize," the guard said to Alex, "Fraser gave you the nasty jobs because you are a nasty Scot, do you not?"

The young guard was on his back on the ground in the next second, and Alex's boot was on top of his chest. "Call me a filthy Scot again," he snarled, "and I'll cut out *yer* tongue. Do ye ken me?"

"Yes," the guard gasped, clutching at his neck.

Alex lifted his boot and ordered, "Leave me." The moment the man shuffled away, Alex kneeled down in front of Angus. "Got yerself caught, did ye?"

"It seems so," Angus said to Alex Fraser as relief that it was who he had hoped filled him. Alex was a good man, and if he was here, he had to be aiding Simon.

"How long before ye can untie us?" Angus asked, desperate to get to Lillianna and Allisdair.

"When the men are asleep," Alex replied. "I kinnae chance doing so before that, lest I draw suspicion to myself and then Simon. Unless Bruce is ready for us to rise?"

Angus shook his head. "Nay. I dunnae believe Robbie even kens ye are working with Simon. I did nae. And Robbie was very specific that Simon must keep his cover and continue to gather information."

"Alex, is yer brother Hector aiding Simon, as well?" Ross asked from where he lay beside Angus.

A fierce scowl settled on Alex's face. "Nay." Angus sensed anger in Alex at Hector, but if Alex did not want to tell them what the dispute was between himself and his brother, it was not Angus's place to ask of personal family matters. Alex shifted his weight forward and settled his forearms on his legs. "I only recently convinced Simon to let me aid him, so I'm nae surprised neither ye nor Bruce did nae ken it."

Angus nodded his understanding, then turned to Ross. "Where are Allisdair and Lillianna?"

Ross, who was lying on his back, turned his face to

Angus. Shadows from the torch danced across his face and accentuated the tight set of his jaw. "Belfaine," Ross spat, his voice rough with emotion. "Belfaine took them."

"Belfaine?" Angus repeated, astonished. A dark fear settled in his heart. Belfaine had long tried to find a way to strike at Angus since Angus had killed the man's father. God's blood! With Allisdair and Lillianna, the man now had a way to hurt Angus. All the images he had tried to suppress earlier of Lillianna being abused and Allisdair being tortured filled his head once more. Every muscle in his body tensed, and a physical ache pulsed in his chest. "Belfaine is wicked," Angus muttered.

"Aye," Alex, Ross, and Grant, who'd not spoken since they'd arrived, said together.

"Grant!" Alex popped up from where he had been kneeling and went back into his tent. "Ye look like hell," Angus heard Alex say to Grant.

"I feel it," Grant replied. "But I'm alive. Angus, I'll help ye to get yer brother and Lillianna back. I swear it."

"Thank ye," Angus said, praying they would reach them before it was too late, before too much damage had been done. He did not fear Belfaine would kill Allisdair or Lillianna, but he feared greatly what else the man might do to them. Belfaine would keep Allisdair alive to use him to try to force Angus to relinquish his castle. As for Lillianna… Belfaine was well-known for his appetite for beautiful lasses. Belfaine would use her in the worst sort of way, and that fear froze Angus's blood in his veins.

Lillianna could hardly stand up when she was dragged off the horse by Belfaine a couple of days later, but when

Belfaine's hand slid around her waist, purposely brushing against her breasts, she willed herself to stay upright. Her skin crawled as she recalled his whispered taunts in her ear throughout the hard, fast journey to Belfaine's stronghold, Castle Blair, of how he planned to use her body. She scanned the long line of warriors who'd traveled with Belfaine, searching for Allisdair. She'd caught glimpses of him on the journey but had not gotten to speak to him, as they had been kept apart. He looked unharmed, but she'd overheard Belfaine speaking and knew he planned to use Allisdair to get Angus to submit his main stronghold, Castle Balmont. She had no notion why Belfaine wanted the castle, but she feared what he would do to Allisdair to obtain it.

When Belfaine's finger brushed her breasts once more, she shoved away from him to the chuckle of his men.

"I can stand on my own," she bit out.

"Excellent," Belfaine said, his voice making her grit her teeth. "Then you will be well enough to come to my bed tonight."

"I'll never be well enough for that," Lillianna countered icily.

"Ye kinnae take a wench to yer bed this night," a female voice called from behind Lillianna.

Lillianna whirled around to see a stunning woman with fiery red hair and emerald eyes strolling into the courtyard toward them. Those green eyes flicked briefly to Lillianna before focusing on Belfaine once more. "Yer wife has returned with her father, and he would be most displeased if ye bedded another woman when his precious daughter is in residence."

The relief Lillianna felt at the blessed reprieve from Belfaine's impending attentions made her legs shake.

"Devil take my wife and Laird Drumlan," Belfaine

growled, then waved a negligent hand at the men standing close to them.

Drumlan!

Anxiety curled within Lillianna and stole her breath. It could not be the same man who had long ago tricked her mother into believing he loved her when he had only wanted to use her power. It could not be the same man as the one who had grasped her mother's brooch off her neck as she fled him.

Lillianna began to tremble all over. She wrapped her arms around her waist in an effort to calm herself, but it was useless. Panic clawed at her.

"All of ye leave me, except Thorton. Ye stay here with the boy," Belfaine barked at his men.

At the mention of Allisdair, Lillianna twirled around and saw him across the courtyard, hands bound behind him, with a guard at his side. Their gazes locked, and her heart twisted for the fear she saw in Allisdair's gaze. But he smiled and notched up his chin. He had the same bravery that Angus possessed.

Belfaine's guards emptied the courtyard in such haste that Lillianna had little doubt Belfaine ruled his clan with fear and an iron hand. Her father had ruled his knights in the same way, and she could feel the underlying tension in the air that came from men in constant worry for their lives.

The woman with emerald eyes sauntered over to Belfaine and rested a hand upon his chest. "Dunnae forget, Brother," she said, her tone a warning one, "that ye need Laird Drumlan as an ally if ye are to ever become Lord of the Isles."

"I will nae forget," Belfaine growled and shoved the woman's hand off his chest.

Lord of the Isles! Dear God above!

Lillianna swallowed repeatedly. Belfaine could not be allowed to become Lord of the Isles. The Lord of the Isles was the ruler of all Highland clans. Lillianna's mind swirled with all the shocking things she was hearing. If this woman was Belfaine's sister, then was this Isla Belfaine, the woman who had betrayed Angus and had made him harden his heart? Lillianna studied the woman from under her lashes. Intense dislike flared in her as Belfaine motioned toward Lillianna. "Take my guest to wash herself," he ordered, looking to his sister.

Isla instantly pouted. "Why me? Have one of the servants wash the wench," she said, eyeing Lillianna critically.

Lillianna had an overwhelming desire to stride over to the woman and slap her. Twice. Once for herself and once for Angus. Instead, for now, she settled with imagining how good it would feel to do so.

"Nay," Belfaine responded. *"The wench,"* he said, with a chuckle, "has nae been cooperative in telling me who she is. I ken ye have yer special ways to get unwilling captives to talk."

Lillianna immediately took a scrambling step back and smacked into a horse who neighed at her.

Belfaine glanced toward her and frowned. "Dunnae cause me trouble, wench, or I'll take out my displeasure with ye on the boy."

Belfaine's words were like a punch to her gut. He would hurt Allisdair if she displeased him, just as her father had hurt her mother. They had to escape as soon as possible. For, if she had to lie with Belfaine to protect Allisdair, she was unsure she could stomach it.

"Did ye hear me?" Belfaine snapped at her.

Lillianna forced herself to nod.

"Excellent," Belfaine replied, motioning toward Lillianna once more. "Dunnae mark her face if ye need to use torture, Isla. Do ye ken me?"

Lillianna's heart clenched at Belfaine's words and the look of utter anticipation that Isla gave Lillianna at the prospect of torturing her. "I ken ye, but that does take some of the fun away."

"Be that as it may," Belfaine said, clearly amused.

"Who's the boy?" Isla asked, pointing behind Lillianna.

Lillianna did not turn to Allisdair for she did not want to portray any care for him that Isla and Belfaine might use against him. Instead, she curled her hands into fists and silently willed him to be brave. Her own heart hammered, and sweat trickled down her back and dampened her underarms.

"That, my dear Isla, is Angus MacLorh's brother."

Isla tensed. Her eyes widened with what appeared to be fright, but she quickly recovered and smiled brightly. Lillianna frowned in confusion. Why would the woman be afraid? Or was she merely dismayed to hear her brother had captured Allisdair? If Isla hated the MacLorhs as Belfaine did, Lillianna would think she would be glad to have Allisdair in their clutches.

"Excellent," Isla purred, interrupting Lillianna's thoughts. "We can finally repay him for killing Father." That was more of the reaction Lillianna would have expected, but was it a real one? She had no notion what to think.

Belfaine nodded. "Aye. And I intend to use the boy to get Angus's castle. And once I have it—"

"Ye will be keeper of the seas," Isla interrupted, "and lord of trade, and then—"

Lillianna's breath caught in her throat at the plans Belfaine had to rule the Highlands.

"I will take the title of Lord of the Isles, which should have been Father's," Belfaine stated with a vehemence that made gooseflesh sweep Lillianna's entire body. He smacked a fist into his open palm. "There will nae be a soul strong enough to deny me, as I'll hold the castle that is in the position to allow their ships to bypass the dangerous Narrows of Yarrow, and without my permitting their passage—"

"They will continue to lose ships against the steep cliffs that line each side of the Narrows. And when they lose ships, they will lose men," Isla said almost gleefully. Bile rose in Lillianna's throat, and Isla grinned. "The Highlanders will nae get the goods to and from the foreign lands they wish to trade with. And then I will be the sister of the most powerful man in the Highlands." She paused and speared Belfaine with a serious look. "Ye vowed to me I could chose the man I wish to wed. *Whatever* man I wish," she clarified, and it seemed most important to her that he agreed, which he did with a nod.

Something about the way Isla said it filled Lillianna with an impending sense of doom. She could not say why, but the feeling was there, like a hunger in the pit of her belly.

"Take the boy with ye and let him observe what befalls someone who dunnae tell me what I wish to ken," Belfaine said, turning his gaze upon Lillianna.

Dread roiled in her stomach at what was to come, but no matter what, she would not give her name, for they may well contact her uncle, and being forced back to him or her father would be a fate worse than death, with or without the brooch in their possession.

"What do ye wish me to discover?" Isla asked, her excitement of the nasty task to come evident in her breathless tone. Instinctually, Lillianna tried to step back once more.

The horse neighed again, and Belfaine shook his head at her.

"Dunnae make me harm the boy more than I need to, wench."

Lillianna swallowed, her throat feeling parched. "I won't," she said.

He smirked at her before saying to Isla, "Discover the wench's name. And what she means to MacLorh. The boy claims she dunnae mean anything, but I dunnae believe him."

Isla whipped her gaze to Lillianna and scowled. "I kinnae see how Angus would be interested in a woman like her. She's plain and nae Scottish. He loves fiery women—women like me."

Lillianna swallowed her shock. Isla Belfaine was jealous of the mere idea of Lillianna meaning something to Angus, which could only mean the woman cared for Angus in her own twisted way. Isla's comment about picking her own husband whispered in Lillianna's head, and the sense of doom for Angus grew so that she had to bite her lip not to cry out.

"Pull in yer claws, Isla," Belfaine said, his tone mocking and warning at once. "Did ye expect MacLorh to wait for ye to return to him forever?"

"Nae forever," Isla replied.

Something about the way she said the words, as if there was a *but* on the end of the sentence, made it seem as if Isla had planned to get Angus in her coil once more. Lillianna sucked in a sharp breath. Could Isla somehow get Angus back?

"Thorton!" Isla screeched. "Take the boy to the high rooms."

The guard obeyed immediately, and Allisdair was

dragged past Lillianna. Their gazes met for a brief second before Isla screeched another command, and two guards appeared from the castle to seize Lillianna on either side.

"Take her to the high rooms, too," Isla said, gazing at Lillianna with an eager look. "Strip her to her underclothing and tie her to the pole with her arms behind her back."

Lillianna tried to keep her heart still, but it galloped, trying to outrace the fear that was consuming her. Digging deep within herself, she lifted up her chin.

A slow, wicked smile spread across Isla's face. "I'm going to enjoy this."

"I'm glad I can provide you with some entertainment," Lillianna spat. And as she was dragged away, she had to fight against herself not to battle the guards for fear of how much worse her resistance could make it for Allisdair. Torture was coming—that much was certain. Whether she survived it or not remained to be seen.

Chapter Fifteen

"Tell her what she wishes to ken!" Allisdair sobbed from in front of Lillianna, where he'd been tied to a chair to watch her be tortured.

Though her head throbbed as if it would explode and every inch of her screamed in agony, she managed to lift her gaze to look at Allisdair. Her head felt as if it remained attached to her body by one extremely frayed string that would snap in two at any minute. Lillianna smiled at Isla, flinching when the woman swung the whip out again and it slashed across Lillianna's stomach, cutting into her skin once more. She looked down, feeling the warmth of blood, and her head seemed to bobble on her neck as the room swam in and out of blackness.

She swallowed against the desire to retch and licked her lips. "I have no worth to Laird MacLorh."

It was true, wasn't it? Her thoughts were so scattered at the moment, she could not recall for certain. She heard the swish of the whip through the air again, and to her humiliation, a whimper escaped her. And this time, when the whip cut through her tender flesh, she blacked out.

Freezing water hit Lillianna's face and awoke her with a

start. She opened her eyes and looked down, confusion muddling her thoughts. She blinked, her vision slightly blurry, and a chair came into focus. She was tied to a chair. Her feet were bound and her hands—Panic swallowed her as she realized her hands were bound behind her back.

Where was she? Her thoughts tripped and then seemed to right themselves. She was being tortured by Isla. But why was she sitting? Was her torture over? Immediately, she glanced up, fear for Allisdair taking her breath, and when she saw him, his shirt had been removed and his chest was bloody from lashes. A horrid scream filled the room, and she winced and gasped when she realized it was her. Her raw throat burned with her effort. How many times had she screamed thusly?

Isla had just raised the whip to hit Allisdair again, but she lowered it and slowly turned toward Lillianna. "Ye're awake," Isla said, matter-of-fact. "I was beginning to wonder how long it would take, and if ye would rouse before I killed the lad."

"Kill him?" Lillianna gasped. "Yer brother wants him alive."

"Aye," Isla said, smiling, "but accidents do happen when ye torture people."

Lillianna tried to surge up to no avail. Isla walked toward Lillianna and kneeled before her, looking up at her with amusement in her eyes. "Ye have the power to stop this. Ye have the power to save Allisdair's life. Tell me," she said, leaning in as if they were friends about to share a secret, "who are ye and what do ye mean to Angus?"

Allisdair's eyes filled with tears, but he shook his head, yet Lillianna could see he was on the verge of breaking. Even if he had not been, she'd rather die than be the reason he was tortured any further. Besides, if Isla and her brother were focused on Lillianna, mayhap it would take their attention off Allisdair long enough for Angus to rescue him.

"My name," she said, fury rising in her, "is Lillianna de Burgh, niece to Richard Og de Burgh, who is—"

"I know who de Burgh is," Isla said. "He is one of the King of England's favored advisors. Excellent. Ye will be a great benefit for negotiating what we desire. Now why were ye with Angus?"

Lillianna's mind raced with what to say. She'd offered enough truth. There was no chance she was going to help Isla figure out that Angus was on a mission to warn Bruce's men. She had no idea if Isla and her clan were loyal to Bruce or Edward. "Angus stole me from the king's castle. He intended to use me to strike at my uncle and the king."

Isla frowned. "Angus would nae do that. He is too honorable to use a woman."

The truth of that statement hit Lillianna hard. Angus *was* honorable and good, and she trusted him. The fact that Isla, who had betrayed him, said so to this day, even after he had killed her father in retribution, reinforced what Lillianna knew to be true. Still, she had to make Isla think she was wrong about him.

"I suppose he's changed since you knew him," Lillianna said. "War does that to men."

Isla nodded, as if that explanation made sense to her. She eyed Lillianna. "And ye're half-Irish, so he need nae be honorable to ye in the same way he was to me."

Lillianna imagined slapping the woman. Her palm tingled as if she had actually done it. Isla Belfaine was in love with Angus, or at least Lillianna thought she was. So why then had she betrayed and used him?

"My brother and Drumlan will be thrilled to hear we have de Burgh's niece as prisoner," Isla said. "Mayhap we can trade ye back to yer uncle for troops to aid us in defeating the MacDonalds and the MacLeods."

Lillianna tensed. Of course Belfaine would want to defeat the MacDonalds and the MacLeods. Those two clans would surely oppose him when he tried to take the position of Lord of the Isles. A MacDonald laird was the current Lord of the Isles, if she recalled correctly, and the MacLeods were their allies.

Isla turned from her, stalked to the door, and motioned the guards who had been stationed outside of the room into it. She pointed to Lillianna. "Ye," she said, motioning to one of the guards, "untie her. And ye," Isla said, indicating the other guard, "take the boy to the dungeon and make certain his wounds are treated. We kinnae have him dying on us…yet."

Isla grabbed Lillianna by the chin, and when she did, a bright light flashed in Lillianna's head and then a series of women's images filled her mind, each disappearing quickly. Each woman had green eyes and brown hair similar to hers, but she recognized only one of them—her mother. The others, she suspected, were her ancestors.

Lillianna… Her mother's voice filled her head. *Open yer heart.*

Lillianna gasped and squeezed her eyes shut, but when she opened them, the light was gone and she could no longer hear her mother's voice.

Isla narrowed her eyes, which gleamed maliciously. "Did I hurt ye?" she asked in a false apologetic tone.

Lillianna nodded, not wishing to reveal what had just happened.

"Good," Isla said, smirking. "Ye'll be coming with me to the great hall," she continued. "I wish my brother to see the prize he has unknowingly captured." She shoved Lillianna at a guard. "Take her!"

When the man touched her, that same shaft of nearly blinding light filled her head, followed by images of her mother and the other women—seeing them again, she was certain they were her ancestors—and her mother's voice once again filled her ears. *Open yer heart.*

Lillianna glanced wildly around the room as the guard dragged her out of it. She half expected to see her mother, but it was only Isla and the guard. She had no time to consider her mother's words or what was happening to her as the man yanked her down the hall, the stairs, and the passage toward the great hall. Though pain radiated from her stomach to every part of her body, and each movement that brought the shredded material of her gown into contact with her skin made her want to howl, her rage was so fierce she knew she could stand the pain. Yet her good sense kept her from fighting back. It would do no good right now, weaponless and surrounded, and in the great hall of the castle. No, it was far better for them to think she was weak and defeated so they would underestimate her. Then, when the opportunity presented itself, she would flee and take Allisdair with her.

Isla's hand came to Lillianna's free arm and jerked it hard. "Hurry yerself! I dunnae have all day for ye."

Lillianna missed a step because of the bright light and images that filled her vision for the third time now. *Open yer heart. Open yer heart*, her mother said, the words louder and more urgent each time.

The guard opened the door to the great hall, pulled her into the room, then up beside him, pressed his hand to her back, and shoved her forward. Lillianna tripped, and fell to her knees. The jarring pain spiraled through her body in dizzying waves, and she stilled, panting, tense with expectation of more images and her mother's voice, but nothing came. Open her heart? To whom? Angus?

"Sister," Belfaine said, annoyed. "I assume ye have news for me if ye're interrupting my meeting with Drumlan."

"Hello, Laird Drumlan," Isla purred. "'Tis good to see ye, as always."

"Isla," a man replied, laughter behind his words. "Who do ye have with ye?"

Lillianna righted herself and came to her feet, then pushed her hair out of her eyes to take in the man before her. If this was Laird Drumlan, then this man was her enemy, as he had betrayed her mother.

Drumlan's dark gaze narrowed upon her, but it widened considerably as he viewed her. "Christ's teeth," he murmured, his ruddy complexion going white as if he had seen a ghost. She looked much like her mother, so she did not doubt he thought he truly was seeing a ghost.

"What's the matter with ye, Drumlan?" Belfaine demanded.

The tall, silver-haired, sharp-eyed man stood and moved toward her and stopped directly in front of her. He gazed at her intently, grasping her by the chin, and this time, the light that filled her mind caused her to cry out in fear more than anything. It was so bright that she could see nothing else, and her head felt as if it would explode from the intensity. Her mother's image flooded her, followed by images of the women who had her hair and eyes. The pictures came swiftly, repeating themselves.

Open yer heart. Open yer heart. Open yer heart, her mother demanded. But why would her mother wish her to open her heart and let in the powers if it just led to betrayal?

"What's ailing ye, lass?" Drumlan demanded.

She could not even talk, the pain in her head was so

great.

"Isla, I told ye nae to mar her face!" Belfaine roared.

The light in Lillianna's head began to fade, and Drumlan's face started to become clear. He surveyed her with what appeared to be awe and excitement. Shivers raced down her spine. He turned her face to the right and then the left. "Christ's teeth," he said again, his voice vibrating with obvious shock. "Ye look just like her."

Lillianna could see that the pulse at his neck had sped, sending his blood through his veins in a rush, lifting his skin in hard pushes she could see. Panic gripped her with its icy fingers. The brooch. He still had it, and he understood what putting it on her would mean. She had no doubt that her uncle had been looking for it—perhaps even somehow had discovered that Drumlan had it—but this man possessed it, and now he wanted to possess her.

"Who does she look just like?" Belfaine demanded, coming to stand beside Drumlan.

Drumlan released his hold on her, but she was left feeling weak and tired.

Isla drew close to her brother and stared at Lillianna. "She's the niece of Richard Og de Burgh," she announced, sounding all too pleased with herself. "That's what I brought her here to tell ye, Brother. Ye have captured a great prize. We can use her to bargain with the king and gain troops to support ye when ye rise against the MacLorhs, and then the MacDonalds and the MacLeods."

"Nay," Drumlan said, his tone hard and ruthless. "Ye will nae trade this lass for troops. I will give ye all the warriors ye need if ye will but give me the lass."

Lillianna's heart thudded wildly, and a damp coolness covered her back and the base of her skull. Dear God above, her worst fear was about to come true.

"Why do ye want her?" Belfaine demanded. "Who is she to ye?"

"I loved her mother," Drumlan said. "And she was taken from me."

Lillianna wanted to shout that he was lying, but she resisted. If Drumlan departed this castle and took her with him, it might be her best—and maybe only—chance to escape, and for Allisdair, she would risk gaining her powers through the brooch. For the boy and for Angus, she would risk it. If she was to be taken with Drumlan, she had to think of an argument to ensure Allisdair came with them.

"She looks just like her mother," Drumlan repeated, jerking her attention back to him. He stared at her with a gleam in his eyes that made her skin crawl. "I want the lass." His gaze raked over her with a look of malevolent possessiveness that made her shudder.

"If I give ye the lass," Belfaine said, "ye will supply the warriors I need to take MacLorh's castle?"

"Aye," Drumlan replied. "I will return home today as planned and rally my troops. We could attack MacLorh's stronghold in two days' time."

Dear God! She had to somehow flee with Allisdair and reach Angus's home to warn his men. Was that even a viable plan? How far was Angus's home from here? She didn't know, but she had to try. Thoughts of Angus made her throat grow tight and her eyes burn as if she might cry. She blinked repeatedly, forcing back the tears. Where was he? Was he alive? What if he had been killed? A raw primitive grief overwhelmed her at the thought. He could not be dead. She refused to even think it.

"Ye can have the lass for the troops," Belfaine announced, his words piercing the fog of misery in which she was floundering.

Lillianna could not decide whether to rejoice that she might have a chance to escape or weep that she might now be turned over to a man who, in all probability, possessed her mother's brooch and undoubtedly intended to make her use the powers that would come with it. And she'd not be able to deny him or lie to him about what she saw. Her mother once told her that to do so would cause such horrific pain that it would bring her to her knees and steal her consciousness.

Belfaine raised his arms wide and glanced upward. "Fate is smiling upon me."

"Fate is a fickle mistress," Lillianna blurted, unable to help herself.

Belfaine shot her a withering stare, and she bit the inside of her cheek at her foolishness for saying such a thing. "If my horse had nae slipped a shoe, I would have been long gone from Ettrick Forest before I heard the fighting and saw ye. Fate *is* smiling upon me."

"Yes," she forced herself to say for fear that if she didn't, he might become angry and do something to hurt Allisdair. "Given that, it does seem Fate is smiling upon you."

"Ah, my dear Fate!" he exclaimed, glancing up once more. "I'd be most pleased if MacLorh himself was killed in the scrimmage." Disgust roiled in Lillianna's gut for Belfaine's obvious dramatics and intent. He glanced at her once more, his eyes assessing her until uneasiness gripped her. "Even if MacLorh is dead, the king likely would love to get his hands upon MacLorh's brother to execute him publicly for MacLorh's sins." Belfaine chuckled, and Lillianna had to clench her teeth so as not to scream her hatred at him.

Drumlan and Belfaine had been watching her, and she feared her expression had revealed her grave concern for

Allisdair. Drumlan cocked his head and continued to study her, then said, "Why nae let me take the lad?" With that, she was certain he knew that she felt protective of Allisdair, and he intended to somehow use him against her.

"I'm set to meet with that turncoat bastard Fraser in a fortnight," Drumlan said. "I can show him the lad as proof that we have possession of him and then get him to make a bargain for ye with the king: the lad for execution in exchange for some coin or land for ye. Of course, Fraser will likely wish coin for his efforts.

Drumlan and Belfaine were men with no honor, but their dishonor would serve her well if Allisdair got to travel with her. All that would be left once, she was reunited with Allisdair and out of this castle, would be to find a way to escape. She bit down hard on her lip at the desire to laugh at the impossibility of her situation.

"Why should I let ye bargain for me? Why should I trust ye that much? For all I ken ye will claim the lass is yer prisoner and gain boons for yerself."

"Ye ken Fraser hates ye," Drumlan said easily. "He would nae acquiesce to meet with ye."

"Och," Belfaine said with a wave of his hand. "The man holds a grudge too long."

"Agreed, but nevertheless, the dislike of ye is there. I have a much better chance of getting Fraser to speak with King Edward and broker a pact in yer favor than ye do."

Lillianna held her breath, fearing Belfaine would disagree. The tight look on his face told her he did not like the idea of relinquishing Allisdair to Drumlan, and undoubtedly his instinct was correct. "What think ye, Sister?" Belfaine asked.

"Fraser will nae ever do a thing to aid ye," Isla said, matter-of-fact. "Ye bedded his wife. A man dunnae forgive or forget that."

Repugnance nearly choked Lillianna. She did not know Simon Fraser, but she knew the man had sacrificed a great deal to aid the Scottish people in gaining their freedom.

"Perhaps ye're right," Belfaine said with a shrug. "Ye can take the lad with ye, but if ye cross me, Drumlan, I'll kill yer daughter."

Lillianna barely held in her gasp that Belfaine had threatened to kill his own wife, Drumlan's daughter.

Drumlan stiffened. "I will nae cross ye," the man said, his voice low.

"Then it's settled," Belfaine exclaimed. "This wench—" he caught Lillianna by the hair, making her scalp sting "—will be yers."

Another brilliant light filled her vision, making her head pound horribly. Images of her mother and ancestors started to roll through her mind and her mother's voice whispered the same words as before in her ear.

"Pity, I had plans to put ye in my own bed," Belfaine said, though his voice was nearly lost in the pounding in her head and her mother's ever-loudening tone. "Alas," he continued, his hot breath washing over her, "I must relinquish ye to gain my rightful place as Lord of the Isles."

"The pity is that ye ever were born," Lillianna spat, trying desperately to pull away from him and failing. She felt as if the pain in her head may well kill her. *And the light!* Her eyes began to water from the intensity of it.

"Watch this one," Belfaine said to Drumlan, releasing her. "There is something about her that makes me uneasy."

Lillianna let out a relieved breath when her contact was broken with Belfaine and the light and images disappeared. Her mother's voice faded away, and Lillianna's vision returned to normal. Her relief was short-lived, however, when she caught Drumlan staring at her with a knowing look. Panic rioted through her. Had she made the right choice not trying to convince Belfaine to keep her in his possession? Had there even been a choice? No, both men were evil, and at least with Drumlan, the chance of escape was greater. She began to pray fervently that Fate, that fickle mistress, would smile upon *her* this time.

Chapter Sixteen

Angus dismounted his horse in the thickness of Blair Woods, which lay behind Belfaine's home of Castle Blair, and glanced up toward the stronghold sitting atop a rocky headland that seemed to reach high into the sky. He inched his gaze up along the cliffs that surrounded the other three sides, trying to discern how the devil they'd get into the castle unseen.

"How do ye want to try to gain entry?" Ross asked, coming immediately to Angus's right as Grant came to stand on Angus's left.

He studied his two comrades in the daylight. Did he look as bone tired as they did? Dark shadows lay under his brother's and Grant's eyes, though Grant's were harder to see, marred with bruises as he was from the beating he'd taken from the English. His cheekbones were still slightly swollen and discolored, but the man had not uttered one complaint during their relentless travels.

And they had been relentless. Angus had pushed himself—and them, he was certain—perilously close to the edge of collapse. They'd traveled hard in the days since Alex had released them, and they'd crept away from King Edward's men. They'd stopped only long enough each day to give the horses water and a few minutes to eat and cool, so they could keep up the grueling pace. They'd slept only long enough to physically keep their eyes open when needed. Angus felt the toll now in an uncommon heaviness of his limbs, but as he thought of what needed to be done, determination flowed through his veins and his weariness faded.

Somewhere in that castle hopefully were Allisdair and Lillianna. If they were there, Angus, Grant, and Ross would rescue them. But getting in would be the tricky part. The previous Belfaine laird had been clever building his stronghold here. There was only one path to the castle that was not treacherous, and that path was manned by warriors all the way up the craggy, rocky headland. The other three sides could only be approached by birlinn or skiff, but it would do the person approaching little good for there was no shore to dock. The steep rocks met straight at the bottom with the deep, freezing waters of the sea, and it was a sea that was not calm today.

"Angus?" Ross prodded.

Angus nodded. "I heard ye. I will scale the rocks. There is nae another way."

"*We* will scale them," Ross emphasized.

Angus opened his mouth to protest, but Grant said, "Dunnae think yer brother and I are going to remain here like lasses while ye scale the cliffs and rescue Lillianna and Allisdair, and then have all the bards weave stories about ye."

"Nay," Ross said. "I will have a story."

"As will I," Grant added.

Angus nodded again, still staring up at the castle. "Thank ye," he said, serious. "Let us hope we all live to hear the story. Come on, then." He looked to his brother and Ross, who were both watching him expectantly. "Now that it's decided, let us make haste. The longer Allisdair and

Lillianna remain inside, the more harm they can come to. We'll climb from the east where the cliff is the shortest distance to the top." And the water was the deepest should they fall from the cliffs. Of course, the waves could still carry them into the rocks, and they could die by being bashed, but that was a chance he was willing to take to save Lillianna and Allisdair.

An image of Lillianna filled his head. Was she harmed? Did she think he would come for her? He had not gotten the chance to convince her to wed him yet, but surely once he rescued her, the lass would see the need she had for a husband. They would wed, and then she would be safe, and his near-obsessive desire for her would relent. But what if it was more than desire that was driving him to distraction?

As a boom of thunder followed a crack of lightning and rain poured down on them, he shoved the thought away. He had neither the time nor the inclination to examine it. The only thing he had time for now was a rescue. After that, he could sort everything else out.

The weather had turned sour, raining, lightning, and thundering, but Drumlan apparently thought himself immune to the forces of nature. His inflated ego suited her needs perfectly. Escaping on a rainy and shadowy day would be far easier than fleeing on a perfect, cloudless one.

The minute they stepped outside, Lillianna scanned the courtyard for the destriers they were to ride, praying she would have her own. Not only did she not see any horses but she did not see Drumlan's warriors. She'd overheard a servant saying warriors had accompanied Drumlan here. They were alone in the courtyard besides Allisdair, who was to Lillianna's left. Both of them were now weaponless, so she supposed Drumlan, who was much larger than her or Allisdair, and who held a sword in his hand, was unconcerned about being alone with them.

"Where are the horses and your men?" she asked.

Drumlan did not answer her. He waved them forward past the courtyard gates. She hesitated for a moment. He cocked his eyebrows at her and pointed his sword toward Allisdair. "Do ye wish me to gut this lad because ye are being uncooperative?"

She shook her head. She exchanged a quick look with Allisdair, who for all his earlier bravado now looked frightened and fatigued, and she gave him a smile as she hastened her pace to match Drumlan. To her surprise, he strode almost to the edge of the steep cliff that faced the east.

Unease started at the base of her spine and crawled up it, making her shiver. The driving rain pelted her, soaking her hair, stinging her skin, and forcing her to squint to protect her eyes. "What are we doing?" she asked, dread swirling in her belly faster than the gooseflesh covering her body.

Drumlan reached inside the neck of his tunic, and she could see a leather strap secured about his neck. She knew what it was before he even began to pull the strap out. Of course he would not want to ever part with the brooch. The dread within her became a pulsing thing that thudded in her ears and stole her breath. Her fingernails curled into the palms of her hands cutting the tender flesh so that she hissed in a surprised breath and forced her hands to relax.

He gave her a hard, cold-eyed smile as he tugged the leather strap over his neck and brought her mother's brooch between them. "I've worn this for so many years that I've lost count. Do you know what this is?" he asked, the brooch dangling from his fingertips as lightning once again illuminated the sky.

Black fright seized her and took her ability to speak for a moment. She swallowed, trembling all over, and beside her, she could feel Allisdair trembling, as well. The boy reached for her hand, and she gripped his cold, wet fingers. "No," she lied, having to raise her voice to be heard over the rain.

Drumlan scowled at her. "The pitch of yer voice changes when ye lie. I'll ask ye again," he said, swiping his hand across his face, "if ye know what this is. But before ye answer, remember that the boy's life is in yer hands."

Allisdair's fingers curled tighter around hers. She had known the only reason Drumlan had wanted Allisdair to come with them was to use him in some way. She hated that she had been right. She inhaled a long, shaky breath, the rain pelting her ever harder. "It's my mother's brooch. You lied to her, you betrayed her, and you stole that brooch from her."

"Technically, I was trying to grasp her and nae the brooch as she ran from me," he said, his tone ruthless. "My fingers caught the leather strap, it broke, and yer mother escaped. I was certain I would catch her, so I did nae rush. She'd shot me, ye see. Did ye ken that?"

Lillianna shook her head, a clump of her wet hair sliding over her forehead to dangle in her eyes. She shoved it back. "No, she didn't tell me all the details." She wished her mother had killed him, but saying that now would be beyond foolish.

"She aimed for my heart with *my* bow," Drumlan spat. "Fortunately, she was a bad shot. She accused me of nae truly loving her because I demanded she tell me my future. She was selfish," he growled.

Allisdair squeezed her so hard that her fingers hurt, but she gave him a squeeze back to try to reassure him.

"I had to betray her," Drumlan continued. "She forced my hand. I wanted to love her." His eyes narrowed, water dripping off his lashes. "But I needed her to prove she was worthy. I needed her to tell me if I would best her father if I stormed his castle." Lillianna held her silence. He was trying to wash away the guilt of what he'd done to her mother, and she refused to aid him. He stepped closer, his gaze clinging to her. "I could hardly believe it when I saw ye."

A ring of white puffed from his mouth, showing the temperature was quickly dropping. Lillianna simply glared at him. She refused to engage in useless chitchat with this man.

He scratched at his soaked beard and looked contemplative. "I did nae have a notion yer mother had born a child, nae that it would have done me much good. I sent mercenaries to try to take her from yer father several times after she first escaped me, but they failed. Fools. I couldn't go myself and risk yer father discovering I had the brooch."

"Of course not," Lillianna bit out.

"And then everyone said yer father killed her not long after he wed her. The whispers were because he loved a servant whom bore him ye. Imagine my shock when several weeks ago I heard someone say Brice de Burgh's daughter was nae a bastard but the product of his union with his dead wife."

"My father hid my mother away," Lillianna said, watching Drumlan. "He hid her because she would not tell him where her brooch was and he did not want anyone who might have the brooch to ever get their hands on her. She lived for years after she fled you—in isolation with no one but the servants of the castle."

"I could have stolen her back," Drumlan said, showing he was as horrid as her mother had said. Lillianna clenched her jaw on the need to scream. "I was trying to discern how I could get my hands on ye, and now here ye are." He leaned a bit closer and whispered, "I have a secret to share with ye. I think I should be Lord of the Isles, and ye are going to look at my future and tell me if I will I will become the leader of the isles if I betray Belfaine." He paused and gave a vicious smile. "I think I'm the one Fate is smiling upon, do ye nae agree?"

Allisdair tensed beside her. "As I said to Belfaine, I think Fate is fickle," Lillianna growled.

"Well, I will soon know what Fate has in store for me," Drumlan said, chortling. "Tell me, does any man hold yer heart?"

She thought immediately of Angus. Did he hold her heart? A piece of it certainly, but all of it? She didn't know, and it was none of Drumlan's affair. "No," she replied through cold, stiff lips, "but plenty hold my hatred."

He thrust the brooch at her. "It dunnae matter. Put this on."

She was so sickened by him that she could not make herself take the brooch.

He frowned with cold fury. "From this day forward, ye will tell me what I wish to ken."

"I'll not," she replied, finding her voice as the wind picked up and the smell of salt filled her nose. She stole a quick glance behind her at the steep drop to the sea below. Waves crashed against rock, and her thoughts raced wildly. There was only one possible way to escape Drumlan, and that was to jump into the sea and risk her life. She'd do it in an instant, because she refused to be held prisoner by this man and forced to read his future and help him destroy people with the knowledge she provided. But she could not leave Allisdair, and she would not risk him.

Unless... She blinked the rain out of her eyes and looked at the brooch her mother had worn, and her mother before her, and her mother before her, all the way back to the original fairy who had first given it to the MacLeod laird. It was gold, formed by two almost perfect half circles that surrounded a large, dark stone that symbolized present and future meeting. If she put on the brooch and touched Allisdair, she would try to see if he would survive them plunging into the sea. She would know if he had a future. And if he did... Her heart thumped madly as she tried to decide what to do.

"Put it on, or I will kill the lad," Drumlan snarled. "I ken ye fear for him. I see it on yer face."

Without another thought, she snatched the brooch from him and slipped the leather band over her head. The cold gold circle settled between her breasts atop the soaked material of her gown. Bright light flashed before her eyes, and her body tingled all over. Then, as before, the images of her mother and her ancestors filled her mind, but her mother's voice did not come. Lillianna curled her hand tighter around Allisdair's, and suddenly Drumlan disappeared. It was as if the world around her had parted to reveal a picture of the future and he was no longer in it. Allisdair was plunging through the air and down through the darkness. She felt his terror, and she cried out as he was swooped up into a crashing wave and nearly bashed against the rocks. But someone grabbed him at the last moment, saving him. The images flashed so fast, she could not keep up until one stilled. Allisdair was kneeling before Elizabeth and Lord Bruce. He was no longer a boy but a young man.

Lillianna cried out in joy at the sight of Elizabeth and

Bruce with crowns upon their heads. Bruce lifted his sword and tapped Allisdair on both shoulders, and Lillianna recognized immediately that Allisdair was being knighted. Then the picture disappeared, replaced by another. This time Allisdair was talking animatedly, relaying a story and waving his hands at something or someone as he did.

She gasped, the air feeling as if it were being sucked from her lungs. She released her hold on him as she turned to him. "Will you trust me?" she whispered, ignoring Drumlan for a moment.

Allisdair looked from the hand she had been holding to her face. Had he felt it? Had he felt the power coursing through her? "Aye," he croaked.

"Did ye see his future?" Drumlan asked, his excitement easily discernible in his voice.

She grasped Allisdair's hand once more and stepped back toward the dangerous ledge. His eyes grew wide with fright, but he moved with her. Her heel hung half off the cliff. Her stomach hollowed, and her heart raced. She had seen Allisdair's future. He would live. The unanswered question was, would she?

"Answer me," Drumlan roared. "Did yer seer powers awaken when ye put the brooch on as they are supposed to? Did ye see the lad's future? Touch me and tell me of mine!"

Her breath seemed to solidify in her throat, but she kept her gaze on Allisdair. "I did see your future, Allisdair, and you will live. So jump!"

Angus reached the bottom of the cliffs where they'd begin their climb. He looked up to search for the best path and he blinked in disbelief at what he saw. High above, near the ledge that overhung to the water below, stood his brother and Lillianna. Joy at confirmation that they were still alive filled him, but then as they seemed to move closer to the edge of the cliff and the storm raged above them, illuminating them, fear gripped him.

"Watch out for the ledge!" he called out uselessly.

And then unbelievably they stepped backward as if there were something there to catch them besides the never-ending blackness. His heart stopped, and his breath ceased. Their bodies dropped at a dizzying pace in an unstoppable fall toward death, one they had purposely taken. Every muscle he possessed clenched, and the desire to look away consumed him, but he just stared, unable to move, unable to make a sound.

Ross cried out, and Angus jerked, feeling the impact of unforgiving water to his own body as they hit the ocean water and disappeared. A thousand pricks tingled his skin as grief tore through him. For one breath, he was frozen in limbo, drowning in sorrow. All decisions, all actions were impossible as he tried to process the unbelievable, and then rage, hot and consuming, broke through his fear, sweeping the gooseflesh away and searing him with urgency. They could be saved. He had to save them. His heart exploded as he turned on the sliver of ledge upon which he stood and dove into the violent ocean.

Immediately, the icy water stole his breath, the waves sucked him up, tumbled him over, and pulled him farther underwater, knocking him into something—no, someone. His pulse exploded as he reached out a hand and grasped flesh. A hand grasped back at his, and he took it, his heart twisting with hope as fine-boned fingers twined with his. Lillianna. He was certain he had her. Now where was Allisdair?

Specks of bright light danced in his vision, warning him of the need for air. He kicked his legs and used his free arm to try to pull them upward, but he needed both hands to reach the surface in the waves. He slid Lillianna's hand to his waist, and it was as if she read his mind and knew his thoughts. Immediately, her arm wrapped around him, and he started to swim them up as he kicked. He could feel her kicking beside him, and when they broke the surface, with a fresh wave about to crash down on them, he roared, "Swim for the rock ledge," before they were tugged under once more.

They were thrown together, and he feared the force of the impact would injure her, but she grasped him by the hand and started to tug him. Together, they breached the surface again, and it was Lillianna who gasped, "To the right! Allisdair is to our right!"

Angus plunged underneath the waves with her and swam toward the right as she had said. When a surge of waves overhead shoved them hard in that direction and broke their grip on one another, he slammed into his brother. Frantic hands grasped his face and neck. Allisdair was panicked. He clawed at Angus, and so Angus drove his right elbow up into his brother's face. Allisdair instantly went slack, and Angus began to swim upward, clutching Allisdair's left arm. It wasn't until he burst through the surface that he realized Lillianna was on Allisdair's other side aiding him.

Waves tossed them and sucked them under several more times before they managed to get close enough to the rock ledge that Ross could reach them. Ross threw the end of his plaid out to Angus, but in order to grab the plaid, he had to release his hold on his brother. "Lillianna," he shouted above the deafening crash and hum of the waves.

"I have him," she yelled, and then her hand clutched Angus's side. "And you," she yelled, her grip on his waist increasing.

He grasped the plaid and pulled them close enough that Ross could touch him, and then Angus grabbed Lillianna's arm and tugged her forward. Allisdair moaned, and Lillianna shouted to Ross, "Take Allisdair first. If he panics again…"

Ross nodded as Grant dropped to the rock ledge beside him and took Allisdair by the arm that Lillianna managed to hold up, and then Grant hauled Allisdair out of the water. But just as he did, Lillianna was sucked back into the sea. Angus released his hold on the plaid and plunged under the water after her. For one moment, icy fear twisted around his heart, but then her hair brushed his foot and he reached downward, grazing her head and then her shoulder. He clutched her as she clasped him, and then they locked hands and kicked to the surface. As they did, her grip on him intensified and she cried out.

Once again, he clasped the plaid that Ross held out as Grant helped Lillianna to the rock ledge. A breath later, he was climbing the rocks as waves battered him and knocked him into the sharp edges. Ross hurriedly helped him to the safety of the ledge. There was no time to waste. He sucked in a deep breath, and they sprinted toward the bank where Lillianna, Grant, and Allisdair were waiting. He waved at them as he and Ross ran. "Head to the horses!"

Grant gave a nod and started up the path to lead Lillianna and Allisdair, but soon, Angus and Ross were behind them, urging them faster. Whoever they had jumped to escape would be coming for them and quickly. Torrential rain continued to fall as they ran, but in the distance, torches blazed one by one along the path that led to the castle, and dread enveloped him.

"They light the path for the warriors to ride out," Grant yelled.

Angus nodded. "Let us abandon the horses and try to run."

"Nay!" Grant argued. "Let us try to get to the horses."

He opened his mouth to tell Grant no when Lillianna suddenly clutched his forearms. Her body went rigid before him, her nails dug into his skin, and her lips parted on a moan.

"Lillianna!" he cried out, moving to release her grip from his forearms. The strength of her hold on him shocked him. She moaned again, and he tugged her closer, seeing that her green gaze had turned golden. "Something's wrong!" he shouted to the others, more fearful in this moment than he'd ever been in his life.

"Nay!" Allisdair shouted. "She's all right."

His blood rushed in his ears as he started to pry her fingers off his arms so he could sweep her off her feet and carry her. The second he released her right hand, she blinked and her gaze cleared. "Go to the horses," she said, her voice eerily calm and certain. "We will reach the horses before they reach us. That's how we will survive. We must get the destriers."

Confusion blanketed Angus's mind. "How the devil can ye possibly—" The horn that called the warriors to arms blew ominously through the night. Angus's eyes locked with hers. Torment and sorrow seemed etched on her face.

"She's seen it!" Allisdair blurted. "She had a vision. She's wearing a special brooch!"

Angus stared at her in shock, his eyes drawn to the brooch nestled between her breasts. Slowly, he reached out to touch it, and he grasped the brooch between his thumb and his forefinger, bringing it as close as he could with it still hooked around her neck. She inhaled sharply but did not stop him. The middle of the brooch seemed to swirl, and he blinked the rain from his eyes, sure he was not seeing correctly. But when he looked again, it still swirled.

"God's teeth," he muttered. Disbelief collided with the reality of what he had just seen happen to her and of the brooch he had just touched. The legend surrounding her was true. He sucked in a breath, released the brooch, and stepped back from her.

"That's why ye jumped off the cliff," he heard himself say, his mind refuting what his eyes told him was true.

She bit her lip but nodded slowly, reluctantly, as if she did not want to admit it any more than he wanted to believe it. "We must go now," she said, confident.

Angus hesitated a moment before nodding, and then, as if in silent agreement, they all turned and ran. The thundering of horses' hooves vibrated under his feet as the Belfaine warriors rode down the path. When Angus and the others reached the destriers they'd left tethered in the woods, he swung Lillianna onto his horse as Ross and Allisdair mounted Ross's and Grant mounted his. Angus straddled the beast and slid one arm protectively around Lillianna's waist. She went rigid under his touch. Was she getting a vision of his future? He recalled her moan and feared the visions might hurt her. "Do they hurt ye?"

"Not so very much," she said, her words stiff. Except how much was not so very much?

"Are ye having another vision?" he asked.

She nodded. "It is the same as before, so if you are looking for me to tell you more of your future, don't bother," she growled.

He blew out a frustrated breath, understanding dawning. Lillianna's wish not to marry suddenly made sense. The small details she had revealed about her mother and father's union made it clear it was not a happy one. He also thought he recalled hearing a story long ago of her mother escaping Drumlan. Had the man tried to use her for her powers? Had he betrayed her? Likely so. No doubt, Lillianna's reason for not wishing to marry had a great deal to do with not trusting men, especially men who knew of her powers. And he was now one of those men. Her life had been filled with men who had attempted to control her and use her. He was certain of it.

They'd have to discuss it later—*after* they escaped.

"Belfaine and Drumlan plan to attack yer castle," Lillianna blurted, surprising him once more. "Or they did. I'm uncertain if they will stick to the plan, given that both men know I heard it. Belfaine wishes to be Lord of the Isles and needs yer castle, but Drumlan, unbeknownst to Belfaine, also wishes to be Lord of the Isles. So—" she looked momentarily contemplative "—I cannot say if he will still join forces with Belfaine or not."

"Did ye see any of this?" Angus asked.

"No," she snapped. "They spoke of it in front of me."

He nodded. "Thank ye," he said, forcing himself to resist the urge to press a kiss to the exposed slender column of her neck. He knew she had her guard well up against him now, and he did not blame her. He understood it, probably better than most men could, given the betrayal of his past. He felt the men would still come, and together unless Drumlan could get to Lillianna first. Then he might betray Belfaine, or wait and betray him after they defeated Angus. They were stronger together.

Focusing on the need to flee, he thought about which way to take to his home. His stronghold was only a half day's ride from Castle Blair, yet Belfaine would be expecting Allisdair and Lillianna to head there. They could circle around and take a longer route. "We'll head west and circle home."

"That'll take too long," Ross objected. "What if Belfaine reaches the castle before we do?"

"Circle around," Lillianna said, turning to look at Angus. "I saw you riding on that path and arriving at Castle Balmont with Grant and your brothers."

Angus frowned. "What of yerself?"

She turned away from him and shrugged. "I did not see myself in the vision."

He didn't need her to see a vision of her future for him to know that her future was with him. And he'd tell her as soon as there was time to convince her and make her see that it had nothing to do with her newfound powers and everything to do with the fact that he could not imagine his life without her. There was no point denying that truth any longer: he cared for the lass. Like it or not, he was entangled with her, but he would damn well control it and he didn't need to see the future to know that.

Chapter Seventeen

Angus's strong thighs caged her in a protective wall that pressed against both of Lillianna's legs. Nauseating, sinking despair filled her. She had seen the look of disbelief, followed by acceptance and then awe on Angus's face after he had witnessed her have a vision. Now he knew her powers were real, that the legend was true. There was no way to take that knowledge back from him, and if Angus spoke of feelings for her now, she would never know if it was because of the power she could wield or simply because of her.

Her heart ached and she clenched her teeth, even as her mind chided her. Angus had proven himself honorable before now. Did the knowledge of her powers and his belief in them now make him dishonorable? No, certainly not. And he had desired her before he knew of the legend, most definitely, but care for her? He had never said as much, and she wished with all her soul that she could know for certain that he had cared for her before he knew the legend was true.

She tensed as light flashed in her mind, and swift images of her mother and her ancestors passed through her head. Her eyes burned, and the forest before her started to part as if someone were pulling on it from both sides, opening up a new world. She tingled all over, and an image of Angus entered her head. He was in a dark passage filled with smoke. Two torches were the only light in the passage. He held one, and Bruce stood in front of Angus holding the other. They were surrounded by a circle of Scots dressed for battle and wielding swords.

"Robbie!" Angus said, gripping Robert by the arm. "How in God's name do ye come to be at Edinburgh Castle? Why have ye nae contacted anyone?"

"Edward has been keeping me prisoner," Robert said, grasping Angus in return. "How do ye come to be here?"

"By horse," Angus said with a chuckle. "Where else would I be after hearing Edward was headed this way to try to take Edinburgh once more? And ye are here now, so ye will be freed from Edward's clutches."

"Nay," Robert replied grimly. "Edward is at the door of the castle with over a hundred thousand men. The English are slaughtering their way inside these walls."

"Good Christ!" Angus said on a ragged breath. "We dunnae ken the numbers."

Robert nodded as the Scots with Angus came closer. "We must get whoever is hiding in the great hall out down the back wall or they will be slaughtered. The king does nae have any mercy this day."

Suddenly the picture shook and disappeared. Lillianna realized the horse had jolted her, but Angus still held her, and light flashed in her mind again. She gritted her teeth. She did not want the image of Angus. Tears filled her eyes as she fought against what was happening to her. A memory of her mother holding her and speaking of her power flooded Lillianna's mind.

"There were times," her mother whispered, running her hand over Lillianna's head as she rocked her, "that I could control what I saw. I could push back against the vision if I focused very hard on something in the past."

Lillianna saw herself in her mother's lap. She was but a child of ten summers.

She looked at her mother with adoring, fascinated eyes. "When, Mother? When could you control your visions of the future?"

Her mother opened her mouth to answer, but the bedchamber door slammed open and her father, his face twisted with anger, strode in.

Light flashed in Lillianna's mind again, and the images of her mother and ancestors begin to appear. Desperate to stay in the present, she conjured up the memory of Angus kissing her in the woods. She felt his lips, his strong arms, his warmth. She smelled his scent of pine, and she inhaled, curling her hands into fists and pushing that image over the one of her mother and ancestors. The light in her mind disappeared, the images of her mother and ancestors disappeared, and all she was left with was the beautiful memory of Angus kissing her.

She had done it! She had stopped the vision. She had no notion if she could do it again, but she had done it this one time. Tears filled her eyes as she felt Angus's powerful arms on either side of her, extended to hold the reins of his horse. His chest felt like stone against her back, and his heat served to fight the chill of the cold night. Relief and happiness that he was alive rose in her. She sucked in a sharp breath, certain now that she cared for this man. It had grown with each day she had been with him, and soon she suspected it could become love if she would but open her heart. Was that what her mother had been telling her? Did she dare hope he care for her in return, truly? Was that foolish or wise? She didn't know.

She lifted a shaking hand to the brooch and ran her fingertips over the smooth surface. She had never once considered that her powers could save the lives of people for whom she cared. She had focused only on the negative things having the powers had brought to the women in her family. The brooch seemed to pulse in her hand as she held it. For a moment, she considered taking it off, but what if they found themselves in another desperate situation? What if she needed to see into the future to save Angus, Allisdair, Ross, or Grant?

With a sigh, she let the brooch slip from her fingers, and the heavy stone settled once again in the valley of her breasts. For now, until they were safe, she would wear it, and then… And then she did not know. Perhaps she would destroy it or throw it into the ocean. Or perhaps she would do as much good as she could with it. Perhaps Fate would finally smile on her. That last thought almost made her laugh.

The thick woods started to become less dense as they rode, and then a path appeared that directed them toward the castle. They galloped toward a bridge with two guard towers, one at the front and one at the end of it.

Angus held up his hand. "Open the gates and sound the horns," he called out. The gates opened immediately as they approached. Once they were all through the gate, they rode down the long stone bridge, which was lined with warriors.

Angus gave orders to the men he passed. "Put the men on alert for enemies in our midst."

"So you think Belfaine and Drumlan will still come?" she asked, breaking the silence that had been between them for nearly the entire ride.

"Aye," he replied. Something in his tone seemed evasive, but she could not say why or what. "See up there?" He pointed to the high rock formations that rose on either side of the castle, which sat low near the sea.

"Yes," she said, looking at the rocks. She could also see men upon them—archers, it appeared.

"That is our first line of defense. They can see a great distance and can shoot down approaching enemies and ships with not only arrows but fireballs. Belfaine and Drumlan want my home because it sits in the only valley that guards the passage to the west and the sea beyond. But ships must get past my home to get to the sea; otherwise, they have to pass through—"

"The Narrows of Yarrow," she finished for him.

Surprise flashed across his face. "Aye," he said as they paused at the end of the bridge to wait for another gate to be opened. "Lillianna…" His voice was heavy with emotions she could not name. "About yer powers—"

"I met Isla," she cut in, unwilling to face what he might have been about to say. What if he said he cared for her? What if he only asked about her powers? Her emotions turned inside of her like the violent waves she had plunged into earlier.

"I'm sorry for that," he said, pulling his horse to a stop in the courtyard that was filling with his warriors.

"She's horrid, but I think she may have been forced to betray you." Lillianna revealed her suspicion because what she really wanted to learn was if he could forgive Isla and still love her if he knew that.

Angus dismounted his horse and looked up at her, his face taut. "Ye kinnae force betrayal, Lillianna. I would die before betraying my family. That is the allegiance ye give to those ye love. That is—"

"Angus!" Allisdair came running to them and then paused awkwardly in front of his brother. It was the first opportunity the lad had to have a moment with Angus. The need to escape, and the speed at which they had ridden here, had prevented it before. Lillianna suspected the lad wanted to embrace Angus but also wanted to appear tough. When Angus reached out and tugged Allisdair to him and gave him a hug, tears blurred Lillianna's vision. Angus was a good man. He was. He was not like her father, Belfaine, or Drumlan.

Angus's men held back from them as did Grant and Ross, and she was certain to give Angus and Allisdair a moment of privacy. When Angus released Allisdair, Lillianna gasped, truly seeing the wounds Isla had given him and only then thinking of her own wounds. Her inner thighs no longer burned, but her new lashes from Isla did, and she was certain Allisdair's did as well. Raw gashes crossed his chest, and she set a hand to her fiery stomach, knowing her own skin must look much the same.

Rage swept Angus's face as he stared at Allisdair. "Who did this to ye?" he growled.

Allisdair's cheeks became blotchy. "The lady Isla. I hate her! I'm ashamed that a lady beat me," he mumbled.

"Aye, I ken well how ye feel, but dunnae feel shame," Angus replied to Lillianna's pleased surprise. "Ye survived the ordeal, so ye did well."

"I only survived because Lady Lillianna told the lady Isla who she was so that she'd quit whipping me."

Angus ruffled his brother's hair, making Lillianna's heart squeeze. "Then ye were lucky that Lillianna was there to watch out for ye."

When Angus's gaze came to her, her heart turned over in response. The admiring look he gave her made her mouth twitch with the desire to grin. She'd never felt as if she'd been so useful in her life.

"I was lucky!" Allisdair exclaimed. "When Lady Lillianna put on the brooch that Drumlan thrust at her, she had a vision. The brooch gives her the power to see the future, and her vision saved me!"

Angus locked eyes with her once more, and the gratitude she saw there stole her breath. If ever there was a reason to wear the brooch, to accept her powers, it was this. Angus's gaze fell to her stomach, and he swore. "God's teeth!" he thundered, reaching toward her stomach where her gown was stained with blood from her wounds.

She jerked away from his touch instinctively, as much in fear of a vision as to avoid the pain his touch would bring because of her injuries. He pulled his hand back, and she could have sworn hurt flashed across his face. Did he care enough about her that she could hurt him? She wanted to explain, yet how could she? She opened her mouth to try but could not find the words.

Instead, Angus said, "I will avenge ye for this." His savage tone and equally enraged face left no doubt in her mind that he meant it.

"Angus! Allisdair!" a woman cried, racing toward them. She had hair the color of Angus's, and it flew behind her as she darted nimbly around his soldiers and came to a stop in front of Allisdair. Her eyes grew wide as she looked at him. "Allisdair! What happened?" She turned to Angus, a question in her eyes.

"Isla Belfaine," Angus said.

The woman's eyes widened with shock, then she spat toward the ground, before narrowing her attention on Lillianna. "Who is this?" the woman demanded.

"That's Lady Lillianna de Burgh," Allisdair piped up. "She's a MacLeod and a seer!"

"Allisdair!" Lillianna gasped. He grinned, and she realized with horror that he thought her powers magnificent and he wanted to tell everyone.

The woman looked at Lillianna with a mixture of interest and uneasiness. Her gaze drew low to the brooch. "The Brooch of Lagothmier," she whispered, her tone almost reverent. Her eyes rose swiftly to Lillianna's once more. "So the legend is true?" She turned to look at Angus, who nodded as his gaze came softly, almost reassuringly, to Lillianna. She felt immediate comfort from him, which surprised her.

"Lillianna, this is my sister, Greer."

"So," Greer said, before Lillianna could offer an appropriate greeting to Angus's sister, "if I recall correctly, the MacLeod seers can gain their powers when they fall in love or when they wear the brooch." Lillianna tensed, unsure where Greer was going with this but sensing it was not somewhere Lillianna cared to tread, especially not with an audience.

Greer pinned Lillianna with her probing gaze. "Did ye gain yer powers first by falling in love or by putting on that brooch?"

Angus could hardly believe Greer had asked Lillianna such a personal question. Yet he found he was keenly interested in her answer, so he did not reprimand Greer and focused instead on Lillianna. Her tense posture and stricken face made it apparent that she did not wish to answer Greer's question. Was it because she feared injuring him with her answer? God's teeth, for a man who did not want to become entangled any more than he already was, he should not care, but the undeniable fact was that he did.

He studied her for a brief moment—arms crossed, lines of tension between her brows. She had agreed with him when he'd said love was a curse, and no wonder! She must have known her uncle would only come for her if he thought he could find the brooch. Her mumbled words in the grip of her fever echoed in his mind. She had said she had worth, almost adamantly. She felt worthless. Had her uncle and father made her feel her only worth lay in the powers she might get, and when she had not, they had been willing to discard her? His chest squeezed for her.

He wanted to drop to his knees before her in reverence, which had nothing to do with her powers and everything to do with the beauty she possessed inside and out. He wanted to vanquish her fears, and—Astonishment hit him full force, robbing him of breath. He wanted her to give him her heart. It was irrational, for he would not relinquish any more of his than she had already taken. Yet, irrational or not, he wanted her heart.

"Are ye going to answer or nae?" Greer demanded of Lillianna, sending Angus's focus back to the current conversation.

"The brooch is the only reason I have my powers," Lillianna bit out, her gaze cold on his sister. Well, her answer was not exactly what he wanted to hear and did not bode so well for getting her to agree to wed him. And he needed her to do so today. He was certain an attack would eventually happen, but even more pressing in his mind was Drumlan and the threat the man posed to Lillianna. He would come for her in desperation to use her powers to get what he wanted, and Angus would not only make her his wife because he wanted it but he would wed her so that his men would fight for her with the loyalty a laird's wife would command from them.

Taking her heart would have to wait until after the wedding. Today, he would have to be satisfied with her agreement to wed him, which he needed to gather his siblings and Father Dunlap for now.

"Enough, Greer," Angus grumbled. "I need to meet with the counsel. A fight with Drumlan and Belfaine is looming. Take Lillianna to the great hall."

"What for?" Greer demanded.

"Because I ordered ye to," he bit out. "Allisdair will go with ye." He flicked his gaze to his younger brother, who nodded. "I will be there shortly. And have a servant fetch Mari so we can have a family meeting. And fetch Father Dunlap, too."

"Father Dunlap?" Greer asked, her eyes narrowing upon him.

"Aye," he bit out, refusing to lay out his intentions in front of his sister or, for that matter, Lillianna. She might bolt if she knew. He couldn't decide whether the last thought was amusing or sobering. He wanted them all in one place when he told them he was marrying Lillianna, and then they would get the deed done quickly.

Greer looked as if she was about to argue, which was no surprise. His eldest sister was incredibly protective, and since Greer was not familiar with Lillianna, she likely did not want her there since Greer thought they would be discussing family matters. "Do as I say, Greer. I trust Lillianna."

"Of course ye do," she snapped. "She is verra bonny, and we all ken ye give yer trust so verra easily to bonny lasses."

The barb stung like a dagger to his heart. He felt his nostrils and his temper flare. "Make yer way to the great hall *now*," he growled, hearing his anger vibrating his voice.

She nodded stiffly and snapped, "Come along," at Lillianna before taking Allisdair by the hand and petting his head. Angus frowned as he watched them leave. Greer coddled Allisdair too much, but he'd not fought it because he knew she saw herself as the mother of the lot of them since their own mother had died. He also knew that Greer blamed him for both their parents' deaths, and rightly so, so he did what he could to make amends for his failings in the past.

Once the women and Allisdair had parted, Angus motioned Grant and Ross to him, who had been standing talking with a group of men near the castle door. Once they stood before him, he said to Grant, "If ye kinnae stay for the battle, I ken it. Ye have yer own clan—"

"I'll stay," Grant interrupted, clasping Angus by the forearm.

"Thank ye," Angus said, meaning it.

"I'll help ye fight Drumlan and Belfaine, and if ye make a mess of things with Lillianna, I'll be happy to take her with me," Grant said with a wink.

"Ye'll nae be taking her anywhere," Angus said, understanding Grant was trying to stir him to say things.

Grant nodded. "I'm gladdened to hear ye say it so adamantly. She deserves such feeling."

Angus clenched his teeth on that statement. He did feel for her, but he would control it. Angus quickly called the council together in the courtyard, and once all the men faced him, he spoke. "Belfaine and Drumlan had planned to attack our home in the next sennight. I think it's less likely that they will do so now that I ken of their plan, but we will proceed as if we are sure they will attack. I want every man on alert." He barked out orders for who was to be in charge of what, and then he motioned to Grant. "This is Grant Fraser. He has generously offered to stay and aid us in our battle. He's renowned for his commands of ground troops, and, Ross, if ye will agree, he can aid ye in the command of ours."

"Aye," Ross quickly agreed.

"Go now and prepare," Angus commanded.

When the last of the council had left, and only Angus, Ross, and Grant remained in the courtyard, Ross turned to Angus, his expression curious. "Why did ye call for Father Dunlap to come to the great hall?" Ross asked. "Ye dunnae usually invite him into our private family discussions."

"I intend to wed Lillianna today," Angus admitted, seeing no reason to hide what he was about to reveal.

"Excellent!" Grant boomed.

Ross nodded. "Verra smart to wed the seer, Brother. If I'd nae seen her have the vision in front of us and then guide us safely home, I'd nae ever have believed the legend to be true."

Angus would not have, either, but Ross's words of why he was wedding Lillianna angered him. He glared at his brother. "Do ye truly believe I'd wed the lass to *use* her? Do ye nae think I have more honor that that?"

Ross paled. "Of course I do, but I ken ye put the clan first always, so I thought…"

"He likes her," Grant teased.

"I dunnae like her," Angus growled, regretting the words that had just flown out of his mouth in irritation.

"Pardon me," Grant said and elbowed Ross with a smile. "He desires her."

"I can see why," Ross said. "She's verra bonny."

"She is more than a bonny lass," Angus barked. "She's braw and honorable, kind and sensitive." When both men gaped at him, he realized what he had revealed of his thoughts aloud, and he quickly added, "And she saved Allisdair's life. My life, too, most likely. And Grant's. And yours, Ross." He narrowed his eyes upon both men and dared them to deny it.

"Aye, that she did," they agreed.

"But," Grant said, "ye saved her from drowning. Twice. So that makes ye even."

"Twice being saved compared to four lives saved dunnae make us even," Angus snapped. "Beyond that, she needs our protection."

"And she is verra bonny," Grant said with a wink, to which Ross chuckled.

"And she does just so happen to be a seer," Ross added, laughing, but then he sobered. "Greer will nae like ye marrying her, as it seems ye hardly ken her."

Angus inhaled a deep breath. He knew Lillianna better than any woman he'd ever known before, including Isla, but that was none of his brother's or Grant's affair.

Ross scratched at the stubble on his face. "Greer will likely accuse ye of losing yer heart again." Angus growled, and Ross held up his hands. "Greer's words, nae mine. Ye ken our sister, as well as I do. She will think ye lost yer—" he stopped and glanced at where Angus's heart beat in his chest "—that thing. And with its loss, ye will be distracted and nae be as effective a leader, which will make us vulnerable."

Angus frowned as he stared at Ross. His brother made it seem as if he was only pointing out what Greer might think, but Angus got the distinct impression that Ross was worried about the same things. "I am nae distracted," he lied. He was, God's truth, he was, but wedding Lillianna would fix that. "And I have nae lost the vital organ that keeps me standing here and leading all of ye. It's right here." He thumped his chest as his annoyance with his brother and the skeptical look that had just appeared on his face mounted.

"And I'll nae be *losing* it. This discussion is over," he ground out.

He shoved past his brother and Grant and stalked all the way to the great hall door, pushing it open with such force that it slammed against the wall as he entered. Lillianna jolted, Mari's eyes grew wide, and Greer studied him as if she saw something she did not care for, which only served to stoke his ire. Father Dunlap, an always affable older gentleman with silver hair, kind blue eyes, and a belly that showed just how much he loved to eat, smiled at him. "Welcome home, Angus!" the man said jovially. "Did ye call me here to give ye penance?"

"*You* confess your sins?" Lillianna asked in a shocked tone that managed to cut through his anger and make him want to laugh.

"Only a few," he replied, winking at her. "If I confessed them all, we'd be here all day."

Lillianna's jaw dropped open, but his sisters, Father Dunlap, and even Allisdair, looked at him as if they didn't know who he was.

"Sit," he commanded the bunch, and everyone but Lillianna immediately obeyed him, which for some reason made him grin. Though the lass would have to learn to heed his commands. He was laird, and he would be her husband. As soon as he convinced her… "Please take a seat, lass," he said to Lillianna. Behind him, he heard footsteps and glanced over his shoulder to see Grant and Ross coming into the great hall.

"I'll stand, thank you," Lillianna replied, which had him turning back to her to receive a petulant look. He felt everyone's eyes on him in expectation.

Uncomfortable with the audience he had called to such a delicate talk, he yanked his hand through his hair, trying and failing to find words. Mayhap he should talk to her in private? Before he could decide, Allisdair said, "Angus dunnae like it when we dunnae obey his orders."

Lillianna scowled at Angus but offered Allisdair a sweet smile. Angus liked that even when she was irritated with him, she was kind to his siblings. It showed that the lass had control of her emotions and a caring heart. She speared Angus with another look. "As I'm not a hound, nor obligated to obey *your brother*, I will decide if I wish to sit or not, and I do not." Her gaze held his, almost defiantly, which made him proud, though he'd never admit it to her.

Greer, who often made known her dislike of following his orders, opened her mouth and said, "I suppose since ye're a seer ye think ye can do as ye wish! My brother gives orders to protect us. Yer verra presence here endangers us because ye take his attention away from where it needs to be!"

"Greer!" Angus bellowed. Lillianna had flinched at Greer's harsh, accusing tone. Lillianna's face grew pale, and her lips were pressed into a hard line. This was not going like he had intended, and he needed to get control of the situation. "My attention is where it should be, so dunnae fash yerself, Greer." Before anyone else could interrupt him, he continued. "Ye can stand if ye wish, Lillianna, of course, but I'd like to hear how Drumlan came to possess the Brooch of Lagothmier, and I assume the telling might take a spell."

"It's simple," she said, crossing her arms as a wary look came to her eyes. "Long ago Drumlan duped my mother into believing he loved her when all he really wanted was to use her for her powers. She discovered his treachery, and when she fled him, he tried to stop her and the leather strap that held the brooch around her neck broke. She fled, leaving the brooch and her powers behind."

"So the legend we heard growing up *is* true," Greer murmured, her face showing her awe.

"I don't know," Lillianna responded, her voice cool. "What precisely did you hear?"

"That yer powers lie dormant until ye fall in love," Mari and Allisdair said in unison. Angus looked to his siblings in surprise. Judging by the worshipful expressions they wore as they stared at Lillianna, they very much believed in the legend to which he had never given any credence. Worry enveloped him. Lillianna surely noted what he did, and it was going to make it that much harder to convince her that he was not marrying her to use her.

"Yes, that's right," Lillianna said, a look that seemed wistful to him passing across her face so fast that he could not be certain his instinct had been correct.

"Is it also true that if ye are betrayed by the one ye love that yer powers disappear, and ye can only ever foretell the future again if ye are wearing the brooch?" Mari asked innocently.

Lillianna was gazing down so Angus could no longer see her face, but her fingers twisted together in front of her. "That's correct," she said, her voice resigned.

"May I touch the brooch?" Mari asked, rushing so quickly for Lillianna and reaching toward the brooch that Angus did not even have time to tell her not to touch Lillianna. But there was no need. Lillianna scrambled backward until there was nowhere to go because the wall blocked her.

"I'm sorry," Mari whispered, sounding stricken. His younger sister had a fragile heart.

The tenseness in Lillianna immediately disappeared, and she offered Mari a reassuring smile. "No. It's me who should be apologizing. It's just that the visions are new to me, and I don't have much control over them yet."

Angus frowned. "So ye have been able to control them a bit?"

Her eyes, which brimmed with hope, met his. "Only when you touched me," she admitted. "I...I was able to make the vision stop."

The unmistakable relief in her voice matched what he felt. He didn't think he would want her having visions of his future every time they touched.

"How did ye stop the vision?" Allisdair asked with the same innocence as Mari.

Lillianna flushed and bit her lip.

"Leave it be," Angus said. Clearly, how she had done it was something that embarrassed her, and he'd not have her shamed just to satisfy their curiosity.

Greer plunked her hands on her hips, glaring at him. "How did ye come to be with this woman? And what happened to Allisdair?" she demanded, shooting Lillianna an accusing look as if she was personally responsible for Allisdair's injuries.

Angus opened his mouth to explain about taking Lillianna from the Palace of Westminster for her safety, but Lillianna beat him to it. "Your brother," she said slowly, "was asked by Lord Bruce to take me to the safety of my clan. My uncle thought to use me, and he didn't mind if he needed to kill me to get what he wanted."

Angus could hear the breathing in the room it was so silent. Lillianna's face was almost unreadable except her eyes. There a fathomless sadness dwelled. She inhaled a long, deep breath. "I suspect my uncle discovered where the Brooch of Lagothmier was, and so he sent a knight after me to bring me back. He would not have done so otherwise. I'm worthless to him without the brooch." She said it with a matter-of-fact tone, as she would state any piece of information that she had no feelings about, but he knew it to be a defense. She cared greatly. Her uncle and her father making her feel worthless had affected her deeply.

Angus interrupted to purposely give her a moment to consider if and what else she wanted to say. He did not want her to feel compelled to answer Greer's demanding questions. "I had to ride to Ettrick Forest first to warn Robbie's men that King Edward's men were coming for them. A battle ensued, and Belfaine was apparently there, though I kinnae say why."

"It was happenstance," Lillianna inserted, glancing Angus's way for one brief moment. "His horse had thrown a shoe on the way to his home, which was why Belfaine was still there. He came upon us"—she motioned between herself and Allisdair—"as we were trying to escape the English."

Allisdair nodded vigorously. "The English who were pursuing us were also trying to kill Ross. He was hanging upside down on his horse, and Lillianna saw him and was turning to save him when Belfaine and his men shot at the English and killed them," Allisdair added, looking meaningfully at Greer. "Belfaine took us when he realized who I was, and he left Ross to tell Angus that he had me. He took Lillianna to…to use her." His face turned red.

Rage filled Angus at the thought of Belfaine thinking he would defile Lillianna.

"But Drumlan was at Belfaine's home because he had brought his daughter back to Belfaine. Drumlan realized who I was right away." Lillianna's eyes took on a sort of glassy look, as if memories swirled in her head. "You see, I look very much like my mother," she almost whispered. "We've the same hair and eyes." She gave herself a little shake and focused on all of them. "He had my mother's brooch." Her hand fluttered to the brooch secured around her neck. "He had kept it all these years. He wore it." She gave a little shudder, and Angus wanted nothing more than to comfort her, but he held himself still and did no more to touch her. He didn't know if his touch would bring her a vision and pain. He didn't want that.

Lillianna brought her wary gaze to him. "Of course he thought to use me, as has every man I have ever known. As Drumlan did my mother. As my own father thought to do to my mother and myself."

"Is that why ye brought her here, Brother?" Greer demanded. "Are we going to use her powers against our enemies?"

Lillianna flinched at Greer's words, and it took all of his will not to stride across the room and shake Greer senseless. "Nay," he bit out. "I will nae use Lillianna's powers. She is here because I vowed to protect her."

"She will bring trouble to our doorstep!" Greer bellowed. "Drumlan will come for her, as will her uncle!"

"Let them come," Angus said in a hard, ruthless voice. He brought his gaze to Lillianna and willed her to understand, to accept that he would never hurt her. "I will kill anyone who dares to try to take you from me."

Lillianna's mouth parted, and her eyes went wide. Total silence descended on the room, broken only when Angus said, "Everyone but Lillianna out of the room. Await me in the hall. Lillianna and I need to talk in private."

Convincing Lillianna to wed him would take more than words, and for what he intended, he did not want an audience.

Chapter Eighteen

Shocked by Angus's words, Lillianna stood almost dumbfounded and watched Allisdair and Angus's youngest sister, Mari, hurry out of the room. Father Dunlap, who seemed rather nice, rushed out behind them, but Ross and Greer stood their ground. Ross stared at his brother while Greer glared at her. She wanted to dislike the woman in return, but it was clear that Lillianna's presence made Greer feel protective and worried for her family. Lillianna admired Greer's obvious love for her family.

"Do ye need me to stay, Brother?" Ross asked, his gaze shifting from Angus to Lillianna and then quickly back to Angus. Did the man think she held some sway over Angus? The thought made her sad because she'd never know. Not truly. He was aware of her powers now, so how could she ever believe him if he were to ever tell her he loved her? Not that there was a chance of that anyway.

"Nay," Angus answered, "and I dunnae need ye to remain, either, Greer."

"But—"

"Nay," Angus said firmly. "I can manage one wee lass." His gaze captured Lillianna's. When his mouth curved in an inviting smile, she had a flash of memory of his mouth on hers, and a blush heated her cheeks to which he gave a knowing, appreciative look.

"Out," he said even more forcefully, and to Lillianna's sudden amusement, he fairly shoved his sister out of the great hall and then shut the door. When he turned back toward her, he was frowning as he came to stand a hairsbreadth from her. "If I touch ye will ye have a vision?" he asked, the worry in his voice surprising her.

"Likely so," she said, "but I can try to control it. Why?"

"I want to touch ye verra badly," he said. He sounded so earnest that she believed it was simply that. "But as much as I long to touch ye," he continued, "I dunnae want to cause ye pain."

His concern made her throat ache with happiness. "It's not so very painful, but..." How could she explain that she did not want visions of him to invade her every time they touched? What if he wanted that? It would kill her to hear it. She bit her lip, afraid to say what was in her heart for fear of what she would hear in return.

He exhaled a long breath. "I would rather ye nae ken my future at all," he said.

She sucked in a sharp breath. Was he telling the truth? Hope blossomed deep in her belly, and she pressed her lips together on the wish to ask why. She wanted him to explain himself. He moved to reach for her, then stilled and started to pull his hand back, but she grabbed it and set his large, warm palm to her cheek.

Light flashed in her mind. The images of her mother and ancestors began. Her body started to tingle, and the world around her started to fade. Her eyes began to burn, and she squeezed them shut, willing the memory of Angus kissing her at the river to the front of her mind. She concentrated on every detail she could recall, down to the way his tongue had curled deliciously around hers, and all her senses returned to normal. When she opened her eyes, he was there in this moment in time, not the future. She exhaled with relief, and he grinned, looking more carefree than she had ever seen him.

"Did it work?" he asked, his eyes so full of hope that she laughed.

"Yes!" she exclaimed. Before she could say more, his mouth slanted over hers. His tongue parted her lips and plunged into her mouth, sending shivers of desire racing through her. The kiss was hungry, possessive, and demanding and she gave herself eagerly to it—and to him. When he pulled back, she was panting, and he looked particularly pleased.

"What are we doing? What are you doing?" she asked more precisely, her emotions swirling within her.

He reached out and brushed a strand of her hair out of her face, and the look he gave her—possessive, primal, promising—curled her toes with longing.

When he didn't answer, she said, "You said you would kill anyone who tried to take me from you. Do you still plan not to take me to the MacLeods?"

"Nay," he said. "Ye will nae be going to the MacLeods."

She had to fight to focus, his closeness so overpowered her thoughts. What was he offering? Was he offering refuge? More? Dare she hope for more? "Your sister is correct that I bring danger to your clan."

"Aye," he said, sliding his hand down her cheek and making her shiver. His hand stopped on her shoulder and cupped it, even as his other hand came to her other shoulder to do the same. "I'm prepared for that, and I will protect ye."

"Why?" she asked, suspicion and hope warring within her.

"Because ye will be mine," he said, matter-of-fact.

"Why do you want to make me yours? To possess me?"

"Aye," he said, his look dangerously seductive. "I want to possess ye, nae yer powers." The hope in her belly grew despite her inherent wariness. "I dunnae give a damn about yer powers. I want ye for ye." He took her face and held it gently. "I want ye, Lillianna, because I desire ye so damn much I kinnae think straight."

"You want only me? Not my powers?" she repeated, fearful she was mishearing him.

He offered a tender, understanding smile. "I wanted ye before I believed in yer powers, and if ye lost the powers tomorrow, I'd want ye still," he said, brushing his lips ever so softly over hers. His tender kiss pulled a moan from her throat, and even though she tried to keep her hands fisted at her sides, she found them twined around his neck, her fingers locked together. "I want ye for ye," he said again, as if he understood how very much she doubted it. "I wish to wed ye, Lillianna."

Instead of feeling fear, hope filled her. However foolish it was, she could not suppress it or stop it. He wished to wed her. He said he wanted her for her. Did she dare believe him? She sucked in her lower lip, thinking back to their past conversations. "You said you did not want a wife. So why have you changed your mind? Do you…" She could not bring herself to ask him if he loved her, besides, the wary look that came to his face left no doubt he was not marrying her out of love.

Underneath her fingertips, his muscles tensed. "I'm nae proposing giving ye my heart, Lillianna." Hurt and humiliation overcame her. She started to pull away from him, but he gripped her upper arms gently. "I will give ye my protection, my body, and my loyalty forever. Would that nae be enough?"

She stared at him, her mind turning. He was not vowing his love; he was not trying to gain hers. Of course, he did not need to as long as she wore the brooch, and he knew it. Yet for some reason, she believed that he wished to wed her to protect her and because he desired her. She should be thrilled, but she wasn't. She had spent her life fearing love, fearing losing control.

Now, standing here with him, she longed to hear him say he wanted to win her heart, for she suspected he was close to doing so already. She was a fool to even contemplate wedding him, but Drumlan would come for her, and likely her uncle and father, too. And who else would try to take her when word spread that the brooch had been found? Was it not better to choose the devil she knew than the one she did not?

And what if she could win the heart of this particular handsome devil? Truly? Then she could freely give hers. What chance of that was there? She forced back the questions that battered her and focused on him. "If I wed you, what exactly is it you would expect me to give you?"

The way his heated gaze slowly raked the length of her body revealed what was at the forefront of his mind. His hands glided over her arms to her back, and he pressed her against him. "I want yer loyalty, yer desire, and yer heart."

Cold air hit her teeth as she gasped. "You want *my* heart, but you will not give me yours?"

He nodded, his stare unwavering and unapologetic.

"Why do you wish to wed me, and do not just say to protect me. That is not enough for me," she said. She needed to see hope for them. They had desire, but she felt deep within they needed at least the hope for more.

"Of course it's nae just to protect ye!" he burst out and yanked a hand through his hair. "I want ye. It's all I can think about. I desire ye so much that I'm driven to distraction. I kinnae think as I should. I kinnae concentrate as I must as laird. Ye are on my mind always now, and I must get control of it. Aye, I want to protect ye, but I also want to bury myself in ye again and again, and I dunnae ever want another man to have ye. Ye have taken a piece of me that I did nae wish to give, but ye have it now."

She stilled. Did he mean a piece of his heart? She thought he might, and wild hope burst within her.

"And I kinnae imagine letting ye go now. I kinnae offer any more than that, Lillianna. I dunnae have it in me."

She bit her lip on the desire to smile, for she thought perhaps he did, and in that, she saw all the faith that she needed.

"Will ye wed me or nae?" he asked, vulnerability glinting in his eyes.

Determination to claim a future she had thought impossible flowed through her. She would win his heart, and then—and only then—would she give hers. "I'll wed you," she said, and before she could say more, he crushed her to him and covered her mouth with a kiss that left no doubt in her mind that he meant to possess her body and soul.

"Ye must wear this to wed my brother," Mari said, thrusting a beautiful gown at Lillianna, who stood in nothing but the clean léine Mari had let her borrow.

Wed.

The word reverberated in Lillianna's mind, and she inhaled a long steadying breath, feeling the bandages that Mari had wound around her wounds restrict the air flow. She took shallow pulls of air, trying to calm her racing heart, but it would not slow. What was she doing? What had she been thinking? Her fingers fluttered to the brooch she still wore on the leather strap around her neck. She had vowed never to wed, and yet, here she was, about to do so and foolishly full of hope.

Fear that her hope would lead to heartbreak made her start to tremble. Mari's eyes went wide, and she clasped Lillianna's hands. Light flashed in Lillianna's mind and her body trembled. The images of her mother and ancestors came, the room before her folding back as a new image of Mari appeared. She was standing next to Allisdair, and they appeared to be in a kitchen cooking. Lillianna's eyes burned, and she squeezed them shut as Mari and Allisdair laughed in her vision. She concentrated on the memory of Angus kissing her, but the vision of the future seemed to only grow stronger. She could see the stark white of the flour, a smudge on Mari's nose. A spoon clanking in a pot and the smell of fresh baking bread filled her senses.

She jerked her hands from Mari's, and the vision disappeared. Mari looked at her with concern. "Did ye have a vision?"

"Yes," she said, her voice horse. "I tried to fight it. I've been able to suppress them with Angus, but with you…"

"Ye kinnae?"

Lillianna shook her head, and Mari's expression turned thoughtful. "Mayhap fighting the vision only works on yer true love."

"I don't love your brother," Lillianna protested, leaving off the *yet*. She was foolish, but not *that* foolish.

Mari gave her a sympathetic look. "He cares for ye. He's simply afraid to admit it, even to himself."

Lillianna was grateful for Mari's words, and while she too thought Angus cared for her, that was quite different than love. He desired her, he was honorable and wanted to protect her, and he had admitted that she had a piece of him, but she wanted all of him. That was what she needed in order to give him all of her.

"We shall see," Lillianna finally said.

Mari nodded. "Does Angus ken that ye can control the visions of him?"

"Yes," Lillianna said, a smile coming to her lips when she recalled his relief. "He seemed glad."

Mari eyed her. "Ye seem surprised."

"I am," Lillianna said honestly. "All I have ever known of the abilities I would inherit is that they would bring me heartache, that men would try to use me to wield my powers. Your brother seems to want nothing to do with my abilities, and frankly, it's refreshing."

The door to the bedchamber squeaked, and Lillianna's gaze flew to it. Greer was just visible through the crack. Their eyes locked, and Angus's eldest sister narrowed her gaze on Lillianna and shoved open the door. Clearly, she had been eavesdropping, but Lillianna pressed her lips together on saying anything. The woman had made her dislike of Lillianna known, and she did not want to do anything to make it worse.

Greer breezed into the room and plunked her hands on her hips. "A relief?" Greer snapped. "Ye have distracted my brother from his duties as laird, and ye will bring enemies to our door, and ye are *relieved* that he will nae use the only thing that gives ye worth!"

"Greer!" Mari gasped, outraged. "Lillianna will be part of this family." She gave Lillianna an apologetic look and held out the sumptuous, blue velvet gown.

Before Lillianna could reach for the gown, Greer snatched it out of her sister's hands. "Ye will nae give her

Mother's gown to wear!"

Mari snatched the gown back and glowered at her sister. "Mother would be appalled by how ye are acting!"

Lillianna stood speechless and horrified watching the sisters argue. She didn't want to intervene and cause Greer to become even angrier with her, nor did she want to stand idly by and watch them fight.

Greer shoved Mari in the shoulder and yanked the gown out of her sister's hands. "Mother saved that gown so each of us could wear it when we were wed. She'd nae want some wench to wear it!"

"Greer!" Angus's voice thundered from the doorway, making Lillianna flinch, as did Mari and Greer. He strode into the room, looking especially handsome in a clean plaid and braies. His wet, dark hair slicked back from his face emphasized his strong jawline, which was shadowed by a light layer of beard growth. He fixed a menacing glare on Greer, which made Lillianna sigh. She was certain to hate her even more now.

He stopped in front of Greer and took the gown out of her hands, turning to give it to Lillianna without a word. When his sensuous gaze met hers and their fingers brushed, her body tingled all over. "Lillianna is nae a wench, and ye will be kind to her. She will be yer family."

"Nae my family," Greer growled. "Mark my words, Brother. She will bring ye heartache, and then we all will suffer as we suffered before for yer mistakes."

"Your brother has guilt enough for his past, Greer!" Lillianna burst out, unable to help herself. She refused to allow Greer to make Angus feel worse than he already did.

All three MacLorhs looked at Lillianna in surprise. Frankly, she was surprised with herself at how vehement she felt about protecting Angus. "I would never betray your brother or you, I vow it," she said. "I would like to earn your trust, if you will just let me."

"Ye want my trust?" Greer sneered. "Fine. Tell me my future. If I'm pleased with what ye see, then ye have my trust."

"Greer!" Angus roared. "Dunnae ever think to use Lillianna for her powers or ye will suffer my wrath!"

Lillianna winced. Part of her was overjoyed that Angus had stood up for her and stated so bluntly that he would not allow anyone to use her, but she also did not want to be the thing to tear his family apart. She stepped forward and held out her hand to Greer. "Give me your hand," she said.

"Nay, Lillianna," Angus said, putting a hand up to stop her, but she pushed his hand away and scowled at him.

"If your sister wants to know her future, I will tell her what I see." Maybe, if she offered this gift to Greer, the woman would start to trust her.

Greer gripped Lillianna's hand, and their gazes locked. As before, bright light flashed before her eyes, and her entire body tingled. The images of her mother and ancestors rolled across her mind, and the room around her disappeared, revealing the future. Yet, it was not Greer she saw; it was herself.

She was in the woods, standing in a circle of men. In the middle of the circle, Angus and Belfaine danced around each other wielding their swords.

She gasped and jerked in confusion. Angus called her name, but he seemed so very far away.

Isla Belfaine stood in front of her with a dagger pointed at Lillianna, and then Isla spoke. "Move out of my way, Greer! I dunnae wish to kill ye."

Greer held a dagger and stood slightly in front of Lillianna. Greer looked from Isla to Lillianna.

"I will rid ye of the problems she brings ye," Isla said. "Simply step aside."

Greer nodded, and black terror descended on Lillianna.

All the air seemed to be gone from Lillianna's lungs, and she struggled to draw a breath. Then the feeling was gone. She released Greer, scrambling away from her only to collide with Angus. She turned her head to him, and he glanced down at her with concern in his eyes.

"Ye almost collapsed," he said. "I had to catch ye."

She nodded, her heart still racing, and looked to Greer once more. "What did ye see?" Greer demanded.

If she told the truth, it would divide her and Greer further. Should she try to lie? She knew what the legend said, what her mother had told her, but she had to try, and perhaps that future would not come to pass.

"Noth—" Pain, consuming, sharp, and nauseating, shot through her mind as if someone had sliced through her head with a sword. She swayed and would have fallen, except Angus grabbed her around the waist. As her power trembled within her, she frantically drew the vision of their kiss to the front of her mind and gained control.

When the intensity had subsided, she opened her eyes to find Mari and Angus staring at her with worried expressions. Greer, however, stared in fascination.

Angus brought a cloth to Lillianna's face, and she had no notion where he had even gotten it. "Yer nose is bleeding," he said, wiping the cloth under her nose. "What happened?"

She bit her lip. "I...I cannot deny telling someone the truth of my vision of them when I see it, and I tried," she finished, looking to Greer.

Greer's eyes widened in surprise. "What did ye truly see?"

"I saw you," Lillianna said flatly, "agreeing to betray me."

⚜

"Await me outside," Angus ordered Greer, furious.

For once, Greer obeyed without argument and quietly departed the room. Angus guided Lillianna to the bed and then looked helplessly between her and the passage where Greer stood. He understood Greer's fear, but fear did not excuse dishonor and betrayal. He had to make that clear, yet he didn't want Lillianna to feel abandoned by him in her time of need or unimportant somehow and not worthy of his support.

"Go," Lillianna said, waving a hand at him. "You need to speak with Greer, and I need to dress for the wedding. Mari will aid me."

"Ye're certain?" he asked, looking between Lillianna and Mari. Both women nodded. He leaned down and brushed his lips to Lillianna's, the contact like an odd jolt to his chest. When he stood, he said, "I'll set Greer straight. Ye need nae fear her."

Lillianna managed a shaky smile. "Don't be too harsh," she urged, and his chest squeezed. Even after seeing a vision of Greer possibly betraying her, Lillianna was standing up for her.

He stepped out into the passage, shut the door, and waited for Greer to turn to him. She slowly did, guilt and defiance on her face. "If I betray that woman in the future, I'm certain she deserves it," Greer growled.

"Listen to me, Sister," Angus said, taking Greer by her upper arms. "I will nae ever repeat the mistakes of my past."

"How do ye ken?" she demanded. "Ye are distracted by

her just as ye were Isla, and soon she will be yer wife, and it will be worse! Ye will fail in yer duty to us because of her."

"Nay!" he said, harshly, not wishing to have this conversation here at the door to where Lillianna was, nor did he wish to have it right before he was to wed. "My duty to ye and the clan motivates my every choice, Greer!" he growled.

Greer's eyes suddenly widened. "Oh, I see. Clever brother."

He frowned. "Clever?"

"Yes." She nodded. "Clever, but…" She pointed toward the closed door of Lillianna's bedchamber. "Ye need nae say more. Come. Let us get ye wed and"—Greer suddenly leaned close and dropped her voice to a whisper—"and the wench bound to ye and under yer control."

He sighed. Greer did not understand at all. He took a deep breath to try again, but Ross came bounding down the passage. "Hector Fraser just arrived."

Angus frowned. "What is Hector Fraser doing here?" Hector was Simon and Grant's cousin, but Angus had never cared for the man overly much. There was something shifty about him that Angus did not like.

Ross chuckled, knowing well how Angus felt about the man. "Dunnae be so skeptical of him," Ross said, clapping Angus on the arm. "He came in search of Alex."

"Oh, aye?" That made sense given Alex told them that he purposely let Hector believe Alex was choosing the side of the English in the war, as he did not trust his brother not to accidentally spill the secret that Alex was working with Simon as a spy. "I'll go make my greetings. What did ye tell him?"

Ross grinned. "That we saw his turncoat brother with Simon, and hopefully they were dead."

Angus nodded, satisfied, then looked to Greer. "We will finish this talk later," he said.

She inclined her head in agreement, and then Angus departed with Ross to receive Hector.

Not long after seeing Hector and relaying the same thing to him that Ross had, Angus stood awaiting Lillianna in the great hall. He glanced at his brothers and sisters, and the council members of his clan and their families, as well as his most trusted warriors. Word of him wedding Lillianna would spread fast through his clan, but he had given specific instructions for the information to remain within the clan for now. He would not tell the rest of his comrades, including Robbie, until he was certain who he could trust among them and who he couldn't. It pained him to keep secrets from the men who had been like brothers to him for years, men he had risked his life for and who had risked their lives for him, but someone had aided de Burgh and Edward in getting the missive to Ross that lured him to Ettrick Forest, and until Angus knew who, he would trust none beyond those of his clan who lived in this castle.

He knew for certain that Robbie had not betrayed him, but Lillianna's cousin had betrayed him and Robbie when she had plotted to send Angus into the woods in the first place. Telling Robbie so would be useless without proof, though. The man was clearly besotted with Elizabeth, and Angus did not trust that she would not somehow use Robbie to get Lillianna away from here.

"Angus," Ross said in his ear. "Pull yer thoughts to the present, Brother. Yer beautiful bride just entered the room."

Angus looked to the door of the great hall. A strange emotion flooded him when he saw Lillianna dressed in his mother's blue velvet gown. She stood proud, his delicate yet strong lass, this woman who could see futures but not his, if she did not wish to. As she moved toward him, his senses seemed to crackle to life, growing stronger the nearer she came. When she stood beside him and he held his arm out to her, she took it, setting every part of him ablaze with desire and something else. It seemed a connection between them had been formed the day they had met, and despite him fighting it and her not wanting it, the bond had grown stronger. He could feel it now, pulling them together and binding them.

But he did not fear it, for he would control it. He would have this woman, and in doing so, he would temper the need for her. Yet as Father Dunlap looked at him and Angus said the vows the priest indicated, his chest grew tight with a deep ache. And when she looked to him and started to speak her vows, her guileless gaze locked with his, contentment unlike anything he'd ever experienced filled him.

"Angus, ye may kiss yer wife," Father Dunlap said.

Angus blinked. He was not a man to lose focus, but Lillianna took all of his. She was a danger and a lure, but in this moment, as he took her in his arms and his lips found her eager warm ones, he realized she had also banished the shadow of guilt that normally haunted him, at least for the time being. All that haunted him now was desire, and he planned to satisfy that need as soon as possible.

Chapter Nineteen

"Your clan is watching," Lillianna hissed as Angus tugged her out of the great hall and into the passage. The powers within her stirred, but she recognized it immediately and focused all her attention on Angus in the here and the now. She was shocked and pleased when the feelings the powers brought lessened without her even having to conjure up every detail of that kiss in the woods.

"Good," he replied, pulling her along the passage at a clipped pace. "Then they will see a man who desires his wife."

He stopped then and turned to her. The wonder she saw on his face made her heart flutter with true hope. "Ye're my wife," he whispered, his voice reverent.

"I'm your wife," she murmured back, rather stunned herself. "I never imagined…"

"Aye," he said, nodding his head. "I did nae, either." He surprised her then by whisking her off her feet and holding her close to his chest.

"Angus! Whatever are you doing?"

"Hastening things," he said with a wink. "I want ye, Lillianna. I've nae hid that fact. I feel as if, well…"

She thought perhaps he did not want to scare her by showing her the depths of his desire for her, but she felt emboldened and pressed a finger to his lips. "I feel as if I will burst if you don't touch me again the way you did that day in the woods."

"Lass," he said, crushing his mouth to hers, swooping his tongue inside, and then giving her a long, drugging kiss. "I have thought of little else myself since that day."

"Then what," she said, boldly brushing her lips against his neck, "are you waiting for?"

With a grin, he strode to the stairs and took them two at a time, as if carrying her were like carrying a feather. His strength and size made her feel safe, but she also had a stirring of concern about the joining.

When he opened the bedchamber door, she gasped. Candles lit the room, flower petals littered the bed, and in the corner of the room, steam rose from a bathing tub. She stared in wonder at the space and then slowly sought him. "Did you do this?"

He looked suddenly uncomfortable. "Aye," he said, setting her on her feet and releasing his hold on her. She caught his fingers. Angus MacLorh was brave enough to face anything except apparently his heart. He cared for her. She was certain of it. He may not love her yet, but to do this for her, he *had* to care.

"How did you know I liked these things? I've never told a soul."

He gave her a devilish look that made her heart dance with excitement. "When ye were taken by the fever, ye revealed it."

"And you remembered what I said?" she asked, astonished.

"*Mo bhean mhaiseach,* I remember everything about ye—from the mistrustful look in yer jade eyes when I first met ye, to the purple bruise on yer right cheek that ye tried to hide with yer hair, to the way yer hot, eager mouth tastes of honey, and the little moans of pleasure ye make when my tongue swirls along your sensitive—"

She launched herself into his arms with an almost violent need. No one had ever made her feel as wanted, as full of worth as this man in this moment. His mouth came down hard upon hers, demanding, searching, and searing. She loved it. The friction of his chest rubbing against hers caused her breasts to become heavy and tingly, but when his hand grazed her stomach, she jerked in pain. He stilled instantly, breaking the kiss, and gazing down at her with eyes so filled with passion that her legs trembled.

"Why did ye nae tell me ye were in pain?" he asked.

She twined her arms around his neck and tried to press their bodies together again, but he held her at a distance. She frowned. "This is why. I did not want you to be too worried to touch me."

"Of course I'm worried to touch ye if I'm going to cause ye pain. Ye ought to ken that by now. Let us cleanse yer wounds, and then I'll put a salve on them and—"

"No!" she said. "You'll see how horrid it looks, and then you'll not want me."

He pulled her to him and slanted his mouth over hers, their tongues tangling, and her pulse racing. His mouth left hers to trail kisses down her neck, over her collarbone, and to the space between her breasts where the brooch was nestled. He took the brooch in his hands. "There is nae a thing in this world that could make me nae want ye, Lillianna."

Her heart thudded in her ears. "Even," she said, "if I threw away the brooch and had no powers?"

"Even then," he assured her, releasing the brooch. He slipped his fingers inside her gown, and pulled it down just enough to expose the top of her chest. Then he traced his tongue over each breast, pulled her gown down farther, and then slid his tongue lower, very close to her nipples but not touching them. It was torture, but it was exquisite. The desire he aroused in her was painful in its intensity.

As he caressed her chest, neck, and mouth, her body flamed, and she roamed her hands over the hard swell of his arms and the broad stretch of his back. But she wanted and needed more. And as he very ably stripped her of her gown, she knew he did, too. She tugged on his plaid as he kicked off his boots, and then they were both pulling down his braies and slipping off her léine. Suddenly, cold air hit her body, and she shivered both from the draft and the realization that she was standing naked in front of Angus. And then, she looked down at his long staff and all thoughts but those of joining with him fled her mind. There was no more fear, only wonder and anticipation.

"Angus?" she fairly moaned, her core tightening and heat pooling there.

"Aye," he said, circling his fingers around one of her straining buds and then the other.

She foggily recalled that he'd said he wanted them to bathe. "Shall we get in the tub?"

"Oh aye, we shall, but nae yet." A wicked gleam sparkled in his eyes. "First," he said, cupping her breasts, "I'm going to worship ye."

When his mouth came over her left breast with a long, hard pull, she lost all coherent thought. The sensation made her back arch, her nails dig into his skin, and her insides spasm with a need to be released from the exquisite anguish.

He suckled on her left breast until she was certain she could stand no more, and then he moved to the right. Her legs gave, but he caught her, a hand gripping her bottom, and then he scooped her off her feet and took her to the bed where he laid her. She was uncertain of his intention when he pulled her bottom to the very edge of the bed, and his hands came between her legs to spread them. She gasped and set a hand on his shoulder to stop him. "Angus, no," she murmured, though her body said yes.

He kneeled between her thighs but paused, his hands braced on on her. "I want to pleasure ye, to give to ye before I take from ye. But if ye dunnae wish it…"

She leaned up on her elbows, the bandages around her stomach tightening. "Surely this is a sin?"

"Well, if it is," he said, his voice rough with desire, "then I'm an eager sinner, and I'm happy to die unrepentant."

She giggled and flopped onto her back, more carefree than she had ever been in her life, than she had ever dreamed possible. "Make me a sinner, then, too, Husband. For I vow that wheresoever you lead me, I shall follow."

"I'll hold ye to that," he said, and then she gasped, her back arching of its own volition, as Angus's fingers came to the innermost intimate folds of her body. He parted her gently, and then to her delighted astonishment, he slid his tongue down her center, over a spot that seemed to contain every nerve she possessed. Her insides clenched, and she screamed out his name as his tongue began to move in slow circles, and then faster and faster until she was thrashing and begging him to give her what she needed, though she hadn't a clue what that was.

He slid his hands under her bottom as her heartbeat resounded in her ears and she panted for breath. Then in a long, suckling stroke of her sensitive center, he sent her spiraling over an edge she had not known existed. Every muscle inside her tightened and then released, and blood pulsed through her core in delicious beats that melded with her heart. Wave after wave of pleasure washed over her, and when she felt too languid to ever possibly move again, he rose, gathered her into his arms, and carried her to the bathing tub.

There, he set her on her feet and slowly unwound her bandages, a long hiss coming from between his teeth. She shook off the remnants of the daze he'd left her in and tried to raise her arms to hide her stomach from his view.

"Dunnae," he said, the word a harsh command. She frowned at him, and his face gentled. He kissed her above and below the wounds. "Dunnae ever hide yerself from me. When I wed ye, I took all of ye. Every scar makes ye who ye are, and ye are the most beautiful lass I have ever kenned, inside and out."

Tears of happiness sprang to her eyes, and his brow furrowed as he wiped away one of the tears rolling down her cheek. "Why are ye crying?"

She laid her cheek against his chest, listening to the steady beat of his heart. "I never thought to feel this way. I have to wonder if it's real."

He kissed her head, and then he cupped her face in his hands and kissed her lips. "It's real. Dunnae fash yerself, *mo bhean mhaiseach.*"

"What does that mean?" she asked him. She'd been too overwhelmed by his omission earlier to ask him. He smiled as he took her hand and helped her into the bathing tub. The warm water enveloped her as she lowered herself into it, and when he stepped in and sat behind her, bringing her between his thighs and into the protective cradle of his arms, the water lapped over the sides to splash on the hardwood.

"It means my beautiful wife," he said, kissing her neck

from behind and then taking a cloth and soaping it up before running it over one of her arms and then the other.

She turned in his arms, ignoring the sting of pain her wounds caused, and put her hands on his chest. Slowly, she smiled, hoping she had mastered looking wicked as he so easily could do. When he cocked his eyebrows and an intrigued grin turned up the corner of his lips, she thought she just might have captured the look she wanted. "I want to pleasure you in the way you pleasured me."

"Ah, lass, I have never heard a sweeter wish in my life, and I will gladly let ye, but first, I will join with ye proper as a husband does a wife, and hopefully, we will make a bairn that looks just like ye." She shuddered, and his grin disappeared. "Ye dunnae wish for bairns?"

"No, it's not that. I just hope we have boys. I want the curse to end with me. I don't want a daughter who has to worry that she has been married not for who she is but for her power."

A determined look settled on his face, and he slid his hands into her hair. "I'm going to prove to ye that I married ye for ye and only ye, and I'll do it first by seduction." He gave her that wicked grin that she was fast becoming accustomed to. "And if we should have a daughter, she shall see by yer happiness that it is possible to give her heart to a man without fear."

He gave her an expectant look, as if she should declare that he had her heart, yet she could not quite let go. She wanted his and he was not willing to even think of the possibility of giving it, so she kissed him with all the passion inside her, and soon they were once again out of the bathing tub and on the bed. But now she was between his thighs, touching him with wonder, and then tasting him as he had tasted her. When she took the length of him in her mouth and began to slide up and down him, the muscles of his neck and chest bulged. She knew he was trying to hold off his release, but finally, he relinquished all control and seemed to slip over the same edge he'd sent her spiraling from earlier.

When he appeared spent and she thought they would lie there in each other's arms, he gripped her by the waist, careful not to touch her wounds, and rolled her on her back to loom over her. "Now," he said, his voice a ragged growl, "I will make ye mine truly and completely."

"As I will make you mine," she promised him, determined.

Chapter Twenty

Never had joining with a woman been as it was with Lillianna. He wanted to savor each moment, memorize each and every curve, hollow, and line of her body. He wanted to watch her face as he brought her to the height of ecstasy again, but this time as they were one. He slid between her thighs, and his chest tightened painfully when she looked up at him, her eyes so trusting and guileless.

Her silken skin grazing his hot flesh sent a surge of lust through him, but he gritted his teeth, determined to keep the slow pace that would bring her to the greatest pleasure. It occurred to him as his gaze skimmed over her wounds that he might hurt her this way, so he grasped her hips and brought her with him as he flipped onto his back.

"What are you doing?" she asked, showing only curiosity, not fear.

"If I take ye as I'd planned, I may hurt yer stomach wounds. This way, I'll nae touch them."

She bit her lip. "Will it be as enjoyable for you?"

Good God. The lass was actually considering bearing the pain so he could have pleasure. That band that felt so snug around his chest already grew tighter. "Aye, lass. Any way I take ye will be pure bliss."

"What shall I do?" she asked, revealing her innocence.

"I'll guide ye," he assured her, thankful no man but him had ever touched her, nor ever would. She was his. Deep in his bones he felt that she was meant for him. He grasped her hips and situated her at the peak of his hard staff, and when he lowered her so that his flesh met her hot, moist skin, a primal need gripped him.

"Angus?" she murmured, her palms coming to rest on his chest. "I'm afraid."

His blood surged through every part of his body, and his mind screamed at him to take her now, but he'd cut off his arms before ever hurting his wife. His *wife*. The band grew tighter around his chest, so that he could only take a ragged breath. "If ye wish me to stop, simply say the word."

"No." She settled more firmly on him so that he breached the edge of her entrance.

"God..." He moaned, unable to contain how good it felt. "Ye are Heaven on Earth," he growled, his fingers tightening around her hips.

She gave him a wicked smile and said, "Shall I simply sink onto you bit by bit?"

"I'd likely die from the sensations," he said, only half joking, "and that will prolong the hurting, which comes from breaking yer maidenhead. If I thrust into ye, the pain will last but a breath, and then ye will become accustomed to me. Will ye trust me?"

"Always," she answered so vehemently and so immediately that he knew it to be true.

A strong feeling swirled inside him like a violent storm, and he recognized immediately it was need for her. He needed her, and not just physically. He could not imagine his life without her. He shoved the thoughts aside for a later time, slid his hands partially under her bottom, and plunged deep within her welcoming heat.

She cried out in pain at the same time he cried out in ecstasy, and though every fiber that made him a man yearned to move, to possess, to pour his seed into her, he stilled and ran his hands up the perfect curve of her back to offer her support. "When ye are ready for me to move," he managed to get out through teeth clenched against the desire to slide in and out of her, "say so." She wiggled ever so slightly, and a guttural groan escaped him. "Lillianna," he said on a ragged breath, "dunnae wiggle unless ye are ready."

"I'm ready," she said, wiggling her sweet, perfect arse once more.

He pulled out all the way to his tip and slid back in, reveling in the whimpers of pleasure that came from her. As he found a rhythm and her body matched it, he kept his gaze on his beautiful wife, and the band around his chest continued to grow tighter and tighter. Her eyelids fluttered shut, her back arched, and she tilted her head back, clinging to his arms as she rode him. His release came so completely, so violently, that he feared for a moment that he had hurt her, but when she looked down at him with a grin and said, "When can we do that again?" he felt connected to her in a way he'd never felt to another person in his life. He brought her into the cradle of his arms and stroked her hair until her breathing became deep and he knew sleep had claimed her.

He closed his own eyes, thinking sleep would claim him, too, but his thoughts were consumed by her: how to keep her safe, how to make her feel worthy, how to ensure his own sister did not do something to harm her.

God's teeth! He opened his eyes and stared at the ceiling. Wedding Lillianna was supposed to make her less of a distraction, not more. Of course, she had only been his wife for a few hours, but all the same…

He laughed at himself, but stilled when she stirred restlessly. He did not relax until she had settled again, and then he found himself staring at the ceiling once more. What had he thought? That he would marry her and one joining would banish the distraction? He clenched his jaw as he realized he had expected just that. It would take time, clearly, and determination on his part.

With that in mind, he decided to rise before dawn and work with his men to prepare them for battle. He would not linger in this bed, no matter how much he wished to.

When Lillianna awoke the next morning, Angus was gone. She thought she must have slept late, so he had simply crept out of bed, to avoid waking her, but when she glanced out the window of their bedchamber, she realized the sun was barely in the sky. She dressed hurriedly, fearing perhaps something had happened and he had been needed, but as she made her way downstairs and into the great hall, she found it all but empty except for Greer, who looked like she had just woken up herself.

Lillianna paused in the doorway, not wanting to have a confrontation with Greer but wishing to learn where Angus had gone. "Have you seen your brother?"

Greer put down the goblet she had just raised to her lips and turned in her seat to look at Lillianna. "Aye," she said, a rather smug smile appearing on her face. "He is training, as he always does when he is home. He rises before dawn, gathers his commanders, and trains them so that they can then train the men they are in charge of." She arched her eyebrows at Lillianna. "Did ye think he would laze his day away in bed with ye? Especially with the threat of an enemy coming our way?"

A blush heated Lillianna's face as she realized she had foolishly hoped he might spend some time with her this morning.

Greer laughed derisively, likely seeing Lillianna's blush. "Ye are his wife, nae one of his warriors. Yer worth to him comes in the night."

Anger flared in Lillianna. She fisted her hands, marched toward Greer, and slapped her palm on the table beside the woman. She understood Greer had endured great loss, but so had she. "Your brother did not marry me simply to bed me," Lillianna said, though the slightest bit of doubt crept in, which infuriated her.

A mocking smile twisted Greer's lips. "Of course he did nae wed ye just to bed ye. He will also use yer powers when the need arises. Mark my words."

Lillianna sucked in a sharp breath. The woman knew exactly what to say to hurt her the most. "I could just take the brooch off and destroy it," Lillianna bit out. "Then I'd have no powers, and you would see that your brother does not even care."

"Do it, then," Greer challenged. "Destroy yer brooch. Take the chance that Angus dunnae care, but if he does…"

Lillianna's belly clenched in fear. She swung away from the woman with the desire to race out of the room, but she didn't want Greer to know just how much she had affected her. "You're wrong, Greer," Lillianna said, hearing the stiffness in her tone. "But I'll not argue with you."

"Thank God for that!" the woman said, slammed her goblet down behind Lillianna, and marched past her and out of the room. Lillianna slumped into the chair that Greer had vacated. She sat there as doubt battered her. Had she been duped?

No! Angus had been honest. He was not going to use her. He did not care about her powers.

Determined not to let Greer steal the happiness she had found with Angus, Lillianna broke her fast. The great hall slowly began to fill with people, and soon Mari came in, and they sat companionably side by side as Mari ate. Then Allisdair joined them, and he offered to show Lillianna how to wield a sword.

"I can show ye how to shoot a bow and arrow, too," Mari said.

"How did you learn?" she asked Mari.

"Angus taught me. He says the greatest worth each member of our clan has is in how they can help the clan, so I asked him to teach me. That way, when a battle comes, I can be of value."

Excitement bubbled inside Lillianna. She would learn how to wield a sword and shoot, and Angus would see how valuable she could be without her powers. But first she wanted to find Angus and, at the very least, simply say good morning. "Mari, can you show me where Angus trains his men?"

Mari looked hesitant. "I can, but he dunnae like to be interrupted during training."

Allisdair nodded his agreement.

"I understand," Lillianna said. "I won't distract him. I simply want to tell him good morning, and then the three of us can go somewhere else to train."

Mari and Allisdair exchanged a doubtful look, but after a moment, Mari nodded.

Not long later, the three of them stood at the edge of a sharp incline. At the bottom of the incline was a large, flat piece of land that sat between two rock walls. Angus was training with six men, one of whom Lillianna could tell was

Ross. Angus and Ross circled each other, swinging their swords, and the other men stood around them. When Ross swung his sword perilously close to Angus's head, Lillianna tensed.

"Do they ever wound each other?" she asked, her heart beating hard.

"Aye," Allisdair answered, only to be elbowed by Mari.

"They are nae bad wounds," Mari added.

"Well, except once," Allisdair said, and then he grunted when Mari elbowed him again.

It was with this worry in mind that Lillianna started down the rocky hill with Allisdair and Mari arguing behind her. A little over halfway down, the siblings really started squabbling after Allisdair let it slip that someone had lost an arm last year in training. At the exact moment Allisdair shared that information, Ross swung his sword at Angus, and it seemed to Lillianna that it would strike Angus's chest. She screamed in fright, missed her step, and went flying down the remainder of the hill, the rocks cutting her as she went.

Angus could do little more than stare at the sight of Lillianna falling down the steep incline that led to where he was training. Her scream had jerked his attention from training, and because he'd not been focused, Ross's sword had sliced Angus's right arm. But the burning pain in his arm did not compare with the near-suffocating terror gripping him as he helplessly watched Lillianna tumble while Allisdair and Mari raced after her.

When she landed with a thud on her back, unmoving, it was as if the terror holding him in place released its grip. He darted to her, reaching her at the same time that Mari and Allisdair did, and as he kneeled beside her, she blinked up at him. He felt himself tremble with relief that she was alive. "Are ye hurt verra badly, lass?"

She wiggled her arms and then her legs, and smiled sheepishly. "No. It's more my pride," she said, her gaze cutting to the rocks she had just tumbled down. She looked back to him. "Well, that could have been bad." Her tone was so casual that anger filled him. She should never be so cavalier about her life.

"Damn it, Lillianna," he roared, not realizing how loud his voice was until Lillianna and his siblings flinched. Behind him, his men had gathered around them, and now they backed away immediately, including Ross. Allisdair and Mari hovered loyally and foolishly by Lillianna's side. Angus was pleased by the attachment they were already forming to her but irritated that they had not given him and his wife some privacy.

"Give me a moment alone with Lillianna," he commanded of his siblings, trying and failing to temper the anger in his tone.

Lillianna sat up, glaring at him, and then scrambled to her feet. "You don't have to be such a brute to Allisdair and Mari!"

He thought perhaps she was embarrassed, but he could not allow her to order him about in front of his men. "Lillianna," he said, struggling to quell his emotion, "dunnae think to ever order me about again."

Mari and Allisdair both cast their gazes down and slowly edged away from him and Lillianna. She set her hands on her hips. "Why not? Because I'm now your wife? Your chattel?"

He ground his teeth at the situation he found himself in.

He could not explain in front of his men that her taking that tone with him, her ordering him about, would cause him to lose respect from his men, and a leader who did not have full respect was less effective. Men in battle may decide not to obey important orders.

"Aye," he bit out. "Ye are my wife; therefore, ye dunnae have the right."

She flinched as if he'd slapped her. "What rights do I have as *yer wife?*"

He looked at her, knowing full well he was in a terrible spot. If he answered as he should in front of the men, he would hurt her. If he answered as he wanted to so as not hurt her, he would look weak to his men.

She made a derisive noise and waved a hand at him. "The right to warm your bed?" she demanded, and he felt himself grow hot at her tone. "The right to foretell the future when you desire it?" An angry tic began at his jaw. "The right to stay out of your way during the day, so as not to distract you?"

"Woman," he growled, barely resisting the urge to shake some sense into his beautiful, fiery wife. She had no notion of her worth, so she assumed he did not think her worth very much. It infuriated him, but he could say none of that now, not with an audience of his commanders. "Ye already distracted me." He jerked his bloody arm forward to show her. "See this?" Her eyes widened, and her mouth parted on a soft cry. "It's lucky for me that my moment of being distracted by yer scream did nae cost me my arm. I kinnae afford to be distracted. I told ye that before."

"Don't worry," she flung out, "I will not distract you again. I merely came here to say good morning, but I suppose that is not something you wish from me." With that, she turned on her heel and started climbing the incline she had just tumbled down. He forced himself to stand there and not go after her, though everything in him longed to do just that. It was because of that overwhelming desire to do so that he stood still. He had to control himself when it came to her, and this was the first step.

He trained most of the day, not relinquishing the task to his commanders' hands as he normally did. Once he had trained them, he worked with each of them and the men they were responsible for. When he was in the thick of the training, all his attention was on that, but the moment they were finished for the day, and he was making his way back to the castle, thoughts of Lillianna took over. What had she done all day? Was she still angry with him?

He washed the sweat and grime off in the sea and then went in search of Lillianna. She was not in their bedchamber, so he assumed she was likely with Mari or Allisdair, and when he saw Ross on the way to the great hall for supper, Ross told Angus that Mari and Allisdair were training Lillianna.

Angus frowned at the news. Training her for what?

He found the three of them by the horse stables, and he stood just behind the trees, watching his wife. She had a determined look on her face as she attempted to shoot an arrow at a target over and over again. She was not a terrible shot, but she had a great deal yet to learn.

Allisdair clapped for her when she skimmed the target, and she grinned at him. "If ye keep this hard work up, Lillianna, ye will be better with the bow and arrow than Mari."

Mari stuck her tongue out at Allisdair. "She could be better than ye with the sword by the end of the week," she teased, feigning a lunge at Allisdair with an invisible sword.

Angus swallowed a knot in his throat. Had Lillianna

asked his siblings to train her? Was this an effort to show him she had worth outside of the legend? God's teeth, he hated himself at the moment for adding to the feelings of unworthiness she was already burdened with. She needed him to let her in more, but how could he do that and not lose more of himself to her? And if he lost more of himself, how much more distracted by her would he become?

He left them then and made his way to supper to await her, determined to somehow show her tonight she was valuable to him and that it had nothing to do with her powers or her body.

When he sat down at the dais that night, Greer turned to him. "I heard ye nearly lost yer arm during training because ye were distracted by yer wife." She gave him an accusatory look.

"I have everything under control," he said, picking up his wine goblet and taking a long drink.

"What do ye have under control?" Mari asked as she, Allisdair, and Lillianna came up to the dais.

Angus indicated the space beside him to Lillianna as he stood. "Ye will sit here. Beside me."

She arched her eyebrows at him. "Are you certain I'm worthy to sit by you, *Laird*?"

"As long as ye are still a seer," Ross said, chuckling.

Lillianna visibly flinched and went pale.

Angus gripped his goblet so hard he thought it might break. "Ross is only teasing, lass. Are ye nae, ye clot-heid!"

Ross's eyes went wide, and he tossed his bread onto his plate. "Aye. I'm sorry, Lillianna. It was unthinking of me. I'm used to teasing my siblings, and we bait each other. I need to remember ye are nae one of us."

A different kind of hurt flitted across Lillianna's face, and Angus thought he would have gladly strangled his brother in that moment if he was not his brother. He knew Ross had only meant to make it better, but he'd made it far worse.

"I don't have much of an appetite," Lillianna said and hurried from the dais. A tense silence fell in her absence, and Angus thought what to say to his siblings.

"Angus, I'm sorry," Ross said.

Angus waved a hand at him. "I ken it, but watch what ye say to her. She needs to feel she has worth," he said, trying to explain. He didn't want to say more and tell them too much about her personal life or how vulnerable he thought she felt. He knew she would not like that. All his siblings nodded, but Greer gave him an odd conspiratorial smile. He thought momentarily to talk to her right then and set her straight on Lillianna, but he wanted to go to his wife. "Greer, come see me in the great hall first thing in the morning. I wish to speak to ye privately."

"Of course," Greer said with surprising cheerfulness.

He shoved back from the table, dismissing his sister's odd behavior, and started for the great hall door after Lillianna. He got no more than four steps when Hector Fraser stood before him.

"I saw yer lovely wife rushing from the room," Hector said.

Angus narrowed his eyes on Hector. "Were ye watching my wife?"

"Nay, nay. I was coming in when she fled. Jealous over her, eh?" Hector chuckled.

When Angus simply glared at the man, Hector began to fumble and fidget. Then he said, "I hear some of the clan whispering that the brooch yer wife wears is the Brooch of Lagothmier and that she has the gift of sight."

"Ye should nae listen to whispers, Hector," Angus said,

bringing his fingers to his sword. "When do ye plan to leave my home?" He'd rather not throw Hector out, given he did have regard for his cousins, and Simon was a fellow Renegade, but Angus's dislike for Hector had increased tenfold in the last few breaths."

"Tomorrow," Hector said. "Likely by nightfall."

"I'll see you in the morning, then," Angus replied, glad he'd soon be rid of the man.

When he opened his bedchamber door, Lillianna was sitting on the edge of the bed in her thin cotton underclothes. Moonlight sent a shaft of light over her face, and it glinted off her necklace. She looked like a nymph with her wide eyes and wild hair. And when the expression on her face turned tense and she seemed to be staring through him rather than at him, he closed the door and went to her, kneeling in front of her. "What is it? Did ye encounter someone and have a vision?"

He regretted mentioning her powers immediately. Wariness settled on her face, and she moved over so his arm was not brushing her leg. He felt her loss acutely, but he did not reach for her, wishing to prove to himself he could control the overwhelming desire to touch her.

"You hurt me today," she said quietly into the silence that had stretched between them.

"I ken," he admitted. He had never been a man to apologize. He was laird. But with her, the rules he lived by had to change a bit. He saw it now in a way he had not previously understood.

She looked at him with obvious surprise and wariness, and took a deep breath. "If you cannot afford to be distracted by me, where does that leave me? Us?"

He tugged a hand through his hair in frustration. "At night, I can be consumed by ye, lose myself in ye, but in the daytime, I must be focused totally on being the laird. I don't want to hurt ye, but it must be this way. I kinnae repeat my past."

"And you think you will do so because of me?" she asked, her eyes beseeching him to explain.

He felt the fragile bond between them as if invisible tethers had formed. He wanted that bond, despite the fact that it would entangle him with her even further, and he feared breaking it with the wrong words. "I think if I allow thoughts of ye to control me in the day, then aye, I could easily make a mistake. Let an enemy best me. Lower my guard when it should be up. Allow ye to defy me in front of my men and lose their respect."

Her eyes widened, and she opened her mouth as if to say something. But then she gave a little shake of her head, and a look of such sadness crossed her face that he felt her pain to the depths of his soul. "What is it?" he asked, wanting to make right what was hurting her.

"I want more," she said simply, a single tear slipping down her cheek.

"More? More of what?" he asked, sensing a gap growing between them.

Her eyes locked with his. "More than you want to give me."

He stood and pulled her up to him, the lengths of their bodies pressing together. She tensed and squeezed her eyes shut. She grew rigid and her face pale, but when she opened her eyes, they were not golden with visions of the future but the green that he loved so much. "Can it nae be enough that I give ye all of me in the night when we hold each other?"

She sighed and rested her cheek against his shoulder. "For now," she whispered. "For now, I will make it enough.

But I've become greedy," she said, tracing her fingers over his chest and then low to the edge of his braies. "You have awakened a part of me I never even knew existed, and I want things I never dared to desire before.

"What sort of things?" he teased, his wife's delectable body bringing his desire for her to the very forefront of his mind.

"This," she said, taking his hand and putting it over her breast. Her heart raced under his touch, and the very air between them seemed to thicken with the yearning they both shared. He wanted to dive headfirst into that bliss, where they could both let go. He cupped her other breast, and the moan it elicited from her sent a white-hot shaft through him. He told himself to go slow, but when he gave her a gentle kiss, she wound her hands around his neck and ground her hips into him. His kiss became immediately ravenous, and soon they were tearing at each other's clothes. She might be just as desperate for him as he was for her!

When they stood bare, she tugged his head close to her breasts and cried out her pleasure when he flicked his tongue over one hard bud and then the other. He decided to tease and torment her until she was screaming for release, but as he left her breasts to kiss his way down between her creamy thighs, she grabbed his shoulder and stopped him.

"No," she said, panting. "This time I will bring you pleasure first." Before he could respond, she scrambled to her knees and took him in her hot mouth, pulling on his shaft with long strokes that made him lose his senses.

All his blood seemed to rush to where she worked her magic, and when she brought him to the edge of where he knew he'd not return, he grabbed her by the arms and lifted her on top of him. With a knowing grin, she took him into her welcoming body. Her core tightened around him, and then he simply could not think. His body took over where his mind left off, and he slid in and out of her, wanting to possess all of her and, God help him, wanting to give her all of him.

Chapter Twenty-One

Early the next morning in the great hall, Angus tugged a hand through his hair in irritation. He glanced at the missive Simon had sent to him this morning. King Edward was set to attack Edinburgh Castle. It stood as a symbol of freedom to the Scottish people and Edward meant to take it. To make matters worse, Robbie was riding by the king's side to be seen as a traitor by all Scots who did not know the truth.

And Robert is now wed to Elizabeth de Burgh.

The words Simon had written still shocked him. Robbie obviously trusted Elizabeth, but Angus still did not. He'd ride out to Edinburgh and rally with the Scots there who would try to defend the castle, and hopefully he'd see Robbie. He'd not tell him of his own marriage, though, not until he could learn for certain if Elizabeth de Burgh was plotting against Robbie.

His need to depart had come sooner than he'd anticipated, and he had to ensure things between Lillianna and Greer were settled before he left, otherwise his mind would be here at his home, with his wife, rather than in Edinburgh and on the battle where it needed to be. When the great hall door squeaked open, he looked up as Greer walked into the room. She pulled the door behind her, and as she started toward him, he rose and met her halfway. He had many things to do before he departed, and he hoped this conversation with Greer would be quick.

He was trying to find the right words when Greer spoke. "What is the plan?" she asked.

He frowned at his sister. "The plan? For what? My defenses against Drumlan and Belfaine should attack come?"

"Ye can cease pretending now," Greer said with a chuckle.

"I can cease pretending what?" he asked, truly baffled.

Greer scowled at him. "That ye wed that wench for any reason other than the fact that she is a seer and will aid us in defeating our enemies."

He stared at his sister in disbelief. How was it that he had failed to see that she truly thought such a thing? He sighed out a long breath. This conversation was going to take longer than he'd wished. He could insist that he did not wed Lillianna for her powers, but he suspected his sister would simply not believe him. He needed to get at the heart of what was making her dislike Lillianna so much, which he suspected was merely her fear that he would repeat the mistakes of his past, as she had told him previously.

"Greer, ye dunnae need to fret. It's different with Lillianna than it was with Isla."

Greer narrowed her eyes at him. "I ken it's different. Ye dunnae care for her."

Images of Lillianna from the day he had first met her until last night as they joined flew through his head. "Nay, Greer. I *do* care for her," he admitted to her, as well as to himself.

"Nay!" Greer moved as if to rush from the room. He caught her gently by the elbow just as she was about to open the door and turned her to face him. Fear swam in her eyes. *Damnation.* He searched for the words to ease Greer's trepidation. "Lillianna is good, Greer, whereas Isla was nae. Lillianna would nae ever do anything to harm ye or—"

"Cease this!" Greer fairly shouted, the emotions on her face stormy. "She is nae different! She's tricked ye! Ye are distracted just as ye were with Isla. And one of us—" Greer took a ragged breath "—one of us will die again. I kinnae take it! I will nae stand it! If ye kinnae stop yerself, I'll stop ye!"

"God's teeth, Greer!" Angus roared. "If ye dunnae listen to reason, I'll be forced to send ye away until ye will. I kinnae be fearful of what ye will do to Lillianna while I'm gone. I need to ken that she is safe, that all of ye are safe, nae be worried that ye are going to betray her."

Greer grabbed his hands suddenly. "Dunnae let her use ye as Isla did. She is the niece of the king's closest friend and advisor! Cousin to the king's goddaughter. Think ye she dunnae conspire against ye? Against us? Dunnae be so foolish and controlled by lust! Use her. Use her visions to defeat our enemies. Ye can make her fall in love with ye, and she will do whatever ye ask. We can finally destroy Belfaine, and then we will nae have to worry anymore that he will hurt us again. Say ye will finally set to rights what ye caused."

Pain and regret squeezed his chest, and he saw clearly what he'd failed to see all these years, or maybe just refused to see because of his guilt and need to punish himself. True love was not a weakness. He had chosen poorly with Isla. He had ignored that she was not a good person because he'd been in the throes of lust. It was not so with Lillianna. She was good and had proven it with every word, every action. She made him stronger.

He *loved* her.

The realization sucked the air from his lungs. He was

not a man to talk of soft emotions, but he'd have to find a way, so he could help soften his sister's heart, which he himself had a hand in hardening.

"I will do as ye ask," he said, squeezing her hand. "I will set to rights what I have caused."

Lillianna stood shaking at the great hall door. She could hardly believe what she had just heard. The thing she had feared most was happening: Angus had agreed to use her. She tore herself away from the door and raced down the passage to the courtyard, bypassing surprised servants along the way. When she barreled through the door, into the fading sunlight, she faltered, her thoughts colliding in her head like violent waves.

Surely, she had misunderstood what she had heard. Her mind replayed the conversation between Angus and Greer, and Lillianna gave a bitter laugh. She did not see how she could have misunderstood their words. And now she had to get away from Angus. She had to get away from him because when he was near, she forgot to be afraid of men and she did foolish things like wed one, open up to him, and want to make him fall in love with her.

Tears blinded her as she ran across the courtyard toward the stables, and as she approached, she almost slammed into Allisdair who was coming around the corner. She stopped just short of colliding with him and reached out a hand, touching his elbow. "I'm sorry, Allisdair."

He frowned as he looked at her. "What's the matter, Lillianna?"

She swallowed the need to complain about his brother. She refused to put anything between them, despite the fact that Angus deserved it. He'd duped her. Or if he hadn't duped her, he'd been all too willing to do so now when asked to by his sister. Lillianna needed to be alone and think. She was wed to him, but did that mean she was stuck here? Could she ride to the MacLeods and seek their protection? The thought of leaving Angus, of never seeing him or being held by him again, ripped her heart open, sorrow and anger spilling out.

"Lillianna?" Allisdair prodded. "Do ye want me to fetch Angus?"

"No! No, I, well, we had a fight," she lied, unable to think of anything else to say. "I simply need to ride out and clear my head. Do you understand? I just need to be alone."

"Aye, but dunnae ride long. Dark is approaching. And dunnae go farther than the cliffs or Angus will be sore that ye risked yer safety. And take my dagger," he said, holding out his blade.

She took the dagger. "He'd only be angry out of fear of losing me because of my powers," she grumbled, then bit her lip on saying the foolish words aloud in front of Allisdair. She drew him into a hug. "I'm sorry, Allisdair. I should not have said that." Though it was true. "I'm vexed."

The boy awkwardly patted her back. "Shall I fetch a horse for ye?"

She shook her head. "No, I can manage."

"All right, but remember what I said: dunnae venture farther than the cliffs."

She nodded and watched as Allisdair walked away. He looked back several times, so she finally called, "I'm all right, truly," but her voice sounded false to her own ears.

It didn't take long to get a destrier, and once she was mounted, she sent the horse galloping out of the courtyard and toward the cliffs. She had half a mind to turn the horse around and ride toward the bridge, past the guards, and all the way to the MacLeods, but she was not so foolish as that. If she was going to flee Angus, she would do so in the early-morning hours so she'd have the safety of light.

She rode to the edge of the cliffs, then dismounted and tethered the destrier to a nearby tree. She headed toward the ledge that overlooked the ocean, the wind blowing a fine mist of salt and whipping her hair against her cheeks. Hot tears coursed over her cold skin, and she raised her arms over her head, capturing her hair and working to fashion it into a knot. Her heart squeezed in anguish as she thought about Angus and all she had imprudently allowed herself to hope. Her silent tears turned to loud sobs. The wind howled around her, and the waves crashed into the cliffs below. The ferocity of the stormy water matched her mood, she thought bitterly, her numb fingers still clumsily trying to tie her hair. She had walked into deception like a fool. The swell of pain enveloping her made her feel ill.

Suddenly, heat enveloped her from behind, and her reckless heart leaped at the thought that it was Angus. She clenched her teeth and whirled around to tell him what she thought of him, but her words died on her tongue. Icy fear twisted through her. A stranger stood there with a dagger pointed at her.

Angus shifted self-consciously as he fumbled with his words to Greer. Trying to talk of love and his heart was more difficult than any battle he'd ever fought. "And so," he said, finishing, "it is nae softness that is bad."

"Love?" Greer asked. "Do ye mean love?"

He jerked his head in a nod, feeling as awkward as a

newborn bairn. "Aye. That... That did nae make me weak, nor make me lose my good sense. I ignored what Isla showed me of her character time and again, because I wanted to ignore it, because I wanted her."

"Ye mean ye lusted for her," Greer clarified, arching her eyebrows.

His neck heated, but he nodded, thinking briefly that he wished Lillianna could have had this conversation with Greer instead of him. Lillianna would have said it better. He could have told her of his heart more easily. He prayed Greer would hear him and accept the words, because he damn sure did not want to try to explain it again.

"How can ye be certain ye dunnae just want Lillianna?" Greer demanded, crossing her arms over her chest and giving him a suspicious look.

"It's different," he said, Robbie's words about his chest tightening suddenly appearing in his memory. "She makes my chest tight. She steals my air. And I have watched her with open eyes. She is good and true. Allisdair, Mari, and Ross all see it."

Greer bit her lip. "Nae anyone liked Isla."

"True," he agreed. "Ross hated her. So did Ma and Da, but I ignored them."

She looked at him, her lower lip started to tremble, and then she began to cry. "I'm sorry, Angus. I will try. Honestly, I will."

Before he could respond, a knock came at the door. "Enter," he bellowed.

The great hall door opened, and Ross strode in. "We've a problem," he said by way of greeting.

"Aye? What is it?" Angus asked.

"One of the men saw some riders in the woods, but when he tried to chase them down, they escaped."

Angus tensed, immediately thinking upon Belfaine and Drumlan. "Did ye—" The horns announcing intruders began to blow, and Angus nodded. "Ye did alert the guards," he said, not needing to ask the question anymore.

"Of course," Ross said with a smug smile. "Ye can rely upon me, Brother. Ye've taught me well. I also told the guards to bring anyone outside of the main gates into the castle grounds."

"Excellent. Let me tell Lillianna I'm riding out, and we will see what enemies we can catch," Angus said, anticipation of hopefully finding and crushing one or both of his enemies filling him.

"Angus," Allisdair said from the door.

Angus looked to the door, not having realized his youngest brother had entered the room. "Aye?" he asked, baffled when Allisdair glared at him.

Allisdair marched into the room, his lips puckered, and folded his arms across his chest. "What did ye do to Lillianna? I saw her at the stables, and she was crying."

"The stables?" Fear shot through him. "God's blood." He started toward the door. "She was nae headed out of the main castle grounds, was she?"

"Nay. I warned her nae to ride farther than the sea cliffs, and she assured me she would nae. I even gave her my dagger for protection from animals. But what did ye do?" Allisdair asked again. "When I said ye'd be angry if she put herself in danger, she said you'd only be angry because ye would fear losing her because of her powers. Angus, is that true?"

"God's bones," Angus muttered, looking from Greer to the door.

Greer's face paled. "She heard us."

"Aye," he said, never more certain of anything in his

life. She had heard what they'd said, though clearly not all of it. And if she had only overheard the bad part, then in her mind, everything she had feared of him was true. Pain lanced through him at how devastated she must feel. "Ross, await me in the courtyard with the men. I need to find Lillianna and speak with her before I ride out. I need to try to explain what she heard."

But would she even believe him?

Chapter Twenty-Two

"Ye'll be coming with me," the stranger growled, thrusting his dagger so close to Lillianna that it snagged her gown at her chest.

She swallowed past her fear, gripping the dagger that Allisdair had given her in her right hand. She hid the blade under her left arm, which was crossed over her right. "Who are you?"

The man bared his teeth in an almost feral smile. "I'm Hector Fraser. The man who ought to be laird of the Fraser clan."

She could not think what use he would have with her for a rivalry with his family. "Where is it you intend to take me, and why?" she demanded, trying to steal a glance behind her to see how close she was to the edge. Her breath froze in her lungs. She was not even one step away from falling, and this time it would certainly be to her death as rocks jutted out from the cliffs at the bottom of the drop.

"Yer uncle," Hector said. "I bring ye to him, and he will help make me laird."

"My uncle," she echoed, fear strangling her. Devil take her uncle! "You would kill your family simply to be laird?" Would men do anything at all for power? Desolation made her want to cry out, but she'd not give this man the satisfaction.

"I'd kill my own mother, were she nae already dead, to rule the clan as I'm meant to. My father should have been laird, but he was weak and a cripple. He lost me my birthright, and now I will simply take it back," the man sneered.

The wind gusted hard, making Lillianna feel as if she would be blown off the cliff by the gale, or perhaps by betrayal. Her thoughts raced as she tried to figure out what to do. If she could slash the man's arm, knock his weapon away, and get around him, she thought she could escape. She sucked in a breath and her pulse increased as she brought the dagger up and flashed it at Hector's arm. The weapon cut through the material of his sleeve and met flesh. Hector bellowed his pain and dropped his dagger, and Lillianna lunged to the right and attempted to dash around him. He grabbed her by the arm, and she tried to yank free, her feet sliding over the hard ground. Her heart exploded with fright as she was tugged toward the ledge, while struggling desperately against Hector.

※

Time slowed with a violent jerk before Angus's eyes. Yet he was still running. His boots pounded the ground, and each step seemed to jar his stopped heart. Lillianna swiveled toward Hector near the edge of the cliff. Was she trying to break free of the man? What in God's name—

Hector tumbled backward, and Angus roared as Hector and Lillianna flew over the ledge and out of view. Consuming fear flooded him, but he pushed harder to close the last few steps that had remained between him and Lillianna. Panic and loss rioted within him. He fell to his knees and looked over the side of the cliff for Lillianna's still body. He cried out and began to shake. Lillianna clung to the ledge directly below him, which jutted out just enough that she had somehow managed to grasp it.

"Hold on!" he cried out, coming to his belly and hanging his arms over to grasp her. When his fingers grazed hers, hope flickered deep within. He scooted a bit closer to the edge and encircled one of her wrists while bracing himself on the ground with his other hand. There was just enough light left that the stark terror in her eyes was visible. "I'll nae let go, lass, I vow it. Release the ledge with one hand and push up."

She nodded and let go of the ledge. Her body swung heavy for one breath, but he shoved his palm into the ground, gritted his teeth, and began to pull her up with his right arm. After a moment, she grew lighter, seeming to have shoved against the ledge with her foot, and then he pulled her the rest of the way up and onto the ground he lay upon.

Sucking in ragged breaths, he pulled her on top of him, needing to assure himself she was alive, but she rolled immediately off him and scrambled to her feet. Her cheek was bleeding and her eyes were wide with pain.

"Did you save me for this?" she demanded, sobbing as she lifted the brooch away from her chest by its leather strap. "My uncle sent Hector to retrieve me for this. All of you want this, want my powers!"

The realization that he had nearly lost her took all of his control. He stepped toward her, and seeing her flinch, he snatched the bauble from her neck, the strap breaking. He twisted around and flung it over the ledge into the raging ocean below. Then he swiveled to the left where she now stood, yanked her to him, and cupped her cheeks. "I should have done that the minute ye told me what the brooch was." Her lips parted, but she said nothing, so he continued. "I love ye," he said, emotion nearly choking him. "I love ye, and I dunnae care about the powers that brooch brought ye. All I care about is ye. Mayhap one day, ye will love me, too."

Hope and fear crashed together and made her thoughts spin almost dizzyingly, and then she froze in shock as her body began to tingle with power. She still had her abilities! Light flashed in her mind, and the image of her mother and then her other female ancestors rolled through her mind.

Yer heart is open, her mother said in a soft, happy whisper.

The world around her faded, and she let it so she could see the vision. She was no longer afraid of the visions or of love. She had worth beyond her power. Angus saw it, but more importantly, she saw it, too. Her powers were a gift that she could use to aid those she loved. She inhaled a long, deep breath and opened her eyes to the future.

Belfaine stood in his courtyard, his warriors facing him. "The most important thing is to get the seer," *he said to his men.* "As long as we capture the seer, I dunnae care if we take MacLorh's castle this day. For the seer will be able to tell me who to fight and when. I need her!"

Lillianna's vision blurred, and a new one immediately appeared.

Angus faced Belfaine, and they slashed at each other as men stood around them, Belfaine's warriors on one side and Angus's on the other.

Lillianna hissed in a breath. She had seen this future before.

Her heartbeat thudded in her ears, and she turned to her right. Greer stood beside her, and Isla Belfaine stood beside Greer. Isla yanked out a dagger and glared at Lillianna.

"They fight for ye only because of yer powers!" she hissed. "And I lose either way! If my brother wins and he takes ye, ye will be a ghost that Angus dunnae ever forget. If Angus wins and he keeps he, I will nae ever have his love again. Ye must die!"

Before Lillianna could respond, Greer gasped and pointed, and Lillianna turned to see Angus's sword arcing down toward Belfaine's head. He struck a hard blow, and Belfaine fell to his knees. A loud cheer went up among Angus's men.

The world parted again, and Lillianna gulped for breath, realizing she was enfolded in the protective embrace of Angus's arms. Then war horns began to blast, splitting the descending night with the sound of impending terror. Angus stiffened and pulled away, but she grasped his arm, their gazes locking. "I love you, too," she vowed, the wonderment and acceptance of it filling her. "I love you, I do."

The relief that swept his face made her laugh with joy. He had thrown her brooch away to prove himself. His mouth claimed hers for a brief second before he broke the kiss. "I must go see what enemy approaches. Get to the castle and—"

"Belfaine," she interrupted. "Belfaine approaches, but he is here for me. He wants me and my powers, Angus. Offer to fight him in one-on-one combat with the winner taking me. That is how ye will stop bloodshed this day."

"Nay!" he said, the response nearly violent in its intensity.

She placed her hand on his heart. "Yes," she assured him as her blood slowed with the realization and acceptance that because of her love for him, and because of her power, she could save countless lives that would otherwise be lost in battle. "I had a vision of your future. Because I love you, I do not need the brooch any longer."

She heard his sharp intake of surprise, to which she nodded. "You must trust me. Meet Belfaine at the bridge and offer to fight him. You *will* win."

"Nay," Angus stubbornly said again. "I will nae chance ye that way."

"You are not risking me, I vow it! I have seen it, Angus. Please listen to me." She could see he was about to deny her once more, and she searched her mind for the words to convince him. "Do not throw good sense to the wind as you did the brooch. I have the power to see the future, and I have seen yours. I would rather die than risk your life. You will prevail and save hundreds of lives by doing what I say!"

His eyes narrowed on her. "Ye're certain?"

"Yes," she said, feeling the truth of her words in her bones.

"Very well," he finally relented, and then grabbed her hand. "Ye did nae happen to see how I could convince Belfaine to agree to one-on-one combat with me, did ye?"

"No, but perhaps I can try to see it now," she said. She grabbed his hands, and then her body went rigid.

When the vision was over, she opened her eyes to find Angus looking at her with concern. She smiled at her husband, feeling empowered by her abilities. "Listen carefully, my love, for I will tell you exactly what to say."

※

Not long later, after leaving Lillianna in the safety of the courtyard with his sisters and some of his warriors, the hooves of Angus's horse clopped against the bridge as he rode away from the rest of his warriors to meet Belfaine in the middle of the bridge that led to the entrance of Angus's castle. At the far end of the bridge, Belfaine's warriors were gathered, while Angus's men were gathered on the end closest to his home. Lillianna was in the courtyard with his sisters where he had left her, despite her protests that she should ride with him. Until he knew Belfaine would agree to one-on-one combat, Angus would not risk her.

He pulled his horse to a stop as Belfaine did the same, keeping his right hand on his sword, ready to engage in battle if needed. "I'm surprised nae to see Drumlan with ye," Angus remarked.

"Ye shoud nae be," Belfaine replied. "I killed him."

"Because of the brooch?" Angus asked, moving the conversation in the direction Lillianna had told him to.

"Aye. He hid that he had the brooch from me all along. He was going to try to defeat me." Belfaine shrugged. "So I killed him, and now I am here to kill ye, take yer castle, and yer wife."

Angus let a slow, hopefully mocking smile curl his lips. "The brooch is gone," Angus said flatly. "Lillianna threw it into the sea so none of us would ever be able to use her again."

Belfaine stared at Angus in obvious disbelief. "Ye lie!"

"Nay," Angus said easily, "I dunnae. She kenned I wished to use her, so she bested me. I dunnae want her for she will nae ever love me, but I'm nae going to just give her to ye. If ye want her, ye must fight me one-on-one. If I win, ye will leave here without a battle this day. I'd rather nae lose good men. And ye will leave here without Lillianna. But if ye win, ye can take Lillianna and return to fight me another day."

Belfaine grinned. "I'll take that offer," he quickly agreed.

"She'll nae ever love ye, ye ken," Angus said, prodding the man's pride as Lillianna had instructed him to do. "She'll nae ever love ye so she will nae ever have her powers."

"Ye underestimate me, Angus," Belfaine said. "I will gain the wench's heart, and then I will ken exactly when to take yer home, and then I will be Lord of the Isles."

"Ye can try," Angus answered, "but we both ken I'm the better swordsman."

"Ha!" Belfaine sneered. "Ye will rue those words this day."

"I'll see ye on the battlefield shortly," Angus responded, and as Belfaine turned his horse away, Angus did the same.

Angus quickly rode to his men, dismounted, and started toward the courtyard where Lillianna was waiting. She came running toward him as he made his way through the gate, and when he nodded and smiled, she let out a cry of joy and threw herself into his arms. He enfolded his wife in his embrace and kissed her. When they pulled apart, he said, "It worked exactly as ye said it would."

She grinned. "Of course it did, Husband. I'm a seer."

―・❦・―

Not long later, in the very spot Angus normally trained his men to meet their enemies, Angus was fighting his longtime foe. Despite the fact that Lillianna had seen this future and knew Angus would prevail, she was very tense.

Lillianna glanced around the large assembly of Angus's and Belfaine's warriors, who stood in a circle around Angus and Belfaine. To Lillianna's left were Greer, Allisdair, Mari, and then Grant. It did not exactly mirror her vision, as Isla was not beside Greer. Not yet.

Lillianna had no doubt Angus would prevail, but still,

her stomach was in knots, so when the first clash of steel resounded, she jumped at the noise. Greer tugged on her sleeve. "Lillianna, does this match what ye saw?"

Lillianna tore her gaze away from Angus, who had just started to circle Belfaine, and glanced at Greer, whose face was lined with fright. On Lillianna's right side stood Ross and then Belfaine's men.

Lillianna thought for one brief moment of her vision of Greer trying to decide whether to betray her or not. That vision had not yet come to pass. Had the future been changed somehow? Her mother had told her once that it was possible but great alterations in how a person felt were required for a path to change. Did Greer no longer hate Lillianna? Her thoughts were pulled from the question by the sound of steel hitting steel once more.

Angus and Belfaine circled each other, their bodies only visible by the light of the moon and the torches the men in the circle were holding. Lillianna knew Angus had given orders to his men that if Belfaine tried to break the agreement they'd made, they were to pour out and fight. Many of them were even hidden on the cliffs around them. She felt certain it would not come to that, but she had to admit knowing that he'd made a contingency plan did bring her comfort.

When Belfaine's sword left a bloody mark across Angus's chest, she cried out, and at that moment, a hand grabbed her arm. Lillianna turned her head to find Isla to her right. Ross was no longer there. Fear snaked through her. The vision did not match, but mayhap they never matched precisely.

Isla showed the flash of a dagger from underneath her cloak. "I'll kill ye," she said. "I'll kill ye, and then Angus will love me once more. I did nae ever want to betray him. My brother threatened to kill our sister if I did nae betray Angus those years ago! I had to do it, and I tried to tell Angus, but he would nae listen. He would nae believe me!"

"No," Lillianna said calmly, "he would not have cared or listened. Loyalty is everything to him, and you betrayed him. You should have trusted him."

"I'm setting things right," Isla growled. "My brother will fall! I have waited what seems like a lifetime for this chance to get close to Angus again. He will protect me. My brother will nae beat Angus, ye will be dead, and Angus will wed *me*. I will nae have to pretend to love my brother a day longer. I hate him!" Isla reached for Lillianna.

Lillianna scuttled to her left and smacked into Greer, who looked from Lillianna to Isla. Greer scrambled in front of Lillianna as if to shield her. Blood roared in Lillianna's ears as her vision from the past collided with the present.

"Move out of the way, Greer," Isla panted. "I dunnae wish to kill ye."

Greer nodded. "I see that," she responded as Ross suddenly appeared behind Isla without her noticing it. Ross's arm encircled the woman's waist, and as she went to slash at him, Lillianna lunged forward and took Isla's dagger.

"You," she said, pointing the dagger at the cursing woman, "have caused enough trouble."

"Lillianna!" Greer gasped, and Lillianna spun toward Angus, certain Greer's summons had to do with him. When she saw Angus on his knees and Belfaine's sword arcing down toward Angus's neck, stark terror surged through her. She'd been wrong! Her vision was wrong! Without hesitation, she lifted the dagger in her hand and flung it toward Belfaine. It struck him in the arm and gave Angus the chance he needed. He rolled onto his back, jumped to his feet, and sent his left foot into Belfaine's knee. The the man fell to the ground as Angus brought his sword swiftly up and then down upon Belfaine's neck in a killing blow.

Shaking, Lillianna ran through the circle of men and into Angus's embrace. As his arms encircled her, she pressed her cheek against his thundering heart, listening to each beat and allowing her fear to calm.

"Ye saved me," he said in awe. "Ye throwing that dagger saved me."

"No," she said, pressing her lips to his. "We saved each other."

"You have been dreaming of this?" she asked later that night as the moon shone into her bedchamber with Angus.

After he and his men had ensured Belfaine's warriors and Isla had left, Angus had come to her and explained the entirety of his conversation with his sister. And somehow, during the time they had been talking, Angus had undressed Lillianna. The heat of his body enveloped her from behind as his warm hand slid around her waist and up between her breasts. His other hand came between her thighs, and he lowered them both to the ground, directing her. "Get on yer knees, aye?"

A thrill of anticipation shot through her as she did what he asked and he eased down behind her on his knees. He tugged her back until her spine pressed against the solid wall of his chest. Then he kissed her neck as his fingers found her center and then began their magic.

As he stoked the passion within her with each gentle circle of his fingers over her sensitive nerves, she writhed against him. His mouth sucked at her neck, and his fingers moved faster and faster, the pressure inside her becoming nearly unbearable. "Angus!"

Behind her, he chuckled, and his hand left her only for the other to come to the center of her back and gently push her forward until her hands were braced against the bed. Then he clutched her by the hips and slid into her with one long, consuming stroke that made her groan. He filled her completely, and when he started to move, she instinctually moved with him, arching into him as he drove into her faster and harder until they both screamed their release.

Panting and with limbs that felt too shaky to hold her up anymore, she climbed up onto the bed and flopped onto it. Angus came up behind her, the bed creaking, as he took her waist and pulled her into the protective circle of his embrace to spoon her. "Did ye like that?"

"Very much," she assured him. "In fact, I would not mind doing that again in bit," she added shyly.

He pushed up suddenly so that he was sitting and looking down at her. "I have to ride out at dusk for Edinburgh." His face and tone were so serious that she knew instantly he was riding to battle.

"For Bruce?" Lillianna asked.

"Aye," Angus said as he looked down into her suddenly worried eyes. The love he felt for her nearly choked him with its power. He traced a finger down her cheek and gently tugged her to her back so he could memorize the way she looked in the moonlight and think upon it all the night they would be parted.

He slid his hand over each breast, down her flat stomach, and over her round hips as he told her of the message he'd received. When he fell silent, a determined look swept across her face, and she placed a hand on his heart and on his cheek. The moment a vision overcame her, he knew. Her body stiffened, her lips parted, she sucked in a sharp breath, and her green eyes glowed golden. When it was over, her gaze turned bright like summer grass, and she focused on him. "Edinburgh will fall," she said, her voice sad and sure. "But you will live, as will Bruce."

The news hit him with a force that stole his ability to speak for a moment. *Edinburgh would fall. God's teeth.* She leaned up and kissed his shoulder, the simple gesture of love soothing him.

"Lillianna, I dunnae intend to tell Robbie we are wed until I can ken for certain if yer cousin betrayed him."

Lillianna surprised him when she nodded. "I know," she said. "I saw you talking to him in my vision, and I was not mentioned."

He expected her to argue with him to tell Robbie, and when she didn't, he said, "Ye're nae going to fight me on this?"

She eyed him askance. "Would I win?"

"Nay," he said, leaning down to brush his lips against his wife's.

She twined her arms around his neck. "I suspected not, given my vision, so I'll not waste my last few hours with you fighting a losing battle. I have something I want to tell you instead," she said, smiling secretively at him.

"What is it?" he asked, enchanted by the beguiling look on her face.

"I not only had a vision of you in Edinburgh but I had a vision of me. I was enormous in the vision, and I was standing in the kitchen cooking with Mari and Greer," she announced with a happy smile.

He frowned, confused by her comment and her apparent happiness about getting enormous. And then his heart clenched as his hand came to her belly. "Do ye mean—"

"Yes," she interrupted, placing her hand over his. "We've made a babe!"

Joy engulfed him as he kissed Lillianna and then pulled back to stare into her eyes. "Did ye see if I would be here? Will it be a boy or a girl?"

She laughed then, and he lay down beside her, drawing her to him. "I don't know," she said. "All I saw was me growing with child, but I need you here for the birth."

"I will be here," he vowed, kissing her forehead. "I will always be here for ye. And I will always love ye."

"And I, you, Angus. With all my heart and all my soul."

Epilogue

"I will not speak to Angus when he returns from Edinburgh!" Lillianna shrieked as another pain gripped her. Where was he? She had sent a message to him that she would give birth on Hogmanay the very day she'd had the vision, and still, he was not home. She clenched her teeth on her ridiculousness. He was at war. What did she expect? She was a silly woman, who wanted her husband.

"Angus," she bellowed, wishing him there.

A cool rag came to her forehead, and then Greer's face appeared. "Ye will speak to him when he returns, and ye ken ye will. He's all ye've talked about the last nine months, so much so that my ears and my head hurt."

Lillianna gritted her teeth against another wave of agony, and when it passed, her eyes filled with tears, blurring Greer's face. "Where is he?" she sobbed, unable to fight her longing for him in her haze of pain. She gave in to her sadness that he was not there. "He vowed to be here. He'd never break a vow to me." She squeezed her eyes shut as another pain ripped through her, greater than any she had felt before.

"The bairn is coming!" Greer said excitedly.

A hand suddenly gripped Lillianna's and squeezed it. "Mari?" she asked on a ragged breath.

"Nay," came Angus's deep reply. "Nae Mari, lass."

Her eyes flew open to find her husband kneeling beside her. He had a dark beard and his hair was pulled back. His face looked thinner, his eyes harder, but then they softened completely as he gazed at her, and she knew that whatever he had seen had changed him, but not so much that he was not the man she loved.

Joy overcame her, and tears spilled from her eyes. "You made it," she said on a strangled whisper.

"Of course I did," he said, rubbing his hand gently over her forehead. "There is nae any war that could hold me back from seeing my bairn born."

She opened her mouth to tell him she loved him, but another pain came, which made her feel she was going to be rent in two, so she screamed instead.

"I see the head!" Mari announced with glee.

Lillianna battled through the pain, squeezing Angus's hand tightly. When she did not think she could push anymore, it was Angus who encouraged her and told her how brave she was. Then with one last push, their baby started to cry.

"It's a girl!" Greer called out, and Lillianna looked to Angus just in time to see his eyes go wide.

"Don't fear, Husband," she told him as Greer brought their daughter to her. Lillianna took the babe and cradled her gently. "We will protect her together, and one day she will find a husband as good as you are."

"Aye," Angus agreed. "When she's thirty summers at least, and nae one day sooner."

Lillianna was too happy to argue, but as she held her new daughter and Angus leaned in to stare in wonder at her, a vision overtook Lillianna's senses. Their daughter would find love, but it would be far sooner than Angus would like.

Lillianna smiled. That was one secret she would keep for now.

Thank you so much for reading Angus and Lillianna's story! I hope you enjoyed it!

If you love Scottish romance, I think you might like my HIGHLANDER VOWS: ENTANGLED HEARTS series. Book 1 in the series is WHEN A LAIRD LOVES A LADY, and you can purchase it by clicking HERE, and start reading it with chapter one below.

Chapter One

England, 1357

Faking her death would be simple. It was escaping her home that would be difficult. Marion de Lacy stared hard into the slowly darkening sky, thinking about the plan she intended to put into action tomorrow—if all went well—but growing uneasiness tightened her belly. From where she stood in the bailey, she counted the guards up in the tower. It was not her imagination: Father had tripled the knights keeping guard at all times, as if he was expecting trouble.

Taking a deep breath of the damp air, she pulled her mother's cloak tighter around her to ward off the twilight chill. A lump lodged in her throat as the wool scratched her neck. In the many years since her mother had been gone, Marion had both hated and loved this cloak for the death and life it represented. Her mother's freesia scent had long since faded from the garment, yet simply calling up a memory of her mother wearing it gave Marion comfort.

She rubbed her fingers against the rough material. When she fled, she couldn't chance taking anything with her but the clothes on her body and this cloak. Her death had to appear accidental, and the cloak that everyone knew she prized would ensure her freedom. Finding it tangled in the branches at the edge of the sea cliff ought to be just the thing to convince her father and William Froste that she'd drowned. After all, neither man thought she could swim. They didn't truly care about her anyway. Her marriage to the blackhearted knight was only about what her hand could give the two men. Her father, Baron de Lacy, wanted more power, and Froste wanted her family's prized land. A match made in Heaven, if only the match didn't involve her…but it did.

Father would set the hounds of Hell themselves to track her down if he had the slightest suspicion that she was still alive. She was an inestimable possession to be given to secure Froste's unwavering allegiance and, therefore, that of the renowned ferocious knights who served him. Whatever small sliver of hope she had that her father would grant her mercy and not marry her to Froste had been destroyed by the lashing she'd received when she'd pleaded for him to do so.

The moon crested above the watchtower, reminding her why she was out here so close to mealtime: to meet Angus. The Scotsman may have been her father's stable master, but he was *her* ally, and when he'd proposed she flee England for Scotland, she'd readily consented.

Marion looked to the west, the direction from which Angus would return from Newcastle. He should be back any minute now from meeting his cousin and clansman Neil, who was to escort her to Scotland. She prayed all was set and that Angus's kin was ready to depart. With her wedding to Froste to take place in six days, she wanted to be far away before there was even the slightest chance he'd be making his way here. And since he was set to arrive the night before the wedding, leaving tomorrow promised she'd not encounter him.

A sense of urgency enveloped her, and Marion forced herself to stroll across the bailey toward the gatehouse that led to the tunnel preceding the drawbridge. She couldn't risk raising suspicion from the tower guards. At the gatehouse, she nodded to Albert, one of the knights who operated the drawbridge mechanism. He was young and rarely questioned her excursions to pick flowers or find herbs.

"Off to get some medicine?" he inquired.

"Yes," she lied with a smile and a little pang of guilt. But this was survival, she reminded herself as she entered the tunnel. When she exited the heavy wooden door that led to freedom, she wasn't surprised to find Peter and Andrew not yet up in the twin towers that flanked the entrance to the drawbridge. It was, after all, time for the changing of the guard.

They smiled at her as they put on their helmets and demi-gauntlets. They were an imposing presence to any who crossed the drawbridge and dared to approach the castle gate. Both men were tall and looked particularly daunting in their full armor, which Father insisted upon at all times. The men were certainly a fortress in their own right.

She nodded to them. "I'll not be long. I want to gather some more flowers for the supper table." Her voice didn't even wobble with the lie.

Peter grinned at her, his kind brown eyes crinkling at the edges. "Will you pick me one of those pale winter flowers for my wife again, Marion?"

She returned his smile. "It took away her anger as I said

it would, didn't it?"

"It did," he replied. "You always know just how to help with her."

"I'll get a pink one if I can find it. The colors are becoming scarcer as the weather cools."

Andrew, the younger of the two knights, smiled, displaying a set of straight teeth. He held up his covered arm. "My cut is almost healed."

Marion nodded. "I told you! Now maybe you'll listen to me sooner next time you're wounded in training."

He gave a soft laugh. "I will. Should I put more of your paste on tonight?"

"Yes, keep using it. I'll have to gather some more yarrow, if I can find any, and mix up another batch of the medicine for you." And she'd have to do it before she escaped. "I better get going if I'm going to find those things." She knew she should not have agreed to search for the flowers and offered to find the yarrow when she still had to speak to Angus and return to the castle in time for supper, but both men had been kind to her when many had not. It was her way of thanking them.

After Peter lowered the bridge and opened the door, she departed the castle grounds, considering her plan once more. Had she forgotten anything? She didn't think so. She was simply going to walk straight out of her father's castle and never come back. Tomorrow, she'd announce she was going out to collect more winter blooms, and then, instead, she would go down to the edge of the cliff overlooking the sea. She would slip off her cloak and leave it for a search party to find. Her breath caught deep in her chest at the simple yet dangerous plot. The last detail to see to was Angus.

She stared down the long dirt path that led to the sea

and stilled, listening for hoofbeats. A slight vibration of the ground tingled her feet, and her heart sped in hopeful anticipation that it was Angus coming down the dirt road on his horse. When the crafty stable master appeared with a grin spread across his face, the worry that was squeezing her heart loosened. For the first time since he had ridden out that morning, she took a proper breath. He stopped his stallion alongside her and dismounted.

She tilted her head back to look up at him as he towered over her. An errant thought struck. "Angus, are all Scots as tall as you?"

"Nay, but ye ken Scots are bigger than all the wee Englishmen." Suppressed laughter filled his deep voice. "So even the ones nae as tall as me are giants compared te the scrawny men here."

"You're teasing me," she replied, even as she arched her eyebrows in uncertainty.

"A wee bit," he agreed and tousled her hair. The laughter vanished from his eyes as he rubbed a hand over his square jaw and then stared down his bumpy nose at her, fixing what he called his "lecturing look" on her. "We've nae much time. Neil is in Newcastle just as he's supposed te be, but there's been a slight change."

She frowned. "For the last month, every time I wanted to simply make haste and flee, you refused my suggestion, and now you say there's a slight change?"

His ruddy complexion darkened. She'd pricked that MacLeod temper her mother had always said Angus's clan was known for throughout the Isle of Skye, where they lived in the farthest reaches of Scotland. Marion could remember her mother chuckling and teasing Angus about how no one knew the MacLeod temperament better than their neighboring clan, the MacDonalds of Sleat, to which her mother had been born. The two clans had a history of feuding.

Angus cleared his throat and recaptured Marion's attention. Without warning, his hand closed over her shoulder, and he squeezed gently. "I'm sorry te say it so plain, but ye must die at once."

Her eyes widened as dread settled in the pit of her stomach. "What? Why?" The sudden fear she felt was unreasonable. She knew he didn't mean she was really going to die, but her palms were sweating and her lungs had tightened all the same. She sucked in air and wiped her damp hands down the length of her cotton skirts. Suddenly, the idea of going to a foreign land and living with her mother's clan, people she'd never met, made her apprehensive.

She didn't even know if the MacDonalds—her uncle, in particular, who was now the laird—would accept her or not. She was half-English, after all, and Angus had told her that when a Scot considered her English bloodline and the fact that she'd been raised there, they would most likely brand her fully English, which was not a good thing in a Scottish mind. And if her uncle was anything like her grandfather had been, the man was not going to be very reasonable. But she didn't have any other family to turn to who would dare defy her father, and Angus hadn't offered for her to go to his clan, so she'd not asked. He likely didn't want to bring trouble to his clan's doorstep, and she didn't blame him.

Panic bubbled inside her. She needed more time, even if it was only the day she'd thought she had, to gather her courage.

"Why must I flee tonight? I was to teach Eustice how to dress a wound. She might serve as a maid, but then she will be able to help the knights when I'm gone. And her little brother, Bernard, needs a few more lessons before he's mastered writing his name and reading. And Eustice's youngest sister has begged me to speak to Father about allowing her to visit her mother next week."

"Ye kinnae watch out for everyone here anymore, Marion."

She placed her hand over his on her shoulder. "Neither can you."

Their gazes locked in understanding and disagreement.

He slipped his hand from her shoulder, and then crossed his arms over his chest in a gesture that screamed stubborn, unyielding protector. "If I leave at the same time ye feign yer death," he said, changing the subject, "it could stir yer father's suspicion and make him ask questions when none need te be asked. I'll be going home te Scotland soon after ye." Angus reached into a satchel attached to his horse and pulled out a dagger, which he slipped to her. "I had this made for ye."

Marion took the weapon and turned it over, her heart pounding. "It's beautiful." She held it by its black handle while withdrawing it from the sheath and examining it. "It's much sharper than the one I have."

"Aye," he said grimly. "It is. Dunnae forget that just because I taught ye te wield a dagger does nae mean ye can defend yerself from *all* harm. Listen te my cousin and do as he says. Follow his lead."

She gave a tight nod. "I will. But why must I leave now and not tomorrow?"

Concern filled Angus's eyes. "Because I ran into Froste's brother in town and he told me that Froste sent word that he would be arriving in two days."

Marion gasped. "That's earlier than expected."

"Aye," Angus said and took her arm with gentle authority. "So ye must go now. I'd rather be trying te trick only yer father than yer father, Froste, and his savage knights. I want ye long gone and yer death accepted when Froste arrives."

She shivered as her mind began to race with all that could go wrong.

"I see the worry darkening yer green eyes," Angus said, interrupting her thoughts. He whipped off his hat and his hair, still shockingly red in spite of his years, fell down around his shoulders. He only ever wore it that way when he was riding. He said the wind in his hair reminded him of riding his own horse when he was in Scotland. "I was going to talk to ye tonight, but now that I kinnae…" He shifted from foot to foot, as if uncomfortable. "I want te offer ye something. I'd have proposed it sooner, but I did nae want ye te feel ye had te take my offer so as nae te hurt me, but I kinnae hold my tongue, even so."

She furrowed her brow. "What is it?"

"I'd be proud if ye wanted te stay with the MacLeod clan instead of going te the MacDonalds. Then ye'd nae have te leave everyone ye ken behind. Ye'd have me."

A surge of relief filled her. She threw her arms around Angus, and he returned her hug quick and hard before setting her away. Her eyes misted at once. "I had hoped you would ask me," she admitted.

For a moment, he looked astonished, but then he spoke. "Yer mother risked her life te come into MacLeod territory at a time when we were fighting terrible with the MacDonalds, as ye well ken."

Marion nodded. She knew the story of how Angus had ended up here. He'd told her many times. Her mother had been somewhat of a renowned healer from a young age, and when Angus's wife had a hard birthing, her mother had gone to help. The knowledge that his wife and child had died anyway still made Marion want to cry.

"I pledged my life te keep yer mother safe for the kindness she'd done me, which brought me here, but, lass, long ago ye became like a daughter te me, and I pledge the rest of my miserable life te defending ye."

She gripped Angus's hand. "I wish you were my father."

He gave her a proud yet smug look, one she was used to seeing. She chortled to herself. The man did have a terrible streak of pride. She'd have to give Father John another coin for penance for Angus, since the Scot refused to take up the custom himself.

Angus hooked his thumb in his gray tunic. "Ye'll make a fine MacLeod because ye already ken we're the best clan in Scotland."

Mentally, she added another coin to her dues. "Do you think they'll let me become a MacLeod, though, since my mother was the daughter of the previous MacDonald laird and I've an English father?"

"They will," he answered without hesitation, but she heard the slight catch in his voice.

"Angus." She narrowed her eyes. "You said you would never lie to me."

His brows dipped together, and he gave her a long, disgruntled look. "They may be a bit wary," he finally admitted. "But I'll nae let them turn ye away. Dunnae worry," he finished, his Scottish brogue becoming thick with emotion.

She bit her lip. "Yes, but you won't be with me when I first get there. What should I do to make certain that they will let me stay?"

He quirked his mouth as he considered her question.

"Ye must first get the laird te like ye. Tell Neil te take ye directly te the MacLeod te get his consent for ye te live there. I kinnae vouch for the man myself as I've never met him, but Neil says he's verra honorable, fierce in battle, patient, and reasonable." Angus cocked his head as if in thought. "Now that I think about it, I'm sure the MacLeod can get ye a husband, and then the clan will more readily accept ye. Aye." He nodded. "Get in the laird's good graces as soon as ye meet him and ask him te find ye a husband." A scowl twisted his lips. "Preferably one who will accept yer acting like a man sometimes."

She frowned at him. "*You* are the one who taught me how to ride bareback, wield a dagger, and shoot an arrow true."

"Aye." He nodded. "I did. But when I started teaching ye, I thought yer mama would be around te add her woman's touch. I did nae ken at the time that she'd pass when ye'd only seen eight summers in yer life."

"You're lying again," Marion said. "You continued those lessons long after Mama's death. You weren't a bit worried how I'd turn out."

"I sure was!" he objected, even as a guilty look crossed his face. "But what could I do? Ye insisted on hunting for the widows so they'd have food in the winter, and ye insisted on going out in the dark te help injured knights when I could nae go with ye. I had te teach ye te hunt and defend yerself. Plus, you were a sad, lonely thing, and I could nae verra well overlook ye when ye came te the stables and asked me te teach ye things."

"Oh, you could have," she replied. "Father overlooked me all the time, but your heart is too big to treat someone like that." She patted him on the chest. "I think you taught me the best things in the world, and it seems to me any man would want his woman to be able to defend herself."

"Shows how much ye ken about men," Angus muttered with a shake of his head. "Men like te think a woman needs *them*."

"I dunnae need a man," she said in her best Scottish accent.

He threw up his hands. "Ye do. Ye're just afeared."

The fear was true enough. Part of her longed for love, to feel as if she belonged to a family. For so long she'd wanted those things from her father, but she had never gotten them, no matter what she did. It was difficult to believe it would be any different in the future. She'd rather not be disappointed.

Angus tilted his head, looking at her uncertainly. "Ye want a wee bairn some day, dunnae ye?"

"Well, yes," she admitted and peered down at the ground, feeling foolish.

"Then ye need a man," he crowed.

She drew her gaze up to his. "Not just any man. I want a man who will truly love me."

He waved a hand dismissively. Marriages of convenience were a part of life, she knew, but she would not marry unless she was in love and her potential husband loved her in return. She would support herself if she needed to.

"The other big problem with a husband for ye," he continued, purposely avoiding, she suspected, her mention of the word *love*, "as I see it, is yer tender heart."

"What's wrong with a tender heart?" She raised her brow in question.

"'Tis more likely te get broken, aye?" His response was matter-of-fact.

"Nay. 'Tis more likely to have compassion," she replied with a grin.

"We're both right," he announced. "Yer mama had a tender heart like ye. 'Tis why yer father's black heart hurt her so. I dunnae care te watch the light dim in ye as it did yer mother."

"I don't wish for that fate, either," she replied, trying hard not to think about how sad and distant her mother had often seemed. "Which is why I will only marry for love. And why I need to get out of England."

"I ken that, lass, truly I do, but ye kinnae go through life alone."

"I don't wish to," she defended. "But if I have to, I have you, so I'll not be alone." With a shudder, her heart denied the possibility that she may never find love, but she squared her shoulders.

"'Tis nae the same as a husband," he said. "I'm old. Ye need a younger man who has the power te defend ye. And if Sir Frosty Pants ever comes after ye, you're going te need a strong man te go against him."

Marion snorted to cover the worry that was creeping in.

Angus moved his mouth to speak, but his reply was drowned by the sound of the supper horn blowing. "God's bones!" Angus muttered when the sound died. "I've flapped my jaw too long. Ye must go now. I'll head te the stables and start the fire as we intended. It'll draw Andrew and Peter away if they are watching ye too closely."

Marion looked over her shoulder at the knights, her stomach turning. She had known the plan since the day they had formed it, but now the reality of it scared her into a cold sweat. She turned back to Angus and gripped her dagger hard. "I'm afraid."

Determination filled his expression, as if his will for her to stay out of harm would make it so. "Ye will stay safe," he commanded. "Make yer way through the path in the woods that I showed ye, straight te Newcastle. I left ye a bag of coins under the first tree ye come te, the one with the rope tied te it. Neil will be waiting for ye by Pilgrim Gate on Pilgrim Street. The two of ye will depart from there."

She worried her lip but nodded all the same.

"Neil has become friends with a friar who can get the two of ye out," Angus went on. "Dunnae talk te anyone, especially any men. Ye should go unnoticed, as ye've never been there and won't likely see anyone ye've ever come in contact with here."

Fear tightened her lungs, but she swallowed. "I didn't even bid anyone farewell." Not that she really could have, nor did she think anyone would miss her other than Angus, and she would be seeing him again. Peter and Andrew *had* been kind to her, but they were her father's men, and she knew it well. She had been taken to the dungeon by the knights several times for punishment for transgressions that ranged from her tone not pleasing her father to his thinking she gave him a disrespectful look. Other times, they'd carried out the duty of tying her to the post for a thrashing when she'd angered her father. They had begged her forgiveness profusely but done their duties all the same. They would likely be somewhat glad they did not have to contend with such things anymore.

Eustice was both kind *and* thankful for Marion teaching her brother how to read, but Eustice lost all color any time someone mentioned the maid going with Marion to Froste's home after Marion was married. She suspected the woman was afraid to go to the home of the infamous "Merciless Knight." Eustice would likely be relieved when Marion disappeared. Not that Marion blamed her.

A small lump lodged in her throat. Would her father even mourn her loss? It wasn't likely, and her stomach knotted at the thought.

"You'll come as soon as you can?" she asked Angus.

"Aye. Dunnae fash yerself."

She forced a smile. "You are already sounding like you're back in Scotland. Don't forget to curb that when speaking with Father."

"I'll remember. Now, make haste te the cliff te leave yer cloak, then head straight for Newcastle."

"I don't want to leave you," she said, ashamed at the sudden rise of cowardliness in her chest and at the way her eyes stung with unshed tears.

"Gather yer courage, lass. I'll be seeing ye soon, and Neil will keep ye safe."

She sniffed. "I'll do the same for Neil."

"I've nay doubt ye'll try," Angus said, sounding proud and wary at the same time.

"I'm not afraid for myself," she told him in a shaky voice. "You're taking a great risk for me. How will I ever make it up to you?"

"Ye already have," Angus said hastily, glancing around and directing a worried look toward the drawbridge. "Ye want te live with my clan, which means I can go te my dying day treating ye as my daughter. Now, dunnae cry when I walk away. I ken how sorely ye'll miss me," he boasted with a wink. "I'll miss ye just as much."

With that, he swung up onto his mount. He had just given the signal for his beast to go when Marion realized she didn't know what Neil looked like.

"Angus!"

He pulled back on the reins and turned toward her. "Aye?"

"I need Neil's description."

Angus's eyes widened. "I'm getting old," he grumbled.

"I dunnae believe I forgot such a detail. He's got hair redder than mine, and wears it tied back always. Oh, and he's missing his right ear, thanks te Froste. Took it when Neil came through these parts te see me last year."

"What?" She gaped at him. "You never told me that!"

"I did nae because I knew ye would try te go after Neil and patch him up, and that surely would have cost ye another beating if ye were caught." His gaze bore into her. "Ye're verra courageous. I reckon I had a hand in that 'cause I knew ye needed te be strong te withstand yer father. But dunnae be mindless. Courageous men and women who are mindless get killed. Ye ken?"

She nodded.

"Tread carefully," he warned.

"You too." She said the words to his back, for he was already turned and headed toward the drawbridge.

She made her way slowly to the edge of the steep embankment as tears filled her eyes. She wasn't upset because she was leaving her father—she'd certainly need to say a prayer of forgiveness for that sin tonight—but she couldn't shake the feeling that she'd never see Angus again. It was silly; everything would go as they had planned. Before she could fret further, the blast of the fire horn jerked her into motion. There was no time for any thoughts but those of escape.

Series by Julie Johnstone

Scottish Medieval Romance Books:

Highlander Vows: Entangled Hearts Series
When a Laird Loves a Lady, Book 1
Wicked Highland Wishes, Book 2
Christmas in the Scot's Arms, Book 3
When a Highlander Loses His Heart, Book 4
How a Scot Surrenders to a Lady, Book 5
When a Warrior Woos a Lass, Book 6
When a Scot Gives His Heart, Book 7
Highlander Vows: Entangled Hearts Boxset, Books 1-4

Renegade Scots Series
Outlaw King, Book 1
Highland Defender, Book 2

Regency Romance Books:

A Whisper of Scandal Series
Bargaining with a Rake, Book 1
Conspiring with a Rogue, Book 2
Dancing with a Devil, Book 3
After Forever, Book 4
The Dangerous Duke of Dinnisfree, Book 5

A Once Upon A Rogue Series
My Fair Duchess, Book 1
My Seductive Innocent, Book 2
My Enchanting Hoyden, Book 3
My Daring Duchess, Book 4

Lords of Deception Series
What a Rogue Wants, Book 1

Danby Regency Christmas Novellas
The Redemption of a Dissolute Earl, Book 1
Season For Surrender, Book 2
It's in the Duke's Kiss, Book 3

Regency Anthologies
A Summons from the Duke of Danby (Regency Christmas Summons, Book 2)
Thwarting the Duke (When the Duke Comes to Town, Book 2)

Regency Romance Box Sets
A Whisper of Scandal Trilogy (Books 1-3)
Dukes, Duchesses & Dashing Noblemen (A Once Upon a Rogue Regency Novels, Books 1-3)

Paranormal Books:

The Siren Saga
Echoes in the Silence, Book 1

About the Author

As a little girl I loved to create fantasy worlds and then give all my friends roles to play. Of course, I was always the heroine! Books have always been an escape for me and brought me so much pleasure, but it didn't occur to me that I could possibly be a writer for a living until I was in a career that was not my passion. One day, I decided I wanted to craft stories like the ones I loved, and with a great leap of faith I quit my day job and decided to try to make my dream come true. I discovered my passion, and I have never looked back. I feel incredibly blessed and fortunate that I have been able to make a career out of sharing the stories that are in my head! I write Scottish Medieval Romance, Regency Romance, and I have even written a Paranormal Romance book. And because I have the best readers in the world, I have hit the USA Today bestseller list several times.

If you love me, I hope you do, you can follow me on Bookbub, and they will send you notices whenever I have a sale or a new release. You can follow me here:
bookbub.com/authors/julie-johnstone

You can also join my newsletter to get great prizes and inside scoops!
Join here: https://goo.gl/qnkXFF

I really want to hear from you! It makes my day!
Email me here:
juliejohnstoneauthor@gmail.com

I'm on Facebook a great deal chatting about books and life.
If you want to follow me, you can do so here:
facebook.com/authorjuliejohnstone

Can't get enough of me? Well, good! Come see me here:
Twitter:
@juliejohnstone
Goodreads:
https://goo.gl/T57MTA

Made in the USA
Middletown, DE
27 December 2018